About the Author

Cat Schield lives in opiniated Burmese Winner of the R Golden Heart® for she's not writing Boon, she can be found on the Croix River or in more exotic locales like the Caribbean and Europe. You can find out more about her books at www.catschield.net

In 2002 **Janice Maynard** left a career as a primary teacher to pursue writing full-time. Her first love is creating sexy, character-driven, contemporary romance. She has written for Kensington and NAL, and is very happy to be part of the Mills & Boon family—a lifelong dream. Janice and her husband live in the shadow of the Great Smoky Mountains. They love to hike and travel. Visit her at www.JaniceMaynard.com

Cathy Williams is a great believer in the power of perseverance as she had never written anything before her writing career, and from the starting point of zero has now fulfilled her ambition to pursue this most enjoyable of careers. She would encourage any would-be writer to have faith and go for it! She derives inspiration from the tropical island of Trinidad and from the peaceful countryside of middle England. Cathy lives in Warwickshire with her family.

Secrets and Seduction

Secrets and Seduction:
The Lying Game

CAT SCHIELD

JANICE MAYNARD

CATHY WILLIAMS

MILLS & BOON

First Published in Great Britain 2022
By Mills & Boon, an imprint of HarperCollins*Publishers,* Ltd
1 London Bridge Street, London, SE1 9GF

www.harpercollins.co.uk

HarperCollins*Publishers*
1st Floor, Watermarque Building,
Ringsend Road, Dublin 4, Ireland

SECRETS AND SEDUCTION: THE LYING GAME
© 2022 Harlequin Books S.A.

Seductive Secrets © 2019 Cat Schield
Bombshell for the Black Sheep © 2019 Janice Maynard
A Virgin for Vasquez © 2016 Cathy Williams

ISBN: 978-0-263-30405-3

MIX
Paper from
responsible sources
FSC® C007454

This book is produced from independently certified FSC™ paper to ensure responsible forest management.

For more information visit: www.harpercollins.co.uk/green

Printed and Bound in Spain using 100% Renewable electricity at CPI Black Print, Barcelona

SEDUCTIVE SECRETS

CAT SCHIELD

One

Paul Watts entered the hospital elevator and jabbed the button for the fourth floor with more force than necessary. In two hours he was leaving Charleston to attend a week-long cybersecurity conference. His gut told him this was a mistake. His eighty-five-year-old grandfather's medical situation wasn't improving. Grady had been hospitalized six days earlier with cerebral edema, a complication arising from the massive stroke he'd suffered three months earlier that had affected his speech and left one side of his body paralyzed. In the midst of this latest medical crisis, the family worried that Grady wouldn't last much longer. Which was why Paul was rethinking his trip.

Despite the excellent care he was receiving from the doctors, the Watts family patriarch was failing to rally. At first the doctors and physical therapists had agreed that the likelihood of Grady making a full recovery was better than average given his excellent health before the stroke and his impossibly strong will. But he hadn't mended. And he hadn't fought. The stroke had stolen more than his voice and muscle control. It had broken Grady Watts.

Although he'd stepped down as CEO of the family shipping empire a decade earlier and turned over the day-to-day running of the corporation to Paul's father, Grady had remained as chairman of the board. Not one to slow down, he'd kept busy in "retirement" by sitting on the boards of several organizations and maintained an active social life.

Accustomed to his grandfather's tireless vigor, stubbornness and unapologetic outspokenness, Paul couldn't understand why Grady wouldn't strive to get well, and thanks to the strained relationship between them, Paul was unlikely to get answers. Their estrangement was an ache that never went away. Still, Paul refused to regret his decision to pursue a career in cybersecurity rather than join the family business. Stopping bad guys satisfied his need for justice in a way that running the family shipping company never would.

The elevator doors opened and Paul stepped into the bright, sterile corridor that ran past the nurses' station. He offered brief nods to the caregivers behind the desk as he strode the far-too-familiar hallways that led to his grandfather's private room.

His steps slowed as he neared where Grady lay so still and beaten. No one would ever accuse Paul of being fainthearted, but he dreaded what he'd find when he entered the room. Every aspect of his life had been influenced by his grandfather's robust personality and Grady's current frailty caused Paul no small amount of dismay. Just as his grandfather had lost the will to go on, Paul's confidence had turned into desperation. He would do or support anything that would inspire Grady to fight his way back to them.

Reaching his grandfather's room, Paul gathered a deep breath. As he braced himself to enter, a thread of music drifted through the small gap between the door and frame.

A woman was singing something sweet and uplifting. Paul didn't recognize the pure, clear voice and perfect pitch as belonging to anyone in his family. Perhaps it was one of the nurses. Had one of them discovered that his grandfather loved all kinds of music?

Paul pushed open the door and stepped into his grandfather's dimly lit room. The sight that greeted him stopped him dead in his tracks. Grady lay perfectly still, his skin gray and waxy. If not for the reassuring beep of the heart monitor, Paul might've guessed his grandfather had already passed.

On the far side of the bed, her back to the darkened window, a stranger held Grady's hand. Despite her fond and gentle expression, Paul went on instant alert. She wasn't the nurse he'd expected. In fact, she wasn't any sort of ordinary visitor. More like someone who'd wandered away from an amusement park. Or the sixth-floor psychiatric ward.

Pretty, slender and in her midtwenties, she wore some sort of costume composed of a lavender peasant dress and a blond wig fastened into a thick braid and adorned with fake flowers. Enormous hazel eyes dominated a narrow face with high cheekbones and a pointed chin. She looked like a doll come to life.

Paul was so startled that he forgot to moderate his voice. "Who are you?"

The question reverberated in the small space, causing the woman to break off midsong. Her eyes went wide and she froze like a deer caught in headlights. Her rosy lips parted on a startled breath and her chest rose on an inhalation, but Paul fired off another question before she answered the first.

"What are you doing in my grandfather's room?"

"I'm…" Her gaze darted past him toward the open door.

"Geez, Paul, calm the hell down," said a voice from behind him. It was his younger brother, Ethan. His softer tone suited the hospital room far better than Paul's sharp bluster. "I heard you all the way down the hall. You're going to upset Grady."

Now Paul noticed that his grandfather's eyes were open and his mouth was working as if he had an opinion he wanted to share. The stroke had left him unable to form the words that let him communicate, but there was no question Grady was agitated. His right hand fluttered. The woman's bright gaze flicked from Paul to Grady and back.

"Sorry, Grady." Paul advanced to his grandfather's bedside and lightly squeezed the old man's cool, dry fingers, noting the tremble in his knobby knuckles. "I came by to check on you. I was surprised to see this stranger in your room." He glanced toward the oddly dressed woman and spoke in a low growl. "I don't know who you are, but you shouldn't be here."

"Yes, she should." Ethan came to stand beside Paul, behaving as if introducing his brother to a woman dressed in costume was perfectly ordinary.

This lack of concern made Paul's blood pressure rise. "You know her?"

"Yes, this is Lia Marsh."

"Hello," she said, her bright sweet voice like tinkling crystal.

As soon as Ethan had entered the room her manner had begun to relax. Obviously she viewed Paul's brother as an ally. Now she offered Paul a winsome smile. If she thought her charm would blunt the keen edge of his suspicion, she had no idea who she was dealing with. Still, he found the anxiety that had plagued him in recent days easing. A confusing and unexpected sense of peace trickled through him as Grady's faded green eyes focused on Lia Marsh. He seemed happy to have her by his side, weird costume and all.

"I don't understand what she's doing here," Paul complained, grappling to comprehend this out-of-control situation.

"She came to cheer up our grandfather." Ethan set a comforting hand on their grandfather's shoulder. "It's okay," he told the older man. "I'll explain everything to Paul."

What was there to explain?

During the brothers' exchange, the woman squeezed Grady's hand. "I've really enjoyed our time together today," she said, her musical voice a soothing oasis in the tense room. "I'll come back and visit more with you later."

Grady made an unhappy noise, but she was already moving toward the foot of the bed. Paul ignored his grandfather's protest and shifted to intercept her.

"No, you won't," he declared.

"I understand," she said, but her expression reflected dismay and a trace of disapproval. Her gaze flicked to Ethan. A warm smile curved her lips. "I'll see you later."

Embroidered skirt swishing, she moved toward the exit, leaving a ribbon of floral perfume trailing in her wake. Paul caught himself breathing her in and expelled the tantalizing scent from his lungs in a vigorous huff. The energy in the room plummeted as she disappeared through the doorway and, to his profound dismay, Paul was struck by a disconcerting urge to call her back.

Now just to get answers to the most obvious questions: Why was she dressed like that and what was she doing in Grady's room? But also why had she chosen to tattoo a delicate lily of the valley on the inside of her left wrist? He wondered how his brother could be taken in by such guileless naivete when it was so obviously an act.

This last point snapped Paul out of whatever spell she'd cast over him. Grabbing his brother's arm, Paul towed Ethan out of the hospital room, eager to get answers without disturbing Grady. Out in the hall, Paul closed the door and glanced around. Lia Marsh had vanished and he noticed that didn't bring him the satisfaction it should have.

"Who is she?" Paul demanded, his unsettled emotions making his tone sharper than necessary. "And what the hell is going on?"

Ethan sighed. "Lia's a friend of mine."

Paul dragged his hand through his hair as he fought to control the emotions cascading through him. He focused on his anxiety over his grandfather's condition. That feeling made sense. The rest he would just ignore.

"You've never mentioned her before," Paul said. "How well do you know her?"

A muscle jumped in Ethan's jaw. He looked like he was grappling with something. "Well enough. Look, you're seeing problems where there aren't any."

"Have you forgotten that Watts Shipping as well as various members of our family have been cyberattacked in the last year? So when I show up in Grady's hospital room and there's a strange woman alone with him, I get concerned."

"Trust me—Lia has nothing to do with any of that," Ethan said. "She's really sweet and just wants to help. Grady has been so depressed. We thought a visit might cheer him up."

Paul refused to believe that he'd overreacted. And Ethan was transitioning into the CEO position at Watts Shipping, replacing their father who planned to retire in the next year. Why wouldn't his brother take these various cyber threats seriously?

"But she was dressed like a…like a…" It wasn't like him to grapple for words, but the whole encounter had a surreal quality to it.

"Disney princess?" Ethan offered, one corner of his mouth kicking up. "Specifically Rapunzel from *Tangled*."

"Okay, but you never answered my question. Where did you meet her?" Paul persisted, making no attempt to rein in his skepticism. Ethan's persistent caginess was a red flag. "What do you know about her?"

When meeting people for the first time, Paul tended to assess them like it was an investigation and often struggled to give them the benefit of the doubt. Did that mean he was suspicious by nature? Probably. But if that's what it took to keep his family safe, then so be it.

"Can you stop thinking like a cop for two seconds?" Ethan complained.

Paul bristled. It wasn't only Grady who hadn't supported his decision to join the Charleston PD after college and several years later start his cybersecurity business.

"What's her angle?"

"She doesn't have one. She's exactly like she seems."

Paul snorted. A cosplay fanatic? "What else do you know about her?"

"I don't know," Ethan complained, growing impatient. "She's really nice and a great listener."

"A great listener," Paul echoed, guessing that Lia Marsh had taken advantage of Ethan's distress over their grandfather's illness. "I suppose you told her all about Grady and our family?"

"It's not as if any of it is a huge secret."

"Regardless. You brought a complete stranger, someone you know almost nothing about, to meet our dying grandfather." Paul made no effort to temper his irritation. "What were you thinking?"

"I was thinking Grady might enjoy a visit from a sweet, caring person who has a beautiful singing voice." Ethan gave him such a sad look. "Why do you always go to the worst-case scenario?"

Paul stared at his brother. Ethan behaved as if this explanation made all the sense in the world. Meanwhile, Paul's relentless, logical convictions prevented him from grasping what sort of eccentricities drove Lia Marsh to parade around as a storybook character.

"She was dressed up. I just don't understand…"

Ethan shrugged. "It's what she does."

"For a living?"

"Of course not," Ethan countered, showing no defensiveness at all in the face of his brother's sarcasm. In fact, he looked fairly smug as he said, "She dresses up and visits sick children. They love her."

Paul cursed. Actually, that was a damned nice thing to do.

"How did you meet her?"

Ethan frowned. "I'm a client."

"What sort of a client?"

"None of this matters." Ethan exhaled. "Lia is great and your trust issues are getting old."

A heavy silence fell between the brothers as Paul brushed aside the criticism and brooded over Ethan's caginess. He hated being at odds with his brother and wasn't sure how to fix the disconnect. With less than a year between them in age, he and Ethan had been tight as kids despite their differing interests and passions. Paul was fascinated by technology and could spend hours alone, turning electronic components into useful devices, while Ethan was more social and preferred sports over schoolwork.

Both had excelled through high school and into college. And while they'd never directly competed over anything, once Paul decided against joining the family business, a subtle tension started growing between the siblings.

"You might as well tell me what's going on because you know I'll investigate and find out exactly who Lia Marsh is."

Lia Marsh blew out a sharp breath as she cleared the hospital room and fled down the empty hallway, noting her thudding heart and clammy palms. While Ethan hadn't glossed over his brother's suspicious nature, she hadn't been prepared for Paul's hostility or the way his annoyance heightened his already imposing charisma. Unaccustomed to letting any man get under her skin, Lia studied the phenomenon like she would a fresh scratch on her beloved camper trailer, Misty. Unexpected and undesirable.

Usually her emotions were like dandelion fluff on the wind, lighter than air and streaked with sunshine. She embraced all the joy life had to offer and vanquished negativity through meditation, crystal work and aromatherapy, often employing these same spiritual healing tools with her massage clients. Not all of them bought into new age practices, but some surprised her with their interest. For instance, she never imagined a businessman like Ethan Watts opening his mind to ancient spiritual practices, but his curiosity demonstrated that it was never wise to prejudge people.

Someone should share that warning with Paul Watts. He'd obviously jumped to several conclusions from the instant he'd spotted her in his grandfather's hospital room. The unsettling encounter left her emotions swirling in a troubling combination of excitement and dread, brought on by a rush of physical attraction and her aversion to conflict.

Distracted by her inner turmoil, Lia found it impossible to sink back into her role of Rapunzel as she stole along the corridor lit by harsh fluorescent lights. Her gaze skimmed past gray walls and bland landscapes. Recycled air pressed against her skin, smelling of disinfectant. She longed to throw open a window and invite in sunshine and breezes laden with newly cut grass and bird song. Instead, she dressed up and visited sick children, offering a much-needed diversion.

Heading down the stairs to the third-floor pediatric wing, Lia collected her tote bag from the nurses' station.

Since signing up to volunteer at the hospital these last few months, she'd been a frequent visitor and the children's care staff had grown accustomed to her appearances. They appreciated anything that boosted their patients' spirits and gave them a break from the endless rounds of tests or treatments.

The elevator doors opened and Lia stepped into the car. She barely noticed the mixed reactions of her fellow passengers to her outfit. Minutes later Lia emerged into the late afternoon sunshine. She sucked in a large breath and let it out, wishing she could shake her lingering preoccupation with her encounter with Paul Watts. Lia picked up her pace as if she could outrun her heightened emotions.

The traffic accident that had totaled her truck and damaged her beloved camper had compelled her to move into a one-bedroom rental on King Street until she could afford to replace her vehicle. Her temporary living arrangement was a twenty-minute walk from the hospital through Charleston's historic district. She focused on the pleasant ambience of the antebellum homes she passed, the glimpses of private gardens through wrought iron fencing, and savored the sunshine warming her shoulders.

Caught up in her thoughts, Lia barely noticed the man leaning against the SUV parked in front of her apartment until he pushed off and stepped into her path. Finding her way blocked, her pulse jumped. Lia had traveled the country alone since she was eighteen and had good instincts when it came to strangers. Only this was someone she'd already met.

Paul Watts had the sort of green eyes that reminded her of a tranquil pine forest, but the skepticism radiating from him warned Lia to be wary. Despite that, his nearness awakened the same buzz of chemistry that she'd noticed in the hospital room.

He wasn't at all her type. He was too obstinate. Too grounded. Merciless. Resolute. Maybe that was the attraction.

"You were hard to find," Paul declared.

Ethan had told her Paul was a former cop who now ran his own cybersecurity business. She suspected his single-minded focus had stopped a high number of cybercriminals. Her skin prickled at the idea that he'd do a deep dive into her background where things lurked that she'd prefer remained buried.

"And yet here you are," she retorted, dismayed that he'd run her down in the time it had taken her to walk home.

She wasn't used to being on anyone's radar. To most of her massage clients she was a pair of hands and a soothing voice. The kids at the hospital saw only their favorite princess character. She relished her anonymity.

"Is everything all right with Grady?"

"He's fine." Paul's lips tightened momentarily as a flash of pain crossed his granite features. "At least he isn't any worse."

"I didn't know him before his stroke, but Ethan said he was strong and resilient. He could still pull through."

"He could," Paul agreed, "except it's as if he's given up."

"Ethan mentioned he'd become obsessed with reuniting with his granddaughter these last few years," Lia said. "Maybe if you found her—"

"Look," Paul snapped. "I don't know what you're up to, but you need to stay away from my grandfather."

"I'm not up to anything," Lia insisted, pulling her key out of her bag as she angled toward the building's front door. "All I want to do is help."

"He doesn't need your help."

"Sure. Okay." At least he hadn't barred her from connecting with Ethan. "Is that it?"

She'd unlocked the door and pushed it open, intending to escape through it when Paul spoke again.

"Aren't you the least bit curious how I found you?" he asked, his vanity showing. Given her minimal electronic footprint, tracking her down left him puffed up with pride. No doubt he wanted to brag about his prowess.

Despite the agitation making her heart thump, Lia paused in the doorway and shot him a sidewise glance. While Paul exuded an overabundance of confidence and power, she wasn't without strengths of her own. She would just have to combat his relentlessness with freewheeling flirtation.

While teasing Paul was a danger similar to stepping too near a lion's cage, Lia discovered having his full attention was exhilarating.

"Actually." Pivoting to face him, Lia summoned her cheekiest smile. Everything she'd heard from Ethan indicated that Paul was ruled by logic rather than his emotions. Challenging the cybersecurity expert to confront his feelings was bound to blow up in her face. "I'm more intrigued that you wanted to."

Two

King Street melted away around him as Paul processed his response to Lia's challenging grin. Her expression wasn't sexual in nature, but that didn't lessen the surge of attraction that rocked him, demanding that he act. He clenched his hands behind his back to stifle the impulse to snatch her into his arms and send his lips stalking down her neck in search of that delectable fragrance. Frustrating. Intolerable. This woman was trouble. In more ways than he had time to count.

What was her endgame? Money, obviously.

Based on the fact that she'd chosen to live in one of downtown Charleston's priciest neighborhoods, she obviously had expensive taste. After meeting Ethan, she'd obviously targeted him, using their grandfather's illness to ingratiate herself. Was she planning on getting Ethan to pay off her debt or to invest in some sort of business?

"Ophelia Marsh, born March first—" he began, determined to unnerve her with a quick rundown of her vital statistics.

"Fun fact," she interrupted. "I was almost a leap-day baby. My mom went into labor late on February twenty-eighth and everyone thought for sure I would be born the next day, which that year was February twenty-ninth. But I didn't want to have a birthday every four years. I mean, who would, right?"

Her rambling speech, sparkling with energetic good humor, soured his mood even more. "Right." He had no idea why he was agreeing. "Born March first in Occidental, California..."

"A Pisces."

He shook his head. "A what?"

"A Pisces," she repeated. "You know, the astrological sign. Two fish swimming in opposite directions. Like you're a goat," she concluded.

Paul exhaled harshly. Horoscopes were nothing but a bunch of nonsense. Yet that didn't stop him from asking, "I'm a goat?"

"A Capricorn. You just had a birthday."

He felt her words like a hit to his solar plexus. "How did you know that?"

Her knowing his birthday filled him with equal parts annoyance and dismay. *He* was the security expert, the brilliant investigator who hunted down cybercriminals and kept his clients' data safe. To have this stranger know something as personal as his birth date sent alarm jolting through him.

"Ethan told me."

"Why would he do that?" Paul demanded, directing the question to the universe rather than Lia.

"Why wouldn't he?" She cocked her head and regarded him as if that was obvious. "He likes to talk about his family and it helps me to picture all of you if I know your signs. You're a Capricorn. Your mother is a Libra. She's the peacekeeper of the family. Your father is a Sagittarius. He's a talker and tends to chase impossible dreams. Ethan is a Taurus. Stubborn, reliable, with a sensual side that loves good food."

This quick summary of his family was so spot-on that Paul's suspicions reached even higher levels. Obviously, this woman had been researching the Wattses for some nefarious purpose. What was she up to? Time to turn up the volume on his questioning.

"You don't stay in one place for very long," he said, remembering what he'd managed to dig up on her. "New York, Vermont, Massachusetts, now South Carolina, all visited in the last twelve months. Why is that?"

In his experience grifters liked to work an area and move on when things became too hot. Her pattern fit with someone up to no good. She might be beautiful and seem to possess a sweet, generous nature, but in his mind her obvious appeal worked against her. He knew firsthand how easily people were taken in by appearances. He was more interested in substance.

"I'm a nomad."

"What does that mean?"

"It means I like life on the road. It's how I grew up." She paused to assess his expression and whatever she glimpsed there made her smile slightly. "I was born in the back of a VW camper van and traveled nearly five thousand miles in the first year of my life. My mother has a hard time staying put for any long period of time."

Paul was having a difficult time wrapping his head around what she was saying. For someone who belonged to a family that had lived within ten square miles of Charleston for generations, he couldn't fathom the sort of lifestyle she was talking about.

"Was your mother on the run from someone? Your father? Or a boyfriend?"

"No." Her casual shrug left plenty of room for Paul to speculate. "She was just restless."

"And you? Are you restless, too?"

"I guess." Something passed over her features, but it was gone too fast for him to read. "Although I tend to stay longer in places than she did."

Follow-up questions sprang to Paul's mind, but he wasn't here to dig into her family dynamic. He needed to figure out what she was up to so he could determine how much danger she represented to his family. He changed subjects. "Where did you and Ethan meet?"

"He's been a client of mine for about a month now."

"A client?" Paul digested this piece of information.

"I work for Springside Wellness," she said, confirming what Paul had already unearthed about her. The company was a wellness spa on Meeting Street that operated as both a yoga studio and alternative treatment space. A lot of mind, body, soul nonsense. "Ethan is a client."

This confirmed what Paul had gleaned from his brother's explanation about how he knew Lia. Still, Paul had a hard time picturing his brother doing yoga and reflexology. "What sort of a client?"

"I'm a massage therapist. He comes in once a week. I told him he should probably come in more often than that. The man is stressed."

Her answer took Paul's thoughts down an unexpected path. "Well, that's just perfect."

Only it wasn't perfect at all. A picture of Lia giving Ethan a massage leaped to mind but he immediately suppressed it.

"I don't understand what you mean," she said, frowning. "And I don't have time to find out. I have to be at work in an hour and it takes a while for me to get out of costume. Nice to meet you, Paul Watts."

He quite pointedly didn't echo the sentiment. "Just remember what I said about staying away from my grandfather."

"I already said I would."

With a graceful flutter of her fingers, she zipped through the building's front door, leaving him alone on the sidewalk. Despite her ready agreement to keep her distance, his nerves continued to sizzle and pop. Logic told him he'd seen the last of Lia Marsh, but his instincts weren't convinced.

Paul shot his brother a text before sliding behind the wheel, urging him to reiterate to Lia that Grady was off-limits. Thanks to this detour he was going to have to hustle to keep from being late for his charter flight.

Ethan's terse reply highlighted the tension between the brothers that seemed to be escalating. The growing distance between them frustrated Paul, but he couldn't figure out how to fix what he couldn't wrap his head around.

Pushing Ethan and the problem of Lia Marsh to the back of his mind, Paul focused his attention on something concrete and within his control: the upcoming conference and what he hoped to get out of it.

As much as Ethan had thoroughly enjoyed seeing his brother utterly flummoxed by Lia in a Rapunzel costume, as soon as Paul headed off to dig into her background, Ethan's satisfaction faded. Leave it to his brother to chase a tangent rather than deal with the real problem of their grandfather's condition. In the same way, Ethan's brother had neatly avoided dealing with Grady's disappointment after Paul chose a career in law enforcement over joining Watts Shipping and eventually taking his place at the helm of the family business. Nor had Paul understood Ethan's conflicted emotions at being the second choice to take up the reins.

While Ethan recognized that he was the best brother to head the family company, he wanted to secure the job based on his skills, not because Paul refused the position. Also, it wasn't just his pride at issue. Ethan was adopted and in a

city as preoccupied with lineage as Charleston, not knowing who his people were became a toxic substance eating
away at his peace of mind.

Although no one had ever made him feel as if he didn't
belong, in every Watts family photo, Ethan's dark brown
hair and eyes made him stand out like a goose among
swans. Not wishing to cause any of his family undue pain,
he kept his feelings buried, but more and more lately they'd
bubbled up and tainted his relationship with Paul.

He'd shared some of his angst with Lia. She was a good
listener. Attentive. Nonjudgmental. Empathetic. Sure,
she was a little quirky. But Ethan found her eccentricities
charming. That Paul viewed them as suspect made Ethan
all the more determined to defend her.

Clamping down on his disquiet, Ethan reentered his
grandfather's hospital room and noted that Grady's eyes
were open and sharp with dismay. Had he heard the brothers arguing in the hallway? Although Grady never shied
away from confrontation, before the stroke, he'd confided to
Ethan that he was troubled by his estrangement from Paul
and also the growing tension between the brothers. Ethan
knew Paul was equally frustrated with the rift, but none of
them had taken any steps to overcome the years of distance.

"Sorry about earlier," Ethan murmured, settling into the
chair between Grady's bed and the window. "You know
how Paul can get."

He didn't expect Grady to answer. In the weeks following the stroke, Grady had made some progress with the pa-
ralysis. He still couldn't walk or write, but he'd regained the
ability to move his arm, leg and fingers. It wasn't so much
his body that had failed him, but his willingness to fight.

Grady's lips worked, but he couldn't form the words for
what he wanted to express. For the first time in weeks this
seemed to frustrate him.

"He worries about you," Ethan continued. "Seeing Lia

here was a bit of a shock." He couldn't suppress a grin. "Did you like her Rapunzel costume? The kids down on the pediatric floor really loved her."

Grady started to hum a toneless tune Ethan didn't recognize. And then all at once he sang a word.

"Ava."

Ethan was shocked that Grady had spoken—or rather sung—his daughter's name. "You mean Lia," he said, wondering how his grandfather could've confused his daughter for Lia. Blonde and green-eyed Ava Watts bore no resemblance to Lia, with her dark hair and hazel eyes. Then Ethan frowned. Had Lia ever come to visit as herself or was she always in costume? Maybe Grady thought she was blonde. And then there was the age difference. If Ava had lived, she'd be in her forties. Of course, the stroke had messed with the left side of Grady's brain where logic and reason held court. Maybe he was actually mixed up.

Ava had been eighteen when she'd run away to New York City. The family had lost track of her shortly thereafter. And it wasn't until five years after that that they found out she'd died, leaving behind an infant daughter. The child had been adopted, but they'd never been able to discover anything more because the files had been sealed.

"Ava...baby," Grady clarified, singing the two words. How had he learned to do that?

"You think Lia is Ava's daughter?" While Grady nodded as enthusiastically as his condition allowed, Ethan's stunned brain slowly wrapped itself around this development. Grady was obviously grasping at thin air. With each year that passed he'd grown more obsessed with finding his missing granddaughter.

"Ava's daughter is here?" Constance Watts asked from the doorway. "Where? How?"

Ethan turned to his mother, about to explain what was going on, when his grandfather's fingers bit down hard

on Ethan's wrist, drawing his attention back to the man in
the bed. Grady's gaze bore the fierce determination of old,
sending joy flooding through Ethan. What he wouldn't give
to have his grandfather healthy and happy again.

"Ethan?" his mother prompted, coming to stand beside
him.

"Lia…" Grady sang again, more agitated now as he tried
to make himself understood.

"Lia?" Constance stared at her father-in-law, and then
glanced at her son for clarification. "Who is Lia?"

But when the answer came, it was Grady who spoke
up. "Ava…baby."

After her run-in with Paul Watts the day before, the last
place Lia expected to find herself was seated beside Ethan
in his bright blue Mercedes roadster on the way to the hospital to visit his grandfather. Overhead, clouds dappled the
dazzling February sky. Around them the sweet scent of
honeysuckle and crab apple blossoms mingled with the
sound of church bells coming from the Cathedral of Saint
Luke and Saint Paul. It was a glorious day for driving with
the top down, but this was no joyride.

"I'm really not sure this is the best idea," Lia said, shuddering as she pictured her last encounter with Paul Watts.
"Your brother was pretty clear that he didn't want me anywhere near your grandfather."

"Paul's occupation makes him suspicious," Ethan said.
"And Grady's illness has made him even more edgy. Add
to that the fact that he doesn't like surprises and that ex-
plains why he overreacted at finding a stranger visiting his
grandfather." Ethan shot her a wry grin packed with boyish
charm. "And you were dressed like Rapunzel so that had
to throw him off, as well."

Lia rolled her eyes, unmoved by his attempt to lull her

into giving up her argument. "Are you sure Paul will be okay with me visiting?"

She craved Ethan's reassurance. No one had ever treated her with the level of suspicion Paul Watts had shown.

"He wants Grady to get better just like the rest of us."

"That's not the same thing as being okay with my visiting," she pointed out, the churning in her stomach made worse by Ethan's evasion. Paul's bad opinion of her bothered Lia more than she liked to admit.

"Look, Paul's not in town at the moment so you don't need to worry about running into him. You just visit Grady a few more times and be the ray of sunshine that will enable him to improve and by the time Paul gets back, Grady will be on the mend and Paul will realize it was all due to you."

"I think you're overestimating my abilities," she demurred, even as Ethan's praise warmed her. Each time she'd visited Grady she held his hand and sung to him, pouring healing energy into his frail body.

"Trust me," Ethan declared, taking his espresso-colored eyes off the road and shooting a brief glance her way. "I'm not overestimating anything. Your visits have been transformative."

"But I've only been to see him four times," Lia murmured, determined to voice caution. If Ethan gave her all the credit for his grandfather's improvement, what happened if Grady took a turn for the worse? "I can't imagine I made that much of an impact."

"You underestimate yourself." Ethan spun the wheel and coasted into an empty spot in the parking garage. "He started communicating a little yesterday by singing the way you suggested. That's given him a huge boost in his outlook and he's growing better by the hour. You'll see."

In fact, Lia was excited to see Grady improve. She believed in the power of spiritual healing and trusted that she could tap into the energy that connected all living things and bring about change because she willed it. It didn't always work. Some concrete problems required real-world solutions. For instance, the broken axle on her camper trailer and her totaled truck.

Meditating hadn't gotten Misty fixed. She'd needed money and a mechanic for that. But after asking for help, the universe had found her a wonderful job, terrific coworkers and an affordable place to live. She'd been offered a solution at a point when she was feeling desperate.

Ethan shut off the engine and hit her with an eager grin. "Ready?"

"Sure." But in fact, she was anything but.

When they got off the elevator on the fourth floor, Ethan's long strides ate up the distance to his grandfather's hospital room, forcing Lia to trot in order to keep up.

As they neared Grady's room, Lia spied a familiar figure emerging. "Hi, Abigail," Lia said, as the distance between them lessened. "How is Grady doing today?"

For a moment the nurse looked startled that a stranger had called her by her name, but then she took a longer look at Lia and her eyes widened. "Lia! I didn't recognize you out of costume."

Lia gave an awkward chuckle and glanced at Ethan. "I'm not sure Grady will recognize me, either."

"Mr. Grady will know who you are." The nurse's reassuring smile did little to ease Lia's nerves. "There's a keen mind locked up in there." She glanced at Ethan and when he gave her a confirming nod, Abigail continued, "He's going to be so glad you've come today. Your idea to encourage him to sing has worked wonders. He's so excited to be able to communicate with people again."

Beside her, Ethan radiated smug satisfaction.

"That's great," Lia said, delighted that her suggestion had produced a positive result.

"His family and all the staff are so thrilled that things

started to turn around yesterday. He's doing so much better that the doctor thinks he'll be able to go in a few days."

"Wow," Lia murmured, "that's wonderful news."

"We're so glad she showed up when she did," Ethan declared. "She's worked a miracle."

"Please stop," Lia protested, the praise making her uncomfortable. "The credit really should go to all of you who've been taking such good care of him this whole time."

"There's only so much medicine can do when the will to keep on living is gone," the nurse said.

"Mind over matter," Ethan said. "People don't give it enough credit."

"They certainly don't," Abigail agreed before heading down the hall toward the nurses' station.

Ethan set his hand on Lia's elbow and drew her into Grady's hospital room. As soon as she stepped across the threshold, Lia was struck by the room's buoyant energy. The first time she'd visited Grady Watts, he'd been an immobile lump beneath the covers, unconscious and unaware that she'd taken his hand and softly sung to him. Today as she stepped closer to the bed, she noticed that he was wide awake and eagerly watching her approach. The directness of his gaze reminded her of Paul and she shivered. Ethan had mentioned his grandfather had a sharp temper and forceful manner when crossed.

Grady wiggled his fingers and she took his hand. His dry skin stretched over bones knobby with arthritis. She gave his fingers a light squeeze, shocked at the rush of affection for someone she barely knew. Yet was that true?

Usually she moved on every couple months and rarely got tangled up in people's lives. In this case, her accident extended her time in Charleston, leading to numerous massage sessions with Ethan where he'd spoken at length about his family. As the weeks turned into months, Lia had grown ever more invested in their stories until she almost felt like part of their circle.

"Hello, Grady," Lia said, her voice warbling as affection tightened her throat. "It's Lia. You probably didn't recognize me without my costume. How are you feeling today? You look really good."

Grady's fingers pulsed against hers as he acknowledged her with two sung words. "Ava daughter."

Ethan had explained how Grady had been desperate to reunite with his missing granddaughter before the stroke, even speculating that the patriarch's illness had been brought on by the crushing disappointment of a recent dead end. Since then, Grady had brooded nonstop about what had become of her and the family's failure to bring her back into the fold.

"That's right, Grady," Ethan said, beaming at Lia. His eyes held a wicked twinkle as he added, "Ava's daughter has come home at last."

Delighted by the news, Lia glanced at Ethan and noticed the way the handsome businessman was regarding her with purposeful intent. Her heart began hammering against her ribs as the import of what Ethan was saying struck her. She shifted her attention to the man lying in the hospital bed and she caught her breath to protest. But before she could voice her sharp denial, she saw the love shining in Grady's eyes for her. No. Not for her. For his missing granddaughter.

Head spinning, Lia turned her full attention on Ethan. "What's going on?"

"What's going on is that Grady knows you're his granddaughter." Ethan gripped Lia's elbow with long fingers while his eyes beseeched her to go along. "I explained how Paul located you through one of those genetic testing companies. It's long been Grady's dream to reunite you with your family. And now here you are."

Lia's mind reeled. The position Ethan had put her in was untenable, and to drag his brother into the mix was only going to create more drama. But the sheer joy in Grady's eyes tied her tongue in knots. This could not be happening. She had to tell the truth. She wasn't Ava Watts's long-lost daughter. To claim that she was the missing Watts grand-daughter would only lead to trouble.

"We need to talk about this," Lia growled quietly at Ethan. She put her hand on Grady's shoulder. "We'll be right back."

Leaving a confused Grady behind, Lia fled out into the hallway. To her relief, Ethan followed her. Worried that Grady might overhear their conversation, Lia grabbed Ethan's arm and towed him down the hall toward the wait-ing area near the bank of elevators.

"Have you lost your mind?" she whispered as soon as they reached the empty family lounge. "How could you tell him I'm his granddaughter? And why put Paul in the middle of it? He's going to be furious."

"Grady came to that conclusion all by himself," Ethan explained. "And the reason I gave Paul credit was to help repair the strained relationship between him and Grady."

"Your brother will never go along with this."

"He will when he sees the way Grady is recovering. Overnight his whole prognosis has changed. And it's all because he believes you're his granddaughter. It was his deepest desire to reunite with her and now he has a rea-son to live."

"But I'm not his granddaughter. Why would he think I am? I don't look like any of your family." Lia's heart twisted as she realized her protest might rouse Ethan's angst over being adopted.

"You could be Ava's daughter." Ethan lifted his hands in a beseeching gesture. "We've been trying for years to find her with no luck. I told you that after my aunt died, her baby was adopted and the records were sealed. Believing you're her has given Grady a reason to go on. Do you seriously want to go back in there and break his heart? He's been so depressed since the stroke. In less than a week you've brought him back from the brink of death."

Lia closed her eyes and spent several seconds listening to the pounding of her heart. This could not be happening. And yet it was.

"I just can't do this."

Besides being wrong, even if she agreed to a temporary stint as Grady Watts's missing granddaughter, there was no way Paul was going to let her take on the role.

"You can," Ethan insisted. "Making people feel better is what you do."

"Sure, but not like this," Lia protested. "And I don't want to lie to your family."

"I understand, but they aren't any good at keeping secrets. We've never thrown a successful surprise party or gotten into trouble without everyone in the family knowing about it. For this to work we need to leave them in the dark or else risk that someone will slip up and give you away."

From Ethan's aggrieved tone, this obviously bugged him, and Lia sympathized. Having been isolated from relatives all her life, she couldn't imagine having so many people in her business. Yet there was a flip side. Ethan could also count on his family to have his back.

"And what about Paul?" she quizzed. "Surely he's already dug up enough info on me to know I'm not your cousin."

"Let me handle my brother."

Lia slid sweaty palms along her jean-clad thighs. "Damn it, Ethan. You can't deceive your grandfather this way."

"I can if it means keeping Grady alive," Ethan said and his voice held genuine pain.

"It's a lie," Lia insisted, but she could feel her determination failing beneath the weight of Ethan's enthusiasm. "A big fat dangerous lie. And you know I wasn't planning on sticking around Charleston much longer. Misty is fixed. I almost have enough saved to replace my truck." While this was true, Lia didn't have enough to buy a quality vehicle she could trust. "It's time I got back on the road."

"All you need to do is stay a couple weeks until Grady's completely out of the woods and then we can reveal that a huge mistake was made with the genetic testing service." Something in Lia's expression must have betrayed her weakening resistance because Ethan nodded as if she'd voiced her agreement. "I've thought the whole thing through and I know this will work."

If she hadn't grown fond of the handsome Charleston businessman since he'd become her massage client six months earlier, she never would've agreed to hear him out, much less consider such a wild scheme, but the pain Ethan felt over his grandfather's illness had touched her heart. Plus, he'd made the whole scheme sound so reasonable. A couple of weeks of playacting and then she'd be on her way again. A bubble of hysteria rose inside her. What were more lies on top of the ones she was already telling?

"But I'll be lying not just to Grady, but your whole family. It's a cruel thing to do to all of them."

"I've thought about that, too, but if we do this right, they'll be so happy that Grady is healthy again that it will make the eventual disappointment of you not being family easier to bear." Ethan gripped her hands and hit her with a mega dose of confident charm.

Lia was rallying one last refusal when the elevator doors opened and a slender woman in an elegant suit the color of pistachios stepped off. Instead of immediately heading for the hallway that led to the hospital rooms, she glanced toward the family lounge. Her expression brightened when she spied them.

"Ethan," she said, coming toward them. "Glad to see you here."

"Hello, Mother." Ethan dipped his head and kissed her cheek. "This is Lia."

Constance Watts was every inch a genteel matriarch of the South with her blond hair styled in a long bob and her triple strand of pearls. Her keen blue eyes assessed the jeans and thrift-store T-shirt Lia wore and she braced herself for censure, but Constance only smiled warmly.

"Ethan told me all about you," Constance said, her captivating Southern drawl knotted with emotion.

"He did?" Lia hadn't yet agreed to the scheme and bristled at Ethan's presumption.

"Of course." Constance glanced from Lia to her son. "He said Paul found you through a genetic testing service."

"I'm really—" Lia began.

"Overwhelmed," Ethan broke in, closing his fingers around her hand and squeezing gently. He snared her gaze, his eyes reflecting both determination and apology. "And can you blame her? Finally connecting with her real family after all these years is pretty momentous."

Ethan's need and his mother's elation were a patch of quicksand, trapping Lia. To her dismay, she began nodding.

"Ava's daughter is finally home," Constance murmured, stepping forward and embracing Lia. "You are going to make Grady so happy."

Three

Paul was crossing the hotel lobby on his way to the first panel of the day when his phone buzzed. Incensed at Ethan for bringing a stranger into their grandfather's hospital room, Paul had been ignoring his brother's calls since leaving for the conference. He pulled out his phone and was on the verge of sending the call to voice mail when he spied his mother's picture on the screen. His first reaction was dread. Had Grady's health taken a turn for the worse? Is that why she was calling rather than checking in by text?

"What's wrong?" he demanded, shifting his trajectory toward a quiet nook opposite the reception desk. "Is Grady okay?"

"He's fine. In fact, he's doing better than ever." Constance Watts sounded breathless with delight. "I just wanted to update you that Grady is coming home from the hospital today."

"That's great news," Paul said, stunned by the upswing in Grady's progress. "So he's finally rallying?"

"Thanks to Lia."

"Lia?" Hearing that woman's name was like touching a live wire. The jolt made his heart stop. "I don't understand." Paul believed in cold hard facts not instinct, but at the moment his gut was telling him something bad was happening. "How is she responsible for Grady's improved health?"

"I can't believe you'd have to ask," Paul's mother said. "Ethan told me you found her."

"He did?" Paul responded cautiously. Obviously, his brother had neglected to mention Paul's suspicions about the woman. "Has she been visiting Grady?"

Constance laughed. "She's been by his side constantly for days. Having her there has made his recovery nothing short of miraculous. All the hospital staff are talking about it."

"Grady's getting better?" The volume of Paul's relief almost drowned out the other tidbit his mother had dropped. Lia was visiting Grady despite being told to stay away.

Obviously Paul had underestimated just how intent she was on interfering with his family. Well, he'd send her packing as soon as he returned home.

"...Ava's daughter back in the fold."

Who was back? His mother had continued to prattle on while Paul had been preoccupied. He shook his head to reorient his thoughts.

"I'm sorry, Mother, it's really loud where I am. Can you repeat what you said?"

"I said, Grady is thrilled that you found Ava's daughter," Constance said.

"I found..." Now Paul understood why Ethan had been working so hard to get in touch.

"When are you coming home? Grady's been asking to see you."

For the first time in his adult life, Paul Watts had no words. While his mother waited for his reply, Paul's brain worked feverishly to unravel what could possibly be going on back in Charleston. What sort of crazy stunt was his brother trying to pull? And why? Lia had no more Watts blood than Eth…

Paul shut down the rest of that thought. He and Ethan might not share a biological bond, but they were brothers and Ethan was just as much a Watts as any of them. The same could not be said for a drifter like Lia Marsh.

He hadn't been idle over the last few days of the conference. He'd taken the time to dig into her background and what he'd come up with only reinforced his suspicion that she was some sort of con artist.

"Mother, I need to go." Paul hated to be rude, but he needed to talk to his brother immediately. "Can I call you later?"

"Of course. When are you coming home?"

He was scheduled to return home in three days' time. "I'm going to cut my trip short and catch a flight today."

"That's wonderful."

Paul hung up with his mother and immediately called Ethan. He wasn't surprised when it rolled over to voice mail. Snarling, Paul disconnected without delivering the scathing smackdown his brother so richly deserved. He sent his personal assistant a text about his change of plans so she could organize a flight for him, and then he headed to his suite to pack.

An hour later he was on his way to the airport. A second call to Ethan went unanswered, but this time Paul left an icy message, demanding to know what was going on. The hours between liftoff and touchdown gave Paul plenty of time to check in with the rest of his family and get a feel for what had been going on in his absence.

The situation had progressed further than he'd anticipated. What really burned him was how happy and unquestioning everyone was with the arrival of a stranger claiming to be Ava's daughter. Lia had charmed his parents, aunt and uncle as well as his three Shaw cousins. Nor would any of them listen when he pointed out that they didn't know anything about this woman who'd abruptly appeared in their midst. All they cared about was that Ava's daughter had come home and Grady had magically become healthy.

Eager to get the whole messy situation sorted out, once he arrived in Charleston Paul headed straight from the airport to Grady's estate. He parked on the wide driveway at the back of the property, noting that Ethan's car was absent. The heated lecture Paul wanted to deliver would have to wait.

Paul's breath came in agitated bursts as he wound his way along the garden path and approached the back of the house where a set of double stairs ascended to a broad terrace. Taking the steps two at a time, Paul crossed the terrace to the glass door that led into the kitchen. The room had been remodeled a few years ago to include a massive granite island, abundant cabinets, professional appliances and an updated surround for the fireplace. Two doorways offered access to the interior of the home. Paul chose the one that led into the broad entry hall. Immediately to his left, a set of stairs led upward. Paul's tension rose as he ascended.

The home had been designed with spacious rooms off a wide main hallway. Upstairs, the broad space between the bedrooms was utilized as a cozy lounge area for watching television from the comfortable couch or reading in one of the armchairs that overlooked the rear of the property—as his grandfather's nurse Rosie was doing at the moment. Although Paul recognized that his grandfather didn't require her hovering over him at all hours of the day and night, seeing her whiling her time away over a cup of tea and a novel disturbed him.

"How's he doing?"

Rosie looked up from her book and shot him a wry grin. "Go see for yourself."

Paul approached his grandfather's bedroom, bracing himself for the same dimly lit, hushed space it had become since Grady's stroke. But the scene he stepped into was the utter opposite. Stuttering to a halt just inside the door, Paul gaped in confusion and alarm. What the hell was going on here?

Someone had pulled the curtains back from the windows allowing light to fill the large space. Elvis Presley's "All Shook Up" poured from a speaker on the nightstand, almost drowning out the soothing trickle of water from a small fountain situated on the dresser. The scent of rosemary and lavender drifted toward Paul. As the aroma hit his senses, he noticed a slight boost to his energy and felt a whole lot calmer than he'd been in months. He shook off the sensations and scowled at the source of all his internal commotion.

Paul realized it was Lia who'd transformed Grady's master suite from dark and bleak to bright and festive. And it did seem to be having a magical effect. For the first time since his stroke, Paul's grandfather was sitting upright in bed, propped against an abundance of pillows, his bright gaze fixed on the woman standing beside him. Lia was chattering away while her hands stroked up and down Grady's arm, working the muscles.

A bewildering swirl of emotions cascaded through him at the sight of his grandfather looking so happy and... healthy. Gladness. Relief. Annoyance. This last was due to Lia. She looked so utterly normal without all the theatrical makeup and princess clothing. Today she wore a plain gray T-shirt and black yoga leggings that showed off her lean hips and thighs. A silky ponytail of brown hair swept forward to cascade over one delicate collarbone, while long bangs framed her narrow face with its pixie chin and bright red lips. Silver hoop earrings swung against her delicate jawline.

Paul's immediate impulse was to haul her out of the room and away from his grandfather. He didn't trust her despite finding nothing concrete in her background to support the warning in his gut. Just because she hadn't been caught didn't mean she wasn't up to no good. Nor did it help her case how swiftly she'd charmed his entire family into embracing her as one of their own.

Even as he fumed in frustration, Paul became aware of something hot and disturbing lying beneath his irritation. It was as if his anger had awakened an insistent, instinctive pulse of raw hunger. He cursed the untimely appearance of this single-minded lust for Lia Marsh. Being distracted by physical cravings was the last thing he needed.

As if alerted by his conflicting desires, Lia glanced his way. Within their frame of sooty lashes, her eyes locked on his. Pleasure roared through him as she bit down on her lower lip. Color flooded her cheeks and for a second he pondered what might happen if his awareness was reciprocated.

Paul ruthlessly swept such musing aside. What did it matter if she was attracted to him? But then he dialed back his annoyance. Could he use it to his advantage?

His thoughts must've shown on his face because a wary frown drew Lia's eyebrows together. Irritated that he'd given himself away, Paul scowled in return. With a grimace she shifted her attention to Grady. Her smile brightened with what appeared to be genuine affection. Paul's gut clenched as he took in the tableau.

"Look who's here," she murmured, indicating Paul.

His grandfather turned his head and the warmth in his welcoming smile filled Paul with blinding joy. It was as if all the years of estrangement had been never been.

"Paul."

At hearing his name spoken so clearly by his grandfather, a lump formed in Paul's throat and stuck there. Because the stroke had affected Grady's speech, he'd struggled to make himself understood these last few months. Obviously, the reports of Grady's improvement hadn't been exaggerated. But to credit this interloper was going too far. Lost in his circling thoughts, Paul still hovered where he'd stopped just inside the room until his grandfather tapped out some rhythms on a small drum next to him on the bed.

"That means come," Lia explained.

Completely bewildered by what was happening, Paul crossed to his grandfather's side and gave his arm a squeeze. "How are you feeling today?"

The routine question was completely unnecessary. This man bore no resemblance to the invalid from a week ago. At that point, with Grady growing weaker by the day, Paul would've moved heaven and earth to see the return of a mischievous glint to his grandfather's green eyes, which had so recently been dull with defeat and grief. What he glimpsed in Grady's manner was the exact change he'd longed for. But at what cost?

"Happy." A distinct pattern of tapping accompanied Grady's singing. While his voice was breathy and tuneless, the word came out surprisingly clear. Yet despite his joy, Paul was disturbed by how his grandfather's gaze settled fondly on the young woman massaging his hand. "Lia home."

"What's with the drum?" Paul asked Lia, grappling with his shock at Grady's rapid improvement and his attachment to the stranger who had invaded all their lives. Discomfort formed a hard knot in his chest. Although thrilled by his grandfather's improvement, Paul could see nothing but trouble barreling down the road toward them and cursed his brother for doing something so radical and foolish.

"I did some research on stroke recovery and discovered that music and rhythm can help lift a patient's spirts, enable them to communicate and improve their speech." Lia smiled fondly at Grady. "Tomorrow we're going to learn breathing rhythms and also practice meditating to music."

"What's all that supposed to do?"

"The medical explanation didn't make all that much sense to me," Lia said. "But there was something about how the brain processes information and how music can affect that in a positive way. I think that's why Grady can't speak, but he can sing."

Paul's chest tightened as hope surged and he set his jaw against a blast of raw emotion. From the way his grandfather beamed at Lia, it was obvious what everyone had been saying. Grady's improvement had been inspired by the return of his long-lost granddaughter. Only Lia wasn't Ava's daughter and Paul hated the fraud she and his brother were perpetrating.

So, what was he going to do? Paul had never lied to his grandfather. Many times in the past when he was a kid growing up, he'd done something wrong and no matter how bad the punishment, he'd always told Grady the truth. It was a point of pride to Paul that his grandfather trusted him without question.

If he continued to let Grady believe his granddaughter had returned to her family, what sort of damage was he doing to his relationship with his grandfather? Yet Grady's will to live seemed to have been restored by Lia's arrival. Could Paul figure out a way to get rid of her without causing his grandfather harm?

"Do you have a couple minutes to talk?" he asked as she finished massaging Grady's arm and carefully placed it back on the bed.

"Grady has a session with his physical therapist in ten minutes."

With the number of relatives coming and going these days, Paul didn't want his conversation with Lia interrupted or overheard. "I'll meet you by the pool."

On the flight back to Charleston, he'd prepared a number of ways to extricate her from his family. Now, with Grady's improvement hanging on her continued presence, he wasn't convinced sending her away was the best idea.

While he waited for Lia to arrive, Paul paced the concrete deck, oblivious to the tranquility offered by the turquoise rectangle of water, the lush landscaping and the peaceful twittering of the birds.

This whole situation would be more cut-and-dried if anything suspicious had appeared in her background check. But Paul had nothing concrete to prove that she might not be as transparent as she appeared. While deep in his gut he was certain that she was keeping secrets, Paul was a man who acted on facts not feelings.

When Lia arrived, Paul wasted no time making his position clear. "When I told you to stay away from my grandfather, I had no idea things would get this out of control. I don't know what you and my brother were thinking, but this can't go on."

Because his entire family had embraced her, it fell to Paul to remain detached and keep his guard up. That would be easier if she didn't stir his body and incite his emotions. And if she hadn't worked miracles with his grandfather.

"You're right," she agreed. "I shouldn't have let Ethan talk me into lying to everyone. I'm sorry. It's just Ethan was so desperate to help your grandfather. And believing that I'm his granddaughter has made him better."

Paul watched her expression, determined to see past her guileless facade to the truth. "You've done a good job making sure everyone is attached to you."

Her lashes flickered at his deliberate accusation. "That's to be expected. They all think I'm their long-lost cousin."

She crossed her arms over her chest and lifted her chin. "Have you decided how you're going to break the news about me being an imposter?"

Paul forced air through his teeth in a soft hiss. "I'm not sure I can. The truth would crush Grady."

Her eyebrows went up in surprise. "What are you going to do then?"

"I don't know." He needed to discuss the situation with Ethan.

She narrowed her eyes in confusion. "So why did you want to talk to me?"

Why had he wanted to talk to her?

"I…"

What could he say? That she'd been on his mind the entire time he was gone? That he found her fascinating despite his mistrust? He wanted to know everything about her. And not just because her mysterious background and limited digital footprint awakened his curiosity. Some of her behavior didn't fall into easily explainable patterns. For example, why did she dress up and visit children in the hospital? Something so altruistic was contrary to how an opportunist would behave. Unless she played on the sympathies of parents with sick children to some end. He'd never know unless he got to know her better.

And then there was the pesky physical attraction she inspired in him. Even now, as his thoughts took him down a somber path, he caught himself admiring her long lashes and wondering if her full lips could possibly be as soft as they looked. Her casual outfit showed off a toned body with soft curves. He imagined framing her slim hips with his hands and pulling her close. Dipping his head and running his lips down her neck to the place where it met her shoulder. Hearing her groan in pleasure as he lifted her against his growing erection and plunged his tongue into her mouth…

"Paul?" she said. "Are you okay?"

His name on her lips shocked him out of his lusty daydream. "No, I'm not okay. You and Ethan have put me in the untenable position of having to lie to Grady." A slight breeze flowed toward them from the garden, bringing the sweet scent of honeysuckle and cooling the heat beneath his skin.

"I know and I'm sorry." She put her hand on his arm and the contact seared him through two layers of fabric. "But you won't have to worry about that for too long. In a couple weeks, as soon as Grady is firmly on the road to a full recovery, we'll explain that the genetic testing place made a huge mistake and I'll be gone."

That she and his brother thought they could just snap their fingers and undo the whole situation showed just how impulsive they'd been.

"Why are you doing this?" he demanded, badly needing to understand. "What do you get out of it?"

Something flickered in her eyes briefly before she composed her features into an expression of benign innocence. "Nothing."

Nothing? Paul's muscles bunched as wariness returned. That didn't ring true. Because what he'd glimpsed in that microsecond was all the confirmation that he needed that Lia Marsh was up to no good.

Lia could tell Paul wasn't believing her claim and decided she'd better elaborate. "I really don't want anything from your grandfather or any of your family. I just want to help." She infused this last statement with all her passion, wondering if anything she said would quiet Paul's suspicions.

Earlier when she'd looked up and spied Paul standing in his grandfather's bedroom, her first reaction hadn't been panic, but vivid, undeniable lust. The guy was just so gorgeous. For someone who made his living thwarting cyber-criminals he had an amazing physique. His broad shoulders and imposing height sent her heartbeat racing while his smoldering looks drove her desires into dangerous territory.

Now, as he frowned at her, Lia was struck again by his sex appeal. Sunlight teased gold from his dark blond hair and highlighted his strong bone structure. In those all too brief moments when he wasn't scowling, his features were almost boyishly handsome, and Lia caught herself wishing he'd smile at her. A ridiculous wish considering that he'd made his opinion of her crystal clear.

Before Paul could respond, his phone rang. He glanced down at the screen and grimaced. "I have to take this."

The instant his attention shifted to the call, Lia retreated toward the house. She wanted to check in on Grady before heading back to her rental. Now that Paul had returned home, she decided the less time she spent around him the better for both of them.

As Lia neared the house, she spied Paul's mother descending the wrought iron staircase from the back terrace. Constance's welcoming smile gave Lia an unfamiliar sense of belonging that left her tongue-tied and riddled with guilt over her deception.

"There you are," Constance said. "Isn't Paul with you? Rosie said he'd been up to visit Grady."

"He had to take a call."

"It's probably his office. I swear that son of mine does nothing but work."

"Ethan said he's quite good at what he does."

"He's exceptionally good with computers and dedicated to running down criminals." For a moment Constance's clear blue eyes glowed with maternal fondness, then she sighed. "It caused quite a stir in our family when he opted to go work for the police department out of college rather than join Watts Shipping, but he needed to follow his heart."

"Catching crooks seems to be his passion."

"Yes, but it's grown into more of an obsession these last two years."

"How come?" Lia cursed her curiosity. She should be fighting her interest in the elder Watts brother not delving into his psyche.

"His friend's network services company was hacked and implanted with a bug that affected four million domains, causing them to leak sensitive customer data, including credit card details, for six months before it was discovered. The resulting bad press led to the company losing nearly all their major accounts and forced them out of business."

"Did Paul catch the hackers?"

"Eventually, but not soon enough to stop what happened to Ben."

Although she regretted that the topic had distressed Constance, Lia couldn't stop herself from wanting the whole story. "What happened to his friend?"

"After losing everything, he died in a terrible car accident." Constance's expression turned grim. "Paul thought the circumstances were suspicious because there were no other cars involved. Ben lost control, went off a bridge and drowned. Plus, there was a cryptic email Paul received shortly before the accident. Taken together, he thought perhaps Ben killed himself."

"That's awful."

Constance nodded. "Ben's death hit Paul really hard. After that he became even more committed to shutting down hackers."

Sympathy for Paul momentarily pushed aside her wariness of him. At the same time she recognized this complex man had the power to turn her inside out.

"You know, I can't get over how much you look like your mother," Constance said, the abrupt shift of topic catching Lia off guard.

Lia knew her dark hair and hazel eyes set her apart from the blond and green-eyed Wattses, Ava included. She'd seen pictures of the woman. Yet on Ethan's word, the family had embraced her without question. At least most of them had.

"Tell me about her." Lia couldn't bring herself to say *my mother*.

"She was beautiful and talented." Constance's gaze turned inward. "She played tennis until she was fourteen at a level that she could've competed professionally."

"Why didn't she?"

"She had trouble staying focused on anything," Constance said. "By the time she hit her teenage years Ava was a handful. She grew up without a mother and Grady indulged her terribly. Everyone did because she could be charming when she set her mind to it."

"Ethan said after high school she headed to New York City to pursue modeling."

"She and Grady had a terrible row when he found out she didn't intend to go to college. He gave her a choice—get a degree or find a job. He had such high hopes for her future and wanted to motivate her." Constance sighed. "After years of no contact, Grady hired a private investigator to find her. That's when we learned she'd died. The police never contacted us because Ava did such a good job cutting her ties to Charleston. By the time we discovered Ava had given birth to you, you'd been adopted and the court records sealed."

"And my…father." The last word stuck in Lia's throat. Never mind her fake father—she knew nothing about her own father because her mother had refused to discuss him.

Constance blinked in surprise. "We don't know anything about him. Whatever your mother was up to in New York remains a complete mystery."

Both women lapsed into companionable silence, each occupied with her thoughts. Lia was wondering how to extricate herself without seeming rude when Paul's mother spoke again.

"It's so good to have you here," Constance declared with sudden vehemence. "I'm just sorry it took so long for us to find you."

"I had a good life." For some reason Lia felt compelled to defend her childhood. "A happy life."

"Of course you did," Constance said. "It's obvious that you're a loving, caring person. That sort of thing only happens if you've had the right upbringing. Your aunt Lenora and I were talking last night," Constance said, "and we think that you should move into your mother's old bedroom."

"Oh, well…" Overwhelmed by the thought of having to maintain her deception all the time, Lia scrambled for some polite way to refuse. "I couldn't impose."

"You're family. You wouldn't be imposing. And we have purely selfish reasons to suggest it. We all feel that the more time you spend with Grady, the faster he'll improve."

"Yes, but…"

"He's been without you for too long. You two have a lot of catching up to do."

"Well, sure, but…"

"What are you two talking about?" Paul asked, coming up the gravel path behind them.

Lia turned to confront him, bracing herself for the heat of his displeasure when he found out what his mother had suggested.

"There you are," Constance said. "Rosie mentioned you'd arrived. Have you been up to see Grady? His progress is absolutely amazing."

"Quite amazing," Paul echoed, his distrustful green gaze flickering in Lia's direction.

"And we have Lia to thank."

"So I keep hearing," Paul muttered, his tone neutral.

Seeming unaware of the tension between her son and Lia, Constance continued, "I was just telling her that Lenora and I want her to move in."

"And I was just saying that I don't think that's a good idea," Lia inserted, hoping that he would give her credit for keeping his family at arm's length.

"There's no need to spend money on a rental when there's so much room here," Constance said.

"It's only for a couple weeks," Lia protested. "Then Misty and I will be on our way."

"Misty?" Paul asked.

"She's my camper trailer." She and Ethan had decided to stick close to her original story to avoid slipups.

"You named your camper Misty?" Paul interjected, his lips twisting sardonically.

Lia glared at him. He could insult her integrity all he wanted, but disparage her home and she'd come out swinging. "She's vintage."

Before Paul could reply, his mother jumped in. "Everyone is coming here to have dinner tonight. I hope you can make it."

"I came here straight from the airport," he said, "so I need to run home first."

"Take Lia. I'm sure she'd love to see your home. She's been cooped up with Grady for days. A little sea air would be good for her." Constance turned to Lia. "And on the way back you can pick up your things and get settled in."

"Really, I'm not sure..."

"It will be much better for Grady if you're close by."

Lia caved beneath Constance's firm determination. "Okay."

"Dinner is at seven," Paul's mother said.

"We'll be back in plenty of time." Paul hard gaze flicked to Lia as he bent to kiss his mother's cheek before striding off.

Lia hustled to catch up to him. As soon as they were out of earshot, she said, "I want you to know I didn't put her up to that."

"I know you didn't. Everyone believes what you've done for Grady is a miracle."

"I haven't done anything."

Paul surveyed her for several silent minutes before replying, "On the contrary. You've done plenty."

Despite his rampant disapproval, Paul demonstrated pristine Southern manners by opening the passenger door on his Range Rover and waiting while she climbed in before closing the door and circling to the driver's side.

"I know you aren't interested in spending any time with me so if you want to just drop me at my place—"

"On the contrary, I intend to spend our time away from the estate getting to know the real you."

It took Lia several panicky heartbeats to decide whether to be alarmed or thrilled. Obviously, he hadn't yet decided to go along with Ethan's wild scheme.

"Awesome." She managed the comeback without a trace of irony. "Does that go both ways?"

Paul stopped concentrating on the road and glanced her way. "What do you mean?"

"You want to know everything about me." Something reckless had taken ahold of her. "Are you going to let me get to know you, as well?"

"Why would you want to do that?" While Paul's tone remained neutral, a muscle bunched in his cheek.

"Because it's what normal people do. They exchange information and feel each other out."

Feel each other out? The phrase sounded flirtatious, and heaven knew she'd give anything if he'd just smile at her, but Paul didn't seem to hear it that way.

"Is that what you did with Ethan?" The tightness in his voice took her aback.

"Why would you ask about him?"

"I still can't figure out your relationship with my brother. How much is he paying you for this little charade?"

Now she understood where Paul was going with his questions. "He agreed to cover what I'm losing in income for a couple weeks."

"How much?" Paul asked.

"I don't know." Lia scrunched up her face as she calculated. "No week is the same. I get paid by the client and that varies."

"Ballpark it for me."

"Including tips, it averages to about eight hundred dollars a week."

For the first time Paul looked taken aback. "That's it?"

Spoken like a man who drove a luxury SUV and lived at the beach. No doubt he couldn't fathom Lia's frugal ways any more than she understood paying more for a single pair of shoes than it cost her to eat for an entire month.

"That's it." Lia believed in the equitable exchange of money for goods or services. "All I want is what's fair."

Paul gave her a skeptical look. "What if I paid you fifty thousand dollars to go away and never come back?"

For several seconds Lia pondered the fancy truck she could buy with such an enormous sum. For six months she'd been stuck in Charleston while she saved enough to replace her wrecked vehicle. Accepting Paul's outrageous offer would enable her to return to her nomadic lifestyle in a few days.

"You said you wanted to get to know me better," she said. "Well, the first thing you should know is that I'm not motivated by money."

"Which is exactly what you'd say," Paul countered, "if your endgame would guarantee you a greater payout."

"Are you suspicious of me in particular or people in general?"

"You have to see that I have good reason to doubt you," he said.

"I really don't see it at all," she shot back, wishing that he'd stop toying with her.

Did he know about her past? Bile rose in her throat as she imagined his disgust. But if he'd dug up her secrets, he'd confront her directly. She studied his profile while her heart thundered in her ears and realized that fearing that he knew all about her background was making her come across as guilty. Lia breathed in for a count of four and released the air just as slowly. What did it matter if Paul knew her story? His good opinion shouldn't matter to her.

Paul studied her the whole time she was striving for calm. "You didn't answer me about taking fifty thousand to disappear."

Lia considered what her mother's reaction would have been to Paul's offer. Jen Marsh had a complicated relationship with money and many of her attitudes had rubbed off on her daughter. Lia lived frugally, avoiding debt, buying only what she needed, living with less stuff. But Jen Marsh took her disdain for spending one step beyond obsessive after what she'd experienced growing up.

"You don't have to pay me anything to drop this whole charade and vanish from your lives," Lia said, noticing a subtle easing in the tension around Paul's mouth. The desire to gain his trust prompted her to add, "Whatever you and Ethan decide is fine with me."

Four

"So you'd really go?" Even as he asked the question, Paul recognized exposing her would throw his whole family into chaos. "If I convinced Ethan that you should?"

"Yes." She cocked her head and studied him. "Frankly I'm surprised you haven't done so already."

"He's not taking my calls."

Paul gripped the steering wheel and contemplated Lia's declaration. Would she really leave the decision up to him and Ethan or would she act behind the scenes to win Ethan to her side?

"So you don't know."

"Don't know what?" Paul asked, wondering what else had gone wrong in his absence.

"How this whole situation came about."

Paul glanced her way. "And how's that?"

"Ethan put me in a position where the only choices I had were to go along and pretend to be Grady's granddaughter or tell the truth and risk that he might not recover from the blow."

Although he wasn't surprised that she'd blame the whole situation on Ethan, Paul asked, "Why don't you tell me what happened."

"Ethan set me up. I thought I was visiting Grady as myself. Instead as I stood beside his bed and held his hand, both he and Ethan ambushed me with this whole thing about being Ava's daughter."

"So you're blaming my grandfather for this situation, as well?"

"No. Yes. Sort of. Ethan told me Grady came up with the idea on his own."

"You didn't mention that Grady might be inspired to improve if his granddaughter miraculously appeared?"

Lia's mouth dropped open. "To what end?"

"The Wattses are a wealthy, old Charleston family. We wield both power and influence in this town. You might've liked the idea of being a part of that."

"Hardly," she sniffed. "In fact, it sounds stressful and intimidating. Not to mention having the threat of a simple DNA test hanging over my head all the time."

"Yet here you are." Distracted by their conversation, Paul almost missed the turnoff to Sullivan's Island. "And here I am. Damn it. I hate having to lie to everyone in my family, but most of all to Grady."

"I feel the same way. Your mom and aunt have been welcoming. And your cousins are really nice. It's horrible that I can't be truthful, but then I see how happy Grady is and watch him get a little better every day, and I think the whole messed-up situation might work out okay."

Paul refused to be persuaded by her feel-good justification. "I'm sure this is the logic you and Ethan have used to justify what you've done, but lying is wrong."

"A lot of the time it is, but not always. What about lying to protect someone's feelings? As long as the lie isn't malicious it doesn't do any harm."

It all sounded like a bunch of excuses to Paul, but he'd invited her on this trip to his house to gain insight into her and this conversation was teaching him a lot. "So you don't believe the truth can set you free?"

"Not always. Sometimes it can be painful."

"That doesn't justify lying."

Lia shrugged. "We will just have to agree to disagree."

Paul glanced her way and saw that she was staring out the passenger window at the passing landscape. Despite their opposing opinions, he couldn't shake his fascination with her.

"I guess we will."

An unrelenting silence fell between them that didn't break even as Paul turned the SUV into his driveway and stopped before his house. Switching off the engine, he glanced her way. Lia radiated disappointment and hurt, but Paul refused to be drawn in. Despite her positive effect on Grady, Paul couldn't shake the notion that Lia Marsh was going to cause trouble for his family.

She was working an angle. He just needed to figure out what it was. Which was why he'd decided to move into the carriage house, located near the back of the estate, for the next two weeks so he could keep an eye on her. He intended for Lia to understand that he wasn't taken in by her do-gooder act.

"I'll just be a few minutes," he said. "Do you want to wait here or come in?"

"I'm sure you'd prefer I stay here."

He dismissed her sarcasm with a shrug. "Suit yourself."

But as he headed up the stairs to his front door, he heard her footsteps on the wood boards behind him. The electronic lock on the entrance disengaged as he neared. He opened the door and gestured Lia inside. After suggesting she check out the view, Paul left Lia gawking at the beach beyond the towering floor-to-ceiling windows that made up one wall of his spacious great room. In his bedroom, he unpacked his luggage, swapping the tailored suits he'd worn to the conference for the slacks and button-down shirts he favored for the office.

Before he'd done more than replace his suits in the closet and dump his dirty clothes into the hamper, Paul's phone began to ring. He glanced at the screen, saw Ethan's name and the disquiet he'd been feeling at his brother's snub eased slightly.

Despite their family's expectations, it was Ethan and not Paul who was following in Grady's footsteps as family mediator and key decision maker. Ethan had always been the empathetic brother. Outgoing and social, he tended to be more in touch with the emotions. And despite being the younger brother, everyone turned to Ethan for advice and support.

In contrast, Paul was more comfortable as a lone wolf. He liked technology because of its logic and predictability and had chosen to become a cop because he thrived on the challenge of catching criminals. That doing so also helped people was a bonus, but it didn't drive him. No doubt Ethan would say this attitude made him a jerk.

Would Lia agree?

Paul couldn't imagine what made the question pop into his mind. Nor did he care about some interloper's opinion about him.

"It's about time you called me back," Paul said irritably into the phone, closing the master bedroom door in case Lia decided to eavesdrop.

"Before you go all big brother and start lecturing me about how much I messed up, tell me you don't see a huge change in Grady."

"Fine. I'll admit that Grady's better and that believing Lia is Ava's daughter is the reason, but why the hell did you drag me into it by saying I'm the one who found her?"

"I thought if you got the credit for doing something that would make Grady incredibly happy that it would repair your relationship."

"You're wrong to hope that will make me less furious with you for dragging me into your scheme." Yet even as he spoke, Paul's heart clenched. Despite the tension that had grown between the brothers, Paul appreciated that Ethan had his back. "Have you thought this whole thing through? He's going to be devastated when the truth comes out. And it will because there's no way I'm letting this go on."

"I didn't figure you would, but he'll be stronger in a few weeks." Ethan paused for a heartbeat. "Or she doesn't have to go anywhere." When Paul sucked in a breath to protest, Ethan jumped in. "Hear me out. She spends all her time driving around the country in a vintage camper picking up odd jobs wherever she goes. That's no life. Instead she could stay with us and be our cousin."

"Have you lost your mind?" Paul demanded, wondering what sort of madness had overcome his brother. "We don't know anything about this person."

"I do. She's genuine and kind. Everyone loves her."

"Even you?"

"What?" Ethan exclaimed, following it up with a rough laugh. "Hardly."

Unsatisfied by his brother's answer, Paul asked another. "Is she in love with you?"

"No."

Paul hadn't been entirely satisfied by Lia's denials and he sensed Ethan was holding something back. While it wasn't unusual for Ethan to champion something or someone he believed in, the level of trust he'd afforded Lia compelled Paul to take nothing for granted.

"Are you sure?" Paul pondered the amount of time Lia had undoubtedly spent with her hands roaming over Ethan's naked body. While she'd claimed to be a professional massage therapist, there was something overtly intimate about the experience. "Women tend to fall for you rather quickly."

"That's because I'm nice to them." Ethan's tone was dry as he finished, "You should try it sometime."

For a second Paul didn't know how to respond to his brother's dig. In truth, he had neither time nor interest in a personal life these days. His consulting company grew busier each year as criminals became increasingly bolder and more clever. Technology changed faster than most people could keep up and new threats emerged daily.

On the other hand, Ethan had taken on more responsibility since their grandfather's stroke compelled their father to pick up Grady's chairmanship duties. Although Ethan had been groomed for years to take over one day, having the responsibility thrust on him without any transition period had increased the amount of hours Ethan spent at the office by 50 percent. Yet he still carved out time for family and friends, dating and even attending their mother's endless charity events.

Paul just didn't want to put in the effort. He'd always been solitary, preferring intimate gatherings with his small circle of friends versus the active bar scene or loud parties. Her solitary lifestyle was probably the one thing Paul actually understood about Lia Marsh.

"Are you sure Lia didn't put the idea in your head that she should play the part of Ava's daughter?"

"Trust me—I came up with the plan all on my own."

Paul gave a noncommittal grunt. "She claims she's only planning on sticking around for two weeks." He paused, assessing how much damage would be done during that span.

"That's what we agreed to. I tried to convince her to stay

for a month, but she's determined to go. She doesn't like staying anywhere for more than a few months."

"What's up with that?"

"I don't know. She doesn't talk much about herself."

Paul considered his earlier conversation with Lia. "You don't think that indicates she has something to hide?" While he waited for Ethan to respond, Paul relived his joy in Grady's affectionate greeting. The thought of losing his grandfather's love and approval all over again filled Paul with dread. "Okay, I really hate the situation, but I agree that she's had a positive impact on Grady. As long as it's only two weeks, I'm okay if she stays around and pretends to be Ava's daughter."

"Thanks." Ethan released the word on a long exhale as if he'd been holding his breath. "And don't worry, we've figured out an exit strategy. It's all going to work out. You'll see."

"Both of you keep saying the same thing. I hope like hell that you're right."

"We are." Ethan's smile came through loud and clear. "And be nice to Lia. She's doing us a huge favor."

After he'd hung up with Ethan, Paul chewed over his brother's final statement as he tossed what clothes he'd need for the next two weeks into a duffel. No one would question his decision to stay at the estate. His office was a few blocks away. He'd slept in the carriage house often since Grady's stroke and even before that had utilized the cozy apartment to break for a nap during an intense case when an hour-long round-trip drive to his beach house was time he couldn't afford.

Paul dropped his overnight bag in the foyer and returned to the great room in search of Lia. He looked out the window and saw her standing beside the pool, her arms crossed over her chest, her attention fixed on the Atlantic Ocean. She'd freed her hair and the brisk wind off the water turned the dark strands into a fluttering pennant. He went out to join her.

"I've never been able to decide if I prefer the mountains or the beach," she said, her lips curving into a smile. "I guess that's why I travel so much. There are always new places to discover."

Her tranquil expression transfixed him. He surveyed the freckles dusting her nose and upper cheeks and wondered what about her captivated him. Was it the thrill of the hunt? He'd parlayed his passion for tracking down cybercriminals into a multimillion-dollar company. Lia presented the exact sort of mystery that drove him to work seventy-and eighty-hour weeks to keep his clients' data safe.

And yet here he was, compelled to accept a suspicious stranger as his cousin in order to save his grandfather. Despite Ethan's assurances, Paul knew Lia represented a danger to his family.

So with that foremost in his mind, why did he constantly find himself fighting the urge to touch her? To sample the warmth of her skin. To pull her tight against him and capture her rosy lips in a heated kiss. This unrelenting war between his body and mind was as exhausting as it was troubling.

Had she influenced Ethan the same way? From their earlier conversation Ethan made it clear he trusted Lia. Before she came along, Paul never questioned his brother's judgment. What was it about Lia that roused Paul's suspicions?

"I think my brother might be in love with you."

"What?" She tore her attention from the view and huffed out a laugh. "That's ridiculous."

"Is it?" Paul countered. "He's very protective of you."

"That's because he likes me." Lia turned and studied his expression for several seconds before adding, "I'm a nice person."

Paul's nostrils flared. "Are you sleeping with him?"

"He's my client," she shot back. "I don't sleep with clients."

"But you're attracted to him?"

"He has an incredible body," she mused, with reckless disregard for his escalating annoyance. "Great muscles. Shoulders to die for. Strong thighs." She paused as if taking stock of the impact her words were having. "And as a massage therapist I have to say it's nice when a man takes such good care of his skin."

"So you are attracted to him?"

Lia gave an impatient snort. "Ethan has impeccable manners, a deep, sexy drawl and an overabundance of charm. That I'm not the least bit attracted to him made my coworkers—of both sexes—question my sexual orientation. I'm a professional. I never would've kept Ethan as a client if he'd inspired even a trace of lust. That sort of thing crosses a line for me."

"You forget I've seen you two together. There's something between you."

"He's felt comfortable enough with me to share stuff," she murmured.

"There's more to it than that."

"No, there isn't," Lia declared impatiently before sucking in a deep, calming breath. "Look," she said, giving her shoulders a little shake to relax them. "I feel as if we're dancing around something."

"I don't dance."

"No," Lia muttered wryly. "I expect you don't. Look, for this to work, we really need to find a way to get along." She paused, giving him the opportunity to agree. When he remained silent, Lia chose not to wait him out. "How about if I confess something that's hard for me to admit?" She cleared her throat and gave a nervous half smile. "I find you attractive."

He should've regarded the admission as a clever manipulation and met it with skepticism. Instead, her confession lit up his body like a fireworks finale.

"Why would you tell me something like that?"

"It gives you a little power over me," she said with a sexy, sweet smile that sent an electric pulse zipping along his nerve endings.

"And you think I need that," he countered, bothered that she had him all figured out. Well, maybe not all figured out. But she had a pretty good idea of what made him tick. It served as a reminder that he needed to stay on his guard around her.

"Don't you?" Her presumptive manner bordered on over-confidence. "I think you crave being in control at all times and I'll bet it drives you crazy when things don't go according to plan."

"I don't go crazy," he said, stepping into her space, unwilling to consider his real motivation for what he was about to do. "I adapt."

Lia misjudged the reason Paul closed the gap between them and never saw the kiss coming. Being caught completely by surprise heightened the emotional impact of his soft breath feathering across her skin. An instant later, his lips touched hers and a million stars exploded behind her eyelids. He cradled her head with strong fingers, grounding her while the firm, masterful pressure of his mouth stole her breath and her equilibrium.

Paul's kisses were in a class all by themselves. Never before had she been so swept up in the magic of the moment. The perfection of his lips gliding over hers. The hitch in his breath as she shifted her weight onto her toes and leaned in to him. Lia never wanted the kiss to end, but couldn't explain why. What was it about Paul that called to her? He'd offered her nothing but skepticism and scowls. Yet the clean, masculine scent of him, the gentle sweep of his fingertips against her skin unleashed both joy and hunger.

When he sucked on her bottom lip, she groaned and gave him full access to her mouth. His tongue swept against hers and the taste of him only increased her appetite for more. Lia tunneled her fingers into his hair to keep their mouths fused as he fed on her lips and she devoured him in turn.

His arm banded around her waist, drawing her snugly against his hard torso. While she'd appreciated Paul's powerful body from a safe distance, pressed like this against the unyielding solidity of his strong abs sharpened the longing to feel his weight settle over her.

She'd been kissed enough to recognize she'd never experienced anything like this before. Where moments ago she'd been shivering in the cool breeze coming off the ocean, now her skin burned as fire raced through her veins and sent heat deep into her loins. Paul must've recognized the upward tick in her passion because his hand curved over her butt and squeezed just hard enough to send a jolt of pleasure lancing between her thighs. She gasped and arched her back, driving her breasts against him to satisfy their craving for contact.

His fingers tightened on her, the grip almost bruising, and then he was breaking off the kiss and relaxing his hold. Lia might've cried out in protest, but an icy lash of sea wind struck her overheated flesh, wrenching her back to reality. She shifted a half step back, surprised at the unsteadiness of her knees. Setting her hand on Paul's chest for balance, she noted his rough exhalation. Her own heart was pumping hard in the aftermath of the kiss.

She looked up and caught a glimpse of the twin green flames flickering in his eyes. A moment later all trace of heat vanished from his gaze. Had she imagined it? As much as it pained her to leave the warmth and comfort of his embrace, Lia needed distance to gather her thoughts and make sense of what had just happened. Paul had made it crystal clear that he didn't like her. So, what was he doing?

"Was that meant to determine whether I was telling the truth about being attracted to you?" Lia panted, scanning Paul's expression and hoping that wasn't what the kiss had been about.

"Why would you think I'd do that?" he countered, dragging his thumb over his lower lip.

Mesmerized by the action, Lia shivered as pleasurable aftershocks continued to rock her body. "Because you don't believe anything I say." The bitterness in her tone caught her by surprise. She wished Paul's good opinion wasn't so important to her. "So what's the verdict? Do you think I'm attracted to you?"

"Yes." He waited a beat for her retort. When none came, he raised his eyebrows. "Aren't you going to ask me if the feeling's mutual?"

Lia shook her head and forced her muscles to relax. "I don't want to play those sorts of games with you."

Paul's features looked carved in granite as he regarded her. "I told Ethan I will go along with your subterfuge for now."

"Great." Lia slumped in defeat, unsure why this news bothered her so much. Had she really hoped he'd call her out in front of his family and drive her away? Given who he was, what he believed in, he should. "I'm sure that made Ethan very happy," she murmured.

Paul scrutinized her for several seconds before nodding. "We should be getting back."

The ride to Charleston passed with little conversation between them. Lia needed to sort out her feelings about the kiss, Paul's abrupt acceptance of her temporarily posing as his long-lost cousin and what would happen if her reasons for playing the part ever came to light.

Already Lia suspected her strong attraction to Paul could

develop into an emotional attachment unlike anything she'd known before. She'd never experienced such an unshakable craving to be with anyone. The need scared her a little, but the compelling nature of her desire was impossible to ignore. She couldn't pretend that surrendering to temptation wouldn't have repercussions. Lia couldn't imagine this longing for him would just vanish one day. Even if Paul never found out where she came from and rejected her, she planned to get back on the road in a matter of weeks. For her future peace of mind, she needed to bottle up her feelings here and now.

Yet what was going on between her and Paul wasn't the only emotional time bomb ticking away. The way Paul's mother and aunt had welcomed her into the family had touched Lia in a way she hadn't expected. Despite her guilt at the fraud she was perpetrating on them, the love they'd shown for their missing niece left Lia pondering what her own homecoming might be if she ever reached out to the family her mother left behind in Seattle.

Jen Marsh had struck out on her own shortly after high school and never looked back. Reluctance to linger in any place for long meant she rarely formed any lasting attachments. And neither had Lia.

But even though she lacked experience with lasting familial support, sometimes Lia pined for a family to belong to. Not that she imagined fitting into a large, tight-knit group like the Wattses. The reality was slowly sinking in that she would soon be living amongst them and that they would expect her to share their limelight. Jen Marsh had gone to great lengths to escape her past and create an anonymous life for both her and Lia.

If Paul kept digging into her background, could he jeopardize that? Would a story about the granddaughter of a swindler interest anyone three decades after he went to jail?

Doubtful. But to be sure, she'd better avoid any public attention for the next two weeks.

After a brief stop at her rental to pack up her limited wardrobe, Paul drove straight back to the estate. Constance must've been on the lookout for them because she was on hand in the first-floor hallway to lead the way upstairs to the bedrooms, narrating as she went.

"The Birch-Watts House has six bedrooms and seven bathrooms," Constance said. "It was built in 1804 by Jacob Birch and his descendants lived here until 1898 when Theodore Watts bought it. The home's been in the Watts family ever since."

"Wow, that's a long time." Lia had been present when they'd brought Grady home from the hospital and had been too focused on getting him settled to take in much more than a cursory impression of the grand mansion. "And only Ethan's grandfather lives here?"

It seemed like a lot of empty space for just one person to rattle around in. A house with nearly ten thousand square feet and so many bedrooms should be full of people. And in its heyday, it probably was. But families were smaller now and not so likely to have several generations living under one roof.

"Grady's been alone since he lost Grandma back in the late 1960s," Paul added, "but the Shaw twins live in the caretaker's house on the back corner of the estate. And I spend the night in the carriage house here and there. More often since his stroke."

"He must like having you all close by," Lia murmured, realizing she might be inundated with family members over the next week.

"Both girls are so busy with their careers and social lives." Constance sighed. "Which is why it's wonderful that you've come to spend time with Grady. Did you bring a swimsuit? The pool was recently refurbished and switched to salt water."

"No, I didn't think it was going to be that sort of a visit." Seeing Paul's lips tighten, Lia suppressed a twinge of regret. No matter what he thought, she had no intention of treating her time with his family like a vacation. She intended to do her best to get Grady as healthy as possible in the next two weeks.

"This was your mother's room." Constance led the way into the room on the opposite side of the hall from Grady's master suite. "It's the best guest room in the house."

"Wow!"

The enormous, bright bedroom overlooked the gardens and side lawn with floral curtains framing the four tall windows set into the muted green walls. Lia's gaze darted from the view to the big bed with its matching comforter and the yellow fainting couch at its foot. A giant mirrored armoire dominated one wall and Lia knew without even opening the doors that even with the two bulky costumes she'd brought along, her clothes wouldn't take up half the space.

"You sound like you approve," Constance declared with a delighted smile.

"I've never stayed anywhere so nice. Or so big," Lia said. "It's more space than I'm used to."

Lia was a minimalist by necessity as well as desire. The friends she'd made during her travels marveled at how little she needed, but Lia had never known any other way to be. Traveling around the country in a nineteen-foot camper meant owning a bare minimum of essentials. The only deviation from that rule was her ever expanding collection of princess costumes.

Yet the moment she'd entered the bedroom, Lia had been blown away by the beautiful antiques, the intricate plasterwork around the ceiling and fireplace, the ridiculously comfortable-looking bed and the bathroom that was bigger than her entire camper. For several long seconds she imagined herself spending long hours soaking in the tub. Then reality intruded. She wasn't on vacation. A couple weeks from now she and Misty would be back on the road.

"Get used to it," Constance advised. "You're going to be with us for a long time."

"Um…"

Turbulent emotions rose up in Lia, tightening her throat and making it impossible to speak. Being thrust into the tight-knit Watts family highlighted the isolation in her life-style and brought her into direct conflict with her mother's attitude that just because someone was family didn't mean they gave a damn about you.

"Paul, can you go let Cory know he needs to bring up the rest of Lia's things?"

"This is all there is," Paul answered, setting the boxes containing her costumes on the bed.

"What do you mean?" Constance looked from the boxes to the small duffel that held most of Lia's wardrobe. "How is that possible?"

"Not everyone requires an entire room to hold every outfit they own," Paul remarked dryly.

His mother looked mystified. "But…"

"I don't have much room in my camper," Lia explained. "And I don't really need much."

"That was your life before. You are a Watts now and should dress the part." Constance cast a dubious eye over Lia's yoga pants and T-shirt. "We need to get you some new clothes. The twins can show you all their favorite boutiques."

"There's no need," Lia said, shooting a wary glance in Paul's direction. He would hate that his mother wanted to spend money on her. But his impassive expression tossed her no lifeline. "I'm sure Poppy and Dallas are too busy to take me shopping. Besides, I'm only going to be here a couple weeks."

"Nonsense. You simply have to stay longer than that. Because of you, Grady is getting better every day. No need for you to stay cooped up in the house all the time. The twins and Ethan can take you out so you can meet their friends. I have several events in the next two weeks that all of us will be attending. When word gets around all of Charleston will be dying to meet you."

As Constance spoke, Lia's anxiety ratcheted upward. Chest tightening, on the verge of a mild panic attack, she made another silent appeal to Paul. Why hadn't he spoken up? Surely he'd rather she stay out of sight between now and the time they broke the news that she wasn't a Watts after all. Once again, he remained utterly silent and aloof. Her eyebrows dipped as she realized his refusal to step in was deliberate. He was withholding aid in order to demonstrate the folly of Ethan's plan. As if she needed that pointed out to her.

"I'm feeling really overwhelmed at the moment," Lia protested. "I'm not used to so much attention. If you don't mind, I'd like to focus on helping Grady get better."

"Oh, well, of course." Constance looked surprised and then a bit abashed. "I guess I went a little overboard. We're just so overjoyed to have you home."

At long last Paul took pity on Lia. "Mother, why don't we leave Lia to unpack."

The grateful look she shot him prompted a frown. Honestly, there seemed to be no way to get on the man's good side.

"Of course," Constance said, her gracious smile returning. "Join us downstairs when you're ready." She'd taken several steps toward the door when she suddenly stopped and turned. "I almost forgot. There's a little welcome-home present for you on the nightstand."

Lia's first reaction after glancing at Paul's set expression was to protest that she didn't need any gifts. Then she realized that she could leave behind whatever they gave her. "That's lovely. Thank you."

Left alone, she started to fill the dresser drawers with her meager belongings, but then succumbed to curiosity about the gift. A small, flat box sat beside an elegant sheet of linen notepaper.

This belonged to your grandmother. We thought you should have it.—Constance.

Lia slipped the ribbon off the box and opened it. Nestled on a bed of black velvet was an antique locket. Her heart contracted as she opened the locket and saw that it contained a picture of Ava as a teenager. She sank onto the bed and stared at the photo, pondering all the events that had led her to this moment, wishing she'd done a dozen things differently.

"Hey."

Lia lifted her gaze and spied Ethan standing in the doorway. He looked authoritative in an elegant navy suit and lavender tie.

"Hi."

"Are you okay about staying at the estate for the next two weeks?" Ethan asked as he entered. "Both my mom and Aunt Lenora can be very determined and I don't want you to feel pressured."

Lia blew out her breath. "I plan to spend most of my time with your grandfather so I should be able to handle it for a couple weeks."

Ethan came over and took her hand in his. "I know this isn't what we originally planned on. I owe you a huge debt for helping out like this."

"You really don't," Lia said, some of her angst melting away. "I just want to bring your family some peace."

"You'll definitely be doing that."

"Can you please talk your mom out of introducing me all over Charleston as Ava's daughter, though? That's just going to end up complicating everything and I don't think you want your family to be the subject of gossip."

"Sure, that makes sense." Ethan tugged at the knot on his tie, loosening it. "I'll deal with it."

"Thank you because your brother was no help. I thought for sure he'd want to keep me out of sight."

"I know it's hard to believe, but I think that Paul will come around once he gets to know you."

"I hope so." The memory of their kiss sent heat rushing into her cheeks. Longing spiraled through her. "Because it's daunting how much he dislikes me."

Five

With the successful completion of a year-long investigation into a data breach of one of his company's clients, Paul knocked off early and headed to the estate to see how Grady was doing. Before Lia Marsh had entered their lives, Paul rarely worked a standard eight-hour day. He loved what he did and despite the number of bad actors he and his staff tracked down, there was always another puzzle to unravel, another hacker who'd stolen information. But these days he couldn't concentrate on his day-to-day activities.

When he wasn't following the trail she'd left all over the country, he caught himself ruminating over that stolen moment at his beach house when he'd surrendered to his desire to kiss her. At various times over the last several days, he'd have given anything to escape the distracting memory of how she'd felt in his arms. To forget the softness of her lips as they'd yielded beneath his. To stop imagining his hands gliding over her silky, fragrant skin.

He'd intended for the impulsive act to rattle her, but the

aftermath hadn't offered him any insight into her nefarious plans. Nor in the last week had she made any misstep to confirm she wasn't as genuine as she appeared. The dry facts that summarized her life gave him no sense of her character or her motivation for interrupting her life to act as Grady's granddaughter. He hadn't yet ruled out money, but nothing about the way she dressed or the things she talked about gave her away.

It also occurred to Paul that maybe he was concerning himself with the wrong thing. With only a week left to go in their arrangement, Grady continued to improve. But once they told everyone their story that a mistake had been made at the genetic testing service and Lia wasn't his granddaughter, would Grady's health fade once more?

There was no doubt that her presence had galvanized his recovery, but neither Paul nor Ethan could predict whether Grady's progress would slow or stop when she left the following week. Lia persisted in her belief that once she'd gotten the ball rolling, Grady would continue to improve on his own, but what if she was the oxygen that kept the flame burning on Grady's will to return to full health?

Paul stepped out of his SUV, intending to head straight to the carriage house for a cold beer and more brooding about Lia, when he spotted a flash of yellow coming toward him along the garden path. If he retreated without saying hello to whoever was coming, he'd never hear the end of it. Even as that zipped through his mind, he registered the sound of humming above the crunch of gravel and recognized the source.

Lia.

After that stirring kiss at his house, he'd avoided being alone with her, and he cursed at this untimely meeting. But the woman who emerged from the foliage had a completely different impact on him than what he was used to.

What the hell?

Before he could wrap his mind around her appearance, Lia spotted him and waved. Her infectious smile bloomed as she headed in his direction. His head spun as he took her in. She'd transformed herself into yet another one of her princess characters. Even her movement was different.

"What are you wearing?" he asked, regaining his voice.

"It's a ball gown," she responded as if it was the most ordinary thing in the world to be wearing a floor-length satin and tulle dress in bright yellow with three voluminous tiers, a red wig styled in a fancy updo with ringlets spilling over her bare shoulders and long yellow gloves. "I'm on my way to the hospital to visit the children's ward. I've been so busy with Grady that I missed last week and I can't disappoint them again."

Paul groaned inwardly. It was hard to maintain his skepticism about her when this woman kept proving him wrong. First, she'd brought his grandfather back from the brink of death. Now here was another reminder that she gave of her time to bring joy to sick kids. How was he supposed to resist her?

"Which princess are you today?"

"I'm dressed as Belle. From *Beauty and the Beast*," she explained with exaggerated patience. "The Disney movie about the prince who was turned into a beast and could only be saved by someone who loved him as himself." When Paul continued blankly regarding her, she rolled her eyes in exasperation. "I can tell you don't have children."

"Why do you dress like a Disney character?"

"Because the kids love it. Sure, they appreciate when I just show up to spend time with them, but when I visit dressed as Belle or Elsa or Cinderella…they are so thrilled." She grinned. "For a while they can forget how sick they are."

"How did you get started doing this?"

"I guess you could say growing up I wanted to be a

princess. I imagined that I was like Rapunzel or Sleeping Beauty, locked in a tower taken away from my parents. Hidden away. When I got older, I grew obsessed with getting a job at Disney as one of the princesses."

"So what happened?"

"I became a Disney character." She made a face that told him it had not gone well. "Only I didn't get to be a princess."

"A villain?" he asked, thinking that would be more fun.

"No," she said. "I was Dale." She waited a beat and when he didn't say anything, elaborated, "Of Chip 'n' Dale. They were chipmunks. I wore a big chipmunk head." She used her hands to indicate the costume's size. "It was hot and uncomfortable, but mostly worth it because the kids loved it."

"How did you make the transition from Disney character to massage therapist?" he asked, the thought of her massaging his brother once again flashing unpleasantly through his mind. He recognized that she'd been baiting him when they discussed it, but still he envied his brother.

"I think I mentioned it was hot and stuffy in that costume. Being a character wasn't as glamorous as I'd hoped it would be. One of my coworkers was taking classes in massage therapy and it sounded like a good idea. It was a way for me to help people and that's what I like to do."

"Well, you've certainly had a huge impact on Grady, so I guess you have a knack for making people better."

"Thank you for saying that," she said, showing her appreciation with a bright smile that kicked him hard in the gut.

"How are you getting there?"

"I'm going to walk." She shifted sideways as if to go around him. "It's only fifteen minutes away."

Paul stepped to block her path. "Why don't I drive you instead?"

"Really," she demurred. "It's no problem."

"I insist," he argued, faltering in his week-long battle to avoid being alone with her.

"I like walking."

"So do I. I could walk you there."

She set her hands on her hips and arched one eyebrow. "Don't you have evildoers to chase?"

"Nope. We just wrapped up a huge investigation so I took the afternoon off." Paul held out his arm to her in a gallant gesture that caught her by surprise. "I can't think of anything I'd enjoy more than to watch your performance as Belle."

"But I'm usually there for a couple hours. I'm sure you have better things to do."

"Stop trying to get rid of me," he growled. "There's nothing else I'd rather be doing." And much to his dismay, that was true.

Although she looked like she wanted to voice further protests, Lia gave a little shrug and took his arm. Her delicate grip made such a huge impression that Paul had a hard time concentrating as she told him the story of how Belle and the Beast fell in love.

Fifteen minutes had never gone by so quickly, and all too soon Paul was guiding Lia through the hospital's entrance. Gliding along the corridors, she paid little attention to the stir she caused. The staff greeted her warmly, but Paul couldn't help but notice the way many visitors goggled at her appearance or even laughed at her elaborate costume. He caught himself scowling at a number of them even as he recalled his own initial reaction when he first saw her.

"What?" he demanded, noticing her amused expression as they stood waiting for the elevator to arrive.

"I was just thinking that the way you're glaring makes me think you'd make an excellent Beast."

He forced his facial muscles to relax. "I don't suppose I'm Prince Charming material."

"You could be," she murmured, stepping into the elevator car.

"No," he corrected. "Ethan is Prince Charming." A now-familiar pulse of irritation raised his blood pressure.

"Ethan?" Her snort was an indelicate sound at odds with her royal appearance. "Do you really see him dressing up in britches and a frock coat?"

Not in his wildest imaginings. Paul's lips twitched, but he kept his tone serious. "Maybe for the right woman."

She gave another very unprincesslike snort. "I don't think he'd enjoy playacting."

"I wouldn't, either."

She narrowed her glowing hazel eyes and shot him a piercing glance. "You might be surprised."

Her knowing smile sent a wave of heat through him. Before he could summon a retort, the doors opened and Lia stepped into the corridor of what was obviously the children's floor. She paused for a second, drew in a deep breath, closed her eyes. A moment later, she exhaled and a beatific smile curved her lips. Just like that she'd become someone completely different.

The transformation robbed Paul of words. He trailed after her as she approached the nurses' station and after greeting everyone, introduced Paul. Several nurses accompanied them on the way to the lounge where some of the children had gathered to play. The appearance of a beloved princess in their midst electrified the children.

Mesmerized by the spectacle, Paul stood at the back of the room with a cluster of parents and watched Lia work her way around the space, going from child to child, spreading joy as she went. Some of the kids she called by name, proving that she was indeed a frequent visitor. In every case she lingered, answering questions, asking some of her own.

Nor was Lia's effect limited to the kids. Around Paul several stressed-out mothers teared up at their children's delight and tense fathers relaxed enough to smile. Once again, Lia was demonstrating the incredible magic she'd used to wrest Grady away from the brink of death.

Paul noticed a tightness in his chest and rubbed to ease it. This woman was too much. He recalled Ethan declaring that first day that Lia came off as completely genuine. Confident his brother had been hoodwinked, Paul had done whatever he could to unmask her. Now he was leaning toward her giving her the benefit of the doubt. This hospital visit was the whip cream, sprinkles and cherry on top of the ice cream sundae that was Lia Marsh.

Which made everything so much worse.

Keeping his attraction to her buttoned down had been way easier when he had reason to suspect her character and motives. Now, as she began to sing, Paul's spirits sank. Her clear, sweet voice captivated the children. Their parents looked beyond grateful to see their sons and daughters so happy. And some of the nursing staff were singing along.

Before her topsy-turvy world had intersected with his, Paul never would've imagined himself attracted to a free spirit like Lia. Her ideas about the rejuvenating effects of music and aromatherapies seemed more like wishful thinking than practical fact. Yet he couldn't deny Grady's marked improvement.

Or his own shifting opinion.

Over the next hour Lia demonstrated an extensive repertoire of familiar children's songs. When at long last she signaled the end of the performance with a princess-worthy curtsy and waved goodbye, Paul wasn't surprised at the sharp tug his heart gave when she shifted her full attention to him.

"Sorry that took so long," she said as they headed for the elevator.

"That was something," he remarked, struggling to sort out his muddled emotions as they stepped into the car.

She eyed him while they descended, letting the princess character drop away and becoming Lia in costume once more.

"From your tone I can't tell if that's good or bad."

"The kids really love you."

"Seeing their favorite princess come to life is a wonderful distraction for them."

"And you do this every week?"

Lia nodded. "I try to."

They reached the sidewalk and turned in the direction of the estate.

"Why?"

"You of all people should understand," she said, tugging at the fingers of one long yellow glove.

The movement snared Paul's attention and he noticed an immediate and sharp uptick in his heartbeat as he watched her slide the material down her arm. The practiced move wasn't at all provocative or sexy, but made his breath quicken all the same.

"Why do you think I should understand?"

"Because of all the charity work your family does."

"Philanthropy and wealth usually go hand in hand."

"There's a difference between writing a big check and giving time and energy to a cause. Your family actively participates because that's what's rooted in their personal values."

Yet part of those values was defined by the idea that because of their good fortune the Wattses owed something to those less fortunate. Lia had no largesse, so why was she driven to help others? What compelled her to dress up and sing to children or to help Grady get better?

Despite all the facts he'd gleaned about her, today's hospital visit demonstrated how little he actually knew—or understood—about her.

"Thanks for coming along today," Lia said, rousing Paul from his thoughts.

He noticed that they were nearing the estate and found himself suddenly reluctant to part ways. "Do you want to come in for a drink?"

For a beat she stared at him as if debating how to respond, and then she shook her head. "I can't figure you out."

"The feeling is mutual."

"All week long you've been avoiding me. Now today you come with me to the hospital and invite me for a drink. What's changed?"

What could he say? That he found her charming, her company invigorating? That avoiding her wasn't helping his peace of mind? He already knew their temperaments were completely different. Maybe if they spent more time together her eccentric ways and quirky beliefs would turn him off once and for all.

"Oh," she continued. "I'll bet you're scheming to get me drunk in the hopes I'll slip up and say something damning."

"Now who's the suspicious one," he retorted, wishing this was going more smoothly. As much as he didn't want to put his cards on the table, Paul realized he had to give her a peek at his hand if he hoped to entice her to extend their time together. "Maybe I enjoyed your company this afternoon and don't want it to end."

She blinked at him. "I'm sorry? Did I just hear you right? You enjoyed my company?"

"Do you want to join me for a drink or not?" he grumbled.

She tapped her finger against her lips, making a show of giving consideration to his invitation. "Well, since you asked so sweetly…sure. Let me change and check on Grady. It won't take me more than ten minutes."

"Need any help?" he asked, eyeing the gown's complicated lacings. "I've never undressed a princess before." The declaration came out of nowhere, surprising them both.

"If I thought you actually meant that," she said in a breathless rush, "I'd take you up on your offer."

Paul opened his mouth to either take back his remark or to double down, but before he decided which, Lia threw up both hands and shook her head vigorously.

"No. Don't say anything more." She began retreating toward the house. "I'll be back in ten minutes. That should give you plenty of time to figure out how to get yourself out of trouble."

Lia's buoyant mood lingered as she walked along the garden paths that led to the house. When she'd donned the Belle costume, she'd never imagined such a magical afternoon. She'd spent the last seven days anxious and miserable over Paul's pronounced disapproval, unsure how to cope with her body's irresistible response to his physical appeal or to manage the push and pull of apprehension and lust that kept her off-balance.

Before today, if asked to describe Paul, Lia would have used words like confident and authoritative. Yet at the hospital today he'd shown her a different side, demonstrating he could be reflective and more openminded than she'd imagined. This brief respite from his distrust was a welcome change.

To her relief she encountered no one on the way to her bedroom. Grady's door was closed, indicating he was resting, no doubt worn out from his latest round of physical therapy. Before leaving for the hospital, she'd popped in to show off her costume. His delight at her appearance had been nearly a match for the children.

Although Lia raced through her transformation she took longer than ten minutes. Because the elaborate wig and heavy gown left her feeling sweaty, she grabbed a quick shower and hastily reapplied mascara and red lipstick because she wanted Paul to see her as attractive. Reluctant to keep him waiting too long, she drew her wet hair into a sleek topknot, and just before she headed out the door, swept powder over her nose, obliterating her freckles. She'd noticed how often Paul's gaze focused on the imperfection. No doubt he found them unsightly.

By the time she reached the carriage house, Lia was trembling with anticipation. How many nights had she gone to bed in Ava Watts's old bedroom only to find sleep elusive? Over and over she called herself a fool for letting the cybersecurity specialist get beneath her skin. While the man treated her like a thief out to steal the heirloom silver, she was tormented by fantasies of him making love to her with all the passion and intensity of a man who craved closeness and intimacy. And today, all he'd had to do was show her a little kindness and she was all in.

"Sorry I took so long," she said, covertly scanning his expression in search of reassurance. Was the man attracted to her or not? She couldn't tell. "The wig and dress left me feeling grimy so I showered."

He stepped close and lowered his head, breathing her in. "Damn, you smell good."

A lightning storm of awareness electrified Lia's whole body. She leaned back and peered up at his expression. He watched her through half-lidded eyes, predatory hunger smoldering in their green depths. Her pulse accelerated as his lips took on a sensual curve. The last time she'd seen that smile had been that afternoon at his beach house. Heat raced through her veins, bringing lethargy to her muscles and sparking hope. Emboldened, she reached out and cupped his cheek.

"You are attracted to me," she murmured, awestruck and filled with delight. "What happened last time was real."

"Very real." He wrapped his arm around her waist and

pulled her close. "And something I promised myself would never happen again."

Crushing herself against his hard body, Lia breathed in his masculine scent. She wanted to burrow her hands beneath his clothes and slide her palms along his warm skin. "Why not?"

"You are pretending to be my cousin." His muscles tensed. "My first cousin."

"*Pretending* being the operative word." While Lia recognized that his argument held no water, she'd spent enough time in Charleston to understand that appearances were everything. "As long as we're careful and don't get caught…"

"Do you seriously think that's what I'm worried about?" He took her hands and eased them from his body, his grip gentle despite his frustrated tone. "Getting caught?"

"Isn't it?" She blinked at him in confusion as he set her free and took a half step back.

His bemused expression might have led her to ask more questions if her body wasn't aching with the sharpest longing. Day and night, she'd tormented herself with revisiting that kiss at his beach house, taking things past the moment when he'd stopped. She'd imagined a hundred variations. Them going inside and making love in his bed. Him drawing her into the hot tub and making her come while she floated on a raft of bubbles. Her dropping to her knees to pleasure him in full sight of the beach while he held tight to the deck railing and shouted his pleasure.

"Look, if you're worried that I might fall for you…" She shook her head, hoping she could be convincing. "Don't. I find you attractive. It's just sex."

From the first stirring of physical attraction, she'd accepted that they had no future. Even before she started posing as his first cousin, he'd regarded her with suspicion and she doubted he'd ever fully trust her. In so many ways, from their upbringings to their temperaments, they were completely incompatible. Never in her wildest daydreams could she imagine he'd walk into a public venue and be proud to call her his date much less his girlfriend.

But their chemistry couldn't be denied. That left sex. Great sex. Because after being kissed by Paul Watts, Lia knew the guy would be fantastic in bed. She shivered in anticipation of his strong hands running over her naked body. Just imagining how he would slide his finger through the slippery wetness between her thighs caused her body to clench in pleasure.

"Just sex," he echoed, murmuring the two words in a contemplative tone. "And in a week you'll be gone."

While her heart bucked painfully in her chest, Lia nodded. "That's the plan."

"Nobody could possibly fall for someone that fast." He raked her expression with hard green eyes. "I mean it's only a week."

"Absolutely." Damn the man could talk, but she was starting to see a glimmer of hope. "That's not enough time to get attached."

Lia wasn't sure which of them moved first, but the next thing she knew, he'd cupped the back of her neck in his hand and her fingers had tunneled into his hair. Then they were lip-locked and moaning beneath the onslaught of desire and need.

"That's more like it," Lia murmured a long while later after he released her lips and trailed kisses down her throat. "Damn, you are good at that."

"At what?"

He brought his teeth together on the place where her neck and shoulder joined. Pleasure shot through her at the tantalizing pain of his bite. She groaned as his tongue flicked over the spot, soothing the sting. Desire tore through her. Lia couldn't recall ever feeling so alive or invigorated.

"Kissing," she said. "I thought maybe you were too focused on chasing bad guys to ever make time for a love life."

"So you thought I was inexperienced when it came to women?"

He didn't wait for her to reply before seizing her mouth for another hard, demanding kiss that left her weak-kneed and flushed from head to toe. His fingers dug into her hip as she rocked into him, before he sent his palm coasting downward over her butt. When he lifted her against his growing erection, Lia panted in frustration at the pressure building in her.

His lips moved over the shell of her ear, awakening a million goose bumps. Adrift in pleasure, she didn't expect the sharp nip on her earlobe or the way fireworks detonated in her loins, setting her on fire.

"Have you thought about us together?" he asked, his voice a low purr that sent a riot of tingles along her nerves.

She nodded.

"Is this how it went?"

"Sometimes." She could scarcely speak above a whisper.

"Have you imagined me bending you over and taking you from behind."

The image was only one of a hundred different scenarios she'd toyed with. "Yes."

For a microsecond his whole body went perfectly still. "My mouth between your thighs, driving you crazy?"

"Yes." This time she moaned the word.

His teeth raked down her neck. "I think about your mouth on me."

"Yes," she pleaded. "Oh, yes."

"Wicked girl." He sounded so pleased by her response.

She sighed in relief when his hand slid between her thighs, fingers applying the perfect pressure over the spot where she ached. While she rocked against his palm, his tongue plunged into her mouth over and over. Mindless, her arousal gaining intensity, she rubbed her clit against his hand. With the barrier of her clothes between them, equal parts frustration and delight prompted the incoherent sounds coming from her throat. At last she could take it no more.

"Damn it, Paul," she panted, her desperation giving her voice a shrill edge.

He lifted his head and regarded her from beneath his thick dark lashes. "What?"

Even as she struggled to find the words to tell him what she wanted, he sent his fingers skimming beneath the waistband of her yoga pants and followed the neat landing strip to where she burned. The pleasure was so overwhelming that she huffed out a laugh to relieve some of the strain of keeping her delight bottled up.

"I was just thinking that I should've waxed an arrow to point the way for you."

It was the first thing that popped into her head and one corner of his lips kicked up in a mocking salute.

"Baby, I know exactly where I'm going." Even before he finished speaking, he stroked through her hot core.

The move left her just enough breath for an awestruck curse. "Damn."

"You're incredible," he murmured, raking his teeth over her lower lip. "I can't believe how wet you are. That's so damn sexy."

He stroked his fingers through her slippery wetness, whispering his admiration, letting her know how much he appreciated her. Moaning, she shifted her hips, wanting his fingers inside her. The building pressure was almost too much to bear.

"Please," she panted, gathering a handful of his silky blond hair and tugging. "Make me come."

"My pleasure."

She shuddered in anticipation as he dropped to his knees and dragged her yoga pants and panties down her thighs. A moment later he leaned forward and drew his tongue along the seam that hid her sex from him. Lia's muscles failed her and she would've collapsed without his supportive grip.

"Hold on," he warned, a smile in his voice as his tongue speared into the heart of her.

An old commercial played through her head as Paul drove her excitement still higher. *How many licks does it take to get Lia off? One. Two. Three.* Just that fast she found herself coming. The speed and intensity of her climax blew her mind.

"Paul…" She threw her head back and welcomed the orgasm that blasted through her. Curses fell from her lips at the intensity of the pleasure.

"Wow," he murmured, trailing kisses across her abdomen as her muscles quaked with aftershocks. "You are a firecracker."

Not surprising since she'd had a week of foreplay to prime the pump. To her dismay, he reached down and slid her pants back into place before getting to his feet.

"Are we done?"

He raised his eyebrows at her scandalized tone, but long lashes hid the expression in his gaze. The roughness in his voice, however, gave him away as he breathed, "I hope not."

"Then kiss me again and let's take this thing horizontal."

He put his arm around her, hand sliding to cup her butt while he rubbed his erection against her hip. She savored the hard length of him poking at her and shimmied to add even more friction. The taste of herself on his lips made her eager to have her way with him in turn. Even though she hadn't yet gotten her hands on the bulge behind his zipper, she could tell he was well built.

A staccato horn beeped nearby as someone locked a car.

At the interruption of their thoroughly hot and promising embrace, Paul tore his mouth from hers. Female voices intruded on the sensual fog Lia had gotten caught up in. Paul's hands fell away from her body as he abruptly stepped back. His physical withdrawal left her shivering as if doused with cold water. Her eyes flew open in time to see shutters slam down over his expression. Only his heightened color and his unwillingness to look at her hinted at the passion he'd recently demonstrated.

A second later a knock sounded on the carriage house door and Lia almost whimpered in disappointment as she recognized Poppy's voice.

"Hey, Paul, are you there?"

A muscle jumped in his jaw as he shot a hard look at the door. "I have to answer that."

"Of course." She drew in a shaky breath as his gaze raked over her. Feeling exposed and raw in the aftermath of such all-consuming desire, Lia craved some privacy to recover her wits before facing the twins. "Can I borrow your bathroom?"

"In there." He pointed down the hallway and headed for the front door.

To her dismay, as soon as she met her gaze in the mirror, Lia found herself blinking back a rush of unexpected tears. She braced her hands on the sink and rode the wave of emotions until her breath steadied and she could smile without grimacing.

Although he'd been clear that lying to his family bothered him, Lia recognized that sneaking around added spice to their encounters. And she couldn't imagine Paul being susceptible to such a thing—doubtless he'd never allowed himself to be in a situation like theirs before. And he wasn't the only one.

During her years on the road, she'd had many men look at her lifestyle and view her as a short-term thing. Unlike her mother, who took frequent lovers, Lia needed some sort of a connection and rarely found it. What she'd just had with Paul was worth more than all her experiences combined and it left her wondering—if she'd found this before, would she have stayed put?

Lia loved her life on the road. Traveling around the country satisfied her restless nature and offered her the opportunity to experience places that people often missed because they either flew to their destinations or only visited tourist locations.

Her time stranded in Charleston had given Lia an opportunity to think about what she wanted for the future. Was she going to roam aimlessly for the rest of her life or should she put down roots somewhere? And what was her criteria for staying? She'd found much to like in Charleston, but did it feel like home? Was she drawn to the place or the people or both? Lia's inability to answer told her to move on.

She cracked the door to hear the conversation just in time to recall that she'd committed to spending the afternoon with the twins.

"She's going to tell our fortunes," Poppy was saying to Paul, referring to Lia's promise to bring out her tarot deck and read for them. "You have to come and have your cards read, too."

"It's all foolishness," Paul said, sounding exasperated.

"Come on," Dallas insisted. "I'm trying out some new recipes for Zoe and Ryan's wedding and there will be cocktails. It'll be fun."

"Please," Poppy wheedled. "You never hang out with us anymore."

"Fine. I'll be there."

"Awesome," Dallas said. "Half an hour."

"And leave your skepticism at the door," Poppy said. "The universe might have an important message for you."

Once Paul had ushered out his cousins and shut the door, Lia returned to the great room, a brave smile plastered on her face to hide her disappointment at the change in plans.

"She's right," Lia said, striding toward him. From his closed expression and rigid posture, she guessed the intimacy they'd shared five minutes earlier had been shattered by the twins' visit. "You should come with an open mind. The cards have a way of getting to the truth."

Paul stood with his hand on the doorknob and gazed down his nose at her. "Fortune-telling is all just educated guesses and made-up stuff."

"It can be," Lia agreed, thinking their differences couldn't be any clearer. "But sometimes if you open your heart, the answers will shine like the midday sun."

"Except I don't ask those sorts of questions."

Questions that might encourage him to lead with his heart and not his head. Lia knew nothing she could say would convince him otherwise so she pushed down her disappointment and vowed to only ask of him what she knew he could give.

Six

From Paul's perch on a barstool at the breakfast bar in the caretaker house kitchen, he could observe the shenanigans playing out at the dining room table without appearing to be engaged. He was working his way through the second of the three cocktails Dallas had prepared for them to taste. She'd dubbed this one Love Potion, and with two shots of vodka and one of bourbon mixed with both cranberry and cherry juice, it packed a punch.

Despite being identical twins, with their mother's blond hair and blue eyes, Dallas and Poppy had vastly distinct styles and temperaments. The oldest by ten minutes, Dallas had the Watts family head for business and more than her fair share of ambition. Since graduating college, she'd worked for some of the best restaurants in Charleston with the goal of opening her own place and currently worked as a private chef and caterer.

By contrast, Poppy was a stylist at a high-end salon in downtown Charleston and an active beauty blogger. She was free-spirited and headstrong, with striking pink hair and boundless energy, and whenever her family questioned her about doing something more serious than cutting hair, her quick answer was always a flippant one.

"Hey, Paul," Poppy called, breaking into his musings. "It's your turn."

He blinked several times to reorient his thoughts and noticed that he was the center of attention. "I'm not interested." He hoped his resolute tone would dissuade them from pestering him further, but their eager gazes remained fixed on him.

"Oh come on, we've both done it." Dallas shot Lia a look. "What are you afraid of?"

"Besides," Poppy chimed in. "It's not fair that you've heard all our dark secrets without spilling a few of your own."

"I don't…" Paul trailed off. He'd been about to deny having any dark secrets, but then realized since Lia had arrived, he had more each day. "You know this isn't my cup of tea."

"Ladies, leave him alone," Lia said, no disappointment or censure in her unruffled manner. She gathered up the cards from Poppy's reading and returned them to the stack.

"Obviously he's afraid to face the truth," Dallas said, displaying relentless determination.

For the last hour, while Lia had made credible-sounding predictions for the twins, Paul had grown increasingly skeptical of her glib performance. While her expertise had appeared genuine enough to thoroughly engage his cousins, in Paul's opinion the concept of being able to predict the future based on the turn of a card was nothing but nonsense. Still, as much as he'd wanted to scoff several times over the past hour, he'd held his tongue because Dallas and Poppy were thoroughly enjoying the experience. Or at least they were making a show of doing so. Some of Lia's prognostications had rattled both girls, although they'd laughed and sipped their drinks to cover it up.

"There's no truth I'm afraid to face," Paul declared, his gaze clashing with both his cousins' even as Lia kept her focus on the tarot deck. He was mesmerized by her small hands as she shuffled the deck to clear the energy. Why didn't she chime in? Surely, she was dying to feed him a load of rubbish to get a rise out of him. "I just see all of this as a huge waste of time."

"Since when is having fun a waste of time?" Poppy asked.

"When it comes to Paul," Dallas piped up, "since always."

"Come on, Paul." Poppy got up from where she was sitting across from Lia and gestured for him to replace her. "What does it hurt to have Lia read for you?"

Seeing the two women weren't going to let him escape without taking a turn in the hot seat as Lia had mockingly called it, Paul finished the Love Potion cocktail and made his way to the chair Poppy had vacated. Lia's hazel eyes gleamed as she pushed the cards across the table toward him. From the first two rounds, he knew she wanted him to shuffle the cards. She explained that this would let the cards absorb his energy.

"While you shuffle, think about something you want to ask the cards about." Lia had issued this instruction with both the earlier readings.

"Really," he insisted. "There's nothing."

Lia nodded. "Then just let your mind drift."

Paul handled the cards indifferently, demonstrating that he viewed the whole activity as a grand waste of time, yet while he shuffled the deck, mixing them thoroughly the way he'd watched his cousins do, he found himself besieged by memories of those delicious minutes with Lia in his carriage house. The taste of her. The way she'd given herself over to him. His name on her lips as she'd come.

His body tightened at the vivid images and he shifted uncomfortably on the chair before setting the cards on the silk cloth she'd spread on the dining table. "You know I don't buy into any of this stuff," he muttered with barely restrained impatience.

"You don't believe and that's okay." Lia had been staring at the cards in his hands, but now she lifted her gaze to meet his. The impact made his heart stumble. "But you never know. You might hear something interesting."

A tiny ember of curiosity flared as he wondered what she might tell him. He suspected it would give him insight into her motives. No doubt she'd try to guide him into some sort of behavior the way she had his cousins, telling Dallas that she'd soon be confronted with a difficult decision involving two men in her life and Poppy that she would undergo a transformative period that would shake up her status quo and possibly harm those around her.

Both of these vague but somewhat ominous predictions had puzzled the twins, but they'd eagerly embraced the readings as if they were a road map to their futures.

"Go ahead and cut the cards," Lia instructed. "Make three piles just like your cousins did."

Paul did as she told him and made three similarly sized piles. The ritual of handling the tarot cards had given the process a solemnity that made a strong impression on his cousins.

"Now pick one pile," Lia said.

His immediate instinct was to point to the one in the center, but as his finger was moving to indicate that stack, his gaze veered away.

"This one," he said, indicating the one to the right, unable to explain why he'd changed course.

With a reverent nod, Lia gathered up the deck, placing

the stack he had chosen on the top. Then she began to lay the cards out in a particular order facedown the way she had with his cousins. She'd called it a Celtic Cross and remarked that the layout was one of the most traditional.

"Ready?" she asked.

"Yes." He growled the word from between clenched teeth as he noticed a trace of excitement mingling with anxiety bubbling in his gut. Refusing to fall for Lia's theatrics, he ruthlessly tamped down the emotions.

As if drawn to the drama unfolding at the dining room table, his cousins raced over and took the empty seats on either side of him. Eyes bright with curious intensity, they leaned forward, their full plates and refilled crystal tumblers forgotten.

"We'll start with these two in the center," Lia intoned, indicating the crossed cards.

She pulled the bottom one out first and flipped it over, revealing an old man with a long gray beard and bowed back. He carried a lantern and leaned on a walking stick. The character reminded Paul of Gandalf the Grey from *The Lord of the Rings* trilogy.

"This is the Hermit reversed," Lia said. "It indicates what's currently influencing you. It's crossed by…" A dramatic pause followed as she turned over the next card. "The Fool. It is the first card of the Major Arcana and indicates the beginnings of a journey. The Fool can represent following your instincts despite what might seem the more sensible practice." Lia touched the Hermit card. "As you can see the Hermit is upside down. This indicates that your time of isolation is over. You are ready to rejoin your community."

Paul glanced from Lia to Poppy to Dallas and back to Lia as he absorbed her words. All three women were completely engrossed and he had to resist the urge to snort derisively. Let them have their fun. Nothing Lia said so far pertained to him. He didn't isolate himself. He worked long hours to make sure his clients' data was safe. As for starting a journey…he had no plans to travel anywhere.

Lia flipped over the card below the first two. "This position is the basis of the situation."

"That doesn't look like a very happy scene," Dallas said.

Paul peered at the image on the card and frowned. Two people slogging through the snow, their backs hunched, looking very much as if they were lost and having a very difficult time. Above them was a glowing church window with five circles.

"Many interpret the Five of Pentacles as a dire financial situation," Lia said. "But I often read it as someone who either can't see a helping hand being extended to them or is unable to accept the aid being offered."

As expected, none of this made any sense. Paul forced down his impatience. He wasn't in a situation where he had need of anyone's assistance. With the exception of Lia's appearance in their lives, everything in Paul's orbit ran as smooth as clockwork.

"What's in Paul's past?" Poppy asked, pointing to the card in the nine o'clock position.

Lia turned it over. "The Three of Wands, indicating someone who has achieved much and is now satisfied with all they've done." She lifted her gaze from the cards and regarded Paul. "I think that sums up your past perfectly. You've spent a lot of time working hard on your business and now you get to look forward to what's next. The position above is possible outcome." She flipped the card over.

"Whoa," Dallas murmured. "That's grim."

The card showed a woman standing blindfolded and bound in front of a semicircle of swords. The bleakness of the image made him suddenly glad that it wasn't a definite outcome. Even as that thought crossed his mind, he rejected it. This was nothing more than a foolish pastime. None of this meant anything.

"This is a potential outcome," Lia pointed out.

Poppy worried her lower lip. "It doesn't seem like Paul is destined for a happy ending."

"The key to this card is the blindfold," Lia said. "It symbolizes confusion and isolation. But notice that while her arms are bound, her legs are free. She could walk away from this dangerous situation at any point. Instead, she's choosing to stay where she is." Lia moved on. "This next position is near future. It shows some situation that you will soon have to face, but not with the same certainty as the outcome. However, it can influence how things turn out."

As she finished speaking, she flipped the card over and Paul's heart stopped dead at the sight of the two naked people on the card with the sun shining down and an angel hovering around them.

Poppy squealed with delight. "The Lovers."

"Well, well, well," Dallas said. "Paul, what aren't you telling us?"

To his dismay, he felt a rush of heat beneath his skin. It couldn't be possible. Lia must have managed some trick with the deck. There was no other explanation for why this card had shown up in this position after what had almost happened between them.

After what he wanted to happen between them.

"Looks like I'm going to get lucky," he remarked, retreating into humor to cover his discomfort.

"Good for you," Poppy said, making it sound like he'd been neglecting his sex life.

Dallas nodded her agreement. "Maybe you'll meet someone at Ryan's wedding who you'll click with."

Paul was standing up for his best friend at a small, private wedding in a few days. The speed with which Ryan had fallen for Zoe continued to bemuse Paul, but he had no hesitations about the two being perfect for each other.

"Unlikely," Paul said, "since I know everyone who'll

be there." Yet, even as he spoke Paul couldn't stop himself from glancing Lia's way. In truth, he'd already met someone who intrigued him.

"The Lovers card doesn't always mean the obvious," Lia said, injecting a calm note in the conversation. "In some instances it can be a choice between two things he loves."

"Do you have two things you love, Paul?" Dallas asked.

"The only thing he loves is working," Poppy put in.

He gave each of them a sour look before settling a heavy-lidded gaze on Lia. Since starting the reading, she'd mostly been actively avoiding looking his way, preferring to concentrate on the cards before her, but as soon as the Lovers card had appeared, a trace of color bloomed in her cheeks as if she, too, was thinking about what had happened between them.

"The card at the bottom of the staff indicates self," Lia said, resuming the reading. "The attitude you are contributing to the situation." She flipped the card over exposing a king sitting on a throne with a sword. "Yes," she murmured, "this makes sense. The King represents authority, power and judgment. He likes to rule the world with his keen mind and forceful personality."

"That sounds exactly like you," Dallas said.

"Totally," her sister echoed.

"This next card is your environment." Lia flipped the card over. The Two of Cups.

"I had that one, as well," Dallas said. "You said it stood for romance. Look, it's right next to the Lovers." She pointed to the proximity of the two cards. "It seems like Paul may be headed straight for love."

"What?" Paul muttered, unable to contain his displeasure. "Are you an expert now?"

While Dallas grinned at him in cheeky confidence, Lia shook her head.

"Or it could just mean that he's torn between two things

that are really important to him," she said. "Perhaps he needs to balance his time better between family and his love for chasing criminals."

Her interpretation sounded so reasonable, yet all this talk about romance, love and sex was making him itchy.

"What about the last two cards?" he demanded, impatient to have the whole reading done.

"This position is your hopes and fears." Lia pointed to the second-to-the-last position, and then shifted her finger to indicate the one above it. "And this is your final outcome."

"So what do they say?" Poppy asked, her blue eyes dancing with anticipation.

Lia turned the first card over. From Paul's vantage point, the image appeared to be a man dancing on top of a log, but he realized that he was looking at the card upside down and that the man was actually hanging by his feet.

"That doesn't look good," he said.

"It's not as bad as it looks," Lia countered. "The Hanged Man symbolizes peace and understanding. However, he believes the only way to maintain this state is by withdrawing from society. He's similar to the Hermit. He's serene because he's locked up his emotions for years."

"And the last one?" Paul demanded, ready to be done.

Lia flipped over the final card to reveal a single chalice, balanced on a palm and suspended over the ocean. "The Ace of Cups indicates a time of happiness and love. A gift of joy."

"So," Dallas began, "if I'm hearing this correctly, Paul has been alone too long and he's going to start a new relationship, but he's going to fight his feelings because he's locked up his emotions for so long that he's afraid of them, but in the end it's all going to work out and he'll be very happy."

While Dallas summarized the reading and Poppy nodded her agreement, Lia studied the cards. A frown line appeared between her brows. Had Lia twisted the reading to suit her needs in the hopes that he would believe himself falling for her? If so, she didn't look as pleased as Paul would've expected, given the strong romantic overtones of the cards.

Poppy turned her bright gaze on him. "I can't wait to meet the lucky woman."

Paul very deliberately kept his attention from straying to Lia as he replied, "This isn't a great time for me to focus on my personal life."

Dallas chuckled. "I like the way you believe you'll have a choice." She indicated the cards. "Looks to me like your future is clear. There's romance on your horizon and it's going to change everything."

As Dallas summed up her take on Paul's tarot spread, Lia gathered up the cards and put them away. While she'd been reading for the twins, he'd worn an indulgent half smile. Now, however, he'd retreated behind an impassive expression and only the slight dip in his eyebrows indicated that he was disgruntled.

Either the twins were accustomed to ignoring their cousin's bouts of irritation or they didn't notice that he was troubled. For Lia, Paul's displeasure was palpable. She tried shooting him a reassuring smile, but all that produced was a narrowing of his eyes.

It seemed impossible that she could be falling for someone as serious-minded as Paul Watts. Yet after what had happened between them in the carriage house, Lia recognized that without their growing emotional connection, the earth-shattering orgasm he'd given her wouldn't have been possible. She'd never known that sort of all-consuming passion.

In some ways it terrified her. She was accustomed to

being able to pick up and go whenever the mood hit her.
She didn't have any emotional ties that limited her freedom. Traveling like a leaf on the wind of her whims was
how she'd grown up. Her mother's idea of a perfect lifestyle seemed perfectly rational to Lia given what had happened to Jen Marsh.

No one got close when you moved all the time.

No attachments meant no heartbreak. Or that was how
it was supposed to work.

"What did you think of your first tarot reading?" Lia
asked as they strolled along that path that led away from
the caretaker's house.

"You know I don't believe in any of that stuff."

"I get it." Lia knew his skepticism would continue to
come between them if she reacted defensively. "You're a
logical guy. It's not really your thing."

"All that business about a future romance and having
to choose between two things that I love," Paul continued,
his tone thoughtful rather than dismissive.

As she struggled to make sense of what was bothering
him, Lia realized that Paul had seen enough truth in the
reading to be unsettled by it. How was that possible? He
was too much of a realist to do anything but reject all he'd
seen and heard today.

"If you aren't ready for love then that's not likely to happen for you," she reassured him, despite having seen the
opposite happen when the cards predicted romance. But
if anyone could avoid his emotions or anything that distracted him from business, it was Paul. "Maybe the universe
is just nudging you to work less and spend more quality
time with family and friends." From the way he scowled
at her, Lia should've kept the advice to herself. Awash in
sudden frustration, she threw up her hands. "Look. What
do I know? It's your life."

They walked in tense silence until the path was joined by one that stretched between the house and driveway. Lia started to turn away, but Paul touched his fingertips to her arm, stopping her.

"I know it's last-minute, but I was wondering if you'd like to come with me to Ryan and Zoe's wedding on Saturday."

Lia laid her fist over her rapidly thumping heart. "I thought you wanted me to keep a low profile."

"It's a small gathering of my close friends. None of them will spread gossip around Charleston about you."

His declaration struck her as naive and shortsighted.

"Given how your cousins reacted to the tarot card reading," she said, "there's more interest in your love life than you realize."

"If anyone asks, we'll just say you're a family friend in town for a short visit."

Lia studied his impassive expression, knowing she shouldn't read too much into his offer. Her instincts warned her that spending more time with Paul was a mistake, but the temptation was so strong.

"Let me guess," she said, concealing her jumbled emotions behind mockery. "You were so busy catching bad guys that you forgot to invite anyone and you don't want to go to the wedding alone."

His crushing glare confirmed her hypothesis, but his fingers skimmed down her arm and trailed over the back of her hand. The urge to drag him back to the carriage house and finish what they'd started made her shiver.

"Why do you have to make everything so difficult?" he demanded, his impatient tone at odds with the fire dancing in his eyes.

"Funny," she snorted. "I was thinking the same thing about you."

The air around them sizzled as Lia turned her hand and

placed her palm against Paul's. She barely bit back a groan as he intertwined their fingers. For several silent seconds they stared at each other until Lia's phone chimed, indicating she'd received a text. It took a supreme effort of will to break eye contact with Paul. Glancing down at the screen, she noted that Ethan had sent her a message.

"Something wrong?" Paul quizzed.

"Ethan was going to give me a ride to my camper so I could pick up a costume, and then we were going to go truck shopping, but he has to go into a late meeting so he can't make it." Lia considered her options as she continued, "The nurses are throwing a birthday party for one of the children at the hospital on Saturday and I promised to surprise her with a visit from Elsa."

"I can take you."

"You don't have to do that," she murmured, turning him down despite the craving to spend more time in his company. "Ethan—"

"Forget about Ethan."

His firm command sent a ripple of pleasure cascading through her body. Before meeting Paul, she never imagined herself attracted to someone so authoritative and formidable. He was as set in his ways as a granite boulder while she glided past, a butterfly borne on the winds of chance. The lack of compatibility in their natures offered no reason why they should have the slightest hint of chemistry, yet the pull between them couldn't be denied.

"I don't want to bother you," she protested.

"It's too late for that," he growled, the sound sinking into her bones, turning them to mush. "Text Ethan and tell him I'll take care of you."

Lia shivered at his words, every cell in her body sparkling with delight. "Really, it's okay. I can ask one of the twins…"

"Is there a reason why you suddenly want to be rid of me?"

"I don't want to be rid of you," she retorted in exasperation.

Paul frowned. "Is there a reason why you prefer going out with Ethan over me?"

"It's not that I prefer Ethan's company."

"Then what is it?" Paul persisted.

"The thing is, I think you view me as a tad eccentric—"

"A tad," he agreed, a teasing note in his voice.

Despite his attempt at levity, she remained earnest. "It's just that taking you to where I live is intimate."

All emotion vanished from his expression. "More intimate than what we did earlier?"

"For me, yes. Misty is my safe place. No matter what else changes in my life, she's a constant, my refuge." And being away from the camper, disconnected from the nomadic lifestyle for so many months, had caused a shift in her identity that left her feeling vulnerable and a bit lost.

"And I'm not welcome in your safe place."

"No, I mean…" She scrambled to explain without causing further damage to their fragile rapport.

"But Ethan is?"

"It's different with him," Lia said.

"Different how?"

"We're friends."

"Friends." His jaw worked as if he was grinding the word to dust.

"What I'm trying to say is that I've known him for months and we've talked about a lot of things."

"Are these the sorts of things you don't feel comfortable sharing with me?"

Lia thought about the differences between the two men. Ethan was more like a brother who accepted her oddities. Paul was a shining beacon of all things correct, perfect and gorgeous. From the start he'd been vocal about all her flaws and limitations. Lately she'd glimpsed grudging admiration for how she'd helped his grandfather. At the same time, Lia suspected if Paul hadn't been so suspicious of her from the start, she might never have registered on his radar.

"Ethan sees me. He accepts who I am."

"And you don't think I do?"

When his fingers tightened, Lia realized they were still holding hands. Suddenly aware that they could be discovered by one of his family at any second, Lia tried to tug free.

"You have a bad opinion of me," he declared, looking stunned.

"I don't," she countered.

"On the other hand, you have a high opinion of Ethan."

"Look." Deciding it was fruitless to dance around the truth any longer, Lia stripped all finesse out of her justification. "Ethan isn't likely to judge me for living in a camper."

"But you think I would." Paul released her hand and stepped back. "Let me point out that you are the one jumping to conclusions about me. Which is ironic, considering I spent the last hour watching you read tarot cards and didn't utter a single disparaging remark."

"You're right. I… I'm…"

"Sorry?" He crossed his arms over his chest. "You should be. I've been pretty openminded about all the alternative treatments you've used on Grady. Meditation. Sound baths. Aromatherapy. I've never met anyone who believes in the sorts of things you do, but I've never tried to interfere with anything you've suggested."

"You're right," she repeated. Lia bowed her head and accepted the scolding. "I'm not being fair to you. I know the things I'm into are completely foreign to you and you've been great about all the weirdness." She paused and looked into his eyes, then said, "If you're still willing to take me to pick up the Elsa costume, I'm happy to go for the ride."

"Afterward we'll go truck shopping," he declared, his tone brooking no further discussion. "And then I'll take you to dinner."

"That would be very nice," she said in a small voice, offering him a tentative smile. "Give me ten minutes to put the deck back in my room and get my purse."

He nodded in satisfaction, but his expression had yet to relax. "I'll meet you by the driveway."

Seven

While Paul waited for Lia, he paced from his SUV to the edge of the driveway and back, made restless by his heightened emotional state. Gone were the days when he could summon icy calm and a clear head at will. Just being near Lia disrupted the status quo. The factual logic that had served him all his life was being defeated by things he couldn't see, touch or prove existed. He was actually buying into all her metaphysical nonsense. His tarot reading had struck far too close to home. He'd like to put it down to sleight-of-hand card tricks and guesswork, but she hadn't touched the tarot deck after he'd handled it.

He'd always viewed his suspicious nature as a fundamental part of him like his height and eye color. Innate and something he couldn't change even if he wanted to. He could see how his skepticism created distance from others, but he'd accepted this as a matter of course. He had faith in those who were important to him. His family. Close friends. The rest of the world could go to hell.

But lately he was growing increasingly aware of how his distrust impacted Lia. She lacked the sort of armor those he usually dealt with wore. Her openness and upbeat take on the world displayed vulnerability that charmed everyone she met.

Which made her resistance to letting him see her camper all the more striking.

She didn't trust him.

The revelation stung.

Worse was her blind faith in Ethan. Had she forgotten which brother had landed her in their current predicament? Ethan, not Paul, had been the one who'd perpetuated Grady's incorrect belief that Lia was his long-lost granddaughter. More than any other member of the Watts family, Ethan was the one she should be most wary of.

"Ready?"

Paul had been so lost in thought that he hadn't noticed Lia's approach. She'd done more than grab her purse at the house. While he'd wrestled with his demons, she'd changed into a loose-fitting black-and-white-striped T-shirt dress and white sneakers. With her hair in a loose topknot and dark glasses hiding her eyes, she gave off a cool, casual vibe at complete odds with the turmoil raging in him.

Longing rippled through him. He itched to reach across the distance separating them and haul her into his arms. Instead, stunned by the willpower it took to keep his hands off her, he gripped the passenger-side door handle as if it was a lifeline and gestured her into the SUV. No matter how temptation swelled in him, this wasn't the time or place to cross that line. Why was it so hard to do the right thing around her?

Forty minutes later, Paul drove through the security gate of a boat and RV storage lot and stopped his SUV beside a small vintage trailer painted white and mint green. From

Lia's doting expression, he gathered this must be the famous Misty.

"It won't take me but a second to grab the costume," Lia said, her hand on the door handle. "Do you want to wait here?"

After their earlier quarrel, he intended to prove that he wasn't the judgmental jerk she'd branded him. "No." And then hearing how abrupt that sounded, he added in a more conciliatory tone, "I'd like to see what she looks like inside." He'd picked up Lia's habit of referring to the vintage camper by the feminine pronoun.

"Okay." She drew the word out as she exited the SUV.

Paul noted the matching mint-colored curtains framing the windows as Lia unlocked the camper and stepped inside. He followed her in, surprised that the ceiling height accommodated his six-foot-one-inch frame without him having to stoop.

"This is tiny," he declared, at once shocked by the camper's limited footprint and impressed by how Lia had made efficient use of every inch of it. "How do you live in such a small space?"

"Simply." She flashed him a wry grin and gestured at the boxes piled up in the sitting area toward the back. "It's not usually this cluttered. Normally I store all the costumes in my truck."

"Do you like living with so little?" Paul asked, shifting uneasily in the narrow aisle between closet and kitchen. He became all too aware of the inviting sleeping nook behind him with its extravagance of soft pillows.

"I find it calming." She gave him a quick tour, narrating the camper's history while assessing his reaction the whole time. "What do you think?"

"It's cozy," he ventured, glancing around. "And it suits you."

Into less than one hundred and fifty square feet, she'd

fit a kitchen and bathroom, full-size bed, dinette and a decent-sized closet. Vintage pastel fabrics softened the white walls, tin-tile ceiling and wood-look vinyl flooring. The appliances were the same mint green as the exterior and appeared original to the 1960s' vibe.

"Thank you."

"For what?"

"Being openminded." Her infectious smile bloomed for the first time since Dallas had interrupted them at the carriage house. "You know, we aren't likely to get interrupted anytime soon." While he processed what she'd said, she blew out an exasperated breath. "Are you just going to stare at me?" Giving his shirt a sassy tug, she finished, "Or are you going to take me in your arms and rock my world?"

Relief flooded him. They were going to be okay. Paul wrapped his arm around her waist and hauled her up against him. The breath swept out of her in a soft, satisfying huff. He expected her to get all clingy and press herself against him, but instead she wrapped her arms around his waist and rested her cheek on his chest.

"What are you doing?" Paul asked.

She flexed her arm muscles, embracing him more snugly. "Giving you a hug."

"Why?"

"I want you to know that I like you." Without lifting her cheek from the front of his shirt, she canted her head and gazed up at him. "Before you kiss me. Before I go all weak-kneed and gooey inside. I want you to know I like you. You. Not your money. Or the power your family wields in this town. I'm a simple girl with simple needs. One of them being a gorgeous, sexy man who makes love to her as if she's the most desirable woman he's ever known."

It was both a request and a plea for him to treat her well. But her declaration tempered Paul's all-consuming drive to possess her. He eased his grip, second-guessing everything.

"Why is that important before I kiss you?"

"I don't think this time we'll be able to stop there," she said. "And after whatever happens you'll be even less willing to trust me."

"It's not that I don't trust you..." It was more that he didn't trust himself around her. The feelings she aroused messed with his head.

"You trust that I'm good for your grandfather. But I don't think you'll ever trust that I could be good for you."

With his gaze locked on her lips, he rasped, "That's not true."

But he recognized the reason for her apprehension. He approached decisions with logic; she believed a deck of cards could predict what was to come. She took leaps of faith with little regard for her own safety. He rarely made a move without knowing in advance what the outcome would be. Yet at the moment he felt driven beyond wisdom and sense by his need for her.

"You won't believe that I don't want anything from you," she persisted. "Even when nothing I've done gives you any reason to suspect me."

It should've bothered him that she had him all figured out. Well, maybe not all figured out. But her grasp on what made him tick surpassed what he understood about her.

"I don't have all the answers," he admitted. "You're not like anyone I've ever known before and frankly, you scare the hell out of me."

Her eyes widened. "I don't see how."

"You've brought magic into my life." He braced his hip against her kitchen counter as his admission caused something inside him to snap. Light-headed and reeling, he closed his eyes.

"You don't believe in magic," she murmured.

"I believe in you."

He dropped his head and let his breath flow over her lips

before easing forward to taste her. Anticipating a powerful jolt of desire, he was unprepared for the way his entire
body lit up like he'd backed into a high-voltage generator
marked *Danger*.

Drinking deep of her sweet, sinful mouth, Paul savored
a kiss that reminded him of a quality bourbon, warm and
complex. Heat spiraled through his veins. Her moan gave
him the signal to take the kiss deeper. Lost in the liquid
slide of their dancing tongues, Paul sucked on her lower lip
and smiled as an eager groan broke from her throat. Their
teeth clicked and he slanted his head to adjust the angle of
the kiss so he could continue to devour her unhindered.

Lia's questing fingers dove beneath his shirt and an elec-
trical storm flashed behind his closed eyes. He crackled
with wild thrumming energy.

He came up for air long enough to whisper, "This is
going to complicate things."

"Oh." The anguish in her murmur made him hate that
he'd voiced his concerns. But then she kept going and it
was her throaty yes that sealed both their fates.

He breathed in her laughter, capturing it in his lungs before crushing his mouth to hers. A needy whimper broke
from her as she ground herself against him, her movement
becoming more frantic by the second. She rocked her hips,
as if she'd given herself over to what her body needed and
to hell with pride or consequences.

Paul couldn't get enough of this woman. The chemistry
between them was born of Lia's romantic optimism and
his surrender to everything caring and earnest about her.
Even knowing this stolen moment couldn't last and despite
recognizing her sweetness might shatter his defenses and
leave him open and exposed, Paul could no more stop or
pause than he could fly.

He lowered his lips to hers once more. As her tongue,
hungry and seeking, stole into his mouth, setting him on

fire, he reached up and released her hair from its clip. Threading his fingers through the espresso waterfall of silky strands, he savored the spill of softness against his skin. He breathed in her vanilla scent as she roped her arms around his neck and murmured her appreciation. The sound popped a circuit in his brain, turning his thoughts into white noise that drowned out all things rational.

They tumbled onto her bed, hands skimming beneath the fabric of their clothes to the hot skin beneath. Groaning and panting, they deepened their kisses. Clothing fell away. Paul cupped Lia's breast and pulled her tight nipple into his mouth. With a wordless cry, she arched her back and shifted her hips in entreaty. He wanted to take his time, to put his mouth between her thighs and taste her arousal, but his hunger for her burned too hot. His hands shook as he slid on a condom and shifted her until she straddled him.

Her blissful expression transfixed him. Then she tossed her head back and lowered herself onto his erection. Engulfed by the heat of her, Paul forgot how to breathe. No woman he'd ever known had blindsided him like Lia. She aroused impulsive cravings that couldn't be denied and he'd long since lost the will to resist.

When her orgasm slammed into her, Paul felt the impact shake his soul. In the aftermath, he skimmed his palms over her flushed skin until her lashes lifted. Her eyes glowed with naked joy and absolute trust. At the sight, something rattled loose in his chest, stopping his heart.

"I…"

With a tender smile she set her fingertips against his lips. "Come for me. Please. I need you so much."

Keeping them locked together, Paul flipped Lia onto her back and began driving into her tight heat. With an ardent moan she drove her fingers into his hair and met his deep thrusts with a hunger and enthusiasm that turned his desire into something reckless and unstoppable. He locked his lips to hers and surged into her over and over, feasting on her pleas. She was on the verge of coming again when his climax built to a point of no return.

With her legs wrapped around his hips, her teeth grazing his neck, he held off until a series of tremors detonated through her body and she yielded a soft, keening cry of pleasure. Only then did he let himself be caught in the shattering brilliance of his orgasm.

Contentment settled over Paul as he buried his face in Lia's silky hair and waited for his breath to level out. Trailing his fingertips across her delicate shoulders and down her slender back, he stared at the tin ceiling, then turned his head and took in the cozy pillows they'd knocked to the floor with their passion. Reality intruded, banishing the hazy glow of satisfaction.

They'd agreed she would stay for two weeks. Seven days had already passed. The proof that she would soon depart was all around them. The truth in his heart was that Paul wasn't ready to let her go.

With the wedding Paul had invited her to only two days away, Lia took inventory of her closet and found nothing suitable for an evening wedding featuring a Charleston socialite and a multimillionaire. Dallas had described the private event as a "simple affair," but Lia guessed Charleston "simple" wasn't a barefoot bride in her momma's backyard with a barbecue picnic to follow. No, this wedding would be elegant and classy with a guest list that included the town's elite.

Lia wanted something that would let her blend in with the rest of the Southern women in attendance, but had no idea what that would be. Her best bet would be to reach out to Poppy and Dallas to see if they had recommendations. Once Lia had shot each woman a text, explaining her dilemma, their immediate and enthusiastic response left her second-guessing her decision. In just a few days she'd be bidding them goodbye. Growing closer to the twins was only going to make leaving harder. Not for her. She was all too accustomed to parting ways with those she'd grown fond of.

On the other hand, the Watts family was a tight-knit group who'd been devastated when Ava left. Of course, Grady's daughter had spent her whole life embraced by her family and naturally when she'd fled Charleston, her absence left a void. By the time the story came out that Lia wasn't actually Ava's daughter, they would only have known her for a couple weeks. The loss wouldn't be as profound.

While Lia was pondering her eventual break with the Watts family, she'd received a flurry of group texts. Dallas listed the names of several boutiques in downtown Charleston while Poppy chimed in with her opinion on each one. Lia read the messages with a growing sense of turmoil. At last she jumped in and asked if either one would be available later that afternoon to come shopping with her and give her some tips. An enthusiastic yes from both women left her overwhelmed with fondness and riddled with guilt.

At three o'clock Lia slid into the back seat of Dallas's large SUV while Poppy rode shotgun. The two women exchanged animated opinions as to what would be suitable for the wedding as Dallas drove.

At the first store the twins took her to, Lia could immediately see she was in the wrong place. The clothes had a sexy vibe that she might have explored if her goal was to stand out. When she said as much, the twins exchanged a puzzled look.

"But you've got the perfect body to rock all of this," Dallas said, indicating a short red-orange number with a plunging neckline.

"I don't see why you wouldn't want to show off what you've got," Poppy contributed.

"That's not the first impression I want to make," Lia said carefully. "I was thinking that I wanted to blend in."

"But that's so boring," Poppy cried.

"I think boring is just fine when it comes to a wedding," Lia countered.

"But we're already here. At least try on two things," Dallas said. "Even if you don't buy anything, it'll be fun to try some stuff on."

"Dallas and I will each pick something for you and you can see which you like better."

Poppy's enthusiasm quashed any further protest. What would it hurt for her to indulge the twins? But even as Lia nodded her acceptance, she reflected on their growing camaraderie. Usually her nomadic lifestyle kept her from diving too deep into friendship, but the twins were engaging and endearing. From the first they'd made Lia feel like a part of their inner circle. The fact that she didn't belong, combined with her part in the deception, shadowed Lia's enjoyment of the outing. Still, the twins were a formidable distraction when they combined their persuasive powers and soon Lia surrendered to their enthusiasm.

They didn't allow her to do any browsing of her own and Lia could see that they'd played this game often with each other. Although they were identical twins, their personalities and styles couldn't have been more different. Where Dallas preferred pastel tones and floaty, ruffled dresses that moved as she walked, Poppy adopted a more casual style with bright fabrics that hugged her body and showed off all her assets.

Selections made, the twins herded Lia toward the dressing room. She entered the enclosed space and surveyed each outfit. The first was a strapless bedazzled dress in cobalt blue. While it was beautiful and would no doubt look great with her coloring, it screamed *look at me*. The second dress—a body-skimming red halter with high side split—was no better. If she walked into the party wearing this, everyone would see her and want to know who she was.

Still, Lia had agreed to try both on. She stepped out in the cobalt blue dress first.

"What do you think?" she asked, turning before the three-way mirror.

"I think all Paul's friends will be drooling over you," Dallas said.

That was the last thing Lia was looking for. She didn't want anyone singling her out.

"It's beautiful," she said. "But not exactly what I'm looking for. I feel a little too…" She tugged up the neckline, and then down on the hem. "I would feel a little too exposed in the dress."

"Try the red one on," Poppy said.

Lia returned to the dressing room and swapped dresses. Although the red halter was a little better, she still felt like she was trying too hard to send a message. She came out and had mixed reactions. While Poppy nodded vigorously, Dallas shook her head.

"The color is good on you and it really shows off the muscle tone in your arms, but that slit…"

"Agreed," Lia said. "Let's try somewhere else."

King Street was lined with boutiques and Lia soon learned that at some point, the twins had shopped them all. At the next store they went to the dresses were more in Dallas's style, with lace and ruffle details in pastel fabrics that made Lia look as if she was trying too hard to be someone she wasn't.

"I'm looking for something between these two stores," Lia said, worrying that she was never going to be able to find anything that suited her.

"I have a place in mind," Dallas said.

Lia changed back into her regular clothes and the three women departed for yet another boutique. As soon as they entered, Lia knew this was exactly where she needed to be. This time, instead of letting the twins choose, Lia intended to be part of the search for something she liked. There was a lot for her to pick from, but she settled on one dress in particular.

The gorgeous long-sleeved, ankle-length sheath fit her perfectly. A subtle sparkle ran through the blush-colored fabric that helped define her slender curves without drawing too much attention.

"This one," Lia said, exiting the dressing room to show off her pick.

"It's elegant and understated," Poppy said, but her expression reflected doubt. "Are you sure you don't want something with more pizzazz?"

"Elegant and refined is what I was going for," Lia said, gazing at her reflection in the mirror. "Unfortunately, I can't afford this dress. But you get the idea of what I'm going for."

"You shouldn't worry about the expense," Dallas said, highlighting the stark difference between how the twins lived and Lia's reality.

Despite the fact that both women held down jobs and paid their own expenses, they came from a wealthy family and this gave them a financial edge. Where Lia lived simply and sometimes had to scrape the bottom of her piggy bank when something unexpected happened, she knew all the twins had to do was dip into their extensive reserves.

"It's too much money to spend on something I can't imagine having the chance to wear again," Lia said, pretending not to see the look the twins exchanged.

Since the first day she'd met them, Lia had been dropping hints that she'd soon be leaving Charleston to get back on the road, preparing everyone for the moment when the testing mistake was revealed. Each time she mentioned leaving, one or more of the Wattses deflected her assertion, making it perfectly clear they didn't want her to go. Even though she recognized their affection for her was based on their belief that she was Ava's daughter, Lia had begun to dread the moment when she was no longer part of this family.

She'd always downplayed her need for an emotional support network. Her mother had instilled self-reliance in Lia from an early age. But looking at this way of life through the eyes of the Watts family, she'd started to see its limitations.

Bidding a determined farewell to the blush sheath, Lia settled on a markdown dress in black that skimmed her slim figure and highlighted her shoulders. Both Poppy and Dallas approved the sophisticated style, but best of all, the price was just inside her comfort zone. It wasn't the dress of her dreams but it would definitely do, and she couldn't wait to see Paul's expression when he saw her in it.

Ethan was heading home after another long day at Watts Shipping when he spied the open door to his father's large corner office and stepped inside. Instead of finding his father behind his large mahogany desk, Miles Watts stood near the windows, a drink in his hand, his gaze aimed toward the Cooper River, his mind far beyond the space he occupied.

"Wasn't Mom expecting you home hours ago?" Ethan asked, struck as always by how much Paul resembled his father with their matching tall frames, the family's distinct green eyes and wavy blond hair.

"No," Miles replied, shifting his gaze to his younger son. "She had book club tonight."

"I'm surprised you didn't take the opportunity to head to Chapins."

Chapins was a favorite of the Watts men. An upscale cigar lounge in the heart of downtown Charleston, it offered a large selection of rare and vintage brands.

"I had too much to do here," Miles said, gesturing toward his desk with the crystal tumbler. "Are you heading out?"

"I thought I'd swing by the gym before heading home." But instead of bidding his dad good-night, he advanced into the room. "Is everything okay? You seem distracted."

"Your mom brought one of her lemon pound cakes over to Grady today. You know how he loves her baking."

Ethan smiled. "We all do."

Miles nodded. "She ran into Taylor English while she was there."

While it wasn't unusual for Grady's attorney to visit him, something about the encounter had obviously prompted Ethan's mother to comment on it.

"And?" Ethan asked.

"And nothing." His father threw Ethan a dry look. "You know she wouldn't discuss her business with your grandfather."

"But Taylor must've said something that got you thinking, otherwise you wouldn't mention it."

"It wasn't what she told your mother, it was the questions she was asking about Lia, her background and if Paul had checked her out."

Ethan began to feel uneasy, but kept his tone neutral. "What did Mom tell her?"

"That she assumed Paul had vetted her." Miles glanced toward his son for confirmation before continuing. "But Taylor had all sorts of questions."

"Like what?"

"She pointed out the holes in Lia's adoption story. Would

a court really give a baby to a woman who moved around so much? Isn't there a whole process that happens where she'd have to be evaluated for stability?"

"I'm sure that happened," Ethan interjected, wishing they'd concocted a more run-of-the-mill backstory instead of using Lia's actual past.

Ethan's father didn't look convinced. "Why would Taylor ask so many questions about Lia unless she suspected something was wrong?"

"You know what kind of lawyer Taylor is. She's thorough."

"But why would she need to be thorough? The testing service determined Lia is Ava's daughter. I don't understand why Taylor would question that." His father's eyes narrowed. "Unless she doesn't think the testing service is reliable. Your mother wondered if we should have our own DNA test run."

Although his father had just presented him with the perfect opportunity to explain about the mistake, Ethan hesitated to put an end to their scheme. They'd agreed to a couple weeks. Paul was acting as best man at Ryan and Zoe's wedding the next afternoon and had invited Lia to join him. Both deserved a heads-up before Ethan broke the news that Lia wasn't family.

"Is Taylor right to ask questions?" Miles demanded after Ethan took too long deciding how to answer. And then when Ethan continued to grapple with his conscience, his father cursed. "What is really going on with Lia?"

"Nothing."

Miles crossed his arms and glared. "Do not lie to me."

Ethan sucked in a deep breath and let it ease from his lungs. "Okay, here's the thing…" As he explained the situation, claiming complete responsibility for the scheme, his father stared at him in dismay.

"Damn it, Ethan," Miles raged as he kneaded the back

of his neck. "This is the craziest stunt you've ever pulled. What were you thinking?"

"I did it for Grady," Ethan said, refusing to be treated like a reckless teenager. "And for Paul. Haven't you noticed that things between him and Grady have improved?"

Miles gave a reluctant nod. "And I'm glad, but you can't seriously be planning to pass Lia off as family forever."

"The plan was only supposed to last until Grady improved and he has. Everything will be over in a few days."

"Over how?"

Ethan's concern eased as he realized his father was willing to hear him out before deciding to blow the whistle. "We plan to announce that the testing service got it wrong and she's not Ava's daughter."

"That is going to devastate Dad."

"I know he'll be upset," Ethan said. "But I'm convinced that we would've lost him if he hadn't believed Lia was Ava's daughter. And he's stronger now. I think he'll be okay when he finds out the truth."

"You *hope* he'll be okay," Miles corrected. "Just be ready for the consequences, because if there are any setbacks in Grady's health, that's on Paul and you."

"Not Paul. Just me. By the time Paul found out what was going on we were too far in."

Miles leveled a keen stare on his younger son. "One last thing. You really need to tell your grandfather the whole truth."

Ethan shook his head. "I considered that, but decided that if Grady found out we tricked him on top of losing Ava's daughter, it would be a bigger blow."

"The problem with the whole DNA testing angle," Miles said, "is that Grady will believe Ava's daughter is still out there."

"I've been thinking about that." Ethan opened his brief-case and pulled out the test kit he'd ordered in the days after he'd concocted his scheme to pass Lia off as Grady's grand-daughter. "Maybe you could help me find her for real."

Eight

The morning of his best friend's wedding, Paul spent a few hours at the office, but found he couldn't concentrate. That had been happening all too often in the days since that long afternoon in Lia's camper. Despite the unusual surroundings, or maybe because of them, Paul knew the time with Lia was indelibly etched in his memories. They'd made love for hours, forgoing new truck shopping and skipping dinner. Only after their exertions made their hunger for food more urgent than their appetite for each other did they get dressed and grab a couple burgers at a fast-food restaurant.

He hadn't been exaggerating: giving in to their attraction was going to complicate things. She wasn't like any woman he'd ever known and he hadn't crossed the line with her lightly. This left him with a dilemma. Sneaking around with her compounded his discomfort about the lies they were perpetrating. But the thought of giving her up left him in an ill-tempered funk.

Following the compulsion to see her, Paul left his office

and drove to his grandfather's estate. The sound of feminine laughter reached his ears as he exited his SUV, luring
him toward the pool. Expecting to find his cousins clad in
their customary bikinis, lazily floating on rafts in the turquoise water, he was besieged by wonder and a trace of
amusement at what greeted him instead.

His cousins and Lia balanced on paddleboards in the
middle of the pool, engaged in yoga moves. While both
Dallas and Poppy wore bathing suits, Lia was dressed in
her daily uniform of black yoga pants and a graphic T-
shirt that flattered her lean curves and drew attention to
her high, firm breasts. Given that both his cousins had wet
hair and were wobbling dangerously on the ever-shifting
boards while trying to hold a standing yoga pose, Paul assumed it must be much harder than Lia was making it look.

She moved fluidly on the board, shifting from one pose
to another with barely a ripple in the pool. Her confidence
fascinated him. At every turn she surprised him with a
whole range of unexpected talents from cake decorating
to accompanying Grady's drumming on the harmonica
to assorted art projects geared toward children that now
adorned Grady's bedroom.

With each day that passed, she endeared herself to his
entire family more and more, and even Paul's high level of
skepticism had failed him. Lia was a whirling dervish of
energy and optimism and it was hard to remain detached,
especially when every time they occupied the same room,
she became the focal point of his awareness. His determined distrust had given way beneath the pressure of the
undeniable energy between them. The maddening chemistry was more than sexual. The hunger to be near her was
a fire that burned throughout his entire body.

He found her stories of life on the road fascinating. Her
kindness toward his grandfather wasn't an act. Every minute Paul spent in her company boosted his optimism and

lightened his mood. The tiniest brush of his hand against hers sent a shower of sparks through him. Dozens of times he'd caught himself on the verge of touching her in front of his family. Whenever they occupied the same room, he had to struggle to keep his gaze from lingering on her.

Spying Grady in the shade of the pool house, Paul approached and sat down beside his grandfather's wheelchair. Grady reached out and gave Paul's arm an affectionate squeeze. With the return of his grandfather's love and approval, Paul had no more need to arm himself against the grief that had caused him to guard against personal relationships. Another positive change in his life he could attribute to Lia. Was there no end to her uplifting influence? Did he really want there to be?

Once again Paul was struck by concern for what the future might hold after Lia's departure. While Grady grew more robust with each passing day, finding out that Lia wasn't his granddaughter was certain to hit him hard. Would his depression return?

"What are they doing?" he asked, crossing his ankle over his knee as the afternoon's humid air made its way beneath the collar of his navy polo.

"Yoga," Grady sang, bright amusement in the gaze he flicked toward his grandson.

"Why are they doing it on paddleboards in the middle of the pool?"

"Harder."

Seeing Grady's fond smile, Paul felt a familiar stab of guilt that they were perpetrating a fraud on the old man. His grandfather loved Lia because he believed she was his long-lost granddaughter. That she wasn't ate at Paul more every day.

"I can see that. The twins look like they're struggling."

Even as he spoke, Poppy lost her balance, but before she tumbled into the pool, she dropped to her knees and clutched the edges of the board. She laughed in relief while Dallas and Lia called out their encouragement.

Paul guessed this wasn't Lia's first time doing this because she was rock-solid on the board. "It's good to see you outside," Paul said, tearing his gaze away from her. "How are you feeling today?"

"I'm feeling strong." Grady spoke the words with triumph.

"You're getting better every day," Paul murmured. "That's wonderful."

The two men sat in companionable silence and watched the three women for another half hour, until Lia brought the session to a halt.

"Nice work, ladies," she called, towing the paddleboards toward the storage room at the back of the pool house while his cousins toweled off.

Paul went to help her, eager for a couple seconds alone, somewhere out of the way so he didn't have to guard his expression. He took in the light sheen of moisture coating her skin, tempting him to ride his palms over her sun-warmed arms and around her waist. If he dipped his head and slid his tongue along her neck, he knew she would taste salty. His mouth watered at the memory of her silky flesh beneath his lips.

"You've done that before," Paul said, letting her precede him into the large room crammed with pool toys.

"My mother teaches yoga. I've been doing it since I could stand," Lia said. "You should try it. Besides increasing flexibility and muscle tone, it can reduce stress."

He paused in the act of stacking the boards against the back wall. "Do I seem stressed to you?"

"I was thinking maybe you'd like to improve your flexibility," she teased, shooting him a wry grin.

Paul nodded, letting her score the point without retaliating. She wouldn't be the first person who'd described him as intractable. It's what enabled him to keep pursuing criminals when the trail went cold. At the same time, he recognized being obstinate had created problems in his relationship with his family.

"Grady seems to be doing better every day," he remarked, reaching for her hand. As their fingers meshed, his entire body sighed with delight at the contact. "It's hard to believe that less than two weeks ago we were all worried he wasn't going to last until the end of the month."

"You know he's really proud of you."

His gut twisted at her words. "I don't know that."

"Well, he is," she said, her thumb stroking across his knuckles.

"Even though I didn't join the family business?"

"It makes him happy that you're passionate about what you do." Lia's warm smile eased the tightness in Paul's chest. "And that you help people by making the world safer."

"Thank you," Paul said, tugging her closer.

Entreaty flickered in her eyes, quickly masked by her long dark lashes. His blood heated as he detected an unsteadiness in her breathing. Damn, he badly wanted to kiss her. The need to claim her soft mouth overwhelmed him. Not even the worry that they might be caught could temper the wild emotions she aroused.

Acting before he could convince himself that it was madness, Paul backed Lia toward the wall. A surprised whoosh of air escaped her as her spine connected with the hard surface. He skimmed his fingers down her arms, pinned her wrists to the wall on either side of her hips.

Curses momentarily drowned out his thoughts. "We should get back to the pool before someone comes looking for us."

Releasing his grip on her, Paul flattened his palms against the wall and started to push away, but her reflexes proved faster than his. Before he could escape, she'd locked her hands around his back and tugged him even closer.

"Kiss me first." Her lips curved in a sassy grin that was equal parts sexy and sweet. "Unless you don't want to."

He almost laughed at her words. Not only did he *want* to kiss her, he *needed* to kiss her. Needed it like the air he breathed and the food he ate. She was the most irritating, frustrating female he'd ever known. Thoughts of her distracted him all the time. It took effort to concentrate on his job and for that he couldn't forgive her. Worse, he was ravenous for her in a way that couldn't be denied and with each day his willpower weakened.

Her eagerness was a temptation he couldn't resist and Paul found himself swept into the kiss. Into her warmth and sweetness and enthusiasm. He took what she gave. Unable to stop. Unwilling to stop.

Paul wasn't sure what brought him back from the brink, but soon he lifted his lips from hers and trailed kisses across her cheek.

"I can't stop thinking about being with you again," he murmured, surprising himself with the admission. "But you have that birthday party at the hospital this afternoon, don't you?"

Her chest rose and fell as she stared at him, her beautiful hazel eyes wide and utterly trusting. "You remembered."

Paul stepped back and raked his fingers through his hair. "Do you mind if I tag along?"

"You're always welcome to be my knight-errant."

Even as warmth pooled in his gut, the urge to warn her to be careful of him rose. The things he wanted to do to her weren't romantic or chivalrous. Her love of dressing up as a princess drove home the intrinsic sentimental nature of her true soul.

In fairy tales, princesses got rescued from towers, endless sleep and villains who intended them harm. Paul was no Prince Charming. In fact, he'd acted more like a beast with Lia. And even if his initial disdain had given way to grudging admiration, he didn't deserve her trust.

"That's fine as long as I don't have to wear tights," he grumbled and neither her surprised laughter nor her affectionate hug improved his mood.

On a normal visit to the children's ward at the hospital, Lia would've lost herself in the part of Elsa, the Snow Queen. Bringing joy to children, especially ones who needed to escape reality for a little while, gave her own spirits an enormous boost. But Paul's solemn gaze on her the entire time made her all too aware of the heat and confusion between them.

Every stolen moment with him pushed her further into uncharted territory. She'd never known the sort of urgent craving he aroused in her. In the past, she'd always viewed sex as a pleasurable way to connect with someone she cared about. What she experienced with Paul turned every other encounter into a foggy memory. The crystal-pure clarity of his fingers gliding over her skin. The keen pleasure of his weight pressing her into the mattress. His deep kisses and soul-stirring moans as he slid into her. All of it was etched into her soul never to be forgotten.

Yet all too soon she'd be leaving Charleston, never to see him again. Lia wasn't sure what to do about her growing resistance to the idea of resuming her travels. Never before had she faced a compulsion to stay put. But her growing attachment to Paul was a big part of that. Normally Lia would blindly follow her heart, but this time she recognized that trusting her instincts was impossible. She'd mired herself in a scheme that had only one outcome. Once the genetic test was revealed to be flawed, no member of the Watts family would want her to stick around.

Not even Paul. Despite her longing for a relationship

to developing with him, she feared that if she remained in Charleston, eventually her past would come between them. He'd dedicated his career to hunting criminals. She could imagine his fury when he discovered her grandfather was in prison. And learning what had put him there would confirm Paul's initial opinion of her as an opportunist.

Part of her recognized he was probably still digging into her background. She'd be wise to tell him the truth and face his displeasure before her growing feelings for him made heartbreak inevitable, but as they walked back to the estate, Lia lost her nerve. She was gambling that he wouldn't turn up anything with less than a week until she left Charleston. Better that she stay silent so that his memories of her remained unsullied.

They parted company at the driveway and Lia headed for the house. Upon entering her bedroom, she spied something that hadn't been there when she'd left. A garment bag, twin to the one from the boutique hanging on the armoire door, lay across her bed, along with an envelope. Puzzled, Lia set aside her long ice-blue gloves, opened the envelope and read the note.

We know you loved this dress and wanted you to have it.—Dallas & Poppy.

Overwhelmed by the twins' generosity, Lia slowly unfastened the bag's zipper to reveal the stunning blush gown she'd fallen in love with. Guilt clawed at her. She shouldn't accept the gift. The twins had purchased the expensive dress believing she was their real cousin. Yet to refuse would force awkward explanations.

Lia wanted to scream in frustration. Why did everyone have to be so kind to her? The deception would've been so much simpler if she'd been greeted with the same sort of suspicion that Paul had demonstrated.

After shooting the twins an effusive thank-you text, Lia jumped in the shower. As she applied her makeup and experimented with several hairstyles, she tried to ignore her anxiety over what she might encounter at the upcoming event. Pretending to be Ava's daughter had grown easier these last few days. Not that her subterfuge rode any easier on her conscience, but once she'd answered the tricky questions surrounding her childhood to everyone's satisfaction, she'd been able to lower her guard somewhat.

But attending this wedding with Paul meant she would be under scrutiny once more. Although he'd promised his circle of friends wouldn't ask too many questions about her, Lia suspected that they'd be wildly speculative about any woman he'd bring. Once again, the opportunity to spend more time in his company was a temptation she couldn't resist. Hopefully it wouldn't backfire on them.

The dress fit as perfectly as when she'd tried it on in the shop, reviving Lia's confidence. Tonight she would demonstrate to Paul that she could at least appear as if she fit into his social circle, even if she'd be completely out of her element. As long as she smiled a lot, said little and stuck like glue to Paul's side, she should be fine.

Lia arrived in the formal living room five minutes before she was scheduled to meet Paul only to discover that he'd beaten her there. She had a fraction of a second to appreciate the way his charcoal-gray suit fit his imposing figure and to indulge in a little delighted swoon before he glanced up from his phone and swept a heated gaze over her.

The possessive approval Lia saw there stripped her of her ability to speak or move. As often as she'd donned a costume and played the role of a princess, she'd never truly felt like one before. But now, as she basked in Paul's admiration, she understood what it meant to be treasured.

"You look gorgeous," Paul said, walking over to her. Clearly cautious over the possibility that anyone could stumble on them, he limited his contact to a brief squeeze of her fingers, but even that fleeting touch sent Lia's pulse into overdrive. "I'll have to stay close tonight or my friends will try to lure you away."

"Oh." His low murmur set the butterflies fluttering in her stomach. "No." She shook her head as the full import of his words struck her.

"No?" He looked taken aback.

She shook her head and rushed to explain. "I didn't think I'd stand out in this dress."

Paul's posture relaxed once more. A sensual smile curved his chiseled lips. "You stand out no matter what you wear."

With her skin flushing at his compliment, Lia slid a little deeper into infatuation. Even so, she recognized that the easing of Paul's earlier distrust gave his approval greater significance. Still, there was no fighting the inevitable. She was falling hard for his man.

He took her by the elbow and propelled her toward the door, his confidence muffling her concern. "Relax, you'll be fine."

"That's easy for you to say," she muttered grimly. "This is your world." And she didn't belong.

Twenty minutes later, Lia's mood had lightened. During the short drive to one of the most impressive mansions in Charleston's historic district Paul had shared Ryan and Zoe's inspirational path to love.

Long before the pair met, Zoe had been in the middle of a scandalous divorce. To appear the wounded party and avoid having to pay her alimony, her husband had publicly accused Zoe of infidelity. Eventually the truth of her innocence came out, but by then her reputation was ruined and her finances were in tatters.

Devastated and bitter, Zoe had joined a revenge bargain with two strangers, women who'd also been wronged by powerful men. To deflect suspicion, each woman was tasked with taking down a man she had no connection to.

In Zoe's case, her target had been Ryan and she was supposed to hurt him by damaging his sister's political career.

Zoe hadn't counted on the romance that bloomed with Ryan or the difficulty in extricating herself from the vengeance pact. In the end, because Zoe hadn't been directly responsible for the resulting scandal that harmed Ryan's family, he'd chosen to put aside his anger, unable to imagine a future without her in it.

Paul obviously approved of the union despite its rocky beginning, leading Lia to hope he could set aside his stubborn and judgmental nature when faced with true happiness.

As soon as they went inside, the soothing strains of a string quartet enveloped them. Lush floral arrangements in warm shades of peach and pink decorated every room on the main floor. Lia inhaled the richly scented air as they strolled through the various rooms on their way to the rear garden where the ceremony would be taking place.

Paul introduced her to several people before his best man duties called him away. He left her with Zoe's former brother-in-law the race car driver Harrison Crosby and his fiancée, London McCaffrey. Lia appreciated the couple's easy acceptance of her company as they sipped preceremony champagne before making their way to the area in the garden where the chairs had been set up for the wedding.

The ceremony was short but beautiful. The bride wore a romantic confection of tulle embellished with lace flowers. Her groom stood beside Paul in a charcoal suit and pink bow tie, looking positively gobsmacked as she walked up the aisle toward him. They were emotional as they exchanged vows, bringing both smiles and tears to the thirty or so guests who'd come to celebrate with them.

Lia was still dabbing tears from her eyes when Paul came to find her after the ceremony.

"Are you okay?" he asked, arching an eyebrow at her.

"It was a beautiful wedding," she whispered. "They're so obviously in love."

"They came through a lot to get here," he murmured, his gaze following the bride and groom as they greeted friends and accepted congratulations. "I think it's made them stronger as a couple."

Struck by both his sentiment and the show of obvious affection for his friends, Lia exclaimed, "Paul Watts, you are a romantic!"

He frowned at her accusation. "I wouldn't say that."

"Don't deny it." A happy glow enveloped her. "Here I expected you to have a suspicious view of the whole love-and-marriage thing and you go all mushy on me."

"I'm not mushy."

She ignored his growled denial. "I never imagined you'd be a fan of love and such."

"Calling me a fan is a little over-the-top," he protested, taking her by the elbow and turning her toward the house where the reception dinner and after-party were taking place. "And why is it so surprising that I believe in love?"

"Love requires a leap of faith," she explained, having mulled this topic often in the last few days. "You're so logical."

He looked thoughtful as he considered her point. "It's also about trust," he said, indicating he'd also given the matter some consideration. "Trust of yourself and of the other person."

"But you're not exactly the trusting sort," she reminded him.

"That's not completely accurate when it comes to family and friends."

His single-minded, fierce protectiveness of those closest to him was sexy as hell. She was used to being alone and never considered what it might be like with someone to count on. Lately, however, Lia had pondered the immense sense of security those closest to Paul must feel. She'd never doubted that he was someone who could be counted on to aid and protect, but until now hadn't considered what being the beneficiary of such attention might be like.

That afternoon in her camper, encircled by his strong arms, she'd experienced a sense of well-being unlike anything she'd ever known. At the time she'd put the sensation down to their lovemaking and her joy at being inside the familiar refuge of her camper.

But maybe it had been just as much about gaining Paul's trust. Watching him with his family had offered her insight into his protective nature. He wanted nothing but the best for those he loved. When he'd begun to open up to her in small ways, she'd been thrilled to be gifted with this show of faith.

"So what you're saying," she clarified, "is that once given, your trust is complete?" The power of that took her breath away. "What if someone does something that goes against your principles?"

She was thinking about how Ethan had plotted to introduce her as Grady's granddaughter and the hit Paul was taking to his integrity in going along with the scheme. Yet the animosity between the brothers originated with Ethan. Paul obviously loved his brother and hated their estrangement.

"As much as I wish everything was black-and-white, it's never that simple." Paul stopped beside their assigned places at the dinner table and drew out her chair. "Now, can we drop all this serious talk and have some fun?"

With a nod, Lia abandoned the topic and focused her attention on enjoying the delicious reception dinner Dallas had prepared and marveling at the change in Paul as he socialized with his close friends, trading good-natured quips and contributing his share of funny stories that stretched back to their grade school days.

The depth and breadth of connection these people shared highlighted Lia's isolation. An ache grew in her chest that she recognized as longing. She wanted to belong. To feel the snug embrace of camaraderie. To be in on the private jokes and accepted into the club.

But this was an exclusive group of people, and not just because they'd been friends since childhood. Each one possessed an easy confidence born of privilege. In contrast was Lia as she sat beside Paul, listening attentively while speaking little, a huge fraud in the dress she couldn't afford.

As the waitstaff set plates of wedding cake before all the guests, Lia excused herself and headed to the bathroom. On the way back to the dining room, Dallas appeared in her path. As Lia gushed over the delicious dinner, she immediately sensed that Paul's cousin wasn't paying the least amount of attention to her compliments.

"Is something wrong?" Lia asked, uneasiness sliding across her nerve endings at the older twin's somber expression.

"You and Paul…" Dallas began, her voice scarcely rising above a whisper. "I saw what happened between you when you were putting the paddleboards away."

Cheeks flaming, Lia thought back to those stolen moments. It was her fault that they'd been caught. She'd begged him to kiss her.

"You two were…" Dallas looked horrified. "Kissing."

Lia threw up her hands as if to ward off the undeclared accusation. "It's not what you think—"

"You're first cousins."

"We're not." Stricken by Dallas's accusation, Lia blurted out the denial without considering the wisdom of spilling the truth before she'd spoken to Paul and Ethan about it.

Dallas frowned. "I don't understand."

Lia clutched her evening bag to her chest, struggling with the dilemma she found herself in. "There's a prob-

lem with my DNA test results," she declared in a breathless rush, sick of all the lies. "Ethan and Paul know, but
you can't tell anyone else."

"What sort of a problem?"

"I'm not your long-lost cousin." Lia crossed her fingers
and hoped that Ethan and Paul wouldn't be angry with her
for jumping the gun. "We just found out that there was a
huge mix-up."

Dallas looked appalled. "Why haven't you told anyone?"

"Because Grady has rallied since he thought I was his
granddaughter and we've been waiting for him to be fully
on the path to recovery before saying anything."

"He's going to be so upset," Dallas said. "He's been obsessed with finding Ava's daughter."

Lia hung her head. "We know."

"I can't believe Paul would let this go on."

"He's not happy about it, believe me." Lia grabbed Dallas's hand. "Please don't tell anyone. We've agreed that I'm
only going to stay another few days."

"And then what?"

"Then we come clean about the mistake and I get back
on the road."

Dallas stared at her in silence while emotions flitted
across her face. "I don't understand any of this," she complained at last. "Why do you have to leave?"

"I was never going to stay," Lia reminded her, repeating what she'd been saying all along. "I like traveling the
country too much to stay put anywhere."

"But Grady loves you. We all do."

"He loves his granddaughter," Lia said, her heart aching
at the thought of moving on. Never before had she grieved
for her lack of family ties. "I'm not her."

"What about Paul?"

"What about him?"

"You're obviously the woman from his reading. The one he's supposed to fall in love with."

"No." Lia ignored her pounding heart. "He's not in love with me. Attracted maybe, but we're too different to ever work."

"I think you might be exactly what he needs."

"Are you listening to yourself?" The laugh Lia huffed out fell flat. "A moment ago you were worried he and I were doing something creepy and wrong."

"That's when I thought you were our cousin," Dallas said. "Now that I know you're not, I heartily approve of you two."

"There is no *us two*," Lia corrected, her desperation growing by the second. "Please don't speak about this to anyone. Not even Poppy."

"But we tell each other everything."

"I know, but for now the fewer people who know, the better. And everything will come out in a matter of days." Seeing Dallas was still waffling, Lia gripped her hand. "Please."

"Fine," Dallas groused. "But you really should think about staying. For Paul's sake. And yours."

As Lia returned to Paul, she debated whether to tell him about her conversation with Dallas. She hated to let secrets and subterfuge get between them, but worried that he would keep his distance if he discovered that his cousin had caught them. With her time in Charleston growing short, she self-ishly wanted to soak up his company and if he thought his cousin knew about their deception, that would preoccupy him to the exclusion of all else. She would just have to en-sure that they were more careful around his family.

"Is everything okay?" Paul asked, his green eyes roam-ing her expression.

"Fine." Lia slid into her seat and hid her disquiet beneath a weary smile. "Just a little tired."

"Do you want me to take you home?"

Home. The word sent a spike of electricity through her. She knew he meant his grandfather's estate, but her home was a nineteen-foot camper parked north of the city. A few days from now she'd be hitting the road once more.

"Or maybe back to your house," she said, pushing aside all thoughts of leaving and the disquiet it aroused. "I'd love to spend some time alone with you."

"It's like you read my mind," he murmured. "Let's go."

Nine

The morning after Ryan and Zoe's wedding, Paul was up at dawn, retracing the walk along the beach he and Lia had taken the previous night before he'd dropped her off at the Watts estate. Her mood after leaving the wedding had been reflective, but when he'd asked her what was on her mind, she'd stopped his questions with a passionate kiss.

They'd made love for hours while the moon rose and spilled its pale light across his bedroom floor. He marveled how being in her company kept him grounded in the moment, his thoughts drifting over her soft skin, his focus locked on her fervent cries and the way her body shuddered in climax beneath him.

He'd been loath to take her back to his grandfather's house. Although they'd been together for hours, the time passed too quickly. He wanted to keep her in his bed. To wake up to her sweet face and bury his nose in her fragrant hair. Alone atop the tangled sheets that smelled of her perfume and their lovemaking, he'd spent the rest of a sleepless night staring at the ceiling and probing the dissatisfaction that dominated his mood.

What became crystal clear was that he didn't want Lia to leave. Not that night. Not in a few days. Maybe never.

Now as he looked out at the water this morning, he flashed back to the tarot card reading. The reversed Hermit card, indicating his time of being alone was over. The Lovers in his near future. The final outcome card promising happiness and joy. But there had also been the possible outcome card of the bound woman who Lia said represented confusion and isolation. He had a choice to make. Either maintain his current priorities by giving all his time and energy to his business or take a more balanced approach and open himself to the potential of love.

Appalled at himself for remembering all that New Age nonsense much less giving it the slightest bit of credibility, Paul returned home, showered and then sat down in his home office to lose himself in work. Although he had staff to follow through with the day-to-day business of protecting their clients' data, Paul liked to keep his skill level up to date. As fast as they plugged one hole, the criminals found another to get through.

The morning passed in a blur. He'd left his phone in the kitchen to avoid the temptation to call Lia. Around noon his stomach began to growl so he went into the kitchen to make some lunch.

Ethan had messaged him, asking how the wedding had gone and inviting him for an afternoon of fishing. The offer delighted Paul. It had been a long time since he'd hung out with his brother and he missed the fun times they'd had.

After a quick text exchange to accept, Paul headed west to James Island. Ethan lived in a sprawling four-year-old custom-built house that backed up onto Ellis Creek and offered direct access to Ashley River and Charleston Harbor. With its white siding and navy shutters, reclaimed heart pine floors, white woodwork throughout including kitchen cabinets and built-ins, the home had a more traditional style than Paul expected from Ethan.

A mix of antiques and new furniture filled the rooms, offering a comfortable but conservative feel. Only one room had a purely masculine vibe and that was the entertainment room on the lower level. The room's dark brown walls and red ceiling were the backdrop for a large projection screen, sports-related art and pool table with red felt.

It was in this room Paul found his brother waiting. Because Ethan liked to entertain, the room's location on the creek side of the garage with direct access from the driveway meant that Ethan's friends could come and go from the party spot without traipsing through his entire house.

"So I've been thinking," Paul began, accepting the beer his brother handed him from the beverage cooler built into the wet bar.

"When are you not thinking?" Ethan countered. He flopped onto the leather sectional and took a long pull from his bottle.

Ignoring his brother's jab, Paul rolled the bottle between his hands and paced. "Grady is progressing, but he's far from back to full health."

Ethan's eyebrow rose. "And?"

"We're due to tell everyone there's been the mix-up with Lia's genetic test in a few days and I'm just worried it's too soon and that he'll regress." For the hundredth time Paul wished Lia hadn't had such a profound effect on Grady's health. If she'd never come to stay at the estate, Paul could continue to pretend that he was perfectly content, never knowing how right he felt in her company, never knowing the all-consuming hunger or the raw joy of making love to her. She'd twisted his perceptions and made him question beliefs that ruled his life. Yet he couldn't get over the sense that she was the missing piece that made him whole.

"So you want her to stay longer?" Ethan asked, his eyes narrowing.

"Grady is happy." Paul spoke with deliberate care. "Because he thinks his granddaughter is back."

"I thought you were worried that he'd get too attached."

Paul let out a frustrated sigh, hating that he found himself trapped between a rock and a hard place. "That ship sailed the moment we didn't tell Grady the truth." He paused and drank his beer, picturing his grandfather by the pool the day before, the amused fondness in his gaze as he watched what he thought to be his three granddaughters.

"I don't know," Ethan muttered, sounding more like Paul than Paul at the moment. "The longer we let this go the more we risk the truth coming out. Grady might never forgive us if he thinks we tricked him."

Paul couldn't believe the way the tables had turned. Usually he was the one sounding the alarm. "He'll never know."

"He'll never know?" Ethan echoed, looking doubtful. "What's gotten into you?"

"What do you mean?"

"You were dead set against her pretending to be Ava's daughter at all. Next you'll be suggesting she should stay permanently."

Ethan's remark was a hit Paul didn't see coming.

"Now that's a really bad idea." Paul trusted that he could keep his attraction hidden for another week or two, but pretending she was his first cousin wasn't a long-term solution. In fact, it was more like endless hell. "We can't keep lying to the whole family about her being Ava's daughter."

"About that…" Ethan stared out the windows that overlooked his expansive back lawn. "We're no longer lying to the *whole* family."

Ethan's statement was a streaking comet along Paul's nerve endings. "What does that mean?"

"It means that Mom ran into Taylor English the other day and she had a lot of questions about how Lia's mom came to adopt her."

"Do you think Taylor suspects that Lia's not Ava's daughter?"

"Maybe. I don't know. Mom shared her concerns with Dad and he was worried. So…" A muscle flexed in Ethan's jaw. "I told Dad the truth."

"Damn it, Ethan."

"He suggested running another DNA test," his brother retorted in a reasonable tone that Paul found irritating. "And I was able to explain what we're doing and why. It took some convincing, but I reminded Dad that Grady was on the verge of slipping away from us before he started believing his granddaughter had returned."

Paul sputtered through a string of curses, until the revelation of what Ethan had not said sank in. "He knows we lied about Lia, but he hasn't told anyone?"

"He hasn't told Grady," Ethan said, his precise wording catching Paul's attention. "But I'm guessing he told Mom."

"And his sister?"

"I don't think so," Ethan said. "Can you imagine Aunt Lenora keeping that secret to herself? She might be able to avoid letting it slip with Uncle Wiley, but she talks to the twins about everything."

"Okay." Paul rubbed his temple where a dull ache had developed. "So, you explained the plan to Dad and he was willing to keep Lia's true identity a secret?"

"For a few days." Ethan finished his beer and set it aside. "So you can see why it's probably not a good idea to ask Lia to stay longer."

"Just one more week can't hurt," Paul said, convinced he couldn't make a decision about Lia in a few days. "I'll talk to Dad."

Ethan looked doubtful. "You should also check with Lia. She's pretty keen to get back on the road."

"Speaking of that," Paul said. "I think we should revisit how much we're paying her."

Ethan studied him for a long moment before nodding. "Okay. But I thought you believed she was only in it for the money."

Paul made a dismissive gesture. "That was before I got to know her better."

"How much better?" Ethan demanded, his eyes narrowing.

"Well enough," Paul retorted, unwilling to expound on the time he'd spent in Lia's company. He pivoted the conversation back to something he was comfortable discussing. "She can't leave town without a truck to pull her camper. I've been thinking that our grandfather's health is worth a whole lot more than a brand-new truck, don't you?"

"Okay. Let's get her a truck with all the bells and whistles." Ethan got off the couch and headed for the beverage cooler. "Just don't be surprised when she decides against sticking around longer after she has the means to leave."

Ethan's warning plunged deep into the heart of what had been bothering Paul for days. He didn't want Lia to disappear out of his life. The free-spirited nomad had entangled him in her quirky web of metaphysical nonsense and selfless generosity. Where he kept to himself and focused on business, she told fortunes, spread joy and showered positive energy on everyone she met.

He had yet to decide if being complete opposites would work for or against their romantic future. Since meeting her, Paul had begun noticing the concerns of those around him. He'd spent more time with his family in the last week than he had in the last few months. While he'd done so initially in order to keep an eye on Lia, as his suspicions about her faded, he'd realized how much he enjoyed interacting with his family.

"Do you think the lack of a vehicle is the only thing keeping her in Charleston?" Paul asked.

"That's always been the impression she's given me." Ethan paused and regarded Paul with raised eyebrows. "Has she indicated that she's ready to give up the road?"

"No." And that was the problem. "But you've known her longer. I thought perhaps she'd mentioned what it would take for her to settle down."

Ethan hit him with an odd look. "Why are you so interested?"

"It's just…"

Asking Ethan for romantic advice was harder than he expected. Paul didn't have a lot of practice putting his feelings into words. Nor was he good at sharing what was bothering him. That he wanted to try was another example of Lia's influence.

"Are you asking because you're attracted to her?" Ethan asked.

Feeling cornered, Paul kept his expression neutral. "She's pretending to be our first cousin." Yet he couldn't deny that it was getting harder and harder to avoid letting his feelings for her show.

"She's not our first cousin, though," Ethan countered. "And once the truth comes out the situation will get even more complicated. She's not going to want to stick around."

"No one will blame her for the testing service getting it wrong. Let's just see if she'll delay leaving for another week." Seeing his brother's worried expression, Paul added, "For Grady's sake."

"I'll talk to her," Ethan said. "But you need to be clear about what you want. Lia isn't someone you can toy with until an exciting project comes along that takes all your focus and energy."

"What are you saying?" Paul demanded, bristling at his brother's criticism.

"That if you're leading her on, you can do a lot of damage in a very short period of time."

Even though Ethan had invited his brother to go fishing, by the time their conversation concluded neither one was in the mood to take the boat out. Instead, after Paul left, Ethan wandered into his home office and contemplated the second genetic testing kit he'd ordered, but hadn't yet used.

As much as he wanted to satisfy the ever-intensifying craving to connect with his biological family, he recognized the revelations could come at a cost. Not only did he risk upsetting the people who loved him, but also he could be opening himself up to disappointment and heartbreak. Ethan couldn't explain his pessimism over the outcome, but recognized that not taking the test left him no better or worse off than he was at the moment.

And after watching Paul struggle with his fears and desires concerning Lia, Ethan was even more wary of throwing himself into an emotional maelstrom.

When he'd introduced Lia to his family as Ava's daughter, the last thing Ethan had imagined was that Paul would complicate the situation by developing feelings for her. Paul was too logic-driven to appreciate Lia's spiritual nature and too skeptical to ever trust her motives for helping them. Then again, physical attraction was a powerful thing and could lead to an emotional connection. Even in someone as jaded and pragmatic as Paul.

While Ethan enjoyed seeing his guarded older brother thrown off-balance, concern for Lia tempered Ethan's satisfaction. Although she claimed that traveling around so much kept her from getting too attached to those she met, Ethan sensed that this time was different. If Lia fell for

Paul the way he appeared to be falling for her, she'd throw her heart and soul at him and if Paul didn't wise up, she might end up hurt.

Turning away from the complicated and messy ramifications of his actions, Ethan focused on the trio of good things that had resulted. Grady's improved health. The healing rift between Paul and his grandfather. And one that Ethan hadn't expected, but found himself grateful for—the renewed connection with his brother.

Ethan hadn't realized the cost of pushing Paul away until the scheme with Lia had brought them together again. Setting his fingertips on the genetic testing kit, Ethan shoved it away. Maybe it was time to appreciate the family who loved him and not chase something that might not be out there.

The Sunday morning after Ryan and Zoe's wedding dawned as clear and golden as so many others Lia had experienced in her sumptuous bedroom. Despite her late return to the estate, she was awake with the sun. On a typical morning, she would bound out of bed and begin her day with yoga on the terrace overlooking the lush garden. But today didn't feel typical. Her mind raced, but her body felt sluggish. She curled herself around a pillow and clung to the glow from the previous night with Paul.

Three short days from now the news would break that she wasn't Grady's granddaughter, freeing her from the lies and obligations keeping her in Charleston. In the beginning, with Paul treating her like a criminal, Lia had dreaded the deception and longed for the moment when she could get back on the road. The sheer size and elegance of the Watts estate, not to mention the rules and traditions that operated within its walls, had been overwhelming. She wasn't used to being around people so much and missed the long hours of solitude to meditate or read or daydream.

But one thing that all her traveling to new towns had instilled in Lia was adaptability. Her acquaintances and jobs were constantly changing. So she'd learned how to function within the tight-knit Watts clan with their frequent visits to check on Grady, outgoing natures, busybody ways. And to her surprise, she'd started to enjoy the fun-loving twins, the kind mothering of Lenora and Constance and even Paul's unsettling presence.

Confronted with the reality that she would soon be leaving it all behind, sadness sat like a large stone in her stomach, weighing her down. Yet she couldn't deny there was relief, as well. Living with the lie that she was Grady's granddaughter made her anxious and her attraction to Paul complicated everything.

With her emotions seesawing with each breath she took, Lia struggled to maintain her usual equanimity as she ate with Grady on the back terrace. She knew his family credited her with his daily improvement, but Lia put the credit squarely on his shoulders. His determination was only matched by his enthusiasm to try anything she'd suggested. The singing that had worked in the beginning hadn't been the only method to help him communicate. She'd created a notebook of common words and phrases that he could point to, which sped up conversations and eased frustration all around.

Grady had improved to the point that he intended to join the family for dinner that night. Leaving him to rest, Lia took a taxi to a nearby discount auto sales lot where she'd identified a truck that she hoped might be a good fit. The price was higher than she'd anticipated paying, but she was running out of time to find something that could pull Misty. Unfortunately, when she got to the lot, she discovered that the vehicle had already been sold, and nothing else they had would work.

She was on the verge of heading back to the estate when

Ethan called her. When she explained what she was up to, he offered to act as her chauffeur.

"How was the wedding?" he asked as she slid into the passenger seat of his bright blue Mercedes twenty minutes later.

"It was beautiful. The ceremony was so heartfelt and romantic. I cried." She sighed at the memory. "Silly, isn't it? I don't even know Ryan and Zoe, but all I could think was how they belonged together."

A lump formed in Lia's throat as she recalled the way Ryan had looked at his bride. The love between them was like a stone tossed into a pond, rippling out from the couple to touch all the guests. She trembled as she recalled a moment during the vows when Paul's gaze had found hers amongst the well-wishers. The fleeting connection had sent a shock wave through Lia from head to toe.

"They really do," Ethan agreed. "It's as if everything that they went through created a one-of-a-kind connection between them."

Lia nodded. "That's what Paul said, as well."

"Paul said that?" Ethan blinked in surprise.

"I know, right?" She laughed. "It doesn't seem like him at all."

Ethan considered that for a moment. "I think his emotions go deeper than he lets on. He just needs someone he cares about to start breaking down his walls."

Lia didn't know how to respond, so she fidgeted with her phone. "While I was waiting for you to pick me up, I found a couple options at a dealer west of town."

"We can check those out, but I have a friend who owns a dealership and can get you a deal on something brand-new."

"I can't afford brand-new," Lia insisted.

"Paul and I discussed that and we'd like to help you out."

"That wasn't part of our original deal," she murmured

ungraciously, as she revisited her mixed feelings about accepting the dress from the twins.

Obviously neither Paul nor Ethan understood that she didn't welcome the handout. While part of her acknowledged they perceived their offer as helpful, Lia resented being treated like a charity case.

"Well, we'd like to alter our original deal."

"Alter it how?"

"We were wondering if you could stick around another week."

For days she'd been bracing herself to leave on the date they'd agreed on. Lia contemplated Ethan's offer with a mixture of relief and dismay. As much as she wanted more time with Paul, this increased the risk that someone besides Dallas might suspect something was going on between them.

"Are you sure that's a good idea?" she asked. "Grady is doing so much better. I don't think there's any chance that his health will be impacted when he finds out I'm not Ava's daughter."

"I agree with you," Ethan said. "This was all Paul's idea."

Tears sprang to Lia's eyes, forcing her to turn her gaze to the passing landscape. She knew better than to read too much into what Ethan said. Paul might only be thinking of his grandfather's welfare and not have more personal motives.

"Is something wrong?"

She grasped for some explanation that would convince Ethan of the folly of her staying longer and recalled her conversation with Dallas the night before. Given how tight the twins were, how long could they count on Dallas to keep their secret?

"Something happened last night," she said.

"You don't say."

His tone was so sly that Lia blinked her eyes dry and turned to look at him. Something about his knowing grin sent a spike of anxiety straight through her.

Did he know? She and Paul were playing a dangerous game.

"Dallas knows I'm not your cousin," she blurted out, hoping to distract him.

"Oh."

"Just *oh*?" She'd braced herself to deal with his dismay. "Why aren't you more upset?"

"I guess that means the jig is up."

"Not yet," Lia replied, her frustration rising at his casual manner. Living in fear of being found out for nearly two weeks had taken a toll on her nerves. "I talked her out of telling anyone by promising it would only be a few more days before we tell Grady. So you see why we can't keep going with this."

"I'll talk to her," Ethan said. "Maybe if I explain and let her tell Poppy we can go a little longer."

"What if I don't want to stay?" Lia murmured.

"Is this because Paul didn't ask you himself?"

"Don't be ridiculous." But even as she denied it, heat surged into Lia's cheeks.

"I knew it," Ethan said, looking concerned. "I knew something was going on between you two."

"It's not like that." Even as she spoke, Lia could see that protesting was a waste of breath.

"It's exactly like that. Paul is attracted to you. And it looks as if his feelings are reciprocated."

"Well, yes. But it's just…" She'd almost said *sex*. "It's nothing serious."

"Are you sure?"

Lia fidgeted with her phone. "We're not in the least compatible."

"Here's where you're making assumptions. Has it occurred to you that he doesn't need someone who's like him, but someone who balances him? Someone who's lively and impulsive and knows exactly how to get him out of his head?"

The picture Ethan painted was tempting. Being the yin to Paul's yang appealed to Lia in every way. And it worked in the confines of their secret relationship. Taking things public would bring a whole new series of challenges.

"It might be good for him short-term," she said. "But in the end what he needs is a serious girlfriend. Someone who matches his ambition and his background. Someone he can be proud of."

"You don't think he can be proud of you?" Ethan asked, sounding surprised.

"Look at me." Lia gestured at her denim shorts and graphic T-shirt with its yoga-inspired pun. "I don't bring anything to the table."

"You shouldn't underestimate yourself," Ethan said. "I think you are one of the kindest, most delightful people I've ever met."

Lia forced a laugh. "Paul would say eccentric, impractical and frivolous."

"Maybe that's exactly what he needs."

"It would never work between us long-term," Lia said, musing that in her own way, she was as skittish about emotional entanglements as Paul.

Where he closed himself down and focused on work, she flitted from town to town, never really investing herself in any significant relationships. She was a butterfly. He was a rock. They couldn't possibly work.

"You matter to him," Ethan argued. "I just don't think he's figured out what to do about the way he's feeling. Give him time to adjust. He's never fallen in love before."

Ethan's words electrified Lia, stopping her heart. She pressed her shaking hands between her thighs, terrified that if she bought into Ethan's claim that she would only end up getting hurt. Yet even as she forced herself to be practical, her heart clamored for her to stay in Charleston and be with Paul. Be with him for how long?

"Do you know if he's still investigating me?" she asked, noting that the question surprised Ethan.

"He hasn't said anything. Why do you ask?"

As fast as she was falling for Paul, she needed to know if what was in her past would cause Paul to reject her.

"Paul has made it perfectly clear that he thinks I agreed to pretend to be your cousin because I'm up to no good."

"I'm pretty sure he's changed his mind on that score."

"Maybe." In fact, Lia wanted that to be true because she hated to think that his doubts shadowed the moments she'd spent in his arms. "But I'm afraid he might discover something about me that he won't like."

Ethan frowned. "What sort of something?"

Lia gathered a bracing breath and began to explain about the man who'd swindled people out of hundreds of millions of dollars. Peter Thompson.

Her grandfather.

Ten

When Paul entered Grady's spacious living room prior to the family dinner, he discovered he was the last to arrive. In a matter of seconds he noted the placement of all his relatives throughout the room and had taken two steps toward Lia, following the instinct to be close to her, when his mother intercepted him.

"How was Ryan and Zoe's wedding?" Constance asked, seeming oblivious to the fact that she'd just stopped him from a huge blunder.

"Very nice."

"I never thought she and Tristan Crosby were well matched," his mother continued. "She seems much happier with Ryan."

"They're both happy," Paul declared.

"I don't suppose I'll be helping to plan any weddings in the near future," Constance muttered, casting meaningful glances from Paul to Ethan.

"Isn't wedding planning usually left up to the bride and

her family?" he countered, skillfully turning the conversation to less fraught waters. "You wouldn't want to step on anyone's toes."

"When have I ever overstepped?" Constance asked with studied innocence.

"Never."

But the truth was, Paul's mother was known for getting her way with the various charity events she helped organize. Was it any wonder both her sons had such strong leadership skills? They'd learned how to be in charge from a master.

Dinner was announced before Paul had a chance to do more than wave at his cousins and offer a smile to his aunt and uncle. Paul found himself seated between his father and Dallas, relegated to the opposite side of the table from Lia.

As always, Grady sat at the head. Tonight he was flanked by Lia and Lenora. Grady was in high spirits. Although he still struggled to speak, his eyes twinkled as he observed his family's interaction. The stark contrast in his vitality two weeks earlier lent an even greater festivity to the meal.

From his family's effusive remarks, Paul gathered the food was delicious, but he noticed little of what he tasted. He was preoccupied with Lia and pretending to maintain his interest in the twins' chatter or his father's concern about the imbalance in imports and exports due to the recent tariffs.

As dessert was served, Grady clinked his glass to gain everyone's attention. With each day, he gained more control over his words, but sometimes still relied on singing to produce certain sounds. Having gained everyone's attention, he began in a singsong rhythm.

Reaching for Lia's hand, Grady fixed his gaze on her. "I changed my will to include Lia."

Suspicion ran like poison through Paul's veins while Lia sat in stunned silence, wide eyes glued to Grady's face.

Around the table, there were exclamations of approval. Paul locked gazes with his brother and saw his own concern mirrored there.

"This is quite sudden," Constance murmured with a slight frown. "I mean…" She seemed at a loss as she glanced from one son to the other.

Paul shook his head in an effort to communicate that this wasn't the moment to come clean. If they explained about the testing mistake on the heels of Grady's bombshell announcement, everyone would want to know why the delay in bringing up the issue. They couldn't afford any of the family asking questions that would clue Grady in to their scheme.

"You shouldn't have done that," Lia said, shaking her head. Her dismay seemed genuine. "It's… I don't…"

Her gaze darted Paul's way and just as quickly fled, leaving him unsure that she'd manipulated Grady into changing his will.

"You don't know me," she argued, her panic visibly threatening to choke her.

Grady shook his head, squeezed her hand and gave her a lopsided, reassuring smile. "You're my granddaughter," he announced in definitive tones, suggesting what was done was done.

As everyone finished off the red velvet cake, it was pretty obvious that Grady was fading. Although no one summoned her, Rosie appeared and wheeled him out of the room. Lia followed, but before she could escape upstairs, Paul drew her through the living room and out onto the side terrace.

Lia looked shell-shocked and near tears as she scanned his expression with near-frantic eyes. Paul balled his hands into fists to stop himself from taking her into his arms and soothing away her distress. He had so much to say, but didn't know where to start.

"This is a huge mess," Paul declared, his gut tight with conflicting emotion.

Before Lia could respond, Ethan appeared on the terrace. Her gaze went straight to him and clung like he was her lifeline.

"I had no idea he intended to change his will." Lia's voice was filled with anguish.

"You're sure he didn't mention it at all?" Paul demanded. "Because with a little warning we could've headed off his decision and saved us all a lot of grief."

Seeing her woeful expression, Ethan threw a protective arm around her shoulders and shot Paul a hard look that warned him to back off. "I'm sure if Lia knew she would've told us."

When Lia slumped against his brother's side, Paul felt like he'd been slapped.

"What are we going to do about this?" Irritation gave his voice a bite.

"Tell the truth," Lia said, sending a speaking glance Ethan's way. "The sooner the better."

But once they did Lia wouldn't have a reason to stay in Charleston any longer. He stared at Lia while the conversation at Ethan's house ran through his mind. The thought of her leaving made him ache.

"Let's give it a few days," Paul said. "If we explain about the testing service right now, the timing will look suspicious."

"I agree." Ethan nodded. "The damage is already done. A couple more days won't matter."

Lia grimaced. "I'm not sure that's true."

A significant look passed between Lia and Ethan, turning Paul into an unnecessary third wheel. What happened to the closeness he'd shared with Lia these last few days?

"Am I missing something?" Paul demanded.

"It's more complicated than you know," Lia admitted.

"More complicated how?"

"Why don't you and I grab a drink and I'll fill you in," Ethan said. Then, ignoring Paul's growing impatience, Ethan directed his next words to Lia. "I'll call you in the morning."

"Thank you."

Lia headed for the outside stairs that led to the second-floor terrace and was out of sight before Paul recovered from the bolt of jealousy that shot through him at the easy affection between Ethan and Lia. His resentment even overshadowed the shock of what their grandfather had done.

"What the hell?" Ethan demanded, as they left the house and crunched in the gravel side by side along the garden path on the way to their cars. "Why did you take your frustration out on Lia like that? None of this is her fault."

Paul grappled with dismay and self-loathing at the way he'd taken his shock and jealousy out on Lia. Although his first reaction to her being included in the will had been suspicion, he knew better. Instead he'd acted like she'd manipulated Grady, forcing Ethan to come to her defense.

But instead of owning his mistake, Paul lashed out. "I told you passing off a perfect stranger as Ava's daughter was going to blow up in our faces."

"Fine. You were right as always." Ethan's expression shifted into stubborn lines. "Look, fighting isn't going to do us any good. We need to figure out what to do."

"It's obvious we need to come clean to Grady immediately," Paul declared. "I'll tell him."

"We should both tell him," Ethan said. "It was my idea to let Grady believe she was his granddaughter. You should talk to Lia." Ethan's expression softened with pity. "Although after how you behaved just now, I'm not sure she's ever going to forgive you."

* * *

After leaving Paul and Ethan, Lia escaped to the solitude of her bedroom, intent on digesting the evening's events, and ran straight into more trouble. Dallas stood with her back to the windows, her arms crossed over her chest, wearing a scowl of open hostility. As soon as Lia closed the door for privacy, she rushed to reassure the younger woman.

"Please believe that I never meant for any of this to happen," Lia said, hating the way Dallas's eyes narrowed in suspicion. "I had no idea your grandfather was going to do that."

"This whole thing has gone too far," Dallas said, her voice an angry lash. "You need to tell everyone the truth."

"I agree," Lia assured her. "Ethan and Paul are talking about the best way to handle that right now."

"I really liked you." Dallas turned the declaration into an accusation. "I was so happy you were our cousin."

"The only family I ever had was my mother and since I turned eighteen and struck out on my own, I barely know where she is half the time." The sharp ache in Lia's chest made her next words almost impossible to get out. "You have no idea how much I wanted to be part of your family."

"But you're not." Some of Lia's anguish must have penetrated Dallas's outrage because her next words were gentler. "And that really sucks."

"I'm sorry I upset you, but I never meant for anyone to get hurt," Lia protested, overpowered by loss.

"You should've thought about that before you lied."

Dallas left the bedroom without another word and Lia threw herself facedown on the bed. For several minutes she wallowed in misery while her eyes burned with unshed tears. She'd deserved to be called out for her lies. Lia just wished it didn't hurt so much.

As Lia pondered her next course of action she realized it was time for her to leave Charleston. Earlier that day she'd purchased a truck. Not the fancy brand-new vehicle Ethan had insisted he and Paul wanted to buy for her, but one within her budget. After some determined negotiating, she emptied her savings account and left the lot the proud owner of a five-year-old model similar to the one that had been totaled six months earlier, but with fewer miles on it and a working air conditioner.

The purchase compelled her to confront what she'd been avoiding since the wedding. In the days before the romantic event, as she'd recognized her feelings for Paul were developing into love, she'd toyed with giving up her vagabond ways to be with him. Tonight she'd come to grips with reality. No matter how strong her attachment to Paul, his stark accusation demonstrated that without trust he couldn't love her with the openness and honesty she needed. Settling for anything less would lead to heartbreak.

Halfway through her packing, Lia noticed her duffel held more than when she'd arrived. The fact that she'd begun to collect unessential items revealed a shift in her attitude. There was nothing extravagant or indulgent in the miscellaneous clothes and accessories she'd let the twins encourage her to buy, but the purchases suited the life she'd been living in Charleston.

After stacking her costume boxes and overflowing duffel by the door, Lia crossed the hall and gently knocked on Grady's door. She owed him the truth and an apology before she left.

Later, she would call Ethan and say goodbye. Although she was angry with Ethan and herself for the ruse, he'd been a good friend to her. And he'd worry if she just vanished.

That left Paul. Her heart clenched in regret. Would he even care that she was leaving? She'd been a fool to imagine that she'd won him over, that his poor opinion of her had changed, could change. Instead, his suspicions had merely lain dormant, waiting for something terrible to happen.

No, she couldn't face him again. Couldn't confront the suspicion in his eyes and be devastated by his stubborn refusal to believe that she'd had no interest in financial gain. Now that she was leaving, Lia was overwhelmed with relief that she'd never face Paul's dismay about her grandfather.

When Grady called for her to enter, Lia stepped into the room and crossed to where he sat in bed. Setting aside the book he'd been reading, he smiled at her with such joy that a lump formed in her throat. She might not be his granddaughter, but she loved him and was ashamed that she'd ever lied to him.

At that moment, Lia knew that no matter what the brothers decided over drinks tonight, she had to speak the real truth. Not the story they'd concocted about the mistake with the DNA matching, but the fact that there'd never been a genetic test.

Dropping to her knees beside his bed, Lia touched his arm. "I want you to know that these last couple weeks have been some of the happiest of my life." Her voice faltered, but she cleared her throat and kept going. "You have made me feel welcome and nothing I can say or do could ever repay your kindness."

Grady frowned down at her, obviously perplexed. "What's wrong?"

She couldn't get over how much progress he'd made with his speech, and hated that she was leaving before she could help him make more.

"I'm so sorry." Lia closed her eyes to block out his face for this next part. "The thing is, I'm not your granddaughter."

Grady gripped her hand. "What?"

Lia's heart broke as she continued. "I feel terrible. It's all been a huge misunderstanding. The genetic testing…" She stumbled on her words, needing a moment to collect herself. "We made that up because you were so convinced that I was your granddaughter and you got better because of it. You'd been looking for Ava's daughter for so long, and we just wanted you to be happy. And then you changed your will. And now it's all just a big confusing mess." The words flowed out of her in a great rush. She didn't realize she was crying until Grady's knuckles brushed her cheek and she saw how they came away damp. "I know you must be so upset and I never meant to cause you pain."

She'd surveyed him as she spoke and saw that he was confused and shocked, but her confession hadn't devastated him. In fact, the way he kept patting her hand conveyed he was more concerned that she was so upset.

"We were going to tell you in a few days because you've been doing so much better. Before now we were afraid you'd stop trying to get well again. I know I shouldn't have gone along with it, but Ethan was so desperate and then Paul was forced to keep our secret because he didn't want to put your recovery at risk. It wasn't his fault. And please don't blame Ethan. Your family has been so warm and welcoming. But then you included me in your will and I'm not really your granddaughter." Lia paused to get her ragged breathing under control and peered at Grady. "You are going to be okay, aren't you? Please tell me I haven't made things worse."

"I'm fine."

"Oh good." She squeezed his hand. "I'm glad because I need to leave Charleston and I couldn't go if I thought you might relapse."

"No." Grady shook his head. "Stay."

"I can't. When your family find out I lied about being Ava's daughter, they will all hate me."

"Not everyone," Grady said. "Not me."

The sight of his earnest smile blurred as fresh tears formed in Lia's eyes. If the only opinion that mattered belonged to the patriarch of the Watts family, Lia knew she'd stay and work hard to earn everyone's trust. But she was really running from Paul's reaction, recognizing that he could never trust her because of what lurked in her past.

"The thing is," she whispered, barely able to speak past the raw tightness in her throat. "There's also this issue with my grandfather being a thief and a liar. He's a terrible person and because we're related everyone will think I'm a terrible person, too. Even though I've never met him."

Lia paused to gulp in air, unable to believe she'd blurted out the truth about her grandfather on top of all the other revelations.

"And since I'm confessing everything… I'm in love with Paul and he doesn't love me, so it's too painful for me to stay." Lia pushed to her feet and dropped a fleeting kiss on Grady's cheek. "I want you to know that being a part of your family was the best thing that ever happened to me."

Eleven

Paul barely slept and was on his third cup of coffee when his phone chimed, letting him know he'd received a text. His stomach muscles clenched in reaction. Had Lia finally replied to his messages from the previous night? Her lack of response from the first one had prompted him to send another apology late in the night, asking if they could talk. That she hadn't acknowledged that one either was eating him alive.

A hundred times since last night he'd pledged if she gave him another chance, he would never doubt her again. But as the hours ticked by, he grew less confident that she would give him a hearing.

Glancing at the screen, he discovered the text was from Dallas and not Lia. With the bleak landscape of his future stretched before him, he cued up his messaging app and read his cousin's text.

I did something terrible and now Lia's gone.

Before he could reach out to Dallas about her ominous message, a call from Ethan lit up his smartphone.

"I just talked to Lia," Ethan said, sounding grim.

"She called you?" The words tasted like sawdust. Could he blame her for choosing the brother who'd had her back the night before? "Is she okay? I just got a text from Dallas saying that Lia is gone. Did she say where?"

The night before, he and Ethan had discussed how to handle the revelation that Lia wasn't Ava's daughter and decided to stick to their original story about the testing service getting things wrong instead of telling Grady the truth. She'd been a reluctant coconspirator and shouldn't have to face Grady's anger.

"She's at her camper," Ethan said.

"What's she doing there?"

"I don't think she felt comfortable staying at the estate any longer," Ethan said. "She told Grady the whole story last night."

Paul cursed, remembering how she'd pushed for the truth to come out. "How did he take it? Is he okay?"

"She said he was shocked, but okay when she left. I'm heading over there now."

"Why did she do that?" Paul mused. "We had it handled."

"Maybe because she has more integrity than both of us put together."

Ethan's ironic tone recalled all the accusations Paul had lobbed at her. He knew his brother was right. While they'd all lied, Lia had been the only one who'd done so without selfish motives. She'd declared time and again that she only wanted to help. And that's what she'd done.

Whereas he'd been inspired to sacrifice his own integrity by the desperate need to keep his grandfather alive and the return of Grady's approval. When had guilt stopped eating at him? Somewhere around the first time he'd kissed Lia. After that, he'd been less conflicted about lying to his grandfather and more disturbed by how she affected him.

"Here's the other thing," Ethan continued. "The reason she's at her camper is because she's preparing to leave Charleston."

"Leave?" Paul's chest tightened, robbing him of breath. "When?"

Ethan's tone was hoarse with sympathy as he answered. "She might already be gone."

Blind panic rose at the thought, and after arranging to meet Ethan at the estate in an hour, Paul hung up on his brother. With clumsy fingers he immediately dialed Lia's number, praying that this time she'd answer.

"Ethan says you're leaving," he declared the instant she engaged the call.

"Yes." She sounded shaken, but determined. "I have to."

"No, you don't."

"Grady knows I'm not Ava's daughter."

"I'll make him understand that none of this was your fault."

"But it was my fault. I never should've pretended to be something I'm not." The catch in her voice tore at Paul's heart. "It'll be better once I'm gone. Your family can put it behind you," she finished.

"Don't worry about my family," he said, feeling ragged and unsteady. "Ethan and I will sort everything out. Please don't go. I know Grady won't want you to leave town. He loves you."

Even as he spoke the words, Paul winced. Why hadn't he told her how miserable he would be if she left? Using Grady as an excuse was cowardly.

"Not me. He loves his granddaughter." Her bleak tones told him any attempt to convince her was wasted breath.

"I'm really sorry if I created trouble for you and Ethan by telling Grady the truth," Lia said, a somber warble in her voice.

"Don't worry about Ethan and me. We can take a punch." He stripped all humor out of his voice before saying, "I'm heading to the estate now. Afterward I think you and I need to talk."

"There's nothing more to say."

Oh, there was plenty to say. It just depended on whether he had the guts to declare how he felt about her. "Please don't leave Charleston."

"I have to go," she declared, her urgent need to run coming through loud and clear. "Don't you understand?"

Paul shook his head. He did, but that didn't mean he'd stop trying to persuade her to stay. "Promise me you won't leave town without seeing me first."

"I'll only promise I won't leave today."

That didn't leave him much time. "I'll come by after I see Grady. Where can I find you?"

"I'll be at my camper."

Disconnecting the call with things so unresolved between them was one of the hardest things Paul had ever done, but he trusted her when she promised to stick around until he could get there.

When he arrived at the estate, Paul met his brother near the pool and together they found their grandfather in the library on the first floor. The room was at the back of the house with dual access to the outside terraces. White bookshelves, trim and wainscoting offset the red walls, giving the room a lived-in, cozy feel. Little had changed since his grandmother's death nearly fifty years earlier except for the addition of children's books and thrillers beside the classic novels Delilah Watts had loved.

As soon as they entered the room, Grady spoke. "You lied to me."

"It was all my idea," Ethan explained. "Don't be mad at Paul or Lia. We just wanted you to get better, and from the moment you believed that Lia was your granddaughter, you did."

"It wasn't just Ethan," Paul chimed in, refusing to let his brother shoulder the full blame. "I went along with the ruse, as well. We really did believe it was for your own good."

Grady scowled. "I changed my will."

"We didn't expect that," Ethan admitted, speaking before Paul could. "Our plan had been to tell you this week that the testing service had made a mistake."

"But then you put Lia in your will and everything blew up," Paul added.

"And just so you know, none of this was her idea," Ethan said. "I tricked her that day at the hospital."

"She only went along with it because she wanted to help you." Awash in misery, Paul willed his grandfather to believe that Lia was genuine. "That's all she's ever done."

"I know," Grady said, his words coming with slow, deliberate care. "I don't blame her."

"Does she know that?" Paul asked. "Because she's leaving town. Running away from Charleston. From us." *From me.*

"I told her." Grady shook his head. "She's afraid."

"Of what?"

"Of you."

Paul recoiled from Grady's censure. "I'd never do anything to hurt her."

"Last night—" Ethan began.

"I screwed up." Paul interrupted, glaring at his brother. "And then I made it worse because I got mad when you jumped to her rescue." His irritation faded as he realized how stupid his defense sounded. "I'm an idiot for not believing in her. And she's leaving town because of it." Paul dropped into a chair and let his head fall into his hands. "How do I convince her to stay?"

"Have you told her you're in love with her?" Ethan asked in exasperated tones. "From what I've heard women really go for that."

"I'm not..." he began instinctively, shocked at his brother's revelation. Paul glanced from him to Grady and saw curiosity rather than surprise on his grandfather's lean face.

"Not what?" Ethan demanded. "Not in love? Not sure she'd trust you with her heart? I don't know that I'd blame her."

Paul struggled to wrap his head around what truth lay in his heart. Is this what love felt like? An obsessive hunger to be around her all the time? To revel in blazing joy and suffer terrifying despair in the space of minutes?

And while Lia's generous spirit and upbeat sincerity had gotten beneath his skin, Paul didn't know how to surrender to a relationship that challenged his black-and-white views. Lia's belief in all things metaphysical, her flighty, impulsive need to live a nomadic existence, her lack of substantial ties to people and place ran contrary to what was important to him.

"You're right," Paul said, aching at the thought that she intended to leave him. What could he say or do to convince her to give up her nomadic ways and stay in one place? With him. "I love her, but I messed up big time. She won't stay for me."

Grady shook his head. "She loves you."

For a second Paul couldn't breathe. He shifted his gaze from his grandfather's fond smile to Ethan's exasperated expression. Hope rose.

"Are you sure?" The level of desperation in his voice shook him.

"She's been falling in love with you from the first," his brother said. "I have no idea why. You've been a complete jerk."

"The whole time," Paul agreed, unable to imagine how she'd managed to see something of value in him.

When he wasn't pummeling her with distrust, he'd been battling the unsettling emotions that turned him inside out. He wasn't the least bit lovable. And then he realized the familiar path down which his thoughts had taken him. Damn it. He was still questioning her judgment. Maybe the time had come for him to accept that he had much to learn from her.

"How do I fix this?" he asked the room at large.

"You could start by telling her that you can't live without her," his brother said. "And that you have her back. Then remind her that we all love her and everyone believes she only had Grady's best interests at heart."

"What if I can't convince her?"

Ethan ejected a curse. "When did you become the guy who gives up? Is that what you do when your clients have a data breech?"

"No."

"So why with something that is so much more important than all the hackers you chase put together are you just quitting?"

The question, combined with Grady's disgusted expression, caused Paul's gut to twist in shame. He hated that Ethan was right. Was he really going to let her go? Without a fight? What was wrong with him?

All at once everything became so clear to him. He loved her. She loved him. He just needed to figure out a way to convince her they were meant for each other. In a flash he knew exactly what it would take to convince Lia that he was the man for her. The brilliance of it made him grin.

"I have to go."

"Wait." The single word came from Grady. He pulled something out of his pocket and held it out to Paul. "Give this to Lia."

Feeling slightly light-headed, Paul opened the small box and saw a familiar diamond ring tucked into the black velvet. "This is Grandma's ring," he murmured in awe.

Grady's lopsided smile bloomed as he nodded. "Make her my granddaughter."

Clutching the small box, Paul left the library and raced downstairs.

The trip from the estate to where Lia was keeping her camper felt as if it took forever, but it was only a forty-minute drive. He took advantage of the time to rehearse what he intended to say to her. He started with *I love you* and ended with *Will you spend the rest of your life with me?* What came in between would be all the reasons why she made his life better. Her laugh. Her giving nature. Her sweetness. Her free-spirited ways. Her beauty.

He didn't deserve her. But from now on, he'd work damn hard to.

When he reached the spot where her camper had last been parked, he saw it was gone. He gripped the steering wheel in dismay, unable to believe she'd leave after promising to wait for him. Several seconds ticked by while he brought his doubts back under control.

Lia hadn't left. She'd given her word and she was the type of woman who kept her promises. He turned around and headed toward the shop to find out where the camper had been moved to. To his relief, as he rounded the final corner, he spied it near the water station. She was filling the tanks with water in preparation for starting out.

He parked his SUV so that it blocked her truck and hopped out. Finding himself oddly out of breath, he strode toward her. There was wariness, not welcome, in her hazel eyes as he stopped before her.

"You can't leave," he began, suddenly awkward. Incapacitated by growing panic, he stood looking at her with a pounding heart.

"You have to be kidding," she said, shutting off the water and replacing the hose. "Now that this whole ridiculous scheme is over and everyone knows I'm not Ava's daughter, no one will want me to stay."

"I do." He came over and took her hands in his. "Stay in Charleston with me."

She shook her head and wouldn't meet his gaze. "Why?"

"Because I love you."

Her conversation with Ethan hadn't prepared her for Paul's actual declaration. His open and earnest manner as much as the words he spoke stunned her. Paul loved her. Her heart sang with joy. For days she'd been arguing with herself, seeking ways to make her relationship with Paul work.

If she was too quirky for Charleston society, she could dress differently and learn to discuss what was important to Paul's friends. Giving up the road wouldn't be a hardship if it meant waking up every morning beside the sexy cybersecurity specialist. Already he'd had a grounding influence on her. She'd even imagined herself going to school and becoming an occupational therapist, helping others the way she had Grady.

But then she remembered all that stood between them. She'd deceived his family. Her grandfather had swindled investors out of millions. Their vastly different natures. Any one of those things would create challenges. All three together were insurmountable.

"I don't know..."

"You don't know?" Paul's outrage clearly indicated he

was under the misguided assumption that all he had to do was declare himself and she'd fall at his feet in gratitude. Lia's annoyance gave her the fortitude to resist the romantic longing building in her.

"Ethan said that you've never been in love before," she explained, determined to do the smart thing. "And that you're conflicted."

"Maybe I was before. But that's not how I feel anymore."

"And tomorrow?" she persisted. "When something comes up about my past that triggers your suspicions again?"

He frowned. "What's going to come up?"

"I don't know." She waved her hands around. "My mother could show up and shock you with her passion for taking nude photos of herself. Or you could judge me because I have no idea who my father is." She sucked in a shaky breath and braced herself for his reaction. "Or maybe the fact that my grandfather is Peter Thompson."

His obvious shock at the familiar name confirmed what he'd thought about her all along and sparked her greatest fear. He'd always perceived her as the fruit of a poisonous tree. Still, she couldn't deny a certain amount of relief at getting everything out in the open.

"That's right," she continued. "I'm the granddaughter of one of the country's most notorious swindlers. His Ponzi scheme defrauded investors of hundreds of millions of dollars. The scandal rocked Seattle and devastated my family. It's why my mother changed her name and lives off the grid. It's why I do what I can to help people. I'm related to a liar and a thief who harmed thousands. You were right about me all along."

Paul captured her hands and squeezed gently. "I wasn't right about you at all. That was the problem. I judged you before I knew what a kind, loving, selfless person you are."

"My grandfather is a criminal," Lia said, compelled to point out the obvious.

"A fact that has nothing to do with who you are."

As tempting as it was to accept his breezy dismissal of her background, Lia couldn't believe he'd just let it go. "But it's a scandal that could come to light. I can't imagine your family will appreciate that."

"If it does, we'll deal with it," Paul declared. "You are exactly what I need in my life. Someone to remind me to laugh and to stop working and to enjoy myself. You've made me feel again. Or for the first time. And now that you've opened me up, I need you so I will stay this way."

"But you said it yourself, we're completely different. How long before I start to drive you crazy?"

"Immediately." He laughed and his happiness made her heart pound. "Don't you get it? I'm thrilled that you do. Isn't that what your tarot cards said? For too long I've been burying myself in work. Isolating myself from the people I love and the world at large. You brought me back from the wilderness."

She couldn't believe he remembered the reading much less had taken it so to heart. "Does that mean you believe a little?"

"I'm starting to believe a lot. And that's all because of you."

"But what if I don't want to settle down in one place?"

"I can do my job from wherever," he said. "If you get itchy feet, we'll load up your little camper and take it on the road. Have laptop will travel," he joked, but to Lia's surprise and delight, it looked as if he meant it.

Still, if he'd taught her anything these last few weeks it was caution. "It sounds like a fairy-tale ending," she said. "But I'm not a princess, I just play one for kids who are stuck in the hospital."

"I have an idea." He turned utterly serious. "You read

tarot cards for me and my cousins, but you never did one for yourself."

"I don't generally do my own readings."

"Because you can't?"

"Because I don't want to see what's coming."

"How about for just this once, you take a look. If the cards tell you to get back on the road without me, then you'll know."

She laughed, unable to believe what she was hearing. Paul Watts was going to let his future be shaped by something he claimed not to believe in? "If you truly wanted me to stay, I would think you'd be trying to convince me yourself instead of depending on the cards."

"I haven't stopped trying to convince you. And I think the tarot cards will show you that you belong here. With me. Come on. It'll be fun."

Lia wanted to argue, but the obstinate set of Paul's jaw kept her silent.

"Fine," she said, heading toward the camper. "Let's do this."

In the hours since she'd said goodbye to Grady, she'd restored Misty to her preferred organized state. As she pulled out the tarot deck and sat down at the snug dinette, she noticed the way Paul glanced around, his gaze lingering on the bed where they'd made love the first time. Her heart skipped as stony determination settled over his features. That this man wanted her, loved her, weakened Lia's resolve to make a clearheaded decision. She'd followed her intuition all her life, impulsively jumping into action, but some of Paul's deliberate, logic-driven methodology had rubbed off on her.

Beneath Paul's intense regard, Lia shuffled the cards while asking a simple question. Should she stay in Charleston and be with Paul? Instead of laying out the Celtic Cross spread all at once with the cards facedown the way she'd done in the earlier readings, Lia slowly placed each card faceup, considering the meaning as she went.

The reading started out ordinarily enough with the Fool, signifying the beginning of a journey, covered by the Two of Swords, which had a picture of a blindfolded woman, with arms crossed over her chest, holding two swords. The defensive imagery was clear enough that even Paul blinked in startled understanding.

"The basis of the situation is the Four of Cups," she narrated. "Indicating a situation where someone is apathetic about the same dull situation."

"Meaning it's time for you to leave Charleston?"

Or that she wasn't as enthusiastic to get back on the road as she once might have been. In truth, as she'd prepared the camper to leave, she'd noticed a dullness in her movements, a depression at the idea of leaving behind a city she'd grown to love.

"Possibly," she answered, laying down the card symbolizing the recent past. "The Lovers." Since that interpretation was also incredibly obvious, she moved on to possible outcome. "Eight of Cups." The card showed a man walking away from what had been a happy situation. Lia's heart sank as the message began to materialize.

"The King of Swords," Paul said when he saw the next card. "Is that me in your future?"

Obviously, he'd been paying attention during the readings she'd done for his cousins because there'd been all sorts of kings in their spreads that Lia had interpreted as the significant appearance of strong men in the lives.

"I believe so," Lia said cautiously. In the self position she drew the Six of Swords. It showed a couple traveling across the water in a boat, indicating a journey. The fact that it was reversed suggested the travel would be unsatisfying. "In my environment," she continued, placing another from the sword suit.

"That doesn't look good," Paul remarked, gazing at the Nine of Swords which depicted a woman crying against a backdrop of swords. "In fact, she looks pretty unhappy. Seems like your leaving is going to upset people."

Refusing to give him the satisfaction of agreeing, Lia placed the next card. "Hopes and fears." Her reaction to the card's significance must have shown on her face because Paul eyed her intently.

"What does it mean?"

Lia ground her teeth and debated whether to share that the card indicated the end of a journey or explain the more commonly held understanding that the Eight of Wands quite literally read as arrows of love.

"Action taken in love affairs," she grumbled. "Proposals made and accepted."

Although Lia didn't glance at Paul, she could feel the smugness radiating from him.

"And the outcome card?"

She froze, afraid to see what her future held. So much of the reading confirmed Paul's belief that she needed to stay and give their relationship a chance. How many times had she told people to trust in what the universe was telling them through the tarot deck? To turn her back on such clear mystic advice meant denying what she believed in.

And why?

Because she was afraid to take a risk with Paul.

"Lia?" Paul's gentle prompt brought a lump to her throat. "What's the last card?"

"I'm afraid to find out," she admitted. "In this moment, right here and now, I haven't made a decision that will impact the rest of my life. I'm at a crossroads where I can see my life going either way and there's a certain amount of peace in that."

"Schrödinger's cat," he declared, in all his adorable nerdiness. "Until you see the outcome you are both staying in

Charleston and taking a chance on us while also content to drive off and never look back." Paul plucked the last card from the top of the deck and placed it facedown in its position. "Forget the cards and trust your heart."

That heart was hammering so hard against her ribs that Lia could barely breathe. Loving him consumed her, but she couldn't shake the anxiety that one day he'd wake up and regret asking her to stay.

"It's not my heart I need to trust," she told him, pointing to the King of Swords card that represented him in the near-future position. "You rule your world with the strength of your personality and intellect."

Paul indicated the card that represented her. The Fool. A free spirit. Impulsive. Naive. Trusting that a leap of faith will bring joy and happiness.

"It's why I need someone like you in my life. We've known each other two weeks and I've changed so much in that short period of time. If you leave, I'll just go back to being lonely and isolated, only now that state will make me miserable." He then pointed to the Eight of Cups in her potential outcome position. "Don't leave behind what promises to be a wonderful life with me here."

"But your family," she protested. "I lied to all of them about being Ava's daughter. How can I ever look them in the eye again?"

"Actually, several of them already knew," Paul said. "Ethan told Dad and we suspect he told Mom."

"Dallas confronted me last night and she was really upset that Grady wrote me into his will," Lia admitted, hope fading even as she noted the gentleness that softened the strong lines of Paul's handsome face. "I think she hates me."

"She doesn't. She texted me this morning after she realized you left and knows she handled things badly. My whole family loves you. And I love you. The only question that remains is whether you love us enough to become a permanent member of the Watts clan."

Her breath stopped. "What do you mean by permanent?"

"I mean…" He grinned at her as he slid out of the dinette. Dropping to one knee beside her, Paul popped open the ring box Grady had given him. "Ophelia Marsh, will you do me the honor of becoming my wife?"

The formal words filled her with joy. "I adore you, Paul Watts," she murmured around the thick lump in her throat. "But…" Panic rose; she wanted so badly to belong that she could barely keep it together. "Your family has to approve."

"This is my grandmother's ring," he told her, pulling the circle of white gold and glittering diamonds free of the velvet padding. "Grady gave it to me to give to you. He wants you to be a part of our family. We all do."

Lia stared at the ring, the legacy of an earlier generation's love and fidelity, and something shifted inside her, settling into place, making her whole for the first time in her life. She held out her left hand and let Paul slide the ring onto her finger.

She framed his face with her hands and smiled. "Nothing would make me happier than to spend the rest of my life with you."

As Paul leaned forward to kiss her, he reached out and turned over the outcome card. Lia caught a glimpse of the image an instant before his lips met hers.

The Sun.

Joy. Happiness. Optimism. Energy. Wonder. The card promised all these and more.

Brilliant light exploded behind her closed eyelids as she gloried in the perfection of his kiss and reveled in all the boundless possibilities the future held. As opposites they'd been attracted to each other. Through their differences they'd learned, struggled and eventually changed. Like yin and yang they belonged together, two halves that made up a whole. Their journey had been a blend of destiny and deliberate choices. And as many challenges as they might encounter in the years ahead, Lia trusted they would overcome them together.

Epilogue

In the midst of the party to celebrate their engagement, Paul took Lia's hand and drew her away from the well-wishers. Since arriving at his grandfather's estate, they'd been swarmed by family and friends all eager to congratulate them. It was their first major social event as a couple and he'd been worried how she'd handle all the attention, but her dazzling smile demonstrated that she was gaining confidence by the hour.

Much had happened in the weeks since he'd proposed. Grateful for all she'd done for him, Grady had left Lia in his will, but since she wasn't Ava's daughter, he'd changed the amount intended for her. On the matter of Lia's background, they'd chosen to reveal her family connection to the infamous Peter Thompson. By controlling the way the story came out, they'd gotten ahead of the gossip. Still, when faced with so much unwanted media attention, Paul half expected Lia to bolt for the open road. Instead, supported by the entire Watts family, she'd weathered the news event with grace.

Craving a few minutes alone with Lia, Paul guided her onto the back terrace and into a dark corner away from prying eyes. He didn't expect they'd have more than a few minutes alone before they were discovered. He desperately needed to kiss her. As if her own desires matched his, Lia melted into his embrace, sliding her fingers into his hair and applying pressure to coax his lips to hers.

The scent of her perfume reminded him of the first time they'd met. He realized now that he'd started falling for her in that moment. His tactics for scaring her off would've worked if Ethan hadn't concocted his scheme to pass her off as Grady's granddaughter. Realizing just how close he'd come to losing her made Paul tighten his arms around Lia's slim waist.

"I thought we were done sneaking around," she teased with a breathless laugh when they finally came up for air.

"With a family as large as mine, if we want privacy we're going to have to get creative."

She hummed with pleasure as his lips traveled down her neck. "I like getting creative with you."

The sound of a door opening a short distance away made Paul groan. A second later he heard Ethan's voice.

"Here's where you two disappeared off to."

"Go away," Paul growled, not ready for his interlude with Lia to end. "We're busy."

Ethan ignored his brother's attempts to send him packing and stepped closer. "I thought you both might be interested in learning that we've received a hit from the testing service."

Paul's breath caught as the momentous news hit him like a sharp jab to his gut. Lia clutched his arm as she, too, reacted. Their eyes met and in that moment of connection the rest of the world fell away. Paul reveled in the deep bond developing between them. No matter what happened in the future, Paul knew Lia would be beside him, offering support and performing the occasional tarot card reading.

He grinned down at her. "I love you."

"I love you, too," Lia echoed, her sweet smile setting his heart on fire.

"Did you two hear what I said?" Ethan demanded, his exasperation coming through loud and clear. "We found Ava's daughter."

* * * * *

BOMBSHELL FOR THE BLACK SHEEP

JANICE MAYNARD

For Kathy and Patti:

Families are complicated at times—
understatement! Thanks so much for being the
best sisters ever. Love you both!

One

Hartley Tarleton had made a lot of mistakes in his life, but walking away from Fiona James—twice—had to be the dumbest. He'd had his reasons. Extenuating circumstances. Familial obligations. Still, he'd handled things badly. The woman in question was not likely to be in a conciliatory mood. Even worse, here he was—proverbial hat in hand—to ask for a favor.

Despite a host of misgivings, he parked across the street and a few cars down from her neatly kept bungalow-style home. The middle-class Charleston neighborhood had aged gently, preserving the best of the city's Carolina charm in a price range single people and young families could afford. Fiona was a landscape painter. A very talented one with a quickly burgeoning reputation. Hopefully, her starving-artist years were behind her.

Drumming his fingers on the steering wheel, Hartley rehearsed his speech. The home and the woman drew him, creating a burning ache in his chest. He'd spent two nights in that house, though not in succession. For reasons he wouldn't examine too closely, he recalled every detail.

On difficult days this past year, he had calmed himself by remembering the vintage dinette set in Fiona's tiny breakfast nook. The table was yellow, speckled with gray. He had imagined Fiona, with her naturally curly red hair and wide-set gray-blue eyes, sitting in one of the chairs with the chrome legs, a sketch pad in front of her.

Slowly, he got out of the car and stretched. This momentary procrastination was unlike him. If anything, he erred on the impulsive side. When he was a teenager, people criticized those tendencies as a sign of immaturity. He preferred to think of himself as grabbing the bull by the horns. He liked controlling his own destiny.

A trickle of sweat ran down the center of his back. The day was ridiculously hot and humid. Maybe he had been gone too long. Charleston was his home. Why then, did he feel like an interloper?

His heart hammered in his chest as he crossed the street and walked up the path. He had worried that Fiona might be out and about, but her carefully restored VW Bug sat in the driveway. The car was cotton-candy pink with tiny blue seahorses scattered across the hood. It was a whimsical vehicle, and perfectly suited to the imagination of an artist.

On the porch, he loosened his tie and told himself he wasn't going to lose it. Grief and a host of other emotions bombarded him. His throat was desert dry. Grimly, he reached out and rang the buzzer.

Fiona heard the doorbell and sighed with relief. She had ordered several hundred dollars' worth of new paint—oils and acrylics. The overnight rush fee made her cringe, but it was her own fault for not realizing sooner that she didn't have what she needed to begin a newly commissioned project.

She was wearing a paint-stained T-shirt and ancient jeans with holes in the knees, but the delivery guy had seen her in worse. Her back protested when she sprang to her feet. Sitting in one spot for too long was an occupational hazard. When she was deeply involved in her work, she could paint or draw for hours and never notice the passage of time.

Sprinting through her small house to the front door took a matter of seconds. The only thing that slowed her down was stubbing her toe on the back corner leg of the sofa. *Damn, damn, damn.* The pain had her hopping on one foot. She had to hurry, because the package required a signature.

She flung open the door, breathless and panting, momentarily dazzled by the bright sunshine. The man standing on her porch was definitely not a delivery man. Nor was he a stranger.

It took her a full five seconds to process the unimaginable.

"Hartley?" Her shock quickly changed to anger. "Oh, heck no." This man had bruised her ego and maybe even broken her heart.

She slammed the door on instinct. Or she *tried* to slam the door. One big foot—clad in a size-twelve Italian leather dress shoe—planted itself at the edge of the door frame. The foot's owner grunted in pain, but he didn't give up his advantage.

"Please, Fiona. I need your help."

There it was. Her weakness. Her Achilles' heel. Growing up in a succession of pleasant but unexceptional foster homes had taught her that becoming indispensable to the family in question secured a roof over her head.

She'd been self-sufficient for over a decade now—ever since she had aged out of the system. She had money in the bank, and her credit rating was unblemished. This perfect little house was almost paid for. Pleasing people was a habit now, not a necessity. A habit she had vowed to break.

But when she actually peeked at Hartley's face, her resolve wavered. "You look terrible," she muttered, still with her hand on the door blocking his entrance. Her statement wasn't entirely correct. Even haggard and with dark smudges of exhaustion beneath his eyes, Hartley Tarleton was the most beautiful man she had ever seen. Muscular shoulders, slim hips and a smile that ought to be outlawed on behalf of women everywhere.

They had first met more than a year ago at the wedding of mutual friends, Hartley a groomsman and Fiona his matching attendant. He had escorted her down the aisle during the ceremony. Later that evening, after a raucous reception that involved copious amounts of extremely good wine and plenty of dancing, he had removed her ghastly fuchsia bridesmaid dress…in her very own bedroom. Where she had invited him to join her.

That night, their physical and emotional connection was immediate and seductive—impossible to resist.

When she woke up the following morning, he was gone.

Today, his coffee-colored eyes—so dark as to be almost black—glittered with strong emotion. "Please, Fee." His voice was hoarse. "Five minutes."

What was it about this man that tore down every one of her defensive barriers? He'd walked out on her not once, but twice. Was she a masochist? Normally, she didn't fall for stupid male flattery. But she had actually believed Hartley had been as caught up in the magic of their tantalizing attraction as she'd been.

Sighing at her own spineless behavior, she stepped back

and opened the door wider. "Fine. But five minutes. Not six. I'm busy."

It was a pitiful pretense of disinterest. When he stepped past her, the familiar crisp, fresh scent of his shave gel took her back to a duet of nights she had tried so desperately to forget.

Hartley crossed the room and sprawled on her sofa. She remained standing, arms folded over her chest. The first time they met, he had worn a tuxedo befitting his inclusion in the wedding party. Nine months later when he had shown up on her doorstep without a word of explanation for his long absence, he'd been in faded jeans and a pale yellow cotton shirt with rolled-up sleeves.

Today, his hand-tailored suit screamed money. Despite his almost palpable misery, he looked like a rich man. In other words, not the sort of person Fiona should date. Or sleep with. Or include in any kinds of future plans.

The silence stretched on. Hartley leaned forward, elbows resting on his knees, head bowed. He was a man who always knew what to say. The kind of guy who could summon a woman's interest with one mischievous, wicked quirk of his eyebrow.

Now that she had let the big, bad wolf into her house, he was mute.

The uninterrupted, empty silence finally broke her. "What do you want, Hartley?"

The five words were supposed to be inflected with impatience and disinterest. Instead, her voice trembled. She winced inwardly, hoping he hadn't noticed. If ever there was a time for a woman to seize control of a situation and play the hand on her terms, this was it.

He didn't deserve her sympathy.

At last, he sat up and faced her, his hands fisted on his thighs. There were hollows in his face that hadn't been there before. Unmistakable grief. "My father is dead," he croaked. The expression in his eyes was a combination of childish bewilderment and dull adult acceptance.

"Oh my God. I'm so sorry." Despite her anger, her heart clenched in sympathy. "Was it sudden?"

"Yes. A stroke."

"Were you in Charleston?" They had discovered at the wedding that they both lived in the beautiful low-country city, but clearly they moved in different circles most of the time.

"No. But it wouldn't have mattered. He was gone in an instant."

"I don't know what to say, except that I'm very sorry, Hartley."

"He was old but not *that* old. It never occurred to me I wouldn't get the chance to say goodbye."

She wanted to sit down beside him and hug him, but she knew her own limits. It was best to keep a safe distance. Sliding into Hartley Tarleton's arms made her reasoning skills turn to mush.

His jaw firmed. "I need you to go to the funeral with me. Please." He stood and faced her. "I wouldn't ask if it weren't so important." The muscles in his throat flexed as he swallowed. He needed a haircut. When one thick lock fell over his forehead, he brushed it aside impatiently.

She had seen him naked. Had felt the gentle caress of his big, slightly rough hands on every inch of her sensitive skin. That other Hartley made her body sing with pleasure...made her stupid, romantic heart weave daydreams. But she didn't know him. Not really.

"I don't think it's a good idea, Hartley. We're nothing to each other. You made that abundantly clear. I don't *want* to go with you to the funeral," she said firmly, trying to sound tough and no-nonsense and not at all like the type of woman who let a man disappear for days and weeks on end with no explanation and then three months ago took him back into her bed…again.

"You don't understand." He moved a step in her direction, but she held him off with a palm-out stance.

"No touching," she said, reading his playbook. She wouldn't let him soften her up.

He shrugged, his expression harried. "Fine. No touching. But I need you to go to the funeral with me, because I'm scared, dammit. I haven't seen my brother or sister in over a year. Things have been strained between us. I need a buffer."

"Charming," she drawled. "That's what a woman wants to hear."

"For God's sake, don't be difficult, Fee."

His scowl would have been comical if his behavior hadn't been so atrocious. "*I'm* perfectly reasonable and rational, Mr. Tarleton. You're the one who seems to have lost your mind."

He ran a hand across the back of his neck, a shadow crossing his face. "Maybe I have," he muttered. He paced restlessly, pausing to pick up a nautilus shell a friend had brought her from Australia. It had been sliced—like a hamburger bun—with a fine-gauge jeweler's saw to reveal the logarithmic spiral inside. Hartley traced the pattern with a fingertip, the gesture almost sensual. "This is beautiful," he said.

"I just brought it out of my studio. I've been working on a series of four watercolors…a galaxy, a hurricane, this perfect shell. The pattern occurs in nature more often than you might think."

He closed his palm around the opalescent wonder and shot her a look. "And the fourth?"

Her face heated. "Oddly enough, it's a kind of broccoli... Romanesco."

For the first time, the tension in his broad shoulders eased visibly, and a trace of his trademark grin lightened his face. "I've never met anyone like you, Fiona."

She bristled. "What does that mean?"

"You're special. You see the world in a way us mere mortals don't. I envy you that."

The quiet sincerity in his voice and the genuine compliment reminded her of all the reasons she had fallen for his charms the first time. And the second. His habitual smile was an inexplicable combination of sweet and sexy. For a man who stood six three in his stocking feet and carried himself like an athlete, the hint of boyish candor caught her off guard again and again.

What could it hurt if she accompanied him to his father's service? It was an hour of her life, maybe less. She sighed inwardly, already losing the battle. "What day is the funeral?"

Now he definitely looked guilty. "Today."

She gaped at him. "*Today* today?"

"In an hour and a half."

Her temper ramped to a slow boil. "And you seriously thought you could simply waltz in here, demand my cooperation and get what you want?"

"No," he said forcefully. "No." The second denial was quieter. "I was *hoping*, Fee. Just hoping."

He shoved his hands in his pockets, and he didn't move. She gave him points for that. Everything in her past interactions with him suggested that he could indeed get what he wanted with little more than a kiss. But Hartley didn't try any funny business. All he did was ask.

Before she could formulate an answer, he grimaced. "I know I owe you explanations for my behavior. If you'll do me the kindness of standing beside me this afternoon, I swear I'll tell you whatever you want to know afterward. I won't run out. Not this time."

She searched his face for the truth. "Why are things awkward with your siblings? Isn't your brother your twin? I seem to recall you telling me that. Aren't twins supposed to be tight?"

"I did something to upset my father and Jonathan, my brother. I was written out of the will. And to be honest, maybe I deserved it. But I love my family. They're everything to me. I would like to heal the rift…if that's even possible."

He could have wheedled. Or flirted. Or even pressured. Instead, he simply stood there. Looking at her. So intently that her nipples tightened beneath the soft cotton of her bra. She hadn't imagined the physical connection between them. It was as real today as it was the other times he had blasted into her world. As real as the mantel clock that ticked a steady rhythm.

"Okay. I'll go with you." A platonic date to a funeral didn't mean she was capitulating a *third time.* "I can be ready in half an hour. Will that do?"

He nodded. "Thank you, Fiona." His gaze was sober. "I appreciate it."

"Wait for me here. If the doorbell rings, please answer it. I'm expecting some packages."

Hartley watched her walk away, wishing he could join her in the shower and forget that his life was imploding. It was nothing short of a miracle that she had agreed to go with him. Because of the situation he was in and the looming stress of seeing his family again, he had to slam the lid on all the erotic memories this small house contained.

His gut was in a knot, but the burning dread eased. With Fee beside him, he could get through this afternoon.

Before he could pull out his phone and check his email, a loud knock sounded at the door. The uniformed delivery man on the porch was beaming when Hartley answered the summons, but his smile faded.

"I have some packages," he said.

Hartley didn't call him out on the awkward, unnecessary explanation. "I see that," he said mildly.

The kid, barely twenty at most, tried to peer inside the house. "Fiona needs to sign for this delivery."

Hartley's territorial instincts kicked in. "*Ms. James* is in the shower."

The young man recognized the veiled rebuke. His face flushed. "You could do it, I suppose."

"I supposed I could." Hartley scrawled his name and handed back the electronic clipboard. "I'll tell her you said hello."

Three large boxes changed hands. Hartley gave the poor schmuck a terse nod and closed the door firmly. He couldn't blame the kid for having a crush, but Fiona deserved a man in her life.

The irony of that didn't escape him. In fact, now that he had Fee in his corner, he could spare a moment to wonder what she had been up to in the weeks and months he had been traveling the world. Was there a man somewhere who would protest Hartley's current involvement in her life?

His stomach-curling distaste for that thought told him he was more invested than he wanted to admit. It seemed impossible he could be obsessed with a woman he had known for less than a week, collectively. Yet of all the people in his life who could have been persuaded to accompany him to his father's funeral, Hartley had chosen Fiona.

The momentary peace he experienced deep in his heart told him he had made the right decision.

A lot of things were going to change in the next weeks and months. Even if his brother didn't trust him and his sister would reproach him for being gone so long, the three of them would have to work together to settle their father's affairs.

Only Hartley knew how very difficult that was going to be.

A noise in the hall brought his head up. His breath caught in his throat. "Fiona," he croaked. "You look amazing."

Her classic black dress was sleeveless and knee length. Sexy black sandals showcased slender legs. She had tried to tame her medium-length hair with two antique tortoiseshell combs. Now fiery curls framed her elfin face. "Is this okay?" she asked. "To be honest, I haven't been to a funeral in a very long time." She toyed with the simple pearl earrings that matched the necklace at her throat.

"You're perfect," he said.

Two

Fiona avoided funerals on a good day. Attending this particular one on the arm of the man who had treated her so shabbily didn't make sense.

Yet here she was.

Charleston, in all her low-country charm, basked in the summer sun. The city was a unique amalgam of Southern gentility and a lingering painful past. Palm trees and horse-drawn carriages. Elegant secluded courtyards. And everywhere, the patina of old money. Farther out from the city, pockets of poverty existed, but here in the historic district, wealth and social position held sway.

By the time Fiona and Hartley made it to the upscale funeral home in the heart of town, she knew she was in trouble. Hartley had barely spoken a word the entire time, but she was hyperaware of him at her side.

He drove with careless confidence despite the tightness in his jaw and his palpable air of tension.

It was impossible not to think about the other times they had been together. At least it was impossible for *her*. Presumably, Hartley was too distraught to think about sex.

She was having second and third thoughts about her role this afternoon. "So what do I need to know?" she asked. "I don't want to say anything I shouldn't."

Hartley shot her a sideways glance before spotting an empty spot down the street and parallel parking with ease. "Just follow my lead. My sister will be emotional. For several reasons. She doesn't know why I've been gone."

"Join the club," Fiona muttered.

Hartley ignored her sarcasm. "Mazie's husband is J.B. He's been a friend of ours since we were kids. He and Mazie reconnected recently and fell in love. And to further confuse you, J.B. is my brother's best friend."

"Got it."

"Jonathan, my twin, had serious brain surgery not too long ago, but he's made a complete recovery. His wife is Lisette. She's been working for Tarleton Shipping a long time."

"And your mother? I haven't heard you speak of her." Fiona got out and smoothed her skirt with damp hands. Meeting strangers was not her forte. In this situation, the stakes were much higher than usual. Hartley got out as well and closed his door, resting his arms on the roof of the car as he stared at her. "My mother is not in the picture. The only people you'll have to deal with today are my siblings and their spouses."

If his words were meant to reassure her, they failed. Hartley's air of mystery told her the Tarleton family had more than one skeleton in the closet. Why else would Hartley be so worried about seeing his brother and sister? It was beginning to dawn on Fiona that his brief though startling contact with her was not the only relationship he had abandoned.

They arrived at the funeral home early. Hartley wanted time to speak with his family before the receiving of friends began. When he took Fiona's hand in his as they mounted the steps to the red-brick and white-columned building, she wasn't sure he even noticed.

She tugged him to a halt before he opened the door, squeezing his fingers, trying to extend her support. "It's going to be okay," she said softly. "Every family goes through this. You'll make it. You all will."

His expression was grim. "Death is one thing. Handling the living is something else again."

His odd words stayed with her for the next half hour, illuminating the awkward family reunion.

Mazie was the first person to spot her brother. She ran up to him and threw her arms around his neck, her face wet with tears. "I swear I shouldn't forgive you, but I'm so glad you're here."

Fiona hung back as Hartley embraced his classically beautiful sister. Mazie's skin was fairer than her brother's. And though the family resemblance was strong, her eyes were more golden amber than brown. Her elegance made Fiona feel dowdy in comparison. Mazie wore emeralds that must have cost a fortune.

Hartley reached back and drew Fiona into the small circle. "Mazie, this is my friend, Fiona James. She was kind enough to be my date today."

Fiona grimaced. "I told him no one needs an escort to a funeral, but he wouldn't take no for an answer."

Mazie smiled through her tears. "That sounds like Hartley. Wait a minute," she said. "Fiona James the artist? My husband and I have a couple of your paintings. *The Salt*

Marsh at Sunset. The Bridge at Twilight. I treasure them. You're incredibly talented."

"Thank you," Fiona said. It still startled her to be recognized.

Mazie dried her face with a tissue. "Jonathan is just around the corner. You might as well get this meeting over with."

Hartley's gaze darkened. "Is he really going to be okay?"

"Right as rain," Mazie said. "He didn't even freak out when Lisette told him she had been keeping you in the loop. Apparently, staring death in the face mellows a man."

Hartley curled an arm around Fiona's waist. "Jonathan was misdiagnosed in the beginning, but fortunately, the mistake was caught in time."

"How scary," Fiona said.

Mazie nodded. "Terrifying. We thought we were going to lose him."

They turned down a hallway and more or less ran into the third Tarleton sibling. Jonathan had clearly overheard the end of their conversation.

He lifted a shoulder, his smile laconic. "Apparently, I'm hard to kill."

The two brothers sized each other up. The tension was painful. They were definitely identical twins. No hiding that. But even an outsider would have no problem telling them apart.

Olive skin. Dark brown eyes. Chestnut hair. Those were the commonalities. Hartley's hair was longer…untamed… sun-bleached. And he had the look of a man who spent a lot of time outdoors. Jonathan, on the other hand, was *GQ* handsome. Sculpted jaw. Expensive haircut. Conservative suit.

Two stunningly handsome men in their prime.

Hartley kept an arm around Fiona's waist. "Hello, Jonathan."

Mazie made a huffing noise. "For God's sake. Hug each other."

The brothers ignored her. At last, Jonathan held out his hand. "Welcome home, Hartley."

Even without being privy to all the details, Fiona knew this moment was epic. It was written in Jonathan Tarleton's wary expression and in the rigid set of Hartley's posture.

"Thank you," Hartley said quietly. "I'm glad to be back, but not for this reason. I'm sorry I wasn't here when it happened."

Mazie spoke up, her tears flowing again. "None of us were. Apparently, he died in his sleep. The housekeeper found him."

"Hell," Hartley said quietly. "I knew he wasn't well, but I honestly thought he would go on forever."

"So did we." Jonathan glanced at his watch. "Would you like to see him?"

Fiona felt the shudder that racked Hartley's body. "Yes," he said gruffly.

Moments later, the four of them stood around the casket. Gerald Tarleton had been a large man. But in death, he looked old and frail. Fiona knew he had built a far-reaching shipping empire that would now pass on to his children. Again, she wondered about Mrs. Tarleton. Was she dead or alive?

Soon they were joined by J.B. Vaughan and Lisette, Jonathan's wife. Mazie took care of the introductions. Her husband wrapped her in his arms and kissed the top of her head. "No more crying, honey. You'll give yourself a migraine." He dabbed his wife's cheeks with a handkerchief.

Fiona felt a fierce stab of envy. Would any man ever look at her with such naked devotion?

Her stomach curled with tension. Dozens of floral arrangements flanked the casket and filled the walls on either side. The heavy scent of carnations made Fiona feel ill. A cold sweat dampened her brow.

Could she leave? Could she simply run away? This wasn't *her* family crisis. Suddenly, she knew she needed a moment to gather her composure. But before she could make a break for it, the funeral home director appeared behind them and intruded with a hushed cough.

"Guests are arriving," he said, his tone sepulchral. "If you'll follow me, I'll escort you to an anteroom. We'll open the doors, and then I'll bring you in and arrange the receiving line."

This was Fiona's chance. In the transition, she darted down the hall and found the ladies' room. Once in the stall, she retched and dry-heaved. Oh, God. She felt terrible. Her life was usually placid and peaceful. She *liked* it that way. Damn Hartley for pulling her into the middle of this mess.

When the crisis passed, she put a cold paper towel on the back of her neck and touched up her makeup. All her life she had never done well with confrontation and stress. Lack of stability in her formative years had left her with issues. Duh.

Her psyche craved calm, the kind of steady, peaceful existence her art gave her. She was happiest when she could lose herself in a creative project. Seeing Hartley again and having to negotiate his family storms made her a nervous wreck.

Still, he said he *needed* her. That had been enough to coax her into accompanying him during this difficult afternoon. She'd spent too many years ingratiating herself with different foster families to change her personality overnight.

She was independent now. She didn't have to worry

about housing or food or even winning a kind word from a stranger. But the desire to fit in…to be useful…was never far from the surface.

Fortunately, the crowds of visitors had already overtaken the room where the Tarleton family stood to greet friends and business acquaintances. Fiona was able to slip in unnoticed and take her place at Hartley's side. He gave her a quick intimate glance, but immediately returned his attention to the seemingly endless line of men and women waiting to speak to him.

Fiona smiled and nodded, content to remain in the background. Occasionally, someone questioned Hartley about his long absence from Charleston. Each well-meaning query was deflected with a vague throwaway comment.

The man was a social genius, even if he did have more disappearing acts than Houdini.

At last, it was time to adjourn to the chapel. A couple of songs, some readings and a few words from Jonathan. Finally, it was over.

Fiona couldn't wait to leave. Her stomach still felt iffy, and her head ached. Before she could plan her exit, Mazie appeared at her side.

The other woman's eyes were red-rimmed, but she was calm. "A few of our friends have catered a dinner for us out at the beach house. We'll be headed that way in a few moments. Don't let Hartley escape."

"Oh, no," Fiona said. "This is your family time. I need to go home. It was lovely to meet you."

Mazie frowned and strong-armed Fiona into a nearby corner. "Please, Fiona. You don't know all the details." She paused and grimaced. "To be honest, I don't even know. But Jonathan and Hartley had a huge falling-out about something, something big. This is the first time they've been in the same room in over a year. They *have* to heal this thing. And we need you to be an impartial bystander."

"Why?" Fiona asked, searching desperately for a polite way to make her excuses.

Mazie's eyes filled with tears again, though this time perhaps not for her father's passing. "I adore my brothers. They've been my supporters and protectors my entire life. It kills me to see them so stiff and polite with each other. *Please*, Fiona," she said urgently. "Please have dinner with us."

Hartley walked up to them, overhearing his sister's invitation. "Of course she's coming—right, Fee?"

Fiona knew she was trapped. She gnawed her lip. "If you're sure I won't be intruding." She gave Hartley a pointed stare. "But I can't stay too late. I have a huge project to begin tomorrow, and I want to be in bed at a decent hour."

His gaze was inscrutable. "Understood."

Hartley was no more communicative during the drive to the Tarleton home than he had been earlier en route to the funeral. The silence suited Fiona just fine. She leaned her head back against her seat and closed her eyes.

Unfortunately, shutting Hartley out was not so easy. His masculine scent teased her nose. Her fingers itched to cross the divide between them and stroke his thigh. She *wanted* to help him. She really did. And she wanted to be with him. But her sense of self-preservation warned her to keep her distance.

Instead, she was accompanying him to a meal and a social occasion that was sure to produce strong emotions and any one of a dozen possible outcomes, from uncomfortable silence to vocal recriminations.

If she was lucky, the Tarletons would be on their best

behavior. Fiona would be able to return home and would never again answer her door to a tall, handsome lover.

Despite her misgivings, she was eager to see the beach house. Years ago, Gerald Tarleton had built a walled compound on the tip of a barrier island north of Charleston. Fiona knew of the property in general terms, but when Hartley steered the car through the front gates, she was both taken aback and enchanted.

The structure rested on massive stilts, of course. A sweeping staircase led up to the beautiful double-door entrance. Even from the driveway, Fiona could see the intricate stained glass that incorporated sea turtles, dolphins and starfish. As an artist, she was fascinated.

As a woman, she wanted to run far away.

Hartley shut off the engine and pressed the heels of his hands to his forehead. "This feels so damned wrong."

"I'm sorry." The words were inadequate, but she didn't know how else to help him.

The early evening light illuminated his drawn expression. "I grew up here," he said quietly. "After 9/11, our father was paranoid. He barely let us leave the house for the longest time."

"I can understand that, I suppose. He wanted to protect you." She gazed up at Hartley's family home. It was a far cry from the houses where she had been bounced around.

Her longest tenure was twenty-five months—with a family who had taken in four other foster children besides Fiona. When the wife eventually became pregnant with her own *biological* child, Fiona and her de facto brothers and sisters were reassigned.

Fiona had begged to stay. At thirteen, she was the oldest of the lot and capable of being a help around the house. But the pregnancy was high risk. The doctor said too much stress and chaos would threaten the mother's health.

Fiona's personality was quiet and self-abnegating. No chaos anywhere. But the doctor's orders prevailed.

Fiona's foster mom had cried and cried. She was too hormonal and stressed out to make a good decision. In the end, it was nobody's fault, but Fiona had never again invested so much of herself emotionally.

Hartley touched her hand. "Ready to go inside?"

Even that one quick brush of his fingers against her skin sent shivers dancing down her spine. Why did he have this effect on her? "Shouldn't I be asking *you* that question?"

His low laugh held little humor. "My brother and I are civilized people. You don't have to worry about fistfights."

"I wasn't," she said. "Until now."

Her attempt at humor took some of the darkness from his face. "C'mon," he said. "You'll like the house."

Fiona's sandals had spiky heels, so she didn't protest when Hartley held her elbow as they ascended the stairs. His touch made her knees weak. She had missed him... so very much.

She tried to remember how angry she was about his cavalier treatment of their budding relationship. But the bitterness of his absence winnowed away in the pleasure of having him near again. It was sobering to admit she was perilously close to letting bygones be bygones.

Though it was frustrating not to be able to resist his winsome charm, she liked the woman she was with him. He made her feel sensual and desirable.

Before Hartley was forced to make a decision about letting himself in or ringing the bell, Lisette opened the door and greeted them. Fiona wondered if that was deliberate, so his siblings wouldn't be in the position of welcoming him back to his own home.

"Everyone is gathered in the dining room," Lisette said.

"The food looks amazing. There's enough for half a dozen families."

When the six adults were settled around the table, the housekeeper began setting out the meal on the antique sideboard. The food had come from a top-notch restaurant in the city. Fresh seafood. Ribs. Roasted corn on the cob. The dishes were endless.

The meal and the accompanying conversation progressed in fits and starts. During one awkward pause as wineglasses were being refilled, Hartley leaned in and spoke softly to Fiona. "My siblings are both still relatively new to this marriage gig. Mazie moved in with J.B. after the wedding. Jonathan and Lisette are building their own place." His warm breath brushed her ear, making her shiver. The arm he curled across the back of her chair hemmed her in intimately.

Jonathan overheard the quiet exchange and lifted an eyebrow. "You're curiously well-informed for a prodigal son."

The edge in his voice was apparent.

Hartley shrugged with a lazy smile. "I have my spies."

Fiona forced herself to wade in. Someone needed to defuse the rising tension. "What will happen to the beach house?"

Three

Nobody said a word. As Hartley watched, Fiona's face turned bright red. There was no way to avoid land mines with *this* family around the table. To her, it must have seemed like an innocuous question.

Jonathan spoke up, his smile careful but kind. "It's a little early to be thinking about those decisions. This was our father's fortress, his safe place. He didn't ever tell me what he wanted to do with the house when he was gone, and I didn't ask. I'm sure the lawyers will guide us through probate."

Suddenly, Hartley had reached his limit. They were all on their best behavior because of the funeral, but one thing was certain. Jonathan wasn't opening his arms to let Hartley back into the fold. The unspoken message was clear. Hartley had walked away, and true forgiveness was in short supply.

He stood abruptly. "It was good to see you all. Thanks for the meal. I'd like to take Fiona for a walk on the beach, and then we'll head out."

Mazie looked stricken. "Are you leaving town again?"

Again, that awkward silence.

Hartley shook his head slowly. "No. I'm back for good." There was so much he wanted to explain...so many family secrets to unravel. But how could he upend his siblings' lives for no other reason than to justify his own behavior? It wasn't fair to anyone. Maybe he would *never* tell them.

Fiona stood as well. "It was lovely to meet all of you. Sorry it was not under better circumstances."

Moments later, the ordeal was over.

Outside in the driveway, Hartley looked down at Fiona's shoes. "You can't walk in those on the beach."

"Barefoot is fine." She slipped off her sandals and tossed them in the car, adding her small clutch purse as well.

Hartley removed his jacket, tie, shoes and socks, feeling as if he were peeling away layers of frustration and grief. He had always loved the beach, and this house in particular. "The ground is rough between here and the gate," he said. "Get on my back, and I'll carry you to the sand."

Fiona looked at him askance. "I can walk."

He ground his jaw. "It's a piggyback ride, not foreplay."

"Don't get snippy with me, Hartley. I'm not the enemy."

She was right. He couldn't let Fiona bear the brunt of his mood. "Sorry," he muttered. "Climb on."

He watched as she shimmied her skirt up her thighs. Maybe he was wrong about the foreplay. Fiona's legs were enough to keep a man awake at night. When she moved behind him, he hitched her up on his back and curled his hands beneath her warm, supple thighs.

Fortunately for his self-control, the path beneath the house and out to the gate was not far. Fee reached around him to disengage the lock, and soon they were at the water's edge. He let her slide off his back slowly, steadying her with one hand as she stumbled.

There was no moon. The water seemed dark and menacing. But the whoosh and roar of the waves was a familiar lullaby from his childhood.

He tried to empty his mind of all the sorrow and confusion that had consumed him since he heard the news that his father was dead. Gradually, the inexorable pattern of the tide soothed him.

Fiona stood at his side in silence, her presence both a comfort and a niggling frustration. Twice now, he had made love to her and walked away. The first time, he'd had no choice. The second, he'd been reluctant to embroil her in his family drama. Maybe he sensed that he was using Fiona as a crutch. Maybe he hadn't wanted to let her get inside his head. In both instances, his behavior was logical if not particularly admirable. But what was going to happen moving forward?

If he still wanted to sleep with Fee, and he did, most emphatically, then he needed not only her absolution, but also some notion of what was ahead for him professionally. Anything beyond that was more than he wanted to contemplate right now.

Almost as if she had read his mind, Fiona spoke softly. "What do you do for a living, Hartley? We've flirted and slept together, but I don't really know much about you at all."

Her question prodded an unseen wound. He cleared his throat. "Well, before I left Charleston for an extended period, I was a full partner in Tarleton Shipping. We were working on a proposal to add a boatbuilding arm...pleasure craft. That whole deal was going to be my baby."

"And now?"

He shrugged. "I doubt my brother has any interest in working with me after everything that has happened."

"Because of this mysterious *falling-out*?"

"Yeah." He sighed. "Jonathan is one of the finest men I've ever known. A straight arrow all the way. But as alike as we are physically, our personalities don't always mesh."

"Why did you not live at the beach house?"

"I got tired of butting heads with my father over the business. Jonathan had a knack for handling him with kid gloves. Dad and I only yelled at each other. Several years ago I bought an investment property at a premier golf community north of the city. I was the one who would wine and dine clients. Play a few rounds with them on the course. I liked being outdoors, even if golf wasn't really my thing. But I closed deals and grew the business."

"Who has done that while you've been gone?"

It was a simple question. Not meant to inflict pain. But it hit at the heart of his guilt. "I don't know." Fiona hadn't been the only one he hurt when he'd hared off to Europe. He'd left behind his family and the shipping business and cut all contact. He'd had his reasons. In retrospect, though, he honestly didn't know if he'd done the right thing.

Fiona moved restlessly. "The beach is lovely, Hartley. I really do need to get home, though."

"I promised you explanations. It's late. I don't suppose I could sleep on your sofa?" He threw it out there hopefully. Fiona's little house represented the peace and comfort he had lost in this last year.

"No," she said bluntly. Without another word, she started up the beach toward the gate in the high brick wall.

"Fair enough." He loped up the incline and scooped her into his arms. It was a tougher slog through the loose sand this way, but he persevered. He needed to hold her.

Fiona didn't fight him. As soon as they were back at the car, though, she insisted on wriggling out of his embrace.

After smoothing her hair and brushing the sand from her feet, she put on her sexy sandals.

Then she stood, hands on her hips, and watched him re-dress. "You don't owe me explanations. I told you that."

He rounded the car and cupped her face in his hands. Lightly. Gently. "I *want* to tell you, Fee. And in the spirit of honesty, I'd like to sleep with you again."

"Sleep?"

She had him there. "Sex," he muttered. Even to his own ears, he sounded like a jerk. But he wouldn't dress it up. He couldn't offer her anything more. His life was total chaos. Besides, Fiona would demand full-on honesty and intimacy from any man who shared her life for the long haul. That wasn't him.

Her expression was mutinous. In the glow of the security light, the stubborn tilt to her chin was obvious. *"Sex isn't the answer to all your problems,* Hartley."

"Maybe not, but it would be damned good, and if you're honest, you'll agree. I know I messed up. I won't do that to you again."

"How can I believe you?" Her low laugh held a hint of dismay. "It's a painful cliché, but I'm a kid who came through the foster system. Never got adopted. I have a few abandonment issues. Your recent behavior hasn't helped."

How many women would have the guts to be so vulnerable? He had a lot to answer for and no clear idea how to fix the messes he had created. "I want to kiss you, Fee," he muttered. "But I'm trying my damnedest to respect your boundaries."

Tears glittered in her eyelashes. She sniffed. "Shut up and do it, you aggravating man."

It was all the invitation he needed. He wanted to snatch her up and take everything she had to give. Instead, he kissed her coaxingly, softly. Trying to tell her without words how much he regretted his missteps.

Fiona made a choked little noise in her throat and finally kissed him back. When her slender arms curled around his neck, he felt as if he had won the lottery. She was soft and perfect against his chest. He lifted her off her feet, desperate to make the kiss last.

"I'm sorry," he muttered. "So sorry I hurt you."

"You're forgiven. Doesn't mean I'm a glutton for punishment." She pushed away from him after a few seconds. Reluctantly, he let her go.

"So, what now?" he asked quietly.

"Nothing. At least not today. Or even tomorrow. *Twice*, I let you talk your way into my bed like I was a sixteen-year-old girl with her first crush. That was *my* mistake. I make no guarantees, Hartley. None."

He rolled his shoulders, realizing ruefully that he had been a little unrealistic about where this evening might lead. Even if he'd been saying all the right things, apparently his libido had jumped ahead to more titillating scenarios. "Understood," he sighed.

He started the engine and waited for her to climb into the front seat. The ocean breeze had tousled her hair. It stood up around her head like a nimbus, making her a weary goddess...or a naughty nymph.

Which did he want? The angel or the sexy sprite? In his imagination, she was both.

He turned the radio on for the drive back to Charleston. As they pulled away from his father's home, Hartley glanced in the rearview mirror. Jonathan stood at the top of the stairs, his arms folded across his chest.

Seeing his brother tonight had been surprisingly painful. After all this time, Hartley had been hoping Jonathan might have relented...that he had come to know instinctively that Hartley would never do anything to bring harm to his family.

But apparently, some hurts ran deep. Jonathan wasn't wiping the slate clean. In fact, he hadn't made any mention of the future at all. Hartley was on his own.

When they reached Fiona's street, she gathered her purse and started to climb out as soon as the car rolled to a halt. He took her wrist. "Wait, Fee. Please."

Her body language was wary. "What?"

"Let me take you to lunch tomorrow. I'll tell you the whole story, start to finish." He needed to tell *someone*. The secrets were gutting him. But his family was off-limits until he decided whether or not the truth would be too damaging. Fiona was a neutral player.

"I have to work tomorrow," she said.

"Dinner, then?" He was close to begging on his knees.

She hesitated for far too long. "Fine. But if this story is as convoluted as it seems, we should eat at my house. I'll fix spaghetti."

"I want to treat you," he said.

"You can't spill salacious secrets in the middle of a crowded restaurant. Besides, this isn't a date, Hartley. You seem to have a need to bare your soul, and I've agreed to listen. That's all."

"You're a hard woman."

"It's about time, don't you think?"

"I remember what it's like to make love to you, Fee. You can't blame a guy for wanting to re-create the magic."

"The magic is gone. You killed it."

Her words were harsh, but she was still sitting in his car. He took that as a good sign. "I love spaghetti," he said. "What time?"

"Six o'clock. Don't assume you'll be able to coax me into letting you spend the night. That's off the table."

"Yes, ma'am. You're cute when you're busting my balls."

"Grow up, Hartley. I'm immune to you now."

I'm immune to you now. Fiona had never told a bigger lie in her life. She slept poorly and woke up the following morning disturbed by the vivid dreams that had plagued her. Being with Hartley again kindled a hunger in her belly that no homemade spaghetti was going to fill. She wanted him. Still. After everything he had done. It was a shocking realization.

Despite her unsettled mood, she was a professional artist. That meant working regular hours even when her muse had taken a hike. Today was a case in point. It was harder than it should have been to concentrate on her new project…three massive panels that would hang in one of the main rooms of Charleston's visitor center.

Commissions like this one were her bread and butter. They paid the light bill and kept food in the fridge. But they weren't humdrum. Never that. She poured her heart and soul into every brushstroke.

Because of the size of the canvases, she'd had to buy a special easel that held the work in progress secure. At certain moments, she would have to stand on a ladder to complete the highest portions. Her sketch—the one the city had approved—included historical images all the way from Charleston's founding up until modern times.

A giant undulating current swept through the center of each panel, propelling the milestones of progress from decade to decade. Included in the visual telling were some very painful periods in time. She could see the finished product in her mind. The challenge she faced was being able to successfully translate her vision into reality.

It was her habit to paint for a couple of hours when she

first awoke and then take a break for coffee and a light brunch. After that, she would typically labor for another five or six hours and quit for the day. Hard work and determination had brought her to this place in her career. She was conscious that her success was based on a great many things beyond her control, so she was determined to make the most of her current success.

This morning, though, she found herself swamped with inexplicable fatigue and a draining lethargy that forced her to go in search of calories after only forty-five minutes in her studio.

In the kitchen, an unexpected déjà vu brought her up short. She and Hartley had stood in this very spot and made bacon and eggs amidst much laughter and many hot, hungry kisses.

She put a hand to her chest, trying to still the flutters of anxiety. Hartley wouldn't force her to do anything she didn't want to do. Her problem was far closer to home. It was *her*. Fiona. The woman with the deep-seated need for love and acceptance.

Hartley made her happy, but more than that, he made her wish and dream, and *that* was dangerous.

The fact that she had slept with him twice was no big deal. They'd had fun. Their sexual chemistry was off the charts. He was smart and kind and amusing, and she had never met a more appealing man.

But it was the long view that worried her. Like the deadly undertow out at the beach, Hartley had the power to drag her under…to tear apart the life she had built for herself. She was proud of her independence. She didn't lean on any man for support.

The danger lay in the fact that without even trying, he made her want to throw caution to the wind. When she was with him—and also when she wasn't—the smart, careful, cautious side of her brain shut down.

Even now, all she could think about was how much she wanted to share a bed with him again. Naked and wanton. Losing herself in the elemental rush of sexual desire. Hartley made her *alive*. And she loved it.

But with great joy came the potential for great heartbreak.

With the way she was feeling, it was too much trouble to cook anything. Instead, she opted for cereal and a banana. A cup of hot tea warmed her cold fingers. When she was done with breakfast, she carried a second serving of tea to the living room and curled up on the couch.

Cradling the china cup in her hands, she debated calling off tonight's dinner. Who was she kidding? If Hartley came over, she would sleep with him. Wouldn't she? Did she have it in her to say no?

Sitting here alone, it was easy to see all the problems.

The Tarletons were Charleston royalty. They and J.B.'s family, the Vaughans, had endowed libraries and funded hospital wings and sat on the boards of half a dozen philanthropic organizations across the city. Their bloodlines went back to pre–civil war times.

Fiona appreciated her own worth, but she was a pragmatist. Hartley appeared to have the attention span of a moth. He was interested in Fiona at the moment, because his life was in crisis. And because they had shared a couple of encounters that had all the earmarks of a romantic comedy.

Life wasn't like that, though. In the long run, the chances that he would actually come to love Fiona were slim. Maybe she was his flavor of the month right now, but when the novelty paled, he would be off on another adventure, with another woman, and Fiona might be left with a broken heart if she were foolish enough to fall for him.

Despite all her hashing and rehashing of the facts, she couldn't bring herself to text him and say *don't come*. How pathetic was that? She desperately wanted to see him. And then, of course, there was her curiosity about where he had been all these months.

He had never struck her as a liar. If he had explanations to make today, she had a hunch they would be true. Fantastical maybe, but true.

She finished her tea and stood, only to have the room whirl drunkenly.

With a little gasp, she reached behind her for the arm of the sofa and sat down gingerly. Had she poured bad milk in her cereal? Her stomach flipped and flopped. What was going on?

Five minutes later, she tried again. This time the familiar outlines of her furniture stayed put, but the nausea grew worse. At the last moment, she made a dash for the bathroom and threw up, emptying her stomach again and again until she was so weak she could barely stagger to her bedroom.

She curled up in the center of the mattress, shaking and woozy, and pulled the edge of the comforter over her.

Then it hit her. A possibility that had never once crossed her mind...though it should have. Was she pregnant? She'd had these odd episodes for several weeks now...had written them off as a virus or inner ear trouble or low blood sugar.

Her heart hammered in her chest. Her periods were not regular...never had been. At her gynecologist's urging, Fiona typically noted them on a paper calendar she kept in the bedside table.

When she thought she could move without barfing, she reached for the drawer, extracted what she needed and stared numbly at the unmarked boxes. Back one month. Then two. Then three. At last, she found it. A brief notation in her own handwriting. She'd had her period about ten days before Hartley last showed up at her house.

Dear Lord.

He'd used protection. Hadn't even balked at the idea when she told him she wasn't on the pill. In fact, he'd used protection that night after the wedding, too. He'd been a generous, thoughtful lover.

But no method of birth control was 100 hundred percent. And now that she thought about it, three months ago, they had made love multiple times during the night when they were both half-asleep. Had they messed up? Was there one of those times when his body had claimed hers skin to skin?

Her teeth started to chatter. She couldn't tell him. Not yet. Not until she was sure. He was going to be at her house in a few hours. With a moan of mortification, she buried her face in the pillow.

Yet even as she trembled with fear, excitement and happiness bloomed in her chest. A baby? Was she really pregnant? This could be the future she had always dreamed of…the family she so desperately wanted.

Hartley didn't have to be involved, but he *had* to be told.

Four

Hartley felt like a sailboat with a broken mast. He was home to stay. His time away had always been temporary. But his siblings hadn't known that, because he hadn't told them.

He'd left Charleston in order to be a hero. To fix things. And he'd succeeded in part. All the answers to all the questions had been found, thanks to his extended visit in Europe. Ironically, those answers were too dangerous and painful to explain to Jonathan and Mazie.

Had it all been worth it? Or had he ruined his relationships for nothing? On the day after his father's funeral, he found himself going in circles, or at the very least, becalmed.

What was he going to do with himself? If Jonathan wasn't keen or willing to have him back at Tarleton Shipping, Hartley was lost.

His enormous home adjacent to the world-class golf resort was not *him*. Never had been. At least that was one thing he could change. He spent the day taking care of small maintenance issues, and then called a Realtor and set up an appointment for the following morning.

He was going to sell his house. Immediately.

Maybe he would rent something in Fiona's neighborhood while he figured out his next step. She couldn't help him revamp his life—that was up to him—but sharing her bed would keep him sane. If she allowed it.

By the time four thirty rolled around, he was hot and sweaty but feeling pretty damn good about himself. He jumped in the shower, humming with more enthusiasm than expertise. With the prospect of seeing Fiona tonight, he had plenty of reasons to be upbeat.

His life had taken some unexpected turns, but he would get himself back on course. His siblings were all he had. Fiona was an alluring distraction from his painful family situation. Maybe it was wrong to pursue her. Maybe it was cowardly. Because if he used her and walked away again, he knew in his gut the damage would be permanent.

It would be smarter and kinder to stay away.

Even so, at ten till six, he pulled up in front of her charming home, grabbed the gifts he had brought and locked the car. He thought he saw the edge of a curtain twitch, but maybe not.

When he knocked, she answered almost immediately. "Hi, Hartley. You're right on time." She was wearing a daffodil-yellow sundress that bared her shoulders and emphasized her modest breasts.

He kissed her cheek. "These are for you."

She glanced at the label of his three-hundred-dollar bottle of wine and raised an eyebrow. "A little over-the-top for homemade spaghetti, don't you think? What if we save it for a special occasion? I made iced tea. And there's beer in the fridge…the kind you like."

He was ridiculously pleased that she remembered his preferences. A tiny detail, but a good sign…he hoped. "Sounds like a plan," he said. "Shall I put the flowers in water?" He'd brought her yellow and white roses, a summery bouquet that suited her home and her personality.

"Yes…thanks. You'll find a vase underneath the sink."

The conversation was stilted for two people who had seen each other naked. He wanted to say to hell with dinner and take her straight to the bedroom. "Did you have a good day painting?"

She whirled around, her eyes wide. "Why do you ask that?"

He cocked his head. "You told me you're starting a big new project."

"Oh." She flushed, her gaze skating away from his. "It was fine. Beginnings are always hard."

"Are you okay, Fee?" Now that he thought about it, she seemed pale…and nervous. She hadn't been this skittish the first afternoon they met. At that endless wedding rehearsal.

"Of course I'm okay." Her voice was muffled, because she had stuck her head and shoulders halfway into the fridge.

He glanced at the stove. "Do I need to turn off the heat? The spaghetti is boiling over."

"Oh, damn." She whirled around and rescued the pasta just in time.

He put his hands on her shoulders. "Fiona. Take a breath."

She shrugged out of his grip and put her hands to her cheeks. "Sorry," she muttered. "I'm a little nervous about having you here."

There it was again. That raw honesty. He winced. "I can go. If that's what you want."

They stared at each other across the small kitchen. "No," she said at last. "I don't want you to go."

Thank God. He reached for her hand and linked his fingers with hers. "I swear I'll be on my best behavior."

At last, she smiled at him. It was wobbly, but it was a smile. "I find that highly unlikely." She rested her head against his shoulder. "I'm glad you're here. Really, Hartley. I am."

His hands trembled with the urge to touch her. Coming here was wrong. He knew it. But he couldn't walk away from her a third time. Even if all they had was sexual chemistry, he wanted to erase his past transgressions. He needed to prove he could be trusted.

"Well, that makes two of us," he said heartily. "Now, tell me how I can help with dinner..."

Fiona was embarrassed and relieved at the same time. Hartley had taken her behavior in stride, it seemed. They consumed the simple meal and shared innocuous conversation without incident. Though she felt as if her secret was written on her face, she was clearly overreacting. There was no way for him to know the truth.

She had to get a grip.

"Let's go to the living room," she said when they had cleared the table and loaded the dishwasher side by side. "If you're going to bare your soul, I want a comfy spot."

Hartley followed her, chuckling. "I never promised that."

She curled up on a chair that was only big enough for one. No point in tempting fate. "You don't have to do this," she said.

Hartley shrugged. "You're the perfect listener. A disinterested bystander."

Fiona's heart sank. That wasn't what she wanted to hear at all. Hartley hadn't come to her tonight as a trusted confidante. She was about to be his therapist or his shrink. The distinction was painful.

She swallowed her hurt pride and reminded herself that Hartley wasn't her Prince Charming. Never would be. "Start at the beginning," she said.

Now he was the one to look uncomfortable. Maybe he hadn't rehearsed what he was going to say. "Well…"

"I'll refresh your memory," she offered helpfully. "After the wedding, I invited you here to my house. We both knew what was going to happen. It *happened* three times that night, and when I woke up, you were gone."

"Geez, Fiona. You make it sound so sleazy." He paced restlessly.

"How would you describe it?"

"I had airline reservations for the morning after the wedding. I was supposed to be on a flight out of Charleston at 7 a.m. You were a complication I never expected. I didn't know how to explain."

"Ah."

"It's true," he said.

She stared at him soberly. "Where were you going?"

"London first. I met with a private investigator who used to work for Interpol."

Fiona wrinkled her nose. "I think you've left out some pertinent details. Why would you need a PI?"

Hartley hunched his shoulders, his expression bleak. "Two days before the wedding, I received a blackmail note."

"Seriously?" Her skepticism was warranted, surely.

"The letter threatened to go public with a painful Tarleton family secret if I didn't give the blackmailer a million dollars."

"Hartley. This sounds like a spy novel."

"What you don't know is that my mother has been living in an inpatient mental health facility in Vermont since my siblings and I were preteens. A few people in Charleston know the truth, but not many."

"So you decided to do what?"

"My father's health was failing. Jonathan had been working his ass off at Tarleton Shipping, trying to keep the business afloat. My sister spent her adolescence without a mother. Our family has suffered more than our share of hard times. I didn't want the gossip."

"Everybody knows you can't pay off a blackmailer. Surely you didn't."

"Of course not. But I needed the money in hand just in case. I wasn't sure what else this mystery person might be willing to do. And I didn't know why we were targets."

"What did Jonathan say?"

Hartley's neck flushed. "I didn't tell him. I thought I could handle everything on my own. In retrospect, that wasn't too smart."

"I have to agree. Did you have a million dollars lying around in the bank?"

"Not exactly. I've told you about Jonathan. He's a play-by-the-book kind of guy. Never cut corners. Never bend the rules. If I had told him why I needed the money, he would have asked a ton of questions and then shut me down. I couldn't take that chance."

Her eyes widened. "What did you do, Hartley?"

He shrugged. "I took the money out of our account at work. It wasn't stealing. I own a quarter of the business."

"But you didn't tell Jonathan what was going on."

Hartley heard the criticism in her statement. "No. Like I said, he was under a lot of stress. I wanted to handle this grenade and defuse it. I never imagined that my brother and my father would jump to the absolute worst conclusion."

She shook her head slowly. "That's a lot to ask, Hartley. Blind faith?"

"They know me. Why would I take the money if not for

a damned good reason?" It still pissed him off that he'd immediately been painted the villain. Even worse, it *hurt*.

"Secrets backfire all the time." Fiona's expression was wry. "I can't say that I blame them, Hartley. You didn't trust them enough to believe you could all work together. Surely you see that was a mistake."

Maybe he did now. With the benefit of hindsight. "Well, I can't undo the damage, so it's a moot point."

"Mazie seems to have forgiven you."

"That's only because Dad and Jonathan kept her in the dark. If she knew the truth, she'd probably give me the cold shoulder, too."

"Let's circle back. So you took the money, and you went to London. What next?"

"Eventually, I tracked the letter back to a small village in Switzerland. The blackmailer was a relative on my mother's side. Her uncle, to be exact."

"Why would he want to hurt your family?"

"That's what I needed to know. As it turned out, he was only trying to get my attention. The letter he sent me served its purpose. It got me to Switzerland. Uncle Hans had fallen on hard times. An extended illness had wiped out his savings. He was in danger of losing his house and his dairy farm."

"Did you turn him over to the authorities?"

"How could I? He was a sick man in his late seventies. Frail. No family left. I felt I owed him something."

"So you *did* give him money."

"I paid off his house and put some cash in his bank account. Not much at all by our standards, but he was grateful and it made me feel better. I barely put a dent in the million. I ended up staying with Hans for a couple of months, filling in the blanks. He had a lot of stuff like family Bibles and heirlooms…things he wanted me to see. Items to pass on."

Fiona frowned. "There's something you're not telling me. Why did you come back to Charleston three months ago? And then leave again?"

"I came back to talk to my father and my siblings about why I had been gone. I had information they needed to know. But I chickened out at the last minute. Revealing everything I had learned in Europe was a potential bomb that threatened to blow up in my face. You were the only person I saw or spoke to. After that night in your bed, I went back to Switzerland to pack up my things."

"And then what?"

He shrugged, his eyes bleak with remembrance. "The uncle passed away. Rather suddenly. I found myself in the odd position of having to settle his meager estate."

"Even then, you didn't talk to your family?"

"I couldn't. The conversation was something that needed to be handled face-to-face. But with Hans gone, I began to ask myself if it wouldn't be better to keep everything I had learned to myself."

"What was this terrible secret, Hartley?"

His jaw was carved in stone, his profile no longer the affable man she had come to know. "The woman in that facility in Vermont—the woman who no longer recognizes us because she had a complete breakdown—the woman who is the only mother we've ever known—is *not* our mother."

Fiona couldn't sit still any longer. She jumped to her feet and went to him. Wrapping her arms around his waist, she rested her cheek against his chest, inhaling the pleasant laundry scent of his crisp cotton shirt. "That doesn't even make sense."

He eluded her embrace and continued to wear tracks in her rug. "Apparently, when my siblings and I were toddlers, my father took our mother to Switzerland to visit her family. She hadn't been back since they were married. They left us kids behind in Charleston with a trusted babysitter."

"Okay…" Her mind raced ahead, trying to guess the outcome. But nothing clicked into place.

Hartley's body language was agitated. "According to Hans, my mother committed suicide when they were in Switzerland. Apparently, she had been planning it for some time. There was a note. Hans still had it in the Bible. In her mind, it was better to do the deed where no one in Charleston would know. Maybe she thought my father would invent an accident. Hell, I don't know. She was a very sick woman."

"But I don't understand. Who is living in Vermont?"

He stopped his pacing and faced her. "My *aunt*. My mother's twin sister."

"Good Lord…" Her mind reeled.

"According to Hans, after my mother died, my aunt volunteered to marry my father, return to the States with him and step in as our mother."

"But surely someone would have noticed."

"I told you my father kept the family hidden away. Now all the security and the secrecy make a lot more sense. Maybe he was afraid. He knew keeping the business afloat was all up to him. Maybe he thought being a father was more than he could handle. Or maybe he was so distraught with grief, he wasn't rational."

"It's hard to believe…"

"Hans had pictures of the two women side by side. The sisters were identical. Any household staff here in South Carolina were vetted carefully. And maybe we kids were too young to know the difference."

"I don't know what to say."

"Pardon me for being flip, but being a foster kid doesn't sound so bad now, does it?"

She knew his angry sarcasm wasn't directed at her. "So you're telling me your father lost not one but two wives to mental illness?"

"Yes. And it also makes more sense, I suppose, that he sent the second Mrs. Tarleton so far away when she began to show signs that she might hurt herself or one of us. She wasn't the woman he loved. That tragedy—losing the love of his life—had happened long ago."

"The poor man."

"It's a lot to comprehend. Things were different back then. My father was much older than my mother. I don't think he would have ever considered raising us on his own. He would have been in shock when the suicide happened. Why did my aunt volunteer to take on a ready-made family? Perhaps her life in Switzerland was unhappy. We'll never know, because none of us can get through to her."

Fiona sank onto the sofa, her mind whirling with Hartley's story. Definitely a case of truth being stranger than fiction. "How long were you there after your uncle died?"

"About eight weeks. I sold the house and the farm and settled all the outstanding accounts. I had already shipped several boxes of memorabilia back to the States. I assumed Mazie would be interested one day, even if Jonathan wasn't. All I could think about was coming home, talking to my father, asking him a million questions. And then I got Lisette's phone call. Dad was gone. Now all his secrets are buried with him."

"You *have* to tell Mazie and Jonathan. You have to, Hartley."

He turned and stared at her, his face carefully blank. "I don't know that I do, Fee. I think the kinder thing is to leave well enough alone."

Five

Hartley felt empty…wrung out. Tonight—with Fiona—was the first chance he'd had to work through all of this. Hearing himself say the words aloud settled something in his gut.

He sat down beside her, his body limp with resignation and grief. Without overthinking it, he took her hand in his. Her nails were neatly trimmed but unpolished. Her fingers had calluses in certain spots. She might be small in stature, but she was tough in mind and body. Soft and sensual in bed. A force to be reckoned with when the sun came up.

"Think about it," he said, rubbing her palm with his thumb. "My siblings and I already knew our DNA carried the possibility of mental illness. But *two* sisters in the same family? Twins? That ups our chances of passing on whatever genetic anomaly took our mother from us. The medical community has made huge advances in treatment, but there are no guarantees."

"Isn't that all the more reason to warn them?"

He shook his head. "Mazie and J.B. have been battling infertility already. They may end up adopting. Lisette had a tragic miscarriage only weeks after their wedding and another one two months later. I assume they're trying again, but who knows? I can't be the one who makes those decisions for them. I won't play God. If I tell them what I know, it could change the entire course of their relationships."

"And what about you?" Fiona was milk pale. His story had upset her more than he had anticipated.

"I won't have children," he said bluntly. "All the secrets. All the lies? Families are supposed to love and support each other. I've paid the price for my father's failings. I won't put an innocent child through that."

Her eyes glistened with tears. "Don't you think your brother and sister and their spouses deserve that same clarity?"

He cursed beneath his breath, feeling put upon from all sides. If he'd been able to talk this over with his father, maybe he could have made the right decision. Now all he had were doubts and uncertainties.

"Don't push, Fee. I've been to hell and back. What do you want from me, damn it?"

She stood up slowly, her expression impossible to decipher. "So have I, Hartley. But life goes on. You've had a terrible day…a terrible year. Come to bed with me."

He jerked back, caught between exultation and the absolute certainty that it would be a mistake to sleep with her right now. "I don't need your pity," he muttered. "I'll go."

"Forget the past," she whispered. "Forget the wedding weekend when we met and the night we had after the reception. Forget the moments you spent in this house three months ago. Forget the funeral and the fact that your family is shutting you out. None of that matters right now. I want you, and I think you need me. Let's take tonight for ourselves."

Something about her urgent speech bothered him. Below the surface there was faulty reasoning in the words. But he was finally where he wanted to be, and she was offering him the chance for redemption.

He wasn't a saint—far from it. It was an invitation no mortal man could resist. Fiona. After all these lonely, terrible weeks.

"I came here for dinner, Fee. Nothing more. I swear."

Her smile was wistful. "I think we're both good at kidding ourselves. I can't explain this thing between us other than to call it elemental attraction. You said you wanted to have sex with me again. Maybe what we need is a chance to say goodbye and to have closure."

"Closure?" He mouthed the word with distaste, vaguely alarmed that she was giving him the brush-off in the midst of seducing him.

"I have two huge projects ahead of me," she said. "You have a lot of decisions to make about your life and your relationship with your family. If you're honest, being with me has been an escape for you, nothing more. Your life is one big train wreck right now. I forgive you. I'm not playing games."

He had a choice. He could stand here and argue with her about the future, or he could take what she was offering. In the end, emotional exhaustion won out. He needed her. He wanted her.

She was so beautiful it made his chest ache. Her pale, creamy skin was dotted with the occasional freckle. Those wide-set eyes were a combination of smoke and the sea. The wildness of her fire-kissed hair struck a marked contrast to the serenity she projected.

No woman had ever affected him so immediately, so

deeply. Something about her made him want to make love to her and bask in her peaceful spirit at the same time.

He felt cold inside. Fiona promised him warmth.

"Fine," he said. "Call it whatever you want. I won't say no to you. Not tonight."

She took his hand. He let her pull him to his feet. He was charmed and pleased that she was taking the initiative. In their earlier encounters he'd been the aggressor, the coaxer. Now, his sweet Fiona was staking a claim.

In her bedroom, they faced each other with odd hesitance. They had been virtual strangers before. Things were more *real* now.

"Should we check the doors?" he asked. "Set the alarm?"

She cocked her head. "The doors are locked. I don't have an alarm."

He frowned. "I don't like that. I'll buy you a new system. You need one."

"Hartley…"

"Hmm?"

"Shut up and kiss me. Before I change my mind."

"Yes, ma'am."

Three months. It had been three long months since he tasted her. The memories paled. She melted into his arms, stealing the breath from his lungs. Every part of him hard and taut with wanting. "I've missed you," he said huskily, nipping her lower lip with his teeth, sliding his tongue over hers. "So damn much. I used to lie in bed at night and calculate the distance between Switzerland and South Carolina."

Fiona wrapped her arms around his neck. "At least you knew where I was. All I had were a million questions. Actually, until you showed up on my doorstep three months ago, I didn't know if you were alive or dead. That sucked, Hartley. A lot."

"I'm sorry." His fingers fumbled with the zipper at the back of her bodice. "I'll make it up to you."

"See that you do."

Her teasing smile lit a fire in his gut. He sucked in a sharp breath when he realized that all she wore underneath the sundress was a pair of simple cotton undies. White. Unadorned.

No silk and lace confection could have been more titillating. He let the dress pool at her feet. "Damn, you're gorgeous."

"My boobs aren't very big."

The hint of uncertainty in her gaze brought tenderness into the mix. He kissed her nose. "They're perfect," he said. Carefully, he cupped her curves in his hands, teasing the pert tips with his thumbs.

Fiona's eyelids fluttered shut. She made a sound that was halfway between a purr and a moan. His erection flexed a centimeter more. "Look at me, darlin'. I want you to watch."

His big, tanned hands were dark against her white body. She sucked in a breath, but she obeyed. "I'll watch," she vowed. "It's my turn now." She unbuttoned his shirt and yanked it from his pants. "Get rid of this, big guy."

Sexual urgency told him to take and take until they were both satisfied. But tonight, he wanted to play another tune. Tonight, he wanted to convince her that he wasn't a bad guy. That there was more to him than the lover who ducked out in the night. Hartley Tarleton wanted to make a good impression.

Unfortunately, his patience for having her undress him was eroding rapidly. "I'll do the rest," he said, kicking off his shoes and bouncing on one foot and then the other as he removed his socks.

Fiona—naked but for panties and a smile—watched as he unfastened his belt and pants and shucked them to his ankles. When he lost his balance and nearly fell on his ass, she had the audacity to giggle.

"The man I remember was smoother than you," she said.

"Maybe I'm nervous," he deadpanned. She didn't have to know it wasn't a joke.

"Hurry up, Hartley. I'm getting cold."

It was still eighty degrees outside, even at this hour. And the AC system in Fiona's little house wasn't all that efficient. Perhaps she was nervous, too. She flipped back the simple yellow-and-blue quilt and climbed under the sheets. When she reclined on one elbow and crooked her finger, he was toast.

He was completely naked now. Unable to hide his need even if he had wanted to. Fee stared at his bobbing sex and licked her lips. The reaction didn't seem to be intentional. Her eyes had glazed over, and her chest was flushed.

When he made it under the covers and twined his body with hers in a skin-to-skin hug that fried his synapses, Fiona buried her face in his neck. "You are an impossible man, but Lord knows, you're magnificent. I love touching you." She ran her hands over his back and buttocks as if to make a point.

He found it hard to breathe. "Knock yourself out, Fee." She was warm and supple in his embrace. Her enthusiasm for his body made him glad he was a man. He would die happy if all he had to do was let her experiment with his various appendages.

She pulled back so she could kiss his collarbone. "I'm not even going to ask how many women you slept with while you were abroad."

"Not a one," he wheezed, trying not to come like an untested teenager.

When she zeroed in on the spot that was most eager for her attention, his vision went fuzzy. The sensation of her slender, warm fingers wrapped around his sex was indescribable.

She stroked him up and down, slowly enough to make his forehead damp and his muscles rigid. "I find that difficult to believe."

Was she torturing him on purpose? "I may have walked out on you, Fee, but I've never lied to you. After we met at the wedding, I've been too busy to look at other women."

Fiona wanted so badly to believe him, but she'd been a naive fool twice. Was he playing on her sympathies? Did it really matter tonight? He was here…in her bed. Very much alive. His masculinity was raw and erotic in the midst of her ultra feminine bed. The artist in her wanted to sketch him as he sprawled on his back and watched her.

The woman simply *wanted*. Period.

She reclined beside him and ran her hand from his throat to his hip. Warm golden skin was lightly dusted with just the right amount of hair. He was like a beautiful god, at the height of his physical perfection.

At the moment, her stomach was cooperating, thank heavens. Her earlier fears seemed ludicrous. Of course she wasn't pregnant. A woman would know something like that, right? She couldn't possibly be thirteen weeks along and have survived in blissful ignorance all this time.

Still, the possibility filled her with both anxiety and amazement. A child? A baby with Hartley's big brown eyes? An infant who would possess the best and worst of both of them?

Tremors came to life deep inside her body and spread

outward. She struggled with waves of fear and exultation and sexual arousal. How could she want this man so damn much when he had hurt her twice and had said recently—with perfect clarity—that he was *never* going to have children?

"Do you have a condom?" she asked, feeling her face heat. Hopefully, he would attribute her red-faced mortification to maidenly sexual frenzy. Until she knew for sure about the baby, she wouldn't take chances.

His gaze narrowed. A feral masculine smile accompanied his terse nod. "One second, darlin'." He leaned over the edge of the bed, giving her a stunning view of his tight butt. "Got it," he said triumphantly, brandishing his wallet.

While he was busy tossing the packet on the bedside table, Fiona raked his ass with her fingernails. The soft fuzz was golden, lighter than the hair on his head, as if he might have sunbathed in the nude while he was in Europe.

Thinking of Hartley naked on a beach somewhere made her dizzy. "I'm glad you came back," she whispered. "I missed you, Hartley."

At her words, his expression softened. "And I missed you, sweet Fiona." He moved between her legs and readied himself. "I don't even care if this is pity sex. I've been dreaming about you in my bed for weeks."

When he pushed steadily, filling her, driving himself home until she winced, it was as if everything in her world righted itself for a moment. And then she understood why. This was their pattern, their sexual MO. One frantic, unable-to-wait-a-second-longer coupling followed by a series of languid, self-indulgent second acts.

Hartley was a big man. Everywhere. Her body accepted his eagerly, straining to make the connection last. His urgency was flattering, his attention to detail admirable. Even as he took his own pleasure, he remembered every erogenous zone he had discovered during their earlier encounters.

A nip at her earlobe. A gentle grinding of his pelvis against hers, putting pressure where she needed it to climb even higher. Her breath caught in her throat. A wave of emotion staggered her, making her weak and weepy. He was so dear. So perfect for her. But he *wasn't* hers, and now he never would be. She had to remember that. Had to keep her heart out of this. Sex only.

She'd always heard people say that pregnant women were insatiable when it came to sex. Was that why she was already thinking about round two? Or was this wild urgency all for Hartley and no other reason?

He went still, his body rigid and trembling. "Fee? Are you with me?"

Her mental distraction hadn't gone unnoticed. "I'm here," she whispered. "Don't stop."

He took her at her word. Reaching between their linked bodies, he caressed the aching center of her need and sent her over the edge. The orgasm was off the charts. Incredible. Mildly astonishing.

The ripples went on and on.

Hartley chuckled hoarsely, wheezing as he attempted to speak while balanced on a sexual precipice. "You make a man feel damn good, Fiona. I'd like to spend the whole night reclaiming lost time. We've wasted months."

She smiled lazily, in an expansive, forgiving mood now that he had satiated her considerable needs for the moment. "*We?* Don't blame this one on me, Mr. Tarleton. I've been right here all along. You're the one who went missing."

His smile sent her buzzing again. "You can punish me later."

He withdrew almost completely and then went faster. Groaning, he thrust rapidly until he hit the peak, shuddering and panting in her embrace until he slumped on top of her, his body warm and damp.

She wrapped her arms around him, feeling his heart pound against her breast. As wrung out as he was, she could almost believe he'd been celibate since the last time they were together.

That was dangerous thinking. Such an idea made their brief dalliance more than it was. Why would a man avoid sex for the sake of two isolated one-night stands?

Believing in rainbows, pots of gold, unicorns and happily-ever-afters wasn't who Fiona was anymore. Over the course of her adolescence, she had stomped on her rose-colored glasses. She now viewed the world as it was. Broken. Hurtful. Uncaring.

Maybe that was harsh. She had wonderful friends. But the belief that a man and a woman could form a lasting bond on the basis of a few nights of hot sexual insanity was a fiction she couldn't embrace. She wouldn't.

Idly, she stroked the back of his head, feeling the silky hair slide between her fingers. The other Tarleton twin was a fine figure of a man, but she preferred Hartley's rough-around-the-edges masculinity. He could be brash and unrepentant and frustratingly stubborn, but he tugged at her heartstrings as no other man ever had.

When he could breathe again, he lifted his head. "Damn, woman. You're killing me." He kissed her slow and deep, his tongue mating with hers. "I don't want closure, Fee. I want you."

He punctuated his declaration with a string of kisses down the side of her neck, to her throat, to her breasts. Licking them. Nibbling. Forcing her to acknowledge his mastery of her body.

How could he do it to her so quickly? She was on the verge of climax again. Panic gripped her in a choke hold.

This had to stop. Her mornings were iffy now. She and Hartley couldn't be wrapped in each other's arms when the sun came up. "You should go," she said, blurting out the words with no finesse at all. "It's late." *I can't take the risk you'll stay until morning, see me barf and guess the truth.*

Six

Hartley jerked, stunned. He would have been less shocked if she had slapped his face. He'd been within an inch of giving his sweet Fee a second orgasm when she slammed some kind of door between them.

He gaped. "Are you serious?" Her raspberry nipples were puckered, begging for his attention.

For some reason, Fiona's gaze slid away. "I have to work early in the morning." She slipped out of bed and tugged the coverlet from the foot of the mattress, wrapping it around herself toga-style. "Thank you for telling me why you were gone so long. I hope you and your brother work things out between you."

He staggered to his feet, his brain racing to understand what had just happened. "Are you angry with me?" He frowned, knowing she had every right to evict him, and yet hurt that she could seem so unaffected by what for him had been cataclysmic.

As he reached for his clothes and reluctantly dressed, Fiona shook her head slowly. Smoky blue eyes stared at him. "Of course not. You did what you had to do."

"The past is the past," he muttered. "I'm more interested in what comes next. I'm not done with you, Fee."

Her eyes flashed. "It's not up to you, now is it? I didn't put my life on hold while you were gone. You can't drop back in and expect everything to be the way you want it."

Was this some kind of test? Was he supposed to work for absolution?

Screw that. He owed her an apology, and he had given it, sincerely and wholeheartedly. But he wouldn't crawl. First Jonathan and now Fiona. Was there no one who believed in him?

When he was fully clad, he shot her an angry glare. "I get it," he said. "You don't want to sleep with me anymore. Casual sex isn't your thing, is that it? No worries. Now that I'm home for good, I'm sure there are plenty of available women in Charleston. Good night, Fiona. I'll let myself out."

Even then he thought she might relent. She certainly *seemed* miserable. But she didn't say a word as he stormed out. He heard the *snick* of the dead bolt on the front door after it closed behind him. By the time he reached the sidewalk and headed for his car, the lights inside the house had been extinguished. He stood in the middle of the street... all alone.

In a year and a month and a week that had sucked big time, this was perhaps his lowest point. The investigation was over. Fiona no longer wanted him around. He had reconciled with his family...barely. But there was apparently no longer a spot for him at Tarleton Shipping. That ship had sailed.

He couldn't even laugh at his own stupid joke. Nor

could he face returning to the house that wasn't a home, the house he was going to sell sooner than later.

Instead, he drove aimlessly around Fiona's neighborhood. All her fellow Charlestonians were tucked in for the evening. No teenagers on skateboards. No sweethearts kissing good-night on street corners. Just peace and silence and the sense of a community at rest.

And then he spotted it. A small for-sale sign in front of a three-story brick monstrosity. The house was older than its neighbors and in bad need of repair.

Hartley pulled out his phone and looked up the specs on the Realtor's website. From the pictures, it was no wonder the house had been on the market over a hundred days. It probably had dry rot. Black mold. Maybe even termite infestation.

His spirits lifted. It was exactly the kind of project a man needed when he was looking for an anchor. And it had the added advantage of being under his lover's nose.

If he had genuinely thought Fiona was not interested in a sexual relationship with him, he would have walked away. After all, they had almost nothing in common beyond a visceral attraction. But *she* was the one who invited *him* to her bed tonight. Because the sex was great. Right? Up until that very last part, she had been a willing and eager participant.

It was a puzzle. One he was happy to study until he found the answers. For now, he would give her some space.

Unfortunately, not even a real estate agent hungry for a sale would appreciate a call after eleven at night. Hartley would have to be patient until morning. He decided to make a lowball cash offer, and then while he tried to woo his prickly artist, he would have a project to keep him busy.

Having a plan brought a measure of resolve. He hated

uncertainty…always had. Make a choice, even if it's the wrong one. That's how he operated.

It was late. He knew he needed to go home. But there was one more sore spot he needed to explore.

From Fiona's house, the drive to Tarleton headquarters took no time at all. The building was as familiar to him as his childhood bedroom. He parked right in front. Nothing to hide. Inside, there would be a night watchman somewhere.

At the main entrance, he entered a six-digit code in the electronic keypad and swiped his ID card. To his surprise, the door opened easily. Had Jonathan forgotten to revoke his credentials? Or had he believed Hartley would eventually come home? Either way, it soothed some of Hartley's rough-edged discontent to know he was able to walk inside.

His desk and his office were exactly as he had left them. For the first time, he began to understand how difficult his absence must have been for Jonathan. The questions. The work piling up.

A sound in the outer office had him whirling on his heel. Jonathan leaned against the wall, his expression inscrutable. Clearly, he had gone home after work and come back, because he was wearing old jeans and a T-shirt that had seen better days.

Hartley felt his neck heat. "I was just looking around. I wasn't here to steal the silver."

Jonathan shrugged. "I'm not accusing you of anything."

"Not at the moment." Hartley grimaced. Being at odds with his twin was a physical pain. He cleared his throat. "I'll go. Sorry to have bothered you."

Jonathan held up a hand. "You put the money back yesterday." It was neither a simple statement nor a question, but maybe a blend of both.

"I did, yes."

"Why?"

"I was *always* going to put it back. But neither you nor Dad cared to ask for an explanation. You just assumed the worst."

His brother frowned. "Don't turn this on me. *You* were the one who made off with a million bucks as if it were nothing more than Monopoly money."

"I had my reasons."

"Okay." Jonathan folded his arms across his chest. "Let's hear them. I've got all night."

It was a challenge. Plain and simple. A showdown. But Hartley was going to have to swallow his pride and walk away. He'd already told the story once.

No matter how much he wanted to erase the gaping void between him and his brother, he couldn't dump what he knew on Jonathan. Not without thinking it through.

Maybe Fiona was right. Maybe he owed his siblings the truth. But at what cost? They would both be hurt, as Hartley had been. Unsettled. Dismayed. And without their father to provide answers, this information Hartley had uncovered served no useful purpose.

Hartley cleared his throat. "It's late. The tale will keep for now. Good night, Jonathan."

When he went to slip past the president and CEO of Tarleton Shipping, his brother put a hand on his shoulder. For a moment, they both breathed the same air. Jonathan squeezed briefly, then stepped aside. "I believe you had your reasons. They may not have been good reasons. I'd still like to hear them."

Jonathan was reaching out. Making the first move. Being the bigger man.

Hartley was frozen with indecision. The irony of the situation would have been humorous if the stakes hadn't been so high. Here he was, a guy who believed in always stepping out, sure the path would appear from within the fog.

Now, when it mattered the most, he couldn't do it. The truth had hurt Hartley badly. Why inflict that pain on the man who shared his blood? The brother he loved.

He swallowed hard. "My reasons don't exist anymore. That's why I put the money back. I'm sorry I left you hanging, though. You've carried the brunt of Father's illness and the way that complicated the business. I'm sorry, Jonathan. I really am."

His brother's smile was wry but genuine. "You'd do the same thing again, though. Am I right?"

Hartley considered the question. Ignorance might be bliss, but not for him. He'd done what he had to do to protect his family. Maybe his ultimate task was to be the keeper of the secrets.

"Yes," he muttered. "I'd do it again. Why didn't you tell Mazie about the money?"

Jonathan raked a hand through his short hair, for the first time, betraying exhaustion. He looked beaten. Defeated. "Mazie adores you. I didn't know where you were or why you were gone. The missing money only made it worse. I figured you deserved whatever happened to you, but Mazie's big heart would have been shattered."

"Thank you," Hartley said.

"Don't thank me. I did it for her."

The snap in Jonathan's voice was both startling and depressing. Hartley's twin might have made an overture a few moments ago, but he was still very angry.

Nothing was going to be gained by rehashing old arguments. The untold truth lay between them, terrible and dangerous. It had unmanned Hartley, left him despairing and aching with hurt. Although it had been cathartic to unburden himself to Fiona, he hadn't even let her hear the worst of it. Unless Hartley was willing to tell Jonathan what had transpired in Europe, there was nothing left to say.

"I'll let myself out," he said dully. "Good night."

The morning after Hartley made love to her, Fiona knew without a doubt that she had made the right choice in sending him home. She awoke violently sick, unable to hold down either tea or toast until almost noon. Then, it was all she could do to drag herself to the studio.

She needed to buy a pregnancy test. That was how these situations worked. The thought of getting in a car and driving somewhere was more than she could manage.

So she painted. In short bursts of energy. Twenty minutes here. Thirty minutes here. Astonishingly, the project began to take shape. By late afternoon, she actually felt hungry.

She was cleaning brushes and tidying her work space when her doorbell rang. *Hartley.* Was she irritated by his persistence or flattered that he was back again?

When she opened the door with a neutral smile, the smile faded. Her caller wasn't Hartley. Instead, Mazie Tarleton Vaughan stood on the porch. "May I come in?" she asked, not bothering with social niceties like hellos or explanations.

"Umm…" Fiona felt awkwardly self-conscious, as if Mazie could see the possible pregnancy on her face.

The other woman vibrated with impatience. "I won't stay long."

There was nothing more to say after that, short of being unforgivably rude. "Of course…" Fiona stepped back, allowing her unexpected visitor to enter.

Hartley's sister surveyed the small house, at least the parts she could see from the foyer. "This is nice," she said. "It suits you."

"Thank you, I—"

Mazie interrupted. "We can do the get-to-know-you thing another day, but I'm here to talk about Hartley. Is he okay?"

"What do you mean?" Fiona winced inwardly. She had never been good at prevarication.

"Don't play dumb…please. My own brother has kept me in the dark. I don't need it from you, too. Hartley has a thing for you. Obviously. Which means he must have told you why he left. Right?"

Suddenly, Fiona could see beneath Mazie's imperious demand to the scared sister underneath. "Why don't we sit down?" She steered her guest toward the comfortable sofa and perched on the armchair that had seen better days. "I do know some of it," she said carefully. "But only very recently did he tell me anything. I was as much in the dark as you were. Yes, he's fine. A little lost maybe… after being gone so long."

"He needs to be back at Tarleton Shipping. He belongs there."

"I'm not sure he feels welcome."

Mazie's eyes widened. "What do you mean?"

"Your brothers have some issues to work out. According to Hartley, Jonathan is angry. And not inclined to welcome the prodigal with open arms."

Mazie burst into tears.

Well, crap. Fiona was not equipped to deal with all this family drama. It was why she lived alone. And worked alone. Still, she was not hard-hearted enough to ignore the other woman's distress.

She sat down beside Hartley's sister and handed her a tissue. "It will work itself out. Give them time."

Mazie wiped her eyes and sniffed. "You clearly don't

know my brothers very well. They are both stubborn as sin."

"Well, based on the one I *do* know, I have to agree."

Tears continued to roll down Mazie's cheeks. Somehow, Hartley's sister was as beautiful as ever. Hardly seemed fair. When Fiona cried, her face turned into a blotchy mess.

Mazie sniffed and scrubbed her cheeks with her hands. "Don't mind me. I've been on fertility drugs, and I'm a mess."

"That must be stressful," Fiona said quietly, keenly aware that her own body was out of her control at the moment. "Is there anything I can do for you? A cup of hot tea, maybe? I'm a bit of a connoisseur. Tea always helps me when it's that time of the month, so I keep plenty of bags on hand. I can offer you a wide range of choices."

Hartley's sister sat up straight, an arrested look on her face. She grabbed up her purse, took out her phone and opened a calendar app. "Oh, wow."

"What is it? What's wrong?"

"I've been so upset with the funeral and everything that I haven't paid attention."

"Paid attention to what?"

Mazie's expression was equal parts wonderment and bewilderment. "I missed my period, Fiona. I'm six days late."

Seven

Fiona smiled. "That's good, right?"

Her visitor was pale, her chin wobbly. "We've been disappointed so many times. I can't tell J.B. Not yet." She grabbed Fiona's arm. "Will you do me a favor?"

"Well, I—"

"Nothing big. Everybody in this city knows my family. If I stop in somewhere and buy a pregnancy test, word will get back to my husband before I return home. I don't want to get his hopes up until I know for sure."

Fiona felt like she was in the middle of a bad joke. "You want me to buy you a pregnancy test?"

Mazie's smile was sunny and cajoling, her tears forgotten. "Please. I'll drive. All you have to do is run inside the store and get it for me. Easy peasy."

"How can I say no?" Fiona wanted to laugh, but she didn't dare. "Let me change clothes. I'm speedy. Won't take long."

In her bedroom, she stripped off her jeans and T-shirt

and stared at herself in the mirror. At this particular moment, she didn't *feel* pregnant. Her tummy was flat, her body unchanged. Maybe she had the flu. The summer flu that only happened in the mornings. *Oh, Lordy...*

Mazie was snooping unashamedly when Fiona returned to the living room. She held out a small framed check for fifty dollars. "What's this?"

Fiona dropped her purse on a chair. "It's the first money I ever made as a professional artist. I was dead broke, and I needed so badly to cash it and pay my rent. But I decided to believe in my future and to believe there would be other checks coming. So far, I haven't had to break the glass."

Mazie nodded, returning the small frame to its spot on a bookshelf. "I know what you mean. Not the money part. My family has been fortunate in that way. But when I realized I didn't want to follow the boys into the family business, it was a struggle to decide what I was interested in—and then to make it happen. Now I sell jewelry in the historic district. I love my shop, and I do very well. It makes you proud, doesn't it? Women are always being underestimated. Drives me nuts."

Fiona grinned. Mazie was a firecracker. Fiona liked her. A lot. And although she had never had a real sister, Hartley's sibling was exactly the kind of female Fiona had envisioned when she wished for one.

Mazie handed over two twenties. "I don't know how much they'll cost at a convenience store. I've written down the brand I'd like to have. If you have to pick a second choice, I'll take what I can get."

"Then let's go."

Mazie insisted on driving. Her car was a current-year model that smelled of leather and a whiff of expensive perfume. Fiona settled into the passenger seat with a sigh of appreciation. Her own car was not a clunker, but as cute as it was, the little VW Bug was no match for high-end automotive luxury.

Mazie's driving was the real shock. She tended to talk with her hands, and though she didn't commit any traffic violations, her style was a little too kamikaze for Fiona's comfort.

They pulled up with a screech in front of a gas station mini-mart. Mazie gripped the wheel, her gaze anxious. "Hurry, please. I don't want to take any chances."

Inside the small shop, Fiona found the appropriate aisle quickly. Choices were limited, but the store did have the brand Mazie had requested. Instead of a duo, Fiona grabbed up four, then rounded the corner and plopped them down on the counter in sets of two. "I'll pay for these separately," she said, feeling the heat roll from her chest to her throat to her face.

It was ridiculous to be embarrassed, but this was her first pee-on-a-stick experience. The young store clerk didn't bat an eye. He rang up the two sales, dispensed change and Fiona's credit card slip, and went back to his phone.

Fiona had made a point of bringing a large leather tote instead of the smaller wristlet she often carried. Both women had valid reasons for keeping this little shopping excursion under the radar.

Fiona sauntered back outside as if she bought quads of pregnancy tests every day of the week. She opened the car door, slid into her seat and handed Mazie the white paper bag. "All set," she said breezily.

Mazie chewed her lip. "May I do this at your house?"

Weird. "Why?"

"I told you. I don't want to get J.B.'s hopes up. He hovers. And then it kills him when I'm sad."

"So how many times have you done this?"

"Not as many as you think. Twice maybe. Mostly it's just that my period starts, and then we know we have to wait another month. After this, I'll get out of your way, I swear."

"You're not in my way," Fiona muttered. Though she had to admit the entire scenario was freaking her out. What if Hartley showed up while Mazie was around?

Back at the house, Fiona showed Mazie the tiny guest bath in the hallway. Once Mazie was tucked away, Fiona darted into her studio bathroom and locked the door. Good sense dictated waiting until her guest had departed, but she couldn't.

Her fingers trembled as she opened the box and read the directions. This was a bad sitcom…right? The hero's sister in one bathroom. His lover in another. Both women possibly pregnant.

Fiona did what had to be done and waited. The message on the stick was swift and unequivocal. Positive. *Pregnant*.

She stared at it blankly. One part of her brain acknowledged she was in shock. The other more emotional compartment wanted to scream it from the housetop. She was having Hartley's baby!

Later tonight there would be time for the second test. To double-check. It wasn't really necessary, was it? Her body had already communicated the truth in rare form.

A sound from the other part of the house drew her back to the present. Though she was shaky and weak, she concentrated fiercely. *Wrap the evidence in tissues. Tuck it away. Stash the incriminating boxes in a back corner of the cabinet.*

Then she washed her hands, splashed water on her face and went in search of Mazie.

Hartley's sister was still in the bathroom when Fiona passed by. But moments later, she came out and joined

Fiona in the living room. Instead of being seated, she stood in the middle of the rug, her expression shell-shocked. "I did them both," she whispered. "They were positive."

Hartley had tried to give Fiona her space, really he had. But all day, missing her had been like a throbbing tooth-ache. He still couldn't believe she had tossed him out of her bed.

He'd kept busy. The fixer-upper a few streets over from Fiona's charming bungalow would be his in less than two weeks—a cash sale. His own place out at the golf course already had several offers on the table. Hartley was leaving the minutiae up to the real estate agent. As long as he didn't lose money on the deal, he'd be satisfied.

The one detail he hadn't worked out was where he would live in the meantime. Even optimistically, it would take a couple of months to make his new three-story brick home moderately habitable.

Several of the potential buyers for the golf course house wanted to take possession ASAP. Hartley could go to a hotel, of course. For that matter, J.B. and Mazie would take him in. Still, they were relative newlyweds, even now. Besides, Hartley didn't want to make things awkward between Mazie and Jonathan.

Which left one obvious solution. Fiona.

He pulled up in front of her house and frowned. What was his sister doing here?

Indignation bubbled in his chest. Fiona wouldn't share secrets that weren't hers...would she? He thought he knew her that well, but then again, he hadn't bargained on being booted out of the stubborn woman's warm, comfy bed in the dead of night, so what did he know?

He banged on the door with his fist, unable to decide if he was suspicious or angry, or both. "Fiona! Let me in." When he reached for the knob, it turned easily. He opened the door and found two women staring at him, looking guilty as hell.

Both of them resembled kids with their hands caught in the cookie jar. "What's going on?" he asked.

Mazie and Fiona blushed. His sister looked happy. Fiona's expression was less easily defined. She wasn't smiling at him, and she didn't seem particularly glad to see him.

Mazie broke the silence. "Nothing's going on, silly. I dropped by because I wanted to get to know your girlfriend."

"I'm not his girlfriend," Fiona said quickly. "We're friends. That's all."

Hartley's sister waved a hand. "Friend. Girlfriend. Who cares about labels these days?"

Fiona went on the offensive, her gaze cool. "The question is, Hartley, why are *you* here? It's hard to have closure when you keep turning up like a bad penny. You walked right into my house."

Mazie snickered, her hand over her mouth.

Hartley closed the door and leaned against it. "You were the one wanting closure, Fiona, not me. Do you really want to discuss this in front of my gossipy sister?"

"Hey," Mazie cried. "That's not nice."

Fiona aligned herself with the fairer sex. "Mazie and I were sharing a moment. You're intruding."

Mazie flung herself at Hartley, wrapping her arms around his neck and threatening to strangle him. "No, he's not. I'm so *glad* you're home."

Her tight hug and the kiss on his cheek caught something in his chest and made his eyes damp. "I love you, too, sis," he said gruffly.

His eyes met Fiona's over Mazie's head. "What if I take the two of you to dinner? We can call J.B. and have him meet us at the restaurant. It'll be fun."

Inexplicably, his sister blushed again and looked at Fiona as if for help. "You're sweet to offer, Hartley, but I'll take a rain check. J.B. and I have plans tonight."

Hartley shrugged. "Fair enough. I'd still like to show you something before you leave. We can all three pile into my car. Won't take us long. Twenty minutes, tops."

"So mysterious," Fiona said.

He eluded his sister and curled an arm around Fiona's waist. Her hair smelled like raspberries. He loved raspberries. "I need your artistic expertise." He kissed her nose. She leaned into him. Progress...

Mazie glanced at her watch. "I'm in. But we need to hurry."

As the women climbed into his car, Fiona in the front, Mazie in the back, Hartley realized he was nervous. These two people were important in his life. Their opinions mattered.

When he pulled up in front of the huge dilapidated brick structure with the overgrown yard, he smiled inwardly. Attached to the small for-sale sign was another placard that said Sold. He'd done a lot in twenty-four hours. Moving ahead. Writing off the past.

Mazie leaned over the front seat. "What is this place, Hartley?"

Fiona stared through the windshield, her expression pensive.

He shrugged, gripping the steering wheel. "I bought it today. I'm going to fix it up and live here temporarily. Then sell it later for twice the price if I'm lucky."

"What do you know about renovating an old house?" His sister's concern was valid.

"Not much more than I've seen on TV," he admitted. "But I can learn. I have no illusions about doing all the work myself."

Fiona chewed her lip. "It looks like a wreck. Have you even been inside?"

She nailed him on that one. Perhaps she had already come to recognize his impulsive nature. "I saw lots of pictures," he said. "And I bought it for a rock-bottom price. It's a good investment."

Mazie pinched his arm. "And it's in Fiona's neighborhood…right?"

Fee frowned. "But you have a house. On a golf course somewhere. You told me about it."

"I listed it this morning. Had two offers before lunch and more this afternoon. I'll likely make a handy profit."

Mazie nodded. "He never really liked that house anyway. It served a purpose at the time." She patted his shoulder. "I think it's wonderful, Hartley. I have several friends in the construction business. I'm sure I can round up some experts here and there."

He squeezed his sister's fingers briefly, but his gaze held Fiona's, daring her to look away. "I was hoping Fee would be willing to help me from an artistic perspective. So I can flip it successfully."

Fiona stared at him, her chest rising and falling rapidly as if she were out of breath. "Work is really busy for me right now."

He brushed the back of his hand across her soft cheek, gazing at her with determination and sexual intent. "In the evenings, then. I'll feed you, and I'll pay you for your time."

Mazie fell back in her seat, beaming. "Of course she'll help you. Right, Fiona?"

Fiona felt pressured by the sibling duo. These two thought they could throw money at a problem and everything would break their way. They hadn't a clue what it was like to be hungry or alone or to lack confidence.

Instead of answering directly, she put a hand on the door. "Can we peek in the windows?"

Hartley's face lightened, his enthusiasm contagious. "Of course. Once the paperwork is further along, I'll get the real estate agent to give us a tour."

"Is it even safe?" she asked.

"I suppose we'll find out."

The three of them walked up the path, dodging plants that tried to grab their hair and avoiding broken glass where kids had tossed beer bottles while trespassing. Mazie wrinkled her nose. "How long has this place been empty?"

Fiona surveyed the three-story facade. "I pass by this way now and again. I seem to remember the owner dying a year or more ago. Maybe it's taken this long for the heirs to decide to sell it."

"I can't imagine they would want to keep it." Mazie frowned. "This place is kind of a dump, Hartley. I was imagining a diamond in the rough, not a total disaster."

He tried the front door, but of course it was locked. "The house has good bones. I have faith in her." He took Fiona's wrist and drew her closer. "Peek in this window here. Tell me what you see."

Even from the vantage point of a filthy pane of glass, Fiona was charmed. The house looked like a museum inside, a museum with chunks of ceiling missing and peeling wallpaper, but a museum nevertheless. The ornate cornices and hardwood floors hearkened back to an earlier time. If the double winding staircase at the back of the hallway was intact, Hartley might indeed have found a hidden gem.

"It's got potential," she said grudgingly. What she wanted to say was *Why are you buying a house near me?* It didn't make sense. Hartley was a man without a country, a displaced person. He had come back to his old life, but the world had moved on without him. So he was inventing a spot for himself.

If the only reason he was here with her was because he had no place else to go, she wasn't interested. She'd had a lifetime of not belonging. Now, her small house and her burgeoning career were all hers.

It wasn't that she didn't have room in her life for Hartley. The truth was, if and when she finally fell in love and got married, she wanted a relationship where her husband thought she hung the moon.

Hartley liked having sex with her. She was a handy distraction from his family woes. But she deserved more than that. If she really was pregnant, she *wanted* this baby. More than anything. Yet Hartley had said unequivocally that he wasn't interested in being a father.

If she told him and he tried to *do the right thing*, she couldn't bear it. He'd left her twice. Even if he tried to change his tune, how could she ever trust him or his motives?

Mazie squawked when she glanced at her watch. "Oh, heck. I've got to run. Take me back to my car, Hartley. I still have to go by the shop before I head home. J.B. will shoot me if I'm late."

"Since when is your husband a clock puncher?"

"We've both been working too much lately. We made a pact to have dinner together every night."

In the car on the way back, Fiona glanced over her shoulder. She and Mazie exchanged glances. Hartley's sister had shining eyes and a palpable air of excitement. This meal with J.B. tonight would be momentous.

As soon as Hartley pulled up at the curb, Mazie was out of the car and on her way. Hartley stared after her. "She sure was in a good mood."

Fiona nodded. "Of course she is. She has a husband who adores her. It's a gorgeous day. And her long-lost brother is finally home."

"I wasn't lost," Hartley muttered. "I simply chose to fly under the radar for a few months."

"Your silence hurt them," Fiona said. "If they stumble onto the other secrets you're keeping, it will be even worse this time. Surely you see they need to know what you found out in Switzerland."

Hartley glared at her. "You're not going to give up on this, are you? So what about you, Fiona? Shouldn't you be digging up all your family secrets, sordid or otherwise?"

She gasped, stunned by the attack. "Excuse me," she said carefully. "I'm going in the house now."

He reached for her arm. "Stop. Wait. Dammit, I'm sorry, Fee. I have a temper. You're only trying to help. I get that."

She trembled, close to tears. This was a bad time to fall apart. "Let's get something straight, Hartley. If you're telling the truth when you say you want to be with me, then I need to believe it. So far in our relationship, I've been either a convenient booty call or a buffer for your messed-up family dynamics. Since I'm not interested in either of those roles, I suggest you get your life in order before you come here again."

Eight

Mazie opened the front door of the gorgeous row house that was now *hers*, as well as her husband's, and slipped inside. She wanted to shower and change before running into J.B. Tonight was special.

Upstairs in her decadent walk-in closet, she perused her choices. After their wedding, J.B. had taken one of the smaller bedrooms and converted it for his bride. Now she had a tiny sitting area and plenty of space for her wardrobe.

He spoiled her.

She loved it.

Even now, it was hard to believe she was actually *married* to the handsome hunk who had been her teenage crush. J.B. had been a bit of a rascal in his youth. He'd broken Mazie's heart badly on one particular, memorable occasion. After years of keeping a careful distance from each other here in Charleston, they had reconnected when her little jewelry shop ended up right in the middle of one of J.B.'s big real estate projects.

One thing led to another, and now she was happily married to a reformed bad boy. She smirked as she grabbed a quick shower and changed into black pants and a royal blue silk top. She and J.B. worked hard. This commitment to having dinner together every night had not always been easy, but it was an intimate time they had both come to cherish.

She was ridiculously nervous. Mostly because she hadn't decided whether or not to bring J.B. in on her secret yet. It was too early to get excited. She knew that. She needed an appointment with her ob-gyn before she got her hopes up. No point in telling him when she wasn't absolutely sure.

Over-the-counter pregnancy tests weren't completely reliable.

In the dining room, she found J.B. scrolling through email on his phone while he waited for her. Immediately, he put the phone aside and drew her in for a long, slow kiss. "How's my best girl?" he drawled when she was flushed and breathless. The man was an Olympic-level kisser. World class.

"I'm great," she said. *Maybe really great.*

J.B.'s fiftysomething housekeeper was a Southern-style cook who had learned to tilt her wonderful recipes toward healthier options without sacrificing taste. Mazie might have gained five pounds since the wedding, but it was worth every ounce.

The first course was Caesar salad with freshly made dressing and shaved Parmesan. "I came by the shop this afternoon between site visits," J.B. said, "but you were gone."

"I went to see Hartley's girlfriend."

One masculine eyebrow lifted. "Mazie. I warned you about matchmaking. Hartley's a big boy. He can make his own decisions."

She stabbed a piece of lettuce. "He hasn't done so well this past year," she muttered. "I can't stand to see the way he and Jonathan are with each other. It's *wrong*," she said, her eyes unexpectedly filling with tears. "They're brothers. Twins, for God's sake. Best friends."

J.B. reached across the table and took her hand. "They'll work through it eventually. Hartley's home now. That's a start."

"Can't you talk to them? Either? Both? Jonathan is being all *scowly* and buttoned-up and Hartley is…well, I don't know. He's acting weird. Did you know he bought a house today?"

J.B. blinked. "He has a house."

"Not anymore. He listed it this morning. Already has offers."

"So where is this *new* house?"

"Three blocks away from Fiona."

"Ah. The plot thickens."

"I dropped by to talk to her late this afternoon, and Hartley showed up, insisting that we look at his new toy. It's a huge run-down place. Going to need tons of work."

"Sounds expensive."

She sat back and frowned. "Are you taking any of this seriously?"

J.B. grinned. "I take *you* seriously. They're grown men, sweetheart. Give them time."

"Did Jonathan ever tell you why Hartley left? Or what made Jonathan so angry he will hardly speak Hartley's name?"

"He didn't, my love. Whatever this is feels like a betrayal so deep Jonathan can't get past it."

Mazie chewed her lip. It didn't take a psychologist to see that she was dwelling on this Hartley/Jonathan rift to put off telling J.B. what she suspected was true. It was so scary.

"Fiona knows."

Jonathan frowned. "Are you positive?"

"I asked her. She told me. Not the details," Mazie said quickly. "But that Hartley very recently confided in her."

"So she's important to him."

"Looks that way. But I don't think he knows it yet."

The housekeeper came in with the main course, and the topic was shelved for the moment. By the time dessert rolled around, Mazie had come to a decision. If she was going to wait for confirmation until she could see her doctor, then she wanted J.B. waiting with her.

While he drank his coffee, she watched him. He'd been almost a part of their family since they were all kids. It was impossible to imagine her life without him. He was funny and irreverent and never met a stranger. He would make a wonderful father.

Her stomach flopped and twisted. "J.B.?" she said.

His gaze met hers over the rim of his cup. "Hmm?"

"What if we go upstairs early tonight?"

A dark streak of red bloomed on his chiseled cheekbones. His eyes glittered with strong emotion. "Is that what you want?"

Their sex life had suffered in recent months. It was impossible to make love anymore without thinking about whether or not the baby they so desperately wanted was being conceived. And then every month when Mazie got her period, they both mourned.

"It is," she said.

He lurched to his feet, bumping the table. "I'll tell Mrs. P. to finish up tomorrow. That my dear wife wants my body."

Mazie covered her mouth, laughing. "You wouldn't dare."

"Watch me."

In truth, Mazie had no idea what he said to the housekeeper, but in less than half an hour, the kitchen was pristine and the older woman was gone.

Mazie wandered the living room aimlessly, praying for courage. J.B. found her there.

He paused in the doorway like a gunslinger walking into a saloon. "Alone at last," he said, the words gruff.

She went to him and sighed when he immediately folded her close in his arms. There was no place she would rather be. Not ever.

"I need to tell you something before we go upstairs," she said.

He kissed the top of her head. "I'm listening."

She pulled back, searching his face. Wanting to judge his reaction. "I think I'm pregnant."

His big frame went rigid. "Are you positive?"

"Not a hundred percent. I did a couple of store-bought tests. But I'll need to see my doctor. I can't get an appointment until Tuesday."

He cupped her face in his hands. His eyes were damp. "God, I want this to be true. So damn much. I love you, Mazie."

She swallowed hard. "I'm scared."

His frown was swift. "About what?"

"Lisette has suffered two miscarriages already." Tears she couldn't stem spilled from her eyes. "What if that happens to me?"

"It won't," he said firmly. "We've had trouble *getting* pregnant. There's no reason you should worry about *losing* a baby."

She snuggled into his embrace a second time, drawing strength from the sheer physicality of his body. "I don't *feel* pregnant," she whispered. "Shouldn't I feel something? Shouldn't I know?"

J.B. stroked her hair. "You're gonna have to relax, Mazie."

"I know. I think it would help my stress level if you would play intermediary between Jonathan and Hartley."

"So that's how it's going to be, brat." He took her hand and headed for the stairs. "I get it."

"What?" she cried innocently.

He stopped halfway up to the second floor, his smile lopsided. "You think I'm going to say yes to you for an entire nine months."

"Is that a problem?" She gave him a smug grin, unbuttoning her shirt slowly.

His hot gaze started at her eyes and drifted lower, locking on the curves of her breasts, telegraphing his intent. "Not at all. Because I'm going to keep you on bed rest with me."

She giggled, shoving him in front of her. "That's not even a thing, J.B. Vaughan."

On the landing, he scooped her into his arms and carried her the rest of the way. "Whatever it takes, my love. Whatever it takes."

Fiona nearly called Mazie for advice, a woman she barely knew. That's how freaked out she was. After Mazie dashed away earlier, headed home to rendezvous with her husband, Fiona had made awkward excuses to Hartley and locked herself inside the cottage.

She couldn't face him right now. For all her big words about how wrong it was to keep secrets from his family, Fiona was doing the same thing. Keeping a huge plot twist from the man who might possibly be a father very soon.

That evening, she puttered around the house, dusting... tidying up. Since it was far too early for nesting, the only logical explanation was that she was losing her marbles. Popping her cork. Her well-oiled life was off the tracks.

How could she tell him she might be pregnant? Wouldn't it be smarter to find out for sure first?

And then what? He'd spoken his piece unequivocally. *I won't have children. I choose not to take that chance.*

Remembering his words hurt. Badly. It was as if he was repudiating everything that was happening to her. Of course he didn't know. How could he? That didn't make her anxiety and incredulity any less real and painful.

She managed to keep Hartley at bay over the weekend…barely. He called. He texted. He asked to come by and see her.

Her work was her excuse. She needed blocks of uninterrupted time. He claimed to understand. But each time they spoke, she felt his frustration increase. Worst of all, she missed him. A lot.

Having him in her bed each night would have been a wonderful comfort. Even feeling the way she did, she wanted him. As it was, she slept alone and awoke every morning barely in time to dash to the bathroom.

Her reflection in the mirror was appalling. Her hair was lank and dull. She had lost weight. Cooking was too much trouble. All she could tolerate, even later in the day, was chicken broth and dry crackers. When her stash ran dry, she used a grocery service.

Amid the stretches of feeling sorry for herself—and when she could stand for chunks of time—she worked on her paintings. Only then did she feel anything at all like normal. The repetitive brushstrokes calmed her. The colors that spread forth on the canvas filled the yawning chasm in her chest with purpose and joy.

In her heart, she knew she was pregnant. The doctor's appointment she had wrangled at the last minute for

Wednesday morning was only going to confirm her status as a mother-to-be. So what was she going to do about it?

She wanted the baby. Desperately. There was no doubt about that. Thinking about holding her own tiny infant in her arms made her heart sing. But uncertainty about Hartley's reaction tempered her excitement. Could she be a single mom?

Sunday night, she forced herself to take a shower and wash her hair. The nausea had finally subsided some. But her energy level was nil.

At eight, she put on soft cotton pajamas and curled up to watch a movie. Hartley's text came through before the first credit rolled.

Do you mind if I stop by for a few?

Ah, damn. The way her heart leaped in her chest told her the truth. She couldn't put him off any longer…didn't want to, for that matter.

I'm home. What time will you get here?

I'm in my car out at the street.

His comical emoji actually made her laugh.

Come on in.

She unlocked the door and watched him walk up the path. Everything inside her warmed and settled. Hartley made her world a little better. A lot happier. She could argue with herself all she wanted, but it was true. He was the one she had been waiting for…her knight in shining armor.

Could a black sheep prodigal make the leap to hero?

She gripped the edge of the door, white-knuckled. "Hello."

He paused to kiss her gently. "Hello, yourself. You must have been working hard. Is the project coming along?"

"It is," she said. That wasn't entirely a lie.

"These are for you." He'd brought more roses, blush pink this time. Without asking, he headed for the kitchen and dug out the vase. She followed, standing in the doorway to watch him. Were all women so emotional about the men who made them pregnant?

When he was satisfied with the arrangement, he dried his hands and set the vase on the table. "You look tired. I won't stay long." His smile was sweet, catching her off guard. "I missed you these last few days," he said.

She swallowed. "I missed you, too. Come sit with me in the living room," she said. "I want to tell you something."

Not the whole truth and nothing but the truth. That conversation would have to wait for a few more days. After the official doctor's appointment.

They perched on the sofa together. Hartley wrapped an arm around her shoulders as if it were the most natural thing in the world. Though arousal flooded her veins, it was more like a slow, warm river than licks of fire. Hartley was back in Charleston to stay. They had time. For now.

"How's the new purchase?" she asked.

He yawned and leaned his head against the back of the sofa. "I may have bitten off more than I can chew. Although, I'm discovering that punishing physical labor does wonders for clearing a man's brain. I've been working in the yard since I don't have the keys yet."

"Have you tried to talk to your brother?"

She felt him stiffen slightly. "I ran into him a few nights ago. It didn't go well."

"I'm sorry." The faint bitterness in his voice told her he was wounded by the rift with his twin.

Hartley rubbed the top of her shoulder with his thumb. "What did you want to tell me?"

"I know you disagree with me about whether or not you should tell your siblings about Switzerland. But I have some experience with secrets. It concerns my parents."

He pulled away from her and groaned. "Please don't make me feel worse. I never should have lost my temper. Your past is none of my business."

Her smile was wistful. "You've told me your *sordid secrets*. I think it's time for you to hear mine."

Nine

Sordid secrets. Hell. Now she was quoting his unforgivable words back to him. He felt like whatever was lower than pond scum.

Fiona stood up and wrapped her arms around her waist. Her pj's were not terribly thin, but he could see she wasn't wearing a bra. He was swamped by a wave of tenderness mixed with lust. It was an unfamiliar combo, and he didn't know what to do with the feelings.

"Please don't," he begged. "God knows, you don't owe me any explanations."

She stared at him, big gray-blue eyes filled with feminine emotions he couldn't decipher. "I spent my whole life wondering who I was. I lived in an actual orphanage… a children's home, until I was eight. After that, they had to move some of us out to make room for more. I was labeled *amenable*, so I went into foster care. It wasn't terrible. Some of the families were pretty wonderful. But it was all temporary. I knew it and everyone else did, too.

The odds of getting adopted at that age are like winning the lottery."

She'd barely started and already her story was tearing him apart, leaving him raw inside. While he'd been living in a veritable castle, Fiona had been tossed around by governmental red tape.

"I don't need to hear this," he said. *I don't want to hear it.*

Fiona was on a mission. "When I was seventeen and a half, they told me I could begin the process of applying for my records to be opened. Then, when I reached my eighteenth birthday, I would have the option of knowing or not knowing. My choice."

"And what did you do?"

"I filled out the paperwork, and I started dreaming dreams. Now that I was going to be an adult, I was sure my biological parents would want to know me. I wasn't on drugs. I had graduated near the top of my high school class. I was not going to *ask* them for anything at all. The only thing I wanted was to be able to look them in the eye and see where I came from. To understand why I was allergic to apricots. To know if it was my dad or my mother who gave me my artistic ability, or maybe a grandparent. To finally study my family tree."

"Ah, hell, darlin'—" This story didn't have a happy ending. He knew it before she even told him the rest.

Fiona ran her hands through her hair, her eyes scrunched shut as if she didn't want to remember. "When my birthday rolled around, everything was an open book. The details were sparse, but they were there. I came from a small rural county up the coast. Rampant poverty. Poor schools. High numbers of opioid deaths. My birth mother was fifteen when she had me. She hemorrhaged after the delivery and died before they could save her."

"Good God." The long-ago tragedy was stunning. "And your father?"

"He was in jail for drug possession the night I was born. The following day he was released, but on the way to the hospital, he crashed his car into a tree."

"Because he was high?"

"Yes."

"Surely you had grandparents."

"The official report listed four names. I followed up on each one. All deceased. At that point, I no longer had any interest in looking for cousins or aunts and uncles. I was done."

He went to her and held her, feeling the fine tremors that racked her slender body. "I'm sorry," he said.

Fiona rested her cheek against his chest. "It was wretched," she said. "I felt so foolish for all those silly dreams I had spun in my imagination."

"Dreams are not bad things."

"No. But despite everything I learned, I didn't regret seeking out the answers. I decided I wouldn't be defined by my origin story. There was more to me than that. I set goals, and I pursued my passions, and I made peace with my past. Knowing is *always* better than not knowing, Hartley. That's why you need to tell Jonathan and Mazie about their mother."

He hadn't expected her to turn this on him, but he should have seen it coming. "There's a difference," he said stubbornly, releasing her and going to stare out the window.

"How?"

He shot her a look over his shoulder. "Jonathan and Mazie don't have any 'blanks' like you did. They know who they are. They're *not* wondering and wishing. So they aren't struggling to find answers."

"But the truth they believe is a lie."

He ground his teeth. There was merit in what she was saying. Still, other factors made him leery of sharing the information with his siblings. "Our father just died. I think that's enough trauma for one season. Maybe you and I can agree to disagree on this point."

"I'm pretty stubborn about things that are important to me."

He found a smile, wanting to shift the mood to less volatile topics. "Duly noted." Pulling out his phone, he flipped to the photo icon. "I actually came tonight to ask about you doing a job for me. A commission."

"I've got a couple of big things in the works, Hartley."

"This will be small. Mazie's birthday is coming up in a few weeks, and I wanted to surprise her." He showed her a photo. "This is Mazie and J.B. at their wedding reception. See how he's looking at her. I know she would love to have you paint this for them."

"That's not really what I do. I focus on outdoor subjects. Landscapes. Birds. That kind of thing."

"But you *could* do it…right? Mazie would flip. She's been singing your praises to me. She thinks you're phenomenally talented, and I agree."

"Flattery will get you everywhere," Fiona said. Her laughter loosened the knot in his chest that had appeared when she told him about her parents. "Text me the photo. I'll fool around with a sketch and see what I can do."

"Thank you." He pulled up her number, sent the photo and set his phone on the coffee table. "How about a kiss before I go?"

Fiona didn't want him to go. Not at all. She wanted to burrow into his embrace and feel his hands on her body and forget for a few moments that she was in big trouble.

She cocked her head and stared at him. His innocent expression had to be at least 75 percent fake. He knew what his kisses did to a woman. "Are you asking permission?"

Hartley tugged her toward the sofa again and sat down, tumbling her onto his lap. "I want you, Fee. To a degree that's damn scary. What do you say to that?" Brown eyes stared into hers. The humor was gone now. In its place was pure male hunger. Or maybe not so pure. His expression promised all sorts of mischief. All sorts of pleasure.

Her body responded instantly, softening, yearning. She couldn't even barter for a short-lived fling, because she was growing a baby. A baby who was his. How was she going to tell him? For all her big speeches about the danger of secrets, she was scared spitless to expose hers.

"I want you, too," she said, no longer able to pretend that she didn't. There was no reason to dissemble. Soon enough he would find out that her body was fully prepared to welcome his. Damp heat at her core yearned for his rigid length to fill her and drive her mad.

That's what it was. Madness. She should tell him he didn't need a condom. Explain what happened on that night three months ago. Ask what they were going to do about it.

All the reasons not to make love to him tonight were valid, but she shoved them aside in the pursuit of happiness. Carpe diem. Worry about tomorrow another day.

He twisted one of her curls around his finger. "I care about you, Fiona. This isn't casual for me."

His sober promise should have made her heart sing. At any other moment in her life, that declaration would have been exciting and perfect. As it was, her anxiety ratcheted higher.

"There's nothing wrong with casual. We're both young and unattached. I'm not expecting any commitment at this point."

Her words seemed to bother him. He frowned. "Have you been with a lot of men, Fee? For some reason, I got the impression you were a bit more fastidious about your sexual partners. Am I wrong?"

Now she was caught in the crosshairs. If she said yes, he might ultimately wonder if the baby was his. But a negative response—an admission that he'd been her only sexual partner in the last three years—might reveal more than she was willing for him to know.

She reached up to stroke his masculine jawline. The shadow of a late-day beard gave him a rakish air. "What we stumbled into at the wedding last year and then again three months ago was definitely special. We have chemistry. I'm not denying that. But I have a life and a career that don't really intersect well with yours. Our goals are different." *I have a baby on the way, and I'm thrilled about creating a family.*

"Meaning what?"

"You and I are friends. Temporary lovers. I like plain speaking. I don't need flowery compliments or promises about the future."

"Is this because I'm homeless and unemployed?" His wry grin was boyish and charming and totally unfair.

She rolled her eyes. "You're a wealthy man. I can ignore your money as long as we're playing at this relationship."

"Hell, Fiona. I've never had this level of negotiation before sex. Then again, sex with you is worth a little extra trouble. So what you're saying is that your art and your career are more important than flesh and blood relationships?"

"Of course not. Don't twist my words."

"Then *you* explain it."

How could she? All Fiona wanted was a family and a home of her own. Hartley, on the other hand, was going to be furious when he found out about the baby. If he wanted the unvarnished truth, he could have it. "We had great sex, but that's all it was."

His face darkened with displeasure. "If a man had said that, he'd be pilloried. What are you so afraid of, Fiona? I won't ask for anything you aren't willing to give. We're good together. Admit it."

"I've already admitted it, Hartley."

"If we sleep together right now, are you going to let me spend the night?" His pointed question caught her off guard. Guilt turned her stomach queasy and her face red. He couldn't be here when morning came. Not the way things were with her right now.

She lifted her chin, meeting his gaze calmly. "No. I like my privacy and my personal space. There's nothing wrong with that."

"Okay then." Before she could do more than gasp and flail in his arms, he flipped her onto her back and started unbuttoning her pajama top. She was paralyzed by her need for him. When she was bare from the waist up, he paused and sucked in a breath. "You are so damned beautiful."

He stroked one nipple with a fingertip. His touch made her skin burn. "Hartley..."

"What?" He sprawled beside her, partly reclining beside the low sofa. When he leaned over her, took that same nipple in his teeth and tugged gently, she groaned.

"Don't stop," she whispered. Heat rolled through her body, making her shift restlessly. Had she closed the curtains? Rational thought fled when he dragged her pajama bottoms down her legs along with her plain cotton undies. Now she lay there completely naked, like a not-so-virgin sacrifice.

The look on his face threatened to incinerate her. His

words were ragged. "Each time I leave you I think I might have exaggerated this in my mind. And then we're together again, and I know it's all true. My hands are shaking, and I can barely breathe. That's not normal for a guy my age. I don't know what happens when I touch you…when we touch each other."

The trace of bewilderment in the midst of his arousal reflected her own conflicted emotions. Only now, she had the added bonus of worrying about whether she had a baby bump that would tip him off.

"Enough talking," she muttered.

He chuckled, but stood and ripped off his clothes. His sex was stiff and eager. Had he always been so…*big*? Maybe it was because the lights were on or because he loomed over her.

"Let's go the the bedroom," she pleaded.

A dark flush rode high on his cheeks. The skin stretched taut over the planes of his face. He was the conquering hero…the ravaging marauder. The intensity of his focus on *her* made her shiver.

"No," he said bluntly. "Can't wait."

He moved her like a rag doll, sitting down on the sofa and spreading her legs across his body. Before she could do more than gasp, he entered her with a forceful push. His back arched. He cursed softly. And then he captured her mouth in a frantic, hungry kiss.

This position made her feel deliciously vulnerable. Her hormones went wild, plunging her into a quick, sharp climax that didn't last nearly long enough. "More," she demanded.

"Whatever the lady wants."

Seconds later he tumbled them both to the floor. Her simple rug might never look the same to her again. He lifted one of her ankles onto his shoulder and thrust hard, all the way to her womb. The pleasure was a sharp-edged jolt, so searing, she wondered for a moment if they should be doing this. What did she know about being pregnant?

It was all theoretical until it happened to you.

Then he bit the inside of her thigh and she forgot to worry about anything but the magic they were creating together.

Hartley braced himself on his arms, slowing his movements until both of them were panting.

"Did you lose your way?" she asked, the words undeniably petulant.

Her pique made his masculine grin broaden. "It's called building the tension."

"Did you read this in some manual?"

"Are you criticizing my technique?"

She reached up and brushed the lock of hair from his damp forehead. It fell immediately back over his eyebrow. "This isn't casual for me either," she whispered, admitting defeat.

Her words stunned him visibly. She saw the shift in his gaze. The flare of heat. The exultation.

Gently, he disengaged their bodies and picked her up in his arms, a feat which took considerable strength considering she was on the floor.

"I wasn't done," she complained.

"Patience, Fee." In her narrow hallway, he bumped the bedroom door open with his hip and carried her to the bed. "I need soft sheets for the finale."

"Since when?"

He kissed her nose. "Since I decided to impress you with my romantic prowess."

It wasn't even funny, because it was true. Somehow he had managed to inject tenderness into their sexual insanity. That scared her so very badly. Because he was not going to be able to give her what she wanted and needed. He'd already told her that.

Sex, he could do. Family and forever, not so much.

She'd never had much luck with forevers. Even worse, this particular situation was snakebit from the beginning.

"Come here," she said, holding out her arms.

He settled on top of her with a groan, resting his forehead against hers. There wasn't room between them for a sheet of paper, much less a secret of the enormity of hers.

What was she going to do?

"You're amazing, Fee," he said, filling her again, igniting the flame that had been banked for a time. "Wrap your legs around my waist."

When she did, he slid his hands under her ass and lifted her into his thrusts, giving both of them that extra measure of perfection they craved. She was close, so close.

Hartley shuddered and found his release, his breath warm on her cheek. His scent surrounded her, marking her sheets, making it impossible to pretend he didn't belong here. He was everywhere, filling her feminine bedroom with the force of his personality.

Rolling to one side, he stroked her sex, drawing a quick ragged sigh from her parched throat…sending her over the edge into warm, drowsy completion. "I love how you do that," she said.

"Do what?" he asked, the words slurred as his eyes drifted shut.

"You know exactly how to touch me."

He yawned, turning her and spooning her from behind. "It's my superpower, Fee."

Ten

Fiona woke up some time before dawn. Three things became clear in an instant. A very large, warm man had her wrapped in the pure bliss of his muscular arms. She had to pee. And her stomach had begun its morning calisthenics.

Her choices were limited. She could wake him up and physically shove him out of her house. That seemed mean and cold. She knew he hadn't meant to stay in defiance of her wishes. The two of them had been exhausted, Fiona from being pregnant, and Hartley from working at his new property.

So, if she wasn't willing to kick him out, she had to somehow make it to the bathroom and conceal the fact that morning sickness was about to take its toll. Again.

It was still dark, though the clock on her bedside table told her dawn wasn't far off. Slowly, she began easing out of Hartley's embrace. Even those small movements made her forehead break out in a cold sweat. The timing didn't make sense. Most people were sick during the first twelve weeks and finally got better in the second trimester...or so she had heard.

Then again, she'd known women who struggled with nausea the entire nine months, so who knew? Surely that wouldn't happen to her. She had to work. No work meant no pay. She certainly didn't want to get a reputation for being late on commissioned pieces. That wasn't who she was at all.

How was Hartley going to react? She wanted him to be happy, but that wasn't going to happen. Would he stay away from the child entirely? Or would he want even a minor role?

She had to tell him soon, so they could make plans for the future. Or so *she* could.

How could she keep from breaking her heart again and again if she and Hartley were always connected by this unexpected baby?

Thankfully, Hartley never stirred as she extracted herself from her predicament. Because her house was old, the bathroom was in the hall, not attached to her bedroom. She was able to throw up—twice—wash her face and tiptoe to the kitchen without disturbing her guest.

She didn't turn on the lights. Instead, she heated a mug of water in the microwave, added a tea bag and sat at the table, cradling the cup in her hands. Though it wasn't cold in the house, her shivers came from the inside out. Getting sick so violently left her feeling weak and shaky.

How did women stand this?

Gradually, she sipped her drink and her mood stabilized. Females had been handling this situation since the dawn of time. Fiona, herself, was more resilient that most. She'd had to be. This pregnancy was a curve she hadn't seen coming, but she would deal with it. Somehow.

Hartley startled her when he appeared in the doorway. There was enough light filtering through the window now for her to see that he had pulled on his pants and nothing else. Broad naked chest. Big bare man feet. He was an alien presence in her neatly feminine environment.

He raked a hand through his disheveled hair. "Sorry, Fee. I didn't stay on purpose." His voice was gruff and low, roughened by sleep.

She shrugged. "I know. We were both beat."

"I'll let myself out in a minute. I wanted to say goodbye."

Suddenly, she was teary and emotional. Stupid pregnancy hormones. She patted the table. "Come sit. Make coffee if you want to. Everything is there on the counter."

He glanced at the empty coffeepot. "What are you drinking?"

"Hot tea."

He put a hand on her shoulder and kissed the top of her head. "You doing okay, darlin'?"

His concern made her want to sob. She had to get a grip. "I've been pushing myself too hard lately. Not eating well. Feeling a little rotten today."

Once the coffeepot was burbling, he sat down beside her, rubbing her back. "Poor baby. What can I do to make it better?"

Rewrite the past. Tell me you'd love to have a dozen kids. Go away and never come back.

That last one was a huge, wretched lie. She wanted Hartley, and she wanted Hartley's child growing inside her. The kicker was, she didn't see a way for all of that to happen at the same time. Or ever.

"I'll be fine." She finished her tea, wishing she had a second cup.

"Why don't you take a day off?" he said. "You're the boss…right?"

"Yes. But being self-employed isn't for sissies. I have to think about things like quarterly taxes and health insurance premiums and mortgage payments."

"Ah." He stood and poured his coffee.

Fiona had been afraid the aroma might provoke her nausea, but thankfully, the smell was more comforting than anything else.

When Hartley sat down again, he studied her face. "I have a proposition for you," he said.

"It's too early in the morning for propositions."

He stroked the back of her hand with his thumb, sending tingles all over her body. "I've noticed a few things on the outside of your house…maintenance issues."

She interrupted him, feeling defensive about her beloved bungalow. "I know. I have a gutter that needs repairing. The roof lost a few shingles in that last storm. And the eaves need painting. It's a question of time and money, Hartley. I'll get to it." *Somehow.*

"Hear me out," he said. "I was thinking you might take in a boarder."

"A boarder? I only have one bedroom."

"True. But you have a very nice sofa. My new place is three streets away. It would be damned convenient for me to be close during the renovation. I could pay you rent, *and*," he said, "in the evenings, I could do a few handyman projects around your house."

Fiona closed her eyes. It was too early in the morning to be doing battle with a charmer. "I've already told you. I like my privacy and my space."

"Your studio is in the back of the house. I'll stay out of your way. You won't even know I'm here."

Her brain was muzzy. She could smell the scent of his

sleep-warmed skin. All she wanted to do was go back to bed. *You won't even know I'm here*. Was he kidding? He filled up a room with his smile, which was exactly what got her into this mess in the first place.

From the moment she met the handsome groomsman who was going to walk her down the aisle at their mutual friends' wedding, she'd been a goner. Never had she met someone like Hartley. He was a combo of Viking marauder and Saint Bernard puppy. A stubborn alpha male who shaped the world to his liking but could laugh at himself and coax a woman into his bed with the twinkle in his eye. It was almost impossible for her to get mad at him, because he was so genuinely well-intentioned.

Hartley thought he could control the world, or at least his corner of it. That was why he was now estranged from his brother and why Fiona questioned telling him about the baby. He'd made up his mind not to have kids.

How would he react when she told him it was far too late?

She rubbed her temples. "You have plenty of money, Hartley. Find a hotel nearby. There are dozens of them."

"I lived on the road for over a year. I missed you, Fee. I missed having sex with you. I want to be here. Under your roof. Platonically if necessary until you can trust me again."

"Do you really think I'll sleep in my bed, and you'll be on the sofa? Come on, Hartley. I'm not that naive."

His thumb strayed up her arm, teasing the inside crook of her elbow. "That would be entirely up to you."

She pressed her thighs together. Now that her nausea had abated, arousal settled heavy in her abdomen. "I can't deal with this right now. Take me back to bed. It's too early. My brain doesn't work."

"Whatever you want, Fiona." He picked up her hand and sucked her pinky finger, his teeth raking her knuckle.

Holy hell. Had she always had that erogenous zone, or was pregnancy making her insatiable?

She jerked her hand away with a gasp she tried to turn into a cough. He had far too much ego as it was. No need for him to know he could reduce her to mush so easily. She fled down the hall. It wasn't even seven yet.

When she climbed under the covers, Hartley was right behind her. He nuzzled the back of her neck. "Do you want to sleep or screw?"

Her helpless giggle was mortifyingly girlish. "Do I have a choice?"

He leaned over her on one elbow, his expression dead sober. "You always have a choice, Fee."

"I'm sorry," she said quickly, feeling small. "I know that. I wasn't accusing you of anything. Well, except for being far too hard to resist."

A smile cracked his stoic expression. "A compliment? Wow, Fee, I don't know what to say."

She curled a hand behind his neck and pulled him down for a kiss. "You could say you'll give me a few days to think about this living together thing." *Maybe the morning sickness would subside soon, and Hartley's presence in her house wouldn't be such an issue.*

His tongue mated with hers, stealing her breath. "Fair enough."

Hartley didn't want to leave this woman or this bed at all. But he knew when to back off. If he couldn't win her over with cogent arguments, then he had to play to his strengths.

Though he couldn't take credit for whatever animal

attraction had bewitched them, he'd be happy to use it to advance his cause.

It had alarmed him to wake up this morning and realize he was in bed alone. Fiona had seemed *twitchy* or something when he'd found her in the kitchen. As if he were indeed intruding on her personal space. Gradually, though, she had relaxed.

Now she was warm and affectionate and very clearly inclined to get the day off to a good start. He sifted his fingers through her rumpled curls. "Have I told you how much I love your hair?"

She grimaced. "I hated it for most of my life. I wasn't allowed to go the movies very often, but one of my foster moms had a huge DVD collection. I adored watching Gwyneth Paltrow in *Emma*. Kate Hudson in *How to Lose a Guy in 10 Days*. I envied their blond beauty, because I was the antithesis of that. Skinny and freckled and bashful."

"Neither of them can hold a candle to the woman you are now." He could see that little girl in his mind's eye. She had grown into a stunning human being. "You have a fire in you—maybe it's the creativity, I don't know. The moment we met each other at that damned wedding, I could no more have walked away from you than cut off my own arm. I wanted you desperately. Beyond all reason. Why do you think that is?"

She toyed with the shell of his ear. "Is that a serious question?"

Her touch sent little tingles of fire down his spine to his sex. "I think it is. I've always been suspicious of things I don't understand."

"But…?"

He slid his hand inside her pajama bottoms and found her center. She was warm and wet. He shook with the need to take and take and take until he blacked out from the pleasure. "But I'm learning to live with not knowing."

"Wow. What a sacrifice."

"Has anyone ever told you you've got a mean streak?"

"Most people think I'm adorable." She turned up her nose at him, clearly inclined to make fun of herself.

He chuckled. "Can't argue with that."

Sex with Fiona was never what he expected. In the midst of aching arousal, he still wanted to play endlessly. Her body was soft and supple. Small and yet powerfully feminine, strong enough to make him weak.

He hadn't entirely grown accustomed to the power she wielded. And he was pretty damned sure she had no idea the power was even there. Perhaps for now it was best she didn't. *Because he didn't know what he was going to do about the situation.*

Before climbing into bed, he had shucked his pants and boxers. Fiona wrapped her hand around his erection. His vision blurred. He was breathing like he had run a mile, and they had barely started.

He held his hand over hers. "Easy now. Let me unwrap you first."

"I'll help," she said. "You're being kind of slow."

His laugh was little more than a wheeze.

Between them they ripped off her pjs and clutched each other, naked skin to naked skin. It was enough to make him forget his name and every last one of his troubles.

His world narrowed to this bed. This woman.

Crap. Condoms. Did he have any left? He reached for the floor and his mangled clothing and found one more. Thank God.

His hands shook as he rolled it over his erection. "Fore-play?" he croaked.

She grabbed handfuls of his hair. "Not a chance. Get over here."

He filled her with one wild thrust. It was heaven and hell and every level of torment in between. Burying his face in her neck, he tried to count her heartbeats, to memorize the taste of her skin right below her ear.

Her body welcomed him, drew him in, held him captive. He had never been more glad to be a man. Whatever his sins—and there were many—he must have done something right. "I can't stop wanting you," he groaned.

Fiona sucked his bottom lip, sinking her teeth in just enough to sting. "Works both ways. But we can't stay in bed all day," she said, panting. "We're mature adults. We have to set boundaries."

He braced his weight on his hands for a minute and studied her face. Her cheeks were flushed, her throat abraded by the stubble on his chin. The red hair that was silky and soft fluffed out around her heart-shaped face. Before today, he hadn't noticed how that sweet pointed chin could be so stubborn.

"I never met a boundary I didn't want to smash."

Her eyes widened. The flush deepened. "I always thought of myself as a good girl."

"Just think of me as your black sheep lover. Ready to do any naughty thing your heart desires."

She squeezed his sex with her inner muscles, drawing a ragged groan from his dry throat.

"Make love to me, Hartley," she said. "Now."

It was a demand he was happy to oblige.

The feelings racketing around in his chest were foreign to him, dangerously so. He shoved them away, choosing to concentrate on the physical. When he knew Fiona was at the edge, he reached between their linked bodies and stroked her intimately.

She arched against him and climaxed, whispering his name over and over, making him feel like a king. Seconds later, he lost the fight with his own galloping need and came so hard he actually saw yellow spots dancing behind his closed eyelids.

Without meaning to, he slept again. But when he awoke fifteen minutes later, this time he wasn't alone.

He watched Fiona breathe, her breasts rising and falling almost imperceptibly. Gently, he twisted a curl around his finger, a game that was rapidly becoming one of his favorites.

The springy red-gold strands clung to his skin, alive with the passion he felt in her. In one blinding instant of clarity he understood that he couldn't be the man to break her heart. Not with the disappointments and challenges she had faced in her young life so far.

Fiona was a fighter, yes. Fiercely independent. Generous and brave. The right man could spend a lifetime making her happy…making up for all she had lost.

The big-ass problem was, Hartley didn't know if he was good enough or smart enough or deserving enough to be that guy. He'd been plowing ahead with his laundry list of wants and needs, determined to find his way into her life. But what or who did Fiona need?

When he stroked her cheek with the tip of his finger, her eyelashes fluttered open. Her gaze was dreamy. "Wow."

He couldn't stop his smug grin. "Ditto."

She stretched, causing all sorts of interesting reactions beneath the sheet. "I have to *work*, Hartley. Really, I do."

He rolled to a seated position and held up both hands. "I know, I know. I'm gone. But before I leave, one more thing."

Her hand settled on his thigh, perilously close to his semi-erect sex. "You never give up, do you?"

The temptation was almost overwhelming. Instead of giving in, he tried to be the better man. Lurching to his feet, he dressed clumsily, conscious of her gaze on his naked body. "No, no," he said. "I want to take you out on a date Friday night. It's a charity gala, black-tie. My father is receiving a posthumous award. Apparently, despite everything, my family wants me to be there."

Fiona raised up on her elbows. "Well, of course they do. That's lovely, Hartley."

"I want you to come with me, Fiona. Dinner, dancing. The formalities will be brief."

"I'd love to," she said simply.

"Really?" His disappointment at having to leave her bed was appeased. "I thought we might stay overnight at a small hotel near the event site. So we can indulge in champagne and stroll through the summer night back to our love nest."

His teasing hyperbole made her smile. "That sounds delightful. What time will you pick me up?"

"Well, if I were already staying here..." He trailed off, gauging her mood.

She pulled a robe out of her closet, slipped it on and belted it with a double knot. "You are incorrigible. Not tonight. Not tomorrow. Not this week. After the gala, we'll talk."

He pretended to scowl. "You're a hard woman."

She rounded the bed and slid her arms around his waist. "Patience, Hartley. That new house of yours will take weeks of work. We have all the time in the world."

Eleven

As it turned out, it was *Fiona* who was pressed for time. Not in regard to her work. She'd actually had bursts of energy in the late afternoons and was finding herself wildly productive in those moments. Although her workday had shifted and morphed from her usual pattern, she was not as far behind as she had feared.

The real problem was her clothes. When she dressed Wednesday morning, the jeans that had fit her only the day before were suddenly and mysteriously too tight. She stared in the mirror and ran a hand over her belly.

There was no denying it. Even if the convex shape of her tummy was barely perceptible to the naked eye, her body was changing. Blossoming with new life. The barrage of feelings that knowledge evoked made her feel completely out of her element.

She'd never had a mother, not really. What did she know about giving birth or breastfeeding or how many times was too many to read *Goodnight Moon*? Scarier still was wondering how her baby's father was going to react to the news. Would Friday night or perhaps Saturday morning be the right time to tell him? In the midst of her panic ran a deep, mysterious vein of intense joy.

Though this was a situation she had never anticipated or imagined she wanted, now that her baby was becoming a reality, she was fiercely glad. No matter what happened with Hartley, this child was *hers*. Hers. A family of her own.

In the end, she left her jeans unbuttoned at the waist and chose a loose cotton tunic in navy and orange that would hide any telltale signs. The appointment with her ob-gyn would confirm what she already knew.

Now she understood how Mazie felt the other day... slinking around, hoping no one would see. It was as if she had a giant sign on her back shouting, "I'm pregnant."

An hour later when a no-nonsense nurse called her name, Fiona rose to her feet and followed the woman through a maze of hallways to an exam room. The obstetrician was a female, only two or three years older than Fiona herself. Dr. Anderson was thorough, kind and reassuring. "You're in excellent health, Ms. James. You shouldn't have problems, but of course, you know to call our office immediately if you have any concerns."

The doc handed over a prescription for vitamins and a handful of educational pamphlets, and soon Fiona was out on the street again. She had been certain she was pregnant, but hearing the confirmation from a professional made everything so much more *real*.

As she stood on the sidewalk, her limbs were shaky, and her emotions pinballed. It was impossible to decide which response was the correct one. Jubilation and trepidation seemed equally appropriate.

Since she had already broken up her workday, she decided to consolidate errands. Before leaving the house that morning, she had looked online for maternity shops. There was one nearby, so she stopped in…just to take a look.

She had several tops at home that would probably work for three or four months. What she needed were some stretchy pants on the dressier side. Sometimes she met with prospective clients, so she had to look professional, even if she *was* an artist.

The clothing in this particular shop was wildly expensive, particularly considering she would be wearing maternity pieces for only part of a year. She found one sleeveless shift that she could wear over short-sleeve T-shirts. It didn't look like a tent, so that was a plus. A couple of pairs of pants and she was done for the moment.

It was hard to imagine her body getting big and round. Maybe it would be smarter to wait for the rest.

A more pressing priority than maternity clothes was finding something to wear for Friday night. She owned three relatively formal dresses, but none of them were really exciting. One was a hand-me-down from a friend. Another was the dress she'd worn at the wedding where she and Hartley met, and the third was a heavy winter velvet.

She wanted to look like she was comfortable in his world, even if she wasn't. Since this was definitely a special occasion, she sought out a little boutique where, normally, she only window-shopped. Today, she marched right in and started perusing the racks.

Sequins weren't really her thing. Color was another challenge. Black tended to overwhelm her because of her extremely fair skin and her stature. She wanted something *floaty* and romantic…the kind of gown a woman wore when going out with the man she loved.

The random thought stopped her dead in her tracks. She

didn't *love* Hartley. She couldn't. Sexual attraction was a powerful force, but it wasn't the same as love.

Her stomach churned with nausea, though the baby wasn't to blame. For the first time, she honestly tried to imagine how Hartley was going to react when she told him the truth. She couldn't bear the thought that he would decide to care for her and the baby because he had no choice.

After being taken in by a string of well-meaning foster parents over the years of her childhood and adolescence, she'd had her fill of being someone else's *obligation*. She didn't need Hartley's money, and she didn't need his reluctant parenting.

He was worried about his mother's genetic legacy. Even more than that, his father had created such a mishmash of lies and deceit, Hartley was disgusted by the idea of parenthood. Hartley was determined not to recreate his unorthodox childhood. It made sense. It did. But there was absolutely nothing Fiona could do to alter the present situation. The only option would be to terminate the pregnancy, and that was out of the question.

This baby had already stolen her heart. Making plans for the future was scary and exciting at the same time. After the gala, she told herself. After the gala she would work up the courage to let Hartley know about her pregnancy. Who knows? Maybe the reality of her situation would change his mind.

"May I help you, miss?" A tall, statuesque saleswoman with exquisitely coiffed white hair interrupted Fiona's spate of worrying and gave her a warm smile.

"Yes, thank you. I have a function Friday night. Black-tie. Nothing I have at home will work. Can you point me in the right direction? I don't like anything too fussy, and I'd prefer the more casual side of formal. Am I asking the impossible? My hair clashes with some colors, obviously."

The woman took a step back and surveyed Fiona from head to toe, as if studying a mannequin. "White," she pronounced. "Possibly ivory, but I think white is the shade for you."

"Really? Isn't that a bit too bridal?"

"You must be attending the Chamber Awards Gala Friday, correct?"

"Yes, ma'am." It was hard not to feel like a little kid playing dress up when faced with this paragon of elegance.

"Come with me, young lady. The dressing rooms are this way. You may call me Clarisse."

Fiona trailed in her wake, wondering if she had started something she would regret. Even the changing area was fancier than her bedroom at home. A small antique chandelier. Tall cheval mirrors edged in gilt. Thick, lush carpet underfoot.

Clarisse indicated a small cushioned chair. "Wait here," she said. "Help yourself to fruit water and biscotti."

When the other woman disappeared through plum satin curtains into the bowels of the store, Fiona sat down and pulled out her phone. She was increasingly worried about Hartley. After that first day, he had never again spoken about what he discovered in Switzerland.

Fiona was certain that if he simply told Jonathan the truth about why he had been gone and what he'd learned, his brother would no longer have a reason to be angry. Well, maybe because of the money, but Hartley had put it all back. That shouldn't be a problem in the end.

Clarisse returned with an armful of gowns, effectively ending Fiona's fretting, at least for the moment. The older woman ushered Fiona to a changing room. "Here are the first three," she said. "We can move on quickly if none of these suit your taste."

Fiona stripped down to her undies and surveyed the

haul. One of the ivory dresses caught her eye instantly. It was strapless and fitted from the breasts to the knees, where it flared in a cloud of tulle. The satin had a faux antique patina that appealed to her artistic sensibilities.

But the fit was so tight...

She tried it on, holding her breath.

Clarisse rapped at the door. "Shall I zip you up?"

"Yes, please." Fiona couldn't tell anything at all with the dress open down the back. She clutched it to her chest and waited for the imperious salesclerk to help her.

When everything was tucked and fastened, both women surveyed Fiona's reflection in the glass. The woman looking back at them was wide-eyed and flushed.

Clarisse pursed her lips. "What do you think?"

Fiona touched her hair. Perhaps she could wear it up. "I love it," she said slowly, stunned that a single item of clothing could make her feel so wonderful. Already, she was imagining Hartley's face when he saw her in soft satin and bare skin. The dress made her feel sexy and sophisticated.

Clarisse nodded. "I believe it's perfect for you. But I suggest you try on half a dozen more just to be sure."

"Oh, no," Fiona demurred. "I won't change my mind, I promise. Are you sure I can pull this off? I'm not really accustomed to attending events like the gala. I don't want to feel self-conscious."

"If you're worried about the pregnancy showing, don't be. That tiny baby bump won't be visible at all, even though the dress fits as if it was designed only for you."

Fiona gaped. "You can tell I'm pregnant?" Her mood plummeted. "Maybe I should look for something looser."

Clarisse's expression softened. "I know women's bodies. It's my livelihood. But unless someone sees you naked, I assure you your secret is safe."

Unless someone sees you naked... Fiona gulped inwardly. Not exactly reassuring words given how the evening was likely to end. Hartley in a tux and Fiona dressed to kill? It was going to be their wedding party introduction all over again.

"I'll take the gown," Fiona said firmly. If she was going to be Hartley's plus-one and mingle with his family and friends and business acquaintances, she wanted to look her best.

After paying for her purchase and laying it gently in the back seat of the car, she pulled out her phone and did a search for Mazie's shop. It was a jewelry store in the historic district. As luck would have it, All That Glitters was less than a quarter of a mile away.

Fiona set out on foot. Parking spaces were at a premium in this part of town; plus, she needed the exercise anyway. Though she was by no means a slug, the fact that she was pregnant meant making healthy choices all the way around. She might be inexperienced when it came to babies and mothering, but she was determined to give this little one every advantage.

When she entered Mazie's place of business, the premises were pleasantly cool and scented with the aroma of jasmine. Quiet music played unobtrusively. Can lights overhead illuminated cases of rings and necklaces and bracelets. The atmosphere was everything a weary, overheated female tourist could hope for. Consequently, the place was crowded and buzzing with conversation.

Fiona spotted Hartley's sister right away, but she hung back, not wanting to intrude. When Mazie passed off a happy shopper to the employee at the register who was waiting to ring up and wrap the woman's purchases, Mazie made a beeline for Fiona.

She beamed. "You found me," she said.

"This place is gorgeous. I love how you've used color and light to showcase your merchandise."

"Thanks. Coming from an artist, that means a lot."

Fiona lowered her voice. "How are you feeling? What did J.B. say when he found out you're pregnant?"

The other woman's face was radiant. "I feel amazing. And my husband is over the moon. He barely lets me out of the house, though. Being doted on is great, but I've tried to tell him I'm fine."

"Maybe he'll settle down when he sees how well you're doing."

"I hope so. I love the attention—who wouldn't? Still, I need to breathe." Her smug smile told Fiona that J.B.'s hovering wasn't really a problem.

Mazie took her by the arm. "I need to talk to you," she said. Without waiting for a response from Fiona, she steered her toward the back of the store. "My office is tiny, but no one will disturb us."

Behind the chintz curtain was a jumble of boxes and a nook barely large enough for an antique rolltop desk and a couple of chairs. Mazie motioned Fiona toward one of them. "Water?" she asked.

"Yes, please." The temperature was in the nineties. Her throat was dry. She was either nervous or dehydrated or both. "What's up?" she asked.

Mazie took the other seat and handed Fiona a bottle, then uncapped her own. "I'm worried sick about telling Lisette and Jonathan."

"And Hartley?"

"Him, too. But Lisette has miscarried twice. I don't want to upset her with my news."

"Don't be silly. You have something to celebrate. Lisette will be happy for you. She probably sees pregnant women every day."

"Maybe." Mazie wrinkled her nose. "J.B. and I thought that we'd have all of you over for drinks and hors d'oeuvres before the gala. That way we could tell everyone at once."

Mazie knew instantly this would be a test for her own pregnancy. If Hartley was delighted for his sister, maybe there was hope for Fiona. "We'll be there," she said.

"Excellent." Mazie hopped up and pulled a small box from the shelf behind her shoulder. "I've been meaning to give you one of these," she said. "Sort of a welcome-to-the-family gift. It's clear that my brother is nuts about you."

Fiona wasn't sure this was the time to say that she and Hartley were temporary. So she smiled weakly and opened the offering. It was a delicate seahorse charm, suspended from a beautiful eighteen-inch box chain. "Oh, Mazie. This is lovely."

Mazie hovered. "Put it on. It's white gold. If you'd rather have the more traditional yellow, we can swap it out."

"Oh, no. This is perfect." Fiona fingered the little sea creature. "But I think it's too much. We barely know each other."

"You bought me pregnancy tests. That advances the timeline exponentially."

Fiona chuckled. "Maybe so." She stood and used the small oval mirror on the wall to fasten the chain around her neck. The charm nestled in exactly the right spot. "I love it."

"It's the kind of thing you can wear with everyday outfits. And it suits you. Whimsical and unusual."

"Are you sure that's a compliment?"

Fiona's wry question made Mazie laugh. "Of course it is. That's why my brother is so besotted. No woman he's ever dated is anything like you. You're an original."

"And all those other women?"

Mazie shrugged. "Cookie-cutter debutantes. Rich. Confident. Boring."

"We should all be so lucky," Fiona muttered. "I should go," she said suddenly, feeling weepy for no particular reason except that the life growing inside her was playing havoc with her temperament. "I just wanted to say hello and see where you worked."

"Well, now you know, so don't be a stranger."

When they returned to the main showroom, the crowd had thinned. Fiona wanted badly to share her own secret. But a host of things held her back. This family had a lot of skeletons. For an orphan, it was hard to imagine the kind of blood loyalty that kept a group of siblings together over the long haul.

"Thank you for the invitation," she said. "I'm sure Hartley will be happy for us to come." It wasn't exactly the truth, but she didn't want to add to Mazie's worry about the big reveal. "What time?"

"Probably five thirty. I'll text you both when we nail it down."

"You do realize it's only forty-eight hours from now?"

Mazie grinned. "Not to worry. I'll put my feet up and let J.B. make all the arrangements."

Twelve

Fiona continued to be sick in the mornings. Fitting into the dress she had bought was not a problem. Fortunately, Hartley kept his distance, perhaps hoping his uncustomary reticence would cement her trust.

For two days, it almost seemed as if time stood still. That she had never met Hartley. That her whole life wasn't about to change.

She took advantage of the momentary lull to paint like mad. The work was a welcome distraction. Anxiety about the weekend made her queasiness worse. She had agreed to spend the night with Hartley after the gala. In a romantic, indulgent boutique hotel. What could possibly go wrong?

At the wedding where they first met, and again when Hartley showed up at her house unannounced, the sex and the budding relationship had been wild and thrilling, carried along on a wave of lust and adrenaline and some insane concoction of pheromones.

Friday night would be different. She and Hartley were

invited to socialize with his family. They were going to appear together in public. Neither of them could expect a spontaneous outcome. When a man and a woman dressed up, shared a fancy social occasion, and then checked into a room, what happened next was a done deal.

Fiona was both terrified and giddy with excitement.

In the end, she decided to leave her hair down. Her curls had a mind of their own, and they barely reached her chin. Taming them would take more energy than she possessed at the moment.

She was not a sophisticated woman. No point in pretending.

Friday afternoon she cleaned up her studio and took a shower. She'd bought new undies and a silky nightgown at the maternity shop. Ordinarily, she was more of a tank top and panties sleeper, but tonight she wanted to be someone different. The kind of woman who coaxed a man into bed and made him never want to leave.

She and Hartley had texted back and forth over the past few days, but only briefly. Was he playing games with her? He'd gone from bludgeoning his way into her life to respecting her boundaries. What did it mean? Why was she so suspicious of his motives?

After packing a small overnight bag, she did her makeup and stepped into the fabulous dress. Only then did she realize her problem. With no Clarisse at hand, Fiona couldn't zip up the dress on her own.

Damn, damn, damn.

Hartley was as jumpy as a bullfrog on hot concrete. It felt like weeks, not days, since he had seen Fiona. He was playing the long game, giving her the space she wanted. Had it helped his case?

The only way he managed to survive his self-imposed

separation was by working his ass off packing up his house and getting it ready for closing. All he could think about was whether or not Fiona was going to let him move in. Even if she made him sleep on the sofa, it would be a start. He'd made reservations at an extended-stay condo unit, just in case.

He had mixed feelings about showing up at J.B. and Mazie's house tonight. Lisette and Jonathan would be there, of course. Things were still frosty with his twin. Maybe avoidance was the best policy. Keep the width of the room between him and Jonathan.

Any worry about family squabbles took a back seat when Hartley pulled up in front of Fiona's now-familiar house. He shut off the engine, mentally calculating how many hours and minutes it would be until he and the lovely red-headed artist were alone together. His body tightened and ached as he imagined undressing her.

He had booked the best room in the swankiest, most exclusive hotel in the city. Pulled out all the stops. Tonight would be a slow, sexy buildup to the main event.

If he lived that long. The way he felt right now, he might go quietly insane.

She knew they were good in bed. Why couldn't she admit the benefits of a convenient living arrangement?

He wanted her day and night.

Truth be told, his feelings for Fiona were not entirely comfortable, because he didn't understand them.

When he strode up the path and knocked, no one answered. Seconds passed. He knocked again. "Fiona, it's me."

Suddenly, he heard the sound of the dead bolt being turned. The door opened. But no more than six or eight inches. Certainly not enough for a large man to squeeze through.

Two big eyes in a heart-shaped face peered out at him. "You're early," she accused.

He frowned. "Barely fifteen minutes. What's wrong, Fee?"

The part of her he could see turned bright red. Perfect teeth mutilated a plump bottom lip. "We have a situation."

"Are you sick?" Disappointment flooded his stomach. And then he felt like a jerk for being disappointed.

"I'm not sick."

"Let me in, darlin'. It's hot enough to fry meat on the sidewalk."

"Okay. But wait a minute. And be quick when I let you in." The door closed all the way. Something—maybe an elbow—hit the wood.

He didn't know what the hell was going on, but he wasn't going to get any answers out here. "Fiona…"

Before he could form an objection, the door opened a second time. A small, feminine hand grabbed his wrist and dragged him through the narrow opening. "I need help," she said breathlessly.

When she slammed the door, and he saw her for the first time, he took a blow to the chest. His sweet, usually unadorned Fiona was wearing makeup. She looked unbelievably fantastic. Hot and sultry and gorgeous.

Her eye shadow was smoky gray, a color that made those slate blue irises sparkle. Mascara darkened pale lashes, creating a vision of feminine sexuality. She wore red lipstick, the color of arousal. His mouth dried. "You look amazing."

"Thank you. But I…"

Then he saw it. She was clutching her dress to her breasts. Ivory satin caressed her body. The gown appeared to be undone.

Lord help him.

Fiona's gaze was pleading. "The saleslady fastened me at the store. I never thought about the fact that I'd be home alone. You'll have to zip me up."

He took a step backward. Lust zinged from his sex to his throat, drying his mouth. "Um…"

"It's not a corset," she said. "Just a zipper." Impatience mixed with embarrassment in her voice.

He couldn't do it. He absolutely couldn't do it. All he'd thought about since the last time he stood in this house was how soon he could make love to her again. Now he was hot and horny and frustrated. Dangerously close to the edge. "A neighbor," he croaked. "I can fetch someone."

Confusion darkened her gaze. "Mr. Fontaine on the left is eighty-seven and deaf. My other neighbor has three kids, and they're at soccer practice. What's the problem? We're going to be late."

Well, hell. He could try. He wasn't a slave to his baser instincts. He was a highly evolved, overly educated, twenty-first century gentleman.

She turned her back to him. "Do it, Hartley. Please."

Do it? Was she deliberately trying to drive him out of his mind?

His hands shook so hard he had to clench his fists. "Okay," he muttered. "Don't rush me. I don't want to ruin your dress."

Clearly, Fiona had no idea how she looked from behind. The zipper was a long one. Her soft, pale-skinned back was exposed from the nape of her neck to where her spine took a feminine curve at the top of her ass.

She wasn't wearing anything else but tiny underwear. And even then he got only a peek of lace. Mostly, the view was all Fiona. Naked Fiona.

Gritting his teeth, he took hold of the zipper and wrestled it upward an inch and a half, no more. Fiona made a noise that sounded remarkably like a moan.

He ignored the sexy provocation and tried again. The fabric was slippery. The dress was clearly meant to be fitted to a woman's body with little room to spare.

Suddenly, he had to touch her. Had to see if that magnolia-white skin was as soft as it looked. He traced her lower spine with both thumbs. "We could skip the gala tonight," he muttered, only half kidding.

Fiona shot him a look over her shoulder. "No, we can't." Her eyelids were heavy. The words lacked conviction.

He moved the zipper another inch. His self-control was shot. Wanting her was a living, breathing pain. How was he supposed to resist? He kissed the top of her spine. "Tell me to stop, Fee." His entire body was tense. Braced. As if being stretched on a rack. His sex throbbed beneath the confines of his tux pants.

"Stop what?"

It was a dangerous question, because in her voice he heard the truth. She knew exactly what he was asking.

"Fee…" He pleaded with her.

She dropped her head back against his chest, her curls brushing his chin. "I missed you," she muttered.

He snapped. Completely. His need for her sent him reeling off a cliff. Without conscious thought, he lifted her bodily, freed her from the puddle of satin and kicked it aside.

Spinning her to face him, he ground out the only words he could think of in his delirium. "Speak now or forever hold your peace."

She curled her arms around his neck, her eyes soft with arousal. "I'm going to let you do all the talking," she whispered.

The madness rolled over him like a tide. He shoved her against the door, feasting on one perfect spot at the curve of her neck—careful, though, not to mark her skin. He freed his erection, fumbled with protection and fingered her sex through her panties. She was wet and warm and welcoming.

There was no time to remove her underwear. He tugged at the elastic between her legs and gave himself enough room to maneuver. Then he lifted her and shoved hard, lodging himself all the way to the hilt. Her butt smashed against the door.

Hell and damn. His body was on fire, burning from the inside out. When he moved in her, Fiona whimpered as if afraid he was going to leave her. Not bloody likely. "I'm sorry," he muttered. The weight of his many failings threatened to drown him. She was an angel, and he was nothing but a man enslaved by his need for her body, her soul.

Fee leaned into him and nipped his earlobe with sharp teeth. "I'm not sorry," she said.

Things blurred a bit after that. He remembered hammering into her again and again, muttering words of desperation. Fee's legs tightened around his waist. "Don't stop," she begged.

Half a second later, her sex contracted around his, the sensation exquisite and inescapable. He groaned her name and came with her, burying his hot face in her neck.

When it was over, he set her gently on her feet and kissed her forehead. He was weak, embarrassingly so. He couldn't think of a single thing to say.

Fiona, ever practical, touched his cheek, patting him as if he were a child to be comforted. "I'll use the bathroom in my studio. You can take the one in the hallway."

When she bent over to pick up her dress, he nearly lunged for her again. Instead, he clenched his fists and tried to breathe through the pain. He was falling in love

with her. The knowledge crushed him. Fiona was the kind
of woman who wanted marriage and a family.

He would give her the moon if she asked, but making
babies was out of the question for him.

When he had put himself back together, at least where
his clothing was concerned, he went to her bedroom and
stood in the open doorway. Fee was seated at the antique
vanity adjacent to her bed tidying her curls and freshen-
ing her lipstick. With her arms lifted and her body still
naked, she looked like a painting by one of the old masters.

Woman combing her hair...

"Did I ruin your dress?" he asked. It was tossed across
the bed.

"I don't think so." Her gaze didn't meet his when she
stood. She hadn't bothered with slipping into a robe.

They were lovers. No need to pretend otherwise. Even
so, he averted his eyes when she picked up the heavy satin
and stepped into it. Too much temptation. She gave him
her back. He zipped her up carefully.

"You look beautiful, Fiona." He squeezed her shoulders.

She had wrung him out and used him up, but he was
hard as a pike already and wanted her no less than he had
before.

"Thank you," she said quietly. "We should go. We can
still make it to Mazie and J.B.'s if the traffic is kind." She
picked up a small evening clutch covered in seed pearls.

"Wait," he said, reaching into the pocket of his jacket.
"I almost forgot. Mazie told me the two of you chatted
when you stopped by the store about what you were going
to wear tonight. I pumped her for the color and bought you
this. I hope you like it."

He handed over a velvet box and watched her face as
she opened it.

Her eyes widened. "Hartley…these are gorgeous. But it's too much. I'd be terrified of breaking them."

"Nonsense. Pearls are meant to be enjoyed. They warm with your skin…become part of you. Turn around."

Carefully, he slipped the long double strand over her head. The woman and the dress had been stunning before. Now Fiona looked like a princess. He stood behind her as she examined her reflection in the mirror. Their eyes met in the glass. "I love them," she said. "Thank you, Hartley." When she stroked the necklace with two fingers, he could almost feel her touch against his skin.

He swallowed against a startling lump of emotion in his throat. "I'm glad. I would kiss you, but I don't think we have time for more repairs."

Fiona glanced at the clock on her bedside table and squeaked. "We have to go. Mazie will kill us if we're late."

"What's so important?" He loved his sister, but he was more interested in being alone with Fiona than a round of appetizers and small talk.

Fiona's cheeks turned pink. "Who knows? Your siblings are complicated people."

"So true." While Fee turned off lights and checked doors, Hartley took her small suitcase and put it in the trunk of his car. Only the fact that they were spending the night together kept him in line. It would be far too easy to blow off this gala and let Mazie and Jonathan represent the family.

Truth be told, he still felt guilty about leaving them to do that the whole time he'd been gone. He'd borne a load of his own, but did that balance out the sin of abandoning the family?

In the car, he took Fiona's hand and lifted it to his lips. "Thank you for coming with me tonight. I'll be the most envied man in Charleston with you on my arm."

When he nibbled her knuckles, she jerked her hand back, laughing. "Behave yourself. And don't think ridiculous flattery will let you have your way about everything."

"It's only flattery if it isn't true, Fee. I'm not sure how a woman like you is still unattached."

His praise seemed to bother her. She wrinkled her nose and stared through the windshield. "What does that mean? A woman like me…"

He started the car. "Beautiful. Smart. Talented. Sexy as hell."

"I appreciate the vote of confidence, but I'm not anything special. Don't get me wrong. I have healthy self-esteem. I'm not fishing for compliments."

"Then what *are* you doing?" He frowned, bothered by the fact that she seemed clueless about how she affected him.

"Let's change the subject, please."

He bowed to her wishes, wondering how deeply her early years had marked her. What was it like to be a kid without a home? He couldn't even imagine it.

Yet, he'd *had* a home, and he possessed as many hang-ups as Fiona. Perhaps more. Warning bells sounded in his head. He was getting in too deep. He didn't need to psychoanalyze her to enjoy sex. He needed to back up and look at the big picture.

Fiona was silent for the remainder of the short trip. As always, he wondered what she was thinking. Was she looking forward to sleeping with him tonight? Really sleeping? He was vaguely astonished to realize that he wanted that almost as much as he wanted sex.

Maybe this relationship was temporary. In his gut, he knew it was. That didn't mean he couldn't enjoy it while it lasted.

Thirteen

Fiona was a pile of nerves by the time she and Hartley made it to Mazie's house. The two of them were a full ninety seconds early, a minor miracle considering how they had spent portions of the previous hour.

A uniformed maid met them at the door and escorted them to the dining room. The home was stunning. But Fiona had no time to gawk at the classic architecture and fabulous furnishings. Everyone else was already present. Jonathan and Lisette. And of course, J.B. and Mazie.

Hartley hadn't lost all of his reserve with his siblings. The round of greetings was cordial, but to Fiona's eyes, everyone in the room was carefully on his or her best behavior. She exchanged hugs, too… That seemed to be required. Only Jonathan and Hartley kept a physical distance.

The light appetizers set out on the sideboard were amazing. Fiona could have made a meal out of only this, but she worried about spilling food on her dress. Given how careless she had been with her beautiful new gown already, perhaps she shouldn't press her luck.

When everyone had been wined and dined, J.B. commanded the floor. Fiona expected Mazie to make the big announcement. Instead, her husband grinned widely.

"We're glad you came tonight. Mazie thought this would be a good time to get us all together."

Jonathan looked puzzled. "We're going to the gala— sitting at the same table. I'm not sure what you mean."

Mazie patted her husband's arm and nodded. She glowed. Apparently, that was a real thing. Except for the unfortunate ones like Fiona who were sick as dogs.

J.B. laid a hand on his wife's shoulder. The two of them exchanged a private look that was intimate and smug with happiness. Then J.B., former bad boy and now thoroughly content homebody, cleared his throat. "We're pregnant," he said. "Well, Mazie is. We wanted you all to know."

After a moment of stunned silence, Lisette was the first one to react. She jumped to her feet and smiled broadly. "That's wonderful news. I'm thrilled for you."

Mazie stood as well and embraced her sister-in-law. "I wasn't sure what to say to you, Lizzy. You and Jonathan have been disappointed twice. I feel guilty that I'm the one who's pregnant."

Lisette shook her head slowly. "Silly goose. Your happiness doesn't hurt me. Jonathan and I are fine. We don't know what the future holds for us, but we'll be tickled pink to welcome the first of a new generation of Tarletons."

"And Vaughans," J.B. said. "Don't forget the daddy."

In the midst of laughter and more hugging, Fiona sneaked a sideways glance at Hartley. He was saying and doing all the right things, but he was pale beneath his tan. Had his family noticed? They had all known him far longer than Fiona had. Maybe it was her imagination.

Jonathan picked up a flute of champagne from the sideboard. "To new beginnings," he said. "And to a healthy pregnancy and a perfect little baby—" He halted, an arrested look on his face. "Boy? Girl?"

"Too soon to tell," Mazie said. "Plus, there's always the possibility of multiples given the meds I've taken."

J.B. turned green. "Oh, hell," he muttered. "I forgot about that."

Mazie slid her arm around his waist and chuckled. "I wondered how long it would take you to remember."

Lisette glanced at her watch. "I hate to break up the party, but if we're going to make it in time for the presentation, we'd better head out."

Jonathan nodded. "You're right, sweetheart. One more thing, though. I'll make it quick." When everyone fell silent, Jonathan stared at his twin with a hard-to-read expression.

Fiona had sat down again on the sofa. Hartley perched on the arm beside her. She felt the fine tension in his body when Jonathan spoke.

The CEO of Tarleton Shipping addressed the room. His brown-eyed gaze, so like his sibling's, was focused on his brother. "We've all been through a lot in the past year. Changes and more changes. But one thing stays the same…family." The muscles in his throat worked visibly. "I want you to come back to work, Hartley. The company needs you. I need you. Whatever happened while you were away is water under the bridge. The important thing now is that you've come home."

Fiona was stunned. She squeezed Hartley's hand, silently urging him to accept the olive branch.

He stood up slowly. She had no idea what he was thinking. "I'd like that," he said gruffly. He reached out to his brother. "Thanks, Jonathan."

All the women were misty-eyed as the two men shook hands. There wasn't time to dwell on the tentative truce. Maybe Jonathan planned it that way. Everyone rushed to gather phones and car keys and purses.

Soon, Fiona was in the car with Hartley. "Well, *that* was awesome," she said. "I'm so happy for you."

When Hartley didn't respond, she put a hand on his shoulder briefly. "You okay?" she asked as she fastened her seat belt, taking care not to clip the delicate fabric of her dress in the mechanism.

Hartley pulled out into traffic, his big hands clenched around the steering wheel. "I'm fine." His jaw was granite hard.

"I don't think you are. I thought you'd be excited about returning to Tarleton Shipping."

"I'm pleased," he said tersely. The declaration was hard to believe.

Fiona chewed her lip. "No one is holding a grudge. No one is demanding answers about why you were gone. Your family is wonderfully intact."

"Maybe," he muttered. "He was my best friend. I doubt we'll ever get that back."

"Which is why you have to tell them the truth. You see that…right? Jonathan and Mazie need to know that their mother is not their mother. And that you didn't abandon them for no good reason. This is a critical time for your sister."

Hartley muttered a rude word beneath his breath. "Ignorance is bliss. Trust me on this."

"You are so damned stubborn," she cried. His intractability infuriated her. But they were already pulling up at the event site, so she had to drop the argument.

Crowds of impeccably dressed attendees poured into the building. The venue had once been a trio of row houses.

Careful renovation turned the historic structure into an upscale, sophisticated spot for weddings and other special occasions.

Tonight, the chamber of commerce was celebrating philanthropy in Charleston and honoring Gerald Tarleton with a posthumous award. He would have received the honor in person had he not died so unexpectedly.

As guests entered the building and gathered in a large, bright atrium, screens on four walls detailed the many programs and projects to which the Tarleton patriarch had been a benefactor. The photographs spanned a couple of decades. From the older images, it was easy to see that Jonathan and Hartley resembled their father in his younger days.

The chamber president quieted the crowd and summoned the three Tarleton siblings to the miniature dais. J.B., Lisette and Fiona lingered at the back of the room.

For the first time, Fiona truly understood the place this family held in the story of the port city. The Tarletons were low-country royalty. She was glad all the focus was on the stage. She felt queasy and out of her element.

Hartley was so damned sexy when he stepped up to the microphone and said a few words. She put a hand to her chest to still the ache there. She was such a hypocrite... insisting that he come clean about his trip to Europe. Insisting that secrets were hurtful.

Soon, the brief ceremony was over and huge double doors swung inward, allowing the crowd to progress to the ballroom where a fancy meal was waiting. When the Tarletons rejoined their respective partners, Fiona felt even more like a fraud. She was here under false pretenses. Hartley wanted her. He'd said so in a dozen different ways.

But their fledgling relationship wouldn't stand a chance when the truth came out.

The large room filled rapidly with conversation and laughter. The waiters and waitresses who moved between tables were a welcome distraction. Hartley was seated beside her, but he felt a thousand miles away.

Despite the intimacy he and Fiona had shared earlier, he was only going through the motions now. Behind his pleasant smile she saw a world of confusion. He was hurting, and she didn't know how to help him.

Who was she kidding? She didn't even know how to help herself.

Though the food was wonderful, she ate sparingly. She still had to get through the early morning hours without revealing her *interesting* condition. As much as she wanted to spend the night with Hartley, she was courting danger.

Tomorrow, she wanted to tell him calmly, rationally. Not have him find out about the baby because she was hunched over the toilet losing her breakfast.

Things improved when the lights dimmed and couples began moving onto the dance floor in the center of the room. Crystal chandeliers overhead reflected candle flames from the ornate centerpieces.

Hartley stood and held out his hand. "Dance with me?" he asked gruffly. When she twined her fingers with his, he tugged her to her feet.

"I'd love to," she said.

Hartley was an amazing dancer. She remembered that from the wedding where they met. Though he was big and broad and unabashedly masculine, he moved with confidence across the polished floor.

When she tried to keep a space between them, Hartley simply ignored her self-conscious behavior. "No one's watching us," he said, his breath warm on her temple. "Relax, Fee."

She was pretty sure he was deluding himself. A good

portion of the room—at least the single females from twenty to forty—were eyeing Hartley like he was dark chocolate and they had just finished a ten-day juice cleanse.

Hartley, on the other hand, was flatteringly single-minded. He held her close. His gaze never strayed to other women. His beautiful cognac eyes mesmerized her.

"This is fun," she said, resting her cheek against his shoulder. It wasn't what she *wanted* to say. She wanted to pour out her thoughts and her fears and her questions about the future. She wanted to tell him how he made her life brighter and better. How he made her feel desirable and sexy and *hopeful*.

She wanted to tell him she loved him. Her breath hitched. The knowledge had come to her gradually, but could no longer be ignored.

The words lodged in her throat. Like Cinderella watching the clock, Fiona didn't want to miss a single moment of the magic. She was racing against time, trying desperately to see a solution where there was none.

She *knew*, deep in her heart, that as soon as she revealed the truth about her pregnancy, Hartley would be long gone and she would turn into a fat orange pregnant pumpkin with nothing to show for this crazy affair other than a single glass slipper and a broken heart.

J.B. and Mazie were the first to leave the party. Like Fiona, Mazie had been battling exhaustion. Jonathan and Lisette soon followed.

As the room emptied, Hartley and Fiona remained on the dance floor, swaying from one romantic song until the next. Earlier in the evening, the band had played pop tunes. Top-forty hits.

Now, with the lights low and only two dozen couples still enjoying the music, the old standards were the best.

Especially as a prelude to a cozy overnight rendezvous at a nearby hotel.

Hartley stroked the back of her neck with a single fingertip, reducing her to a puddle of need. "I want you, Fee."

The hoarse words were not surprising. He'd been noticeably aroused for the past hour. She tipped back her head and searched his face. "I want you, too," she said softly. *So. Very. Much.*

They gathered their things from the table and headed for the exit. Numerous people interrupted their progress to say something to Hartley about his father, but finally, they were out on the street in the warm, muggy heat of a Charleston evening.

Hartley had parked the car in a two-tiered garage around the corner from the venue. They strolled there slowly, hands linked like teenagers on prom night. Despite everything that was wrong, Fiona experienced a totally illogical surge of hope.

Maybe Hartley did care for her more deeply than she thought.

Maybe he would be able to handle her shocking news with equanimity.

Maybe she would finally have the family she had always wanted.

At the car, Hartley insisted on carrying both bags. He tucked his smaller case under his arm and picked up Fiona's carry-on. "I'm still holding your hand," he said, giving her his trademark grin. "Tonight is a big romantic gesture. I'm impressing you with my strength and stamina."

She bumped his hip with hers. "Save the stamina for later."

His cheeks flushed. "Duly noted."

Their lodging was a brief walk away. The streets were mostly deserted. When they arrived, a sleepy desk clerk checked them in. Hartley had booked the rooftop suite with a view of the city.

They skipped the elevator and climbed three flights of stairs. Since her escort had his hands full, Fiona unlocked the door and walked in. "Oh, Hartley," she said, delighted. "This is gorgeous." The furnishings were soft and stylish but not too over-the top for a man to feel comfortable. A deep, inviting sofa upholstered in sage green suggested any number of alternatives for adult play. The huge four-poster bed dominated the room.

Beyond the bed, French doors opened outward onto a private patio. Fee kicked off her shoes and went to explore. When Hartley dropped the bags and followed her outside, she leaned over the railing. "This place is perfect."

He wrapped his arms around her waist from behind, tugging her back from the edge. "*You're* perfect."

The absolute sincerity in his voice wooed her, turned her knees to mush. She spun to face him. "Thank you, Hartley. Thank you for thinking of this."

He kissed her nose. "Sit right there. Don't move." The small table was flanked by two metal chairs.

Moments later, he was back carrying a bottle of champagne and two glasses. "This was our welcome gift."

As he started to work on the cork, Fiona felt panic rise. Pregnant women couldn't drink. "None for me," she said. "I want to be awake for the next act. But you have some."

He gazed at her quizzically, setting the bottle aside. "Whatever the lady wants."

She reached across the table and took his hand. "I'll ask it again. Are you okay?"

His expression altered for a split second and then settled back into his habitual lazy grin. Had she touched a nerve?

"Why wouldn't I be?" he said, but his fingers drummed on the table.

"We haven't had a chance to discuss your sister's news. I was afraid it upset you."

His jaw worked visibly. The silence lengthened. "I don't think it's *good* news, if that's what you're asking. But before you start in on me, it wouldn't have changed anything if I had told them the truth. They wanted a baby. Mazie already knows that mental illness runs in our family."

Fiona sighed inwardly. Had she ever met a more stubborn man? "Genetics is a tricky business," she said. "Besides, their baby is half Vaughan. None of us can guarantee a perfect pregnancy ahead of time. It's a roll of the dice."

"Good thing I'm not a gambler."

She glared at him, completely frustrated, but unable to tell him why.

Suddenly, Hartley stood up and paced. "Do you really want to have this argument right now? I thought we were here to indulge ourselves."

He was right. Once she told him the truth tomorrow morning, everything would change. She wanted this one last night. She wanted Hartley. The other could wait. "I'm sorry," she said. She mimed locking her lips and tossing the keys. "From now on, it's all about you and me."

At last, his body language relaxed. "I'm glad to hear it." He moved behind her chair and played with her hair, sifting the strands, his fingers brushing her ears, making her tremble. He had barely touched her, and already she was wild for him.

When she tried to stand up, two big hands settled on her shoulders. "Don't move, darlin'. We're gonna take this slow. We have all night."

It was supposed to be a promise on his part, but to her ears, it sounded dangerous. *All night*? What was she thinking? Morning always came, and with it, a reckoning.

He reached around her and slid his slightly rough man-hands inside the bodice of her dress, cupping her bare curves. She shuddered, biting her lip to hold back a ragged moan. Sounds carried on the night air.

"What are you doing?" she whispered.

"Enjoying myself." The laughter in his voice made her smile, though she was too wound for amusement to take hold.

She exhaled shakily. "Carry on."

He played with her breasts, making her squirm. The nipples were more sensitive now that she was pregnant. When he kissed her neck and nuzzled the spot just below her ear—because he knew she liked it—she reached up and grabbed his wrists. "I want to go inside," she pleaded.

"Not yet." Without warning, he tugged her to her feet. "Let's look at the stars."

Fourteen

Fiona was confused. They were outside. All they had to do was look up. Apparently, that wasn't enough for Hartley. He tugged her toward the edge of the patio where a low stone wall topped with three feet of wrought iron marked a boundary. A century and a half ago, a gentleman might have coaxed a Southern belle up here to see the sights.

The hour was late. Few people roamed the streets below. The ones who did, didn't look up.

Hartley stood behind her, crowding her. "Hold on, Fee." He took her hands and placed them on the smooth, cool metal curlicues. "Don't let go."

Her heart beat faster. Could he see the way her chest rose and fell with her startled breathing? She wanted to question him, to demand an explanation. But another part of her, submissive, aroused, wanted to see how far this would go. Hartley was a modern-day pirate. An adventurer. A man unafraid to push the bounds of propriety.

Even so, she was shocked beyond words when she felt him lift her skirt. Despite the season and the temperature, the air felt cool on her bare legs and the backs of her thighs. "Hartley?" The ragged word was equal parts protest and slurred pleasure. Surely he wouldn't...

Once again, he kissed the back of her neck. "I'll keep you safe, sweet thing. You can trust me."

Her fingers clenched painfully around the unforgiving iron. She might have swooned had twenty-first-century women been given permission to do such a girly thing.

His big hands palmed her butt, squeezing. He made no move to take off her panties, but his thumb traced the crease in her ass through nylon and lace. Goose bumps covered her body.

Her voice was frozen, her breath lodged in her throat. Between her legs, her sex wept for him. She was swollen and hot and damp, unbearably needy. Would he unzip her dress? Here, where they were exposed?

The idea both frightened and seduced her.

Hartley continued to play with her backside as if he had all the time in the world. Just when she thought she couldn't bear another second of his lazy torture, he reached around her and, with a single finger, stroked her to a sharp, vicious climax. She shuddered and groaned.

Afterward, her forehead rested against the metal. She could barely breathe. His hand was concealed by layers of tulle and satin. If anyone on the street below was inclined to gaze upward, nothing would seem amiss.

Hartley moved closer. She felt his arousal at her back. "I told you we'd see stars," he muttered, his voice heavy.

Her body went lax, leaned into his. But still, she held the railing. "How much did you have to drink, Hartley Tarleton? You're out of control."

His laughter was strained. "Possibly." He covered her hands with his.

The visual was enticing and beautiful and painfully perfect. She wanted this man and this life. But she wanted more. She wanted a future full of love and laughter and family squabbles. She wanted everything.

Without warning, he scooped her into his arms. "I'd like to get horizontal now. Any objections?"

Fiona waved a hand, yawning. "Not a single one."

Hartley knew he had met his match. There had never been a female he couldn't walk away from. Not until Fee.

Lust and tenderness and determination swirled in a dangerous cocktail of emotion. He wanted this woman. Maybe forever. The knowledge should have stunned him, but oddly, he recognized it. The need to claim her as his own had been growing underground. He'd told himself he was having fun.

Instead, he'd been making plans.

Fiona had no family of her own. He could share his.

As he carried her over the threshold into their hedonistic bedroom and bumped the door closed with his hip, his heart beat faster, a syncopated rhythm that made him breathe too fast. Was there more to this thing with Fee than sex? Did he want more?

Now they were enclosed in a cool, private lovers' boudoir that smelled of roses and sin. He set her on her feet and kissed her roughly, his hands tangling in her hair, holding her head.

"I never seem to get enough of you, Fiona. Why do you think that is?"

Her sleepy smile was sweet and guileless. "I have no idea. But I'm a fan of your work."

His hands shook. "I may not be able to stop. I may have

to take you all night, again and again. Like that first time we met."

"Do you hear me complaining?"

The sass in her voice inflamed him. Something about this weekend was bringing out his caveman instincts. He backed her up against the carved post at the foot of the bed. Falling to his knees, he knelt between her legs and found his way under her skirt.

Her skin was hot and fragrant with a familiar scent. He nudged her feet apart. Though his body ached fiercely with the need to be inside her, he wanted to give her every ounce of pleasure possible.

When he tasted her intimately, she groaned. Her hands fisted in his hair, making him wince. This time, her orgasm was slower, richer. It rolled over both of them in an endless stream. Hartley felt the quivers in her pelvis, the sharp jerk when her body hit the top.

She collapsed in his arms. He eased her down onto the soft, luxurious rug, wrapping her tightly against him. While Fee struggled to breathe, he pressed kisses to her hot face. "I need you, Fiona James. Tell me you want me, too."

"Of course I do." She blinked at him, befuddled.

"What if we travel the world for a few months? Give you new horizons and inspirations to paint? We'll go wherever the wind blows us."

She flinched. The change in her face was so obvious a blind man would have seen it. While Hartley had been weaving dreams, Fiona had clearly been on a different track. Distress darkened her soft blue-gray eyes. "Your brother asked you to come back to work. You can't abandon him again."

Suddenly, he remembered Fiona's aversion to his spending the night at her house. What kind of fool was he? A woman who wanted her "space" clearly wasn't keen on spending a lot of time together.

The raw hurt in his chest was astounding. Had he really been so clueless about his own obsession and Fiona's ambivalence?

"Forget I said anything," he said lightly, tucking away the heartsick feeling in his gut. "It was the lust talking. You're a very sexy woman. I plead temporary insanity."

"Hartley…" She cupped his face.

He'd be damned if he'd let her see that she had bruised his ego. Jumping to his feet, he dragged her with him. "Enough talking," he muttered.

He stripped the dress and underwear from her body and then removed his own clothes rapidly. After folding back the sumptuous covers, he tumbled her onto the bed. He wanted to prove to himself that his emotions weren't involved.

But when he tried to be rough and impersonal like this was just another encounter with just another nameless female, he couldn't do it. Fee's bottom lip trembled. Her beautiful eyes welled with tears. "I care about you, Hartley. You know I do."

The lukewarm words were like alcohol on a razor cut. He held her wrists in one hand and loomed over her. "Let's put that to the test."

Deliberately, he held her down and pleasured her, made her come three times. Every time she tried to coax him to enter her, he resisted…even though the truth was, he was sick with wanting her.

Finally, his body betrayed him. He'd been aroused for a million hours, desperate to find solace in her arms, her soft, sweet body. He spread her legs and thrust hard, finding himself at the mouth of her womb, buried as deeply as he could go. Wanting to bind her to him. To demand that she acknowledge this incredible connection they shared.

It was over soon. Humiliatingly so.

He visited the bathroom. So did she. After turning out the lights, they climbed into bed. It would have been a fitting end to the evening if he could have turned his back on her. But he was weak in the way only a man could be. He dragged her close and spooned her, already yawning.

They fell asleep without another word.

Fiona awoke at dawn, groggy and needing to pee. It took a moment for her surroundings to register. And then she remembered. The hotel. Hartley.

Panic struck as she assessed her nausea. Unbelievably, her stomach was at rest. Maybe she was turning the corner. It didn't matter anymore, though, did it? Hartley would have to be told about the baby today, and then it was all over.

When she turned on her side to look at him, his eyes were open. He was on his back, arm slung over his forehead, staring at the ceiling.

"What do you want to do?" she asked. They had made plans to enjoy brunch, play tourist at the open-air market, spend a second night at the hotel, make love until they were satisfied.

Hartley didn't even look at her. "I think we should check out of the room. Head home. Separately. We need to back up and take a look at what we're doing. You're right, Fiona. If I'm returning to work at Tarleton Shipping right away, I'll have a lot on my plate."

"You're angry," she said, her heart sinking.

He shrugged. "No."

It was time for the truth. She sat up and wrapped the sheet around her all the way up to her neck. This wasn't an easy conversation to have naked. "I need to tell you something," she whispered.

Shivers racked her body. The nausea threatened to return.

Without warning, Hartley rolled out of bed. "I'm done with talking and listening, Fee. I'm calling a time-out. You in your corner. Me in mine. This relationship is too damn much work."

The next thirty minutes passed in a haze of misery. They took turns showering. Room service sent up coffee and croissants. When both Hartley and Fiona were dressed and ready to go, they carried their bags downstairs and turned in the keys. Fiona's overnight case held a satin gown folded up inside.

Hartley drove her home without speaking a word. He stopped at her sidewalk and left the motor running. There was no choice but to get out, yet something held her back. "Are you done with me?" she asked. "Done with us?"

His expression was inscrutable. "I don't know."

In the days that followed, Fiona lost herself in her work. It was a pattern that had served her well in the past. She felt the urgency of getting all her large commissions finished before the baby came. What did she have? Five months? Six? Babies could come early or late...

She had no idea how she would cope in the beginning. Caring for a newborn was a huge amount of work. And there would be no paid maternity leave for a self-employed artist.

Should she swallow her pride and ask for Hartley's help? He must have thought his travel-the-world plan hadn't interested her. Quite the opposite. It sounded like the most amazing honeymoon.

But preparing for the baby and getting her projects completed didn't leave any time for a months-long jaunt.

And still she hadn't told her baby's father the truth. Though it wasn't entirely her fault, she felt guilty. The longer she waited, the harder it seemed, particularly after the way their romantic weekend had ended.

Despite her distress over the way she and Hartley had parted and her worry about the future, each day brought new reasons to be excited about her pregnancy. Thankfully, she had made it through the worst of the morning sickness. It still caught her off guard at times, but not every day and not as badly as before.

Her breasts were bigger now. The little baby bump was growing more noticeable. Slowly but surely, her body was changing. Soon, telling Hartley would be a moot point. People would begin to notice her shape and draw their own conclusions.

Every morning she told herself today was the day. She would seek him out, give him the news and weather the explosion. After all, this baby linked them, no matter what. But every day she lost her nerve. Seeing the look on his face when he heard the truth would destroy her.

She *wanted* this baby. Desperately. Knowing that Hartley couldn't or *didn't* broke her heart.

Over a week after the gala, Mazie showed up unannounced on Fiona's doorstep. Because she was working, Fiona nearly didn't answer the bell. But her back was hurting, and she needed a break anyway.

She wiped her hands, peeked through the window and felt her heart catch with disappointment. It wasn't Hartley. Of course it wasn't.

Fiona opened the door. "Hey, Mazie. What's up? Come on in. Please excuse the fact that I'm covered with paint. Neatness is not one of my gifts."

Mazie tossed her keys in a chair and put her hands on her hips. Her usual sunny smile was nowhere in sight. "What have you done to Hartley?" She demanded an answer.

The pile of guilt smothering Fiona grew deeper. "Nothing," she said weakly. "I don't know what you mean." She wrapped her arms around her waist, feeling her face heat.

Hartley's sister paced, her stance agitated. "Jonathan is worried about him. He says things are going smoothly at work, but Hartley is distant."

"Well, that makes sense, doesn't it? You're all dealing with the fallout from his being gone. I'm sure it will take some time to get back to the way things were. I wouldn't worry about it."

"That's not all." Mazie scowled, her expression stormy and anxious at the same time. "J.B. is throwing a big party for my birthday soon. I asked Hartley to bring you, and he gave me some weird evasive answer about how you were super busy. It was clearly a lie. What's going on with you two?"

In another circumstance, Fiona might have confessed her pregnancy. She liked Mazie and felt close to her already. But to admit she was pregnant would bring a host of questions and problems. Mazie would rightly want to know why Fiona hadn't told Hartley he was going to be a father—and why Fiona and Hartley weren't living together.

Fiona couldn't explain any of that without divulging Hartley's secrets.

Those secrets weren't hers to tell.

"I'm sure Hartley can find a date for the birthday party. And I'm also sure it's not good for the baby *or* you to get so upset. Give Hartley some space and time to regroup. He'll be fine."

Mazie cocked her head, studying Fiona as if she could see inside her brain. "I was under the impression the two of you were pretty serious."

Fiona bit her lip. Hard. She refused to cry in front of the other woman. "I think Hartley and I want different things out of life. Besides, he needs a chance to get back in the groove at Tarleton Shipping."

"Did you have a fight?"

How was Fiona supposed to answer that? "Not a fight *exactly*. I suppose you could say we had words. But it's over. We're both fine."

Mazie scrunched up her face and ran her hands through her hair. "Why can't anything be simple, dammit? I thought you were perfect for my brother. I can't believe he let you slip through his fingers."

"It was my fault," Fiona said, not wanting Mazie to be disappointed in her brother. "I needed things that Hartley wasn't ready to give. So don't blame him. It's just that he and I are two very different people."

Mazie's face fell. "Well, that sucks. Can you tell me more? Maybe I can knock some sense into him."

"It's personal," Fiona said. "I'm sorry, Mazie. I love your family, and I would have liked to be a part of it. But it's not in the cards." She paused briefly. "I hate to be rude, but I really do need to get back to work."

Mazie's eyes glittered with tears. "He needs somebody."

"You're matchmaking, because you and J.B. are so happy, but not every relationship works out. Hartley will find someone else." Saying those words out loud was an actual physical pain.

"I suppose." Mazie's glum acceptance didn't make Fiona feel any better at all. "I still wish you could come to my birthday party," Mazie said.

"Perhaps you and I should have lunch one day. Just the two of us. A girl can never have too many friends."

"I'd like that. I won't let you slip away simply because my brother is dumb. I'll call you soon. Sorry to interrupt your work."

Fiona said her goodbyes, locked the front door, threw herself down on the sofa and cried…

Fifteen

Unfortunately, tears never solved anything. When her pity party was over, she was no closer than ever to finding answers, and now she had a headache and a stuffy nose besides.

She wiped her face with the hem of her T-shirt and sat up. Reaching in her pocket for her phone before she could change her mind, she sent Hartley a text.

I miss you.

When he didn't answer right away, she reminded herself that he was at work. The important thing was, she had made an overture. Not only did he need to come pick up his birthday gift for his sister, but Fiona needed to see him face-to-face and tell him the truth.

To make sure she didn't back out again, she added a second text.

Mazie's birthday present is ready. Let me know when you want to pick it up.

The dizziness and light-headed feeling she experienced when she hit Send had nothing to do with her pregnancy this time. She was so damned scared.

What would she do if he ignored her entirely? Thankfully, Mazie's painting was Fiona's ace in the hand.

A few hours later as she was fixing herself an early dinner of tomato soup and grilled cheese, her phone finally dinged. Now is good for me, the text said.

Her heart stopped. She wasn't ready. Her hands were clammy and shaky.

Can we make it 6:30?

I'll be there.

With barely an hour to scarf down her food, clean up the kitchen and take a quick shower, she had to hurry. Instead of a sundress, which was her go-to hot-weather wardrobe when she wanted to look nice, she found a pair of new jeans in her closet and paired them with a simple button-up shirt. White. Sleeveless. Nothing to say she wanted to look good in front of an ex-lover.

For courage, she added the seahorse pendant Mazie had given her. The little creature was cool against her hot skin.

Again and again she rehearsed the words she wanted to say when she revealed her pregnancy. All the things she had wanted to say when they were at the hotel but didn't have the chance. Letting Hartley off the hook. Telling him he didn't have to be involved with the baby at all.

All the practice in the world wasn't going to make this confrontation any less painful. What she really wanted to do was get down on her knees and beg him to love her *and* her baby. To plead with him to be happy.

When the knock came at six thirty sharp, she opened the door. Instantly, she knew that Mazie had been right. Hartley looked terrible. Still handsome, of course, but stripped of life. His eyes were dull. The usual joie de vivre that put a twinkle of mischief in his expressive face was gone.

"Come on in," she said. "The painting is on the sofa."

When she closed the door, he stopped in front of her and bent to kiss the top of her head. "Hello, Fee."

Silly tears sprang to her eyes. She blinked them away. His tenderness was more painful than outright hostility. Swallowing the huge lump in her throat, she led him through to the living room. "There it is."

Hartley stopped in his tracks, his expression awed. "My God, Fiona. This is phenomenal." He picked up the small canvas with careful hands and examined it closely. "You've captured the two of them exactly. Mazie will adore it." He turned back to look at her, where she had paused in the doorway. "I knew you were talented, but this is something else again. You're an amazing artist. I don't think I fully understood how gifted you are until now."

His praise warmed the cold places in her broken heart. "Thanks. I'm happy you like it. Shall I wrap it for you?" She had brought the supplies from her studio just in case.

"Yes, please."

He prowled the room for the few minutes it took her to enfold the framed canvas in thick kraft paper and tie it with a fancy golden bow. "There you go," she said. "All ready for the birthday girl." Some tiny part of her still expected him to invite her to the party, but Hartley didn't say a word.

Despite the awkwardness between them, a silly sprig of hope continued to push through her fear. She couldn't procrastinate any longer. "Hartley, I need to talk to you about something."

"Me first," he said. "I need a favor. I know we didn't part on the best of terms, but I need your help."

"With what?"

His expression was bleak. "My siblings and I have been summoned to the lawyer's office tomorrow morning at ten. Something about a letter from our father. Written to me. But the other two are supposed to be there to hear it read aloud. J.B. and Lisette will come with Mazie and Jonathan, of course. I'd like somebody with *me* who is in my corner."

"It's your family, Hartley. Of course they're in your corner. It wouldn't be appropriate for me to intrude."

"I'm going to have to sit there and let my father berate me from the grave. The others may have forgiven me, but my dad died before I even came home. This isn't going to be pleasant." He pressed three fingers to his forehead as if he had a headache.

She swallowed, feeling frustrated and emotional. Finally, she had worked up the courage to tell Hartley about her pregnancy, and he had rerouted the conversation before she could even start.

"You need to eat," she said. "It will make you feel better." There she went again. Trying to make herself indispensable.

In her small kitchen, she waved him to the table and found him a beer. While she made a second version of the meal she had eaten earlier, Jonathan brooded visibly. His masculinity dwarfed the modest room. Or maybe it was his expansive personality.

Hartley was larger than life. He had the family background and the adventuresome spirit to pull off any scheme he chose to pursue. Go racing off to Europe to uncover a decades-old secret. Buy an enormous wreck of a house and blithely decide to renovate it at a moment's notice.

Sweep a bridesmaid off her feet a year ago and make her fall head over heels in love. That last one was his most outrageous affair. Fiona had been an ordinary woman with an ordinary life until Hartley came along.

She sat beside him and sipped a glass of iced tea while he wolfed down the modest meal. He ate as if he were starving.

It was ridiculous to feel sorry for him. The man had plenty of money. Charleston was chock-full of fabulous restaurants that offered takeout. But she loved him, despite the impossibility of their relationship. She wanted him to be happy.

Suddenly, she knew she couldn't procrastinate any longer. She would make love to him one last time and then lay all her cards on the table. "Hartley," she said. She reached a hand across the table and held his wrist. "Would you like to stay the night?"

Hartley nearly choked on his soup. His body went on high alert, sensing danger. Is this why he had come? He could have asked Fiona to deliver the painting via local messenger service. He'd told himself the package was too valuable to entrust to other hands.

The truth was far simpler. He had wanted to see Fiona again. Her three-word text had been all the permission he needed.

Even so, he equivocated. "We always end up fighting afterward."

She lifted his hand and kissed his fingers one by one. "Don't be mean, Hartley."

"Would you rather me be *nice*?" He leaned toward her and curled a hand behind her neck, pulling her close for a searing kiss. The taste of her went to his head like 100 proof whiskey.

He had tried to stay away. He really had. But it was a losing battle. Until another man put a ring on her finger, he was going to fight for what he wanted. And he wanted Fee.

Slowly, he stood, tugging her to her feet. After what had happened at the hotel the night of the gala, he was stunned now to realize that Fiona wanted him as much as he wanted her, not that such a thing was possible.

His body was on fire for her. The hunger consumed him. Something had spooked her when he mentioned *traveling the globe*. He wouldn't make that mistake again. If Fiona was interested in hot and temporary, he would be that guy.

He knew what it felt like to sleep alone. He'd be damned if he would let it happen again. Now that she had offered an olive branch, he was determined to make the most of this extraordinary turn of events.

They navigated the narrow hallway hand in hand. It was still daylight outside. Fiona's bedroom glowed in the late-day sun, even with the curtains drawn. She hadn't made her bed that morning. The tumbled sheets were an erotic invitation.

They barely spoke a word this time. Perhaps because talking always got them in trouble.

He unbuttoned her top. The lacy bra beneath did little to hide pert raspberry nipples. She was softer than he remembered, her breasts fuller and rounder. Maybe absence truly did make the heart grow fonder.

When she was naked, he lifted her into the bed and rapidly removed his own clothes. Climbing in beside her was like coming home.

His breath came in short, jerky gasps. "I won't ask any

questions, Fee. Your reasons are your own. But know that I wouldn't want to be any place else in the world right now."

Her lips were bare. Pale pink. Kissable. Wide eyes stared up at him as he leaned over her on one elbow.

She cupped his cheek. "I was afraid you didn't want me anymore."

His rough curse held incredulity. "I'll never stop wanting you, darlin'. You're the one who seems to have a few issues."

When he reached for a condom, she put a hand on his arm. "You won't need that. I took care of things."

"Whatever you say, Fee."

When he moved between her legs and thrust slowly, the sensation of bare skin to bare skin made him shudder. "I've never been with a woman like this. It feels damned incredible."

"Yes," she whispered. She kept her eyes open the entire time, almost as if she were trying to memorize his face.

He gritted his teeth, clenched his jaw. Tried to stave off the climax that was a desperate convergence of condomless sex and long celibate days without her.

Finally, he rolled to his back, taking her with him. Now he could finger her center, send her over the edge. Her orgasm triggered his own. He came forever. Until he was boneless, helpless.

She collapsed on his chest at the end. He held her tightly, stroking her hair. "Fee…"

He trailed off, not knowing what to say and not wanting to cause another argument. Fiona seemed perfectly content when they were together like this. Why was she so skittish in other ways?

At last, she moved away from him and padded in her bare feet to the bathroom. When she returned, she had pulled a T-shirt over her head. It was long enough to cover the tops of her thighs.

Her face glowed with happiness. "It's only eight o'clock. You want to pop popcorn and watch a movie?"

He raised up on his elbows and grinned at her. "Or have sex again?"

"Can't we do both?" She returned his smile with interest.

"Or I could show you the new house."

"You've made progress?"

"A little."

"Sure," she said. "Let me get dressed. You want to walk? The humidity is down. It's a nice evening."

"I could be persuaded."

Fifteen minutes later, they were outside. The scent of bougainvillea and roses mingled with car exhaust and someone cooking a late-evening steak on the grill. The neighborhood was still busy at this hour. Kids on bikes. Grown-ups sitting on front porches, processing the day.

They walked at a leisurely pace. Even so, Hartley's woebegone house was not more than twenty-five minutes away.

He watched Fiona's face as they approached. Her eyes widened. "You've already closed on the property and done all this?"

"I was motivated." And he was trying to use physical exhaustion as a sedative. Being physically close to Fiona when he was here working had taxed his self-control. He took her hand. "Come see the inside."

When he unlocked the front door, a musty smell greeted them. But it wasn't anything as unpleasant as mildew. More of an old-library odor combined with a house shut up in high temperatures.

"Easy," he said as he steered her around piles of rubbish that he had already accumulated. He gave her the grand tour. Parlor. Dining room. Kitchen. An antiquated bath-room. "We can't go upstairs yet. Too dangerous."

She shook her head. "I thought when you went back to work with Jonathan you would hire a contractor."

"I will…eventually. But I needed something to keep me busy in the evenings."

She didn't react at all to his leading comment. In the front hallway, she leaned against the wall and looked up at the cobwebby chandelier. "So are you really going to flip it or live in it? It's awfully big for a guy who says he doesn't want babies."

"Not every man is cut out to be a father."

"I suppose."

Was it his imagination, or did her face look stricken? Maybe she was disappointed in him.

The golden evening lost some of its shine. "We'd better get back," he said gruffly.

He locked up and checked windows. They reversed their route. Fiona had invited him to stay the night. He wasn't sure it was the thing to do. But who was he kidding? He wasn't going to say no.

In the end, they *did* pop popcorn and watch a movie. With his arm around Fiona and her head on his shoulder, it was almost possible to pretend that everything in his life was perfect.

When it was time for bed, the tension escalated almost imperceptibly. This was the first time he had been ex-pressly invited to spend the night. The moment seemed significant, but in light of everything that had happened, he wasn't sure how.

Fiona rounded up a toothbrush for him. They took turns showering and met in the bedroom. She seemed shy. He was torn in a dozen different directions. Tomorrow's visit to the lawyer loomed, though he thrust the knowledge away, determined not to ruin this night. He wanted her badly. Should he disguise his need until she trusted him more?

His beautiful artist made the decision for him. They had barely turned out the light before he felt her hand slide beneath the covers. She wrapped her fingers around his erection. "Make love to me, Hartley."

The sex was perfect. Their bodies knew each other now. He could make her gasp. She knew how to pull him to the edge of release and keep him there until he was ready to cry uncle. They moved together in silent yearning.

As they drifted off to sleep, he was struck by the inescapable notion that tonight was the last time. Sadness enveloped him. Giving up wasn't his style, but he sensed Fiona pulling away. Her thoughts were a mystery.

In fact, she had wanted to talk to him at the hotel, but he had shut her down.

What was the point of being together if all they had was sex? He used to think it was enough, but now he wasn't so sure…

Sixteen

Fiona awoke with a jerk, her heart racing. Someone was in the house. "Hartley…" She whispered his name urgently. When she reached for him, his side of the bed was empty.

Her heart rate slowed, but now she had a bigger worry. Grabbing up her robe, she slipped it over her naked body and belted it. For some reason, she felt the need to tiptoe in her own house.

She found him in the kitchen. He had put on his boxer briefs, but the rest of him was gloriously naked. Ignoring the ache and zing of completely understandable lust in her pelvis, she went to him and combed her fingers through his sleep-rumpled hair. "You want to talk about it?"

He shot her a tired grin, barely enough wattage to even be called a grin. "Not much to say. This is where my color-outside-the-lines behavior catches up with me. I'd just as soon not have witnesses when the lawyer reads this letter from my father, but it seems I'm out of luck."

"I'm sorry."

Hartley shrugged. "It was my choice to go to Switzerland without telling anyone. It was my choice to borrow the money."

"An incredibly large amount of money," she pointed out.

"I thought you were on *my* side."

She kissed his cheek. "I am. And if you want me with you at the lawyer's office, I'll ignore any strange looks I get from your family. But afterward, I really do need to talk to you."

He frowned. "Why can't we talk now?"

Why indeed? She poured herself a cup of orange juice, keeping her back to him as she opened and closed the fridge. "Because it's three in the morning, and I'm not coherent at this hour. Come back to bed."

He took her hand and whirled her around. "Is that an invitation?"

She wrapped her arms around his neck and yawned. "As long as you won't be insulted if I sleep through your manly moves."

He scooped her up and carried her down the hall. "Challenge accepted."

When Fiona awoke the next morning, Hartley was gone, but he had left a note on the pillow beside her.

Had several things to do before the meeting at the lawyer's office. I'll send a car for you around nine thirty. Text me if that's a problem. When we're done there, you and I can find someplace to talk.

You and I can find someplace to talk. Innocuous words for a conversation that would change her life. Her stomach threatened to act up again, but after a cup of hot tea and some preventative saltines, she felt better.

The dress she had worn to the funeral was getting too tight around the waist. Instead, she put on a pair of the nice black pants she had bought recently—the ones with the stretchy elastic waist—and topped them with a sober gray tunic that had three-quarter-length sleeves and decorative black buttons. The dressy top hit her midthigh and disguised her change of shape.

When she added strappy black sandals and black earrings, she looked entirely presentable for an extremely serious legal meeting. She still thought it was a mistake for her to be there.

They were friends and lovers. After she told him her news, even those designations would be gone. As much as she wanted to think everything was going to turn out okay, in her heart, she knew the truth.

Today would signal the end of her relationship with Hartley Tarleton.

When the driver dropped her off downtown, Hartley was waiting on the sidewalk to greet her. He had showered and shaved and was wearing a suit that was clearly hand tailored. The charcoal-gray fabric emphasized his wide shoulders and his trim waist.

He brushed a kiss against her cheek, but he was distracted.

"You doing okay?" she asked, squeezing his hand.

"I've been better. Let's get this over with."

If any of the Tarleton siblings and their spouses thought it odd for Fiona to be in attendance, they were too well-bred to show it. When Hartley and Fiona joined them in a beautiful reception area, the other four stood and the receptionist ushered them into the lawyer's office.

Here, traditional furnishings reigned. Lots of leather

and dark green, navy and burgundy. Was the palette intentional? Meant to impart gravity?

Fiona had always reacted strongly to color and light. Either positively or negatively, the response was a function of her calling.

Today, in this stuffy, overly formal setting, she felt as if the room was trying to smother her. Maybe Hartley felt the same way, because he looked like his tie was too tight, and he was having trouble breathing.

The lawyer wasted no time greeting them. When everyone was seated in a semicircle facing the large mahogany desk, he opened a legal-size folder and shuffled a few papers.

Jonathan leaned forward, frowning. "I don't understand why we're here. I'm my father's executor. There hasn't been time for the death certificate and other initial documents to work their way through the court. Tell us what's going on. Please. What's so urgent about this letter?"

The lawyer was late fifties, early sixties. He was polite, but not warm. His nod was brief. "As you've been told, Gerald Tarleton left a letter to read in the event of his death. He filed it with my office six months ago. Though it is addressed to Hartley, Mr. Tarleton made it clear that you and your sister were to be here when the contents were revealed."

Mazie frowned as well. "A little too cloak-and-dagger, don't you think? It doesn't sound like my father."

The lawyer bristled. "I assure you, Ms. Vaughan…the letter is entirely legitimate."

Hartley sighed audibly. "We all know what it's going to say." He shot the lawyer a cool stare. "Let's get on with it."

The man nodded. "Very well." He opened a simple white envelope and extracted a single sheet of paper.

Fiona reached out and gripped Hartley's right hand.

His entire body was rigid. This public flogging was cruel, particularly since Jonathan and Hartley had finally begun to mend fences.

When the lawyer stood, she was forced to drag her attention away from Hartley.

The lawyer cleared his throat theatrically.

"My dearest son Hartley:

"If you are reading this letter, it means that I am gone. Though I was very angry with you for leaving and taking the money, in truth, I was angry with myself for my cowardice over the years. I told Jonathan I had written you out of the will, but I did not. I never did. More about that later.

"Some weeks after you disappeared, I discovered you had flown to Europe, and suddenly I understood what was happening in Switzerland. Not the specifics perhaps, but enough to realize that my secret was out.

"I owe all three of you my deepest apologies. I have no excuse other than the fact that I was scared and embarrassed, and I didn't know what to say to all of you now that you were adults.

"I should have done the right thing years ago, but I avoided the pain and let time pass. Now Hartley has to be the one to explain everything.

"Please know that I adored your mother. Losing her nearly wrecked my entire life. I did what I thought I had to do, but I have often wondered if I did all of you a disservice.

"No father could be more proud of his children. Jonathan is the steady hand at the wheel. Hartley has the fire and enthusiasm that propels us all forward. And Mazie, my sweet Mazie, is the heart of the family.

"Whatever you decide about the Vermont situation is up to you. There is no moral high ground. Only regret and sadness.

"Hartley, I addressed this letter to you because I wanted to make absolutely sure you knew that you have never disappointed me. Ever. You have been impulsive at times, but I have come to believe that such impulsiveness is far more admirable than being stuck in endless indecision as I have been.

"Forgive me, son, for letting your brother think ill of you. When I look back at what has happened, I regret that most of all.

"Jonathan will handle the nuts and bolts of dividing the company and the estate. You will all three benefit equally from our collective hard work. Mazie and J.B. have the wonderful house in the historic district. Jonathan and Lisette are building their dream home. To you, Hartley, I leave the beach house. I pray that you will find a partner—a wife—to bring you peace and happiness and many children to carry on your passion for living boldly.

"My plea is that you keep the beach house in the family and that you fill it with joy and laughter and love.

"Goodbye, my dear ones. Please forgive your old father his transgressions and remember me with fondness.

"Much love to each of you,

"Dad

"(aka Gerald Tarleton)"

When the lawyer finished reading and tucked the letter away, dead silence reigned for several moments. Hartley was pale, his gaze haunted. Jonathan's grim expression masked a multitude of emotions. Poor Mazie wept bitterly.

The youngest Tarleton offspring wiped her face. "What money? What was he talking about?"

The lawyer stood. "I have another appointment. You're welcome to talk this over here in my office. Stay as long as you like. Goodbye…"

When the man exited, Mazie repeated her question, looking from one brother to the other and back.

Hartley rolled to his feet and paced. "I stole a million bucks from Tarleton Shipping. Jonathan was pissed, and rightly so."

Jonathan groaned audibly. "Damn it, Hartley." His jaw worked. "Tell us what the hell Father was talking about."

Mazie was pale now, too, and trembling. J.B. was none too happy to see his newly pregnant wife upset. "Jonathan is right," he said. "We need to know."

Fiona stood up beside the man who held her heart. She kissed his cheek. "It's okay," she said. "They can handle it." Then she looked at Jonathan and Mazie. "He didn't want to hurt you. He's kept this terrible secret to himself to spare you pain."

"Tell us now," Jonathan said. "Please."

Fiona nodded, giving the man she loved a reassuring smile. "It's time, Hartley. Let it go."

And so he did. For the next half hour, he talked as if he had been a monk under a vow of silence and finally released. He told them about the blackmail and the hush money and the blackmailer who turned out to be a feeble old man and a relative at that. Then he described the terrible tragedy that happened when they were one and two years old. And about their mother's twin sister. And everything that transpired in the aftermath.

He gave an accounting of everywhere he had been and

everything he had done in the past year. He told of the old man's unexpected death and of settling a stranger's estate. He explained that in a storage unit in North Charleston were cartons of family memorabilia none of them had ever seen.

The only thing he *didn't* mention was how he and Fiona had met and the fact that nine months after that crazy wedding weekend, he had come home for a fleeting visit to tell his family everything. But he chickened out. And instead spent the night with Fiona.

When his incredible tale finally wound to a close, no one spoke for a couple of minutes. Fiona could see on their faces the struggle to accept that a huge part of their lives had been a lie. There were questions, of course. It was a lot to process. Shock made the task more difficult.

Mazie seemed dazed. "So our mother is not our mother…"

Hartley knelt at his sister's feet and took her hands. "I'm so damned sorry, baby girl. You deserved better. We all did."

She shook her head slowly. "But she did care for us while we were growing up."

"I know she did," Hartley admitted. "You have to think, though, she could have injured any one of us or herself there at the end, before Father sent her away. Maybe if she'd had better doctors and treatments early in her life… I don't know. That's why I—"

He stopped suddenly, perhaps realizing at the last moment the insensitivity of explaining to his pregnant sister that he had vowed never to father any biological children of his own.

Jonathan put a hand on Hartley's shoulder, urging him to his feet. When they were eye to eye, Jonathan uttered words that weren't entirely steady. "I'm sorry, Hartley.

God knows I can't ever make this up to you. I should have known. I should have trusted you."

Hartley's face finally lightened. "Hell, Jonathan, even Fiona pointed out to me that expecting blind faith from all of you, given the circumstances, was a lot to ask. I'm ready to be done with this. It's consumed over a year of my life. I just want to get back to normal."

Jonathan hugged him tightly. For a long time. When they separated, both men's eyes were suspiciously bright. Jonathan nodded slowly. "I want that, too. This has been an awful day. We're going to be dealing with this for a long time, each in our own way. But we're family. We'll get through it."

Mazie stood up to join her brothers, the three of them standing arm in arm. She kissed each man on the cheek and gave both of them a brilliant smile. "I *hated* knowing the two of you were at odds. I'm so, so grateful I don't have to watch you both being weird anymore."

The laughter that followed smoothed some of the rough edges in the room. High emotions demanded a break, a way to let off steam after the intensity they had shared.

Lisette joined her husband and addressed the group. "You all know that Jonathan and I are still staying at the beach house for now. Why don't we have a cookout on the beach tonight? Hot dogs, roasted marshmallows. We can watch the stars come out. What do you say?"

There was a resounding yes from almost everyone.

Fiona, on the other hand, was painfully aware that her hard times were just beginning. "It sounds wonderful," she said. "I'll come if I can, but I have a couple of things in the works. I'll have to let you know later today."

Mazie was visibly disappointed. "But you'll be at my birthday party, surely."

"I'll do my best."

If her equivocation confused Hartley, he didn't show it. He hugged each member of his family one at a time and then sighed. "Tonight sounds great. But I think we all need time to debrief between now and then. Fiona and I will see you later."

In the general exodus that followed, Fiona didn't correct his assurance. Sooner or later, Hartley's family would realize that he and Fiona had ended their relationship.

Outside in the parking lot, he stretched his neck and loosened his tie. "I'm shot, but I promised you we'd talk, darlin'. Where do you want to go?"

And there it was. The question of the day. She was torn between a need for privacy and the idea that a public place might serve to quell the worst of the storm.

She glanced at her watch. "I think we're late enough to miss most of the lunch crowd. What about that new little place over near Hyman's? I hear they're giving the big kid on the block a run for its money. They have conch fritters I've been wanting to try. And the booths are comfy." Perhaps she was overselling it.

"Sounds good to me." He took off his jacket and tossed it in the back seat of the car. Then he rolled up his sleeves. To Fiona it almost seemed as if he were shedding all the stress and pain and sorrow of the last months. How could she send him back to the depths again?

But how could she continue to lie to the man by omission? How could she not tell him he had fathered a child?

The restaurant's customers, as predicted, had thinned out. Fiona asked for a quiet booth. The hostess took her at her word and seated them in a tight corner in the back of the second floor. When Hartley excused himself to go to the men's room, Fiona slipped the server a twenty and asked the young man to leave them alone once the food came.

Perhaps her face revealed more than she knew. The kid nodded vigorously. "I won't come by at all, unless you wave your glass and want more tea."

"Thanks," Fiona said.

In the end, the food was amazing. It lived up to all the hype and then some. Hartley devoured a platter of clams and oysters and an enormous salad. Fiona nibbled at her fritters and pretended to eat a bowl of seafood bisque.

She was so nervous she was sweating, despite the efficient AC.

As the minutes passed, Hartley's mood rebounded exponentially. "God, I'm glad that's over. Could have been a lot worse."

He took her hand, lifted it and kissed her knuckles. "Thank you, Fee. You saved my life in there."

His crooked male grin was sweet and sexy and affectionate.

"You're welcome," she said. "Your family is strong. I know it was a lot to have dumped on them with no preparation. But they did well. So did you."

She loved him so much it was tearing her apart. She *had* to change his mind. She had to.

As promised, the server had left them alone while they ate. But time was running out. Fiona and Hartley couldn't sit here all afternoon. After a second drink refill and a puzzled frown from the server, Fiona waved him away with an apologetic smile.

Hartley yawned and stretched out his legs under the table. "One of us was up early," he teased.

"You could have waked me to say goodbye."

"Nope," he said cheerfully. "If you'd been awake, I wouldn't have been able to resist making love to you."

His intense stare unnerved her. She knew exactly what he meant. The two of them were like magnets, unable to occupy the same space without touching. "True…" She trailed off, literally sick with nerves.

Hartley stroked the back of her hand. "What did you want to talk about, Fiona? Are you finally going to give in and let me sleep on your sofa?"

When she didn't smile at his joke, he cocked his head. "Fee?" He frowned. "What is it? Why are you so upset? Whatever it is, I'll help you fix it."

Her lower jaw trembled so hard her teeth chattered. "I'm pregnant, Hartley. I'm sorry. It must have been that day you came back from Europe unexpectedly. We were kind of crazy for twenty-four hours. I guess we weren't careful one of those times, or maybe a condom broke. Nothing is a hundred percent. I know you—"

She ground to a halt abruptly, mortified to realize she was babbling.

Hartley hadn't said a word. He was looking at her, but his eyes were blank, his body frozen.

"Say something," she pleaded. "Please."

Every ounce of color drained from his face. She knew her timing was terrible, but she had waited and waited and then the stupid lawyer letter had come. Putting her confession off for a day or a week or a month wasn't going to make this any easier.

She wanted him to yell at her or curse or lose his cool.

Instead, it was as if the man she knew disappeared. In his place was a robot.

Hartley pulled out his wallet, extracted a hundred-dollar bill and tucked it under the sugar container. Then he slid out of the booth, turned his back on her and walked away.

Seventeen

Hartley went to the cookout at the beach. It was the last thing he wanted to do, but he had caused his family too much pain to let them down in such a simple thing.

So he made excuses for Fiona's absence, roasted his hot dog and his marshmallow, and gave a damned fine performance of a man who hadn't a care in the world.

As soon as he could reasonably leave without being rude, he drove back to the city.

He didn't pass Fiona's house. He couldn't bear to go near her street. Instead, he stopped at a sporting-goods store, bought a thick sleeping bag and drove to his newly acquired residence.

Not a residence so much as a dream. A dream of what his life could be with Fiona by his side and all the secrets finally out in the open. He knew now that he was in love with her. Truly, madly, deeply. Probably had been for some time. But last night had been a revelation. Being with her again had been like one of those crazy cartoons where the character gets knocked on the head with a coconut.

His whole outlook had changed.

Even with the lawyer appointment hanging over his head, he'd suddenly known that he could deal with a dead man's letter as long as Fiona was there, too.

What a naive fool he had been. Life was always waiting in the wings to knock a guy on his ass.

His pain and terror were so deep, they consumed him. He'd seen images in Switzerland. Coroner's photographs. Things he would never be able to erase from his brain. Dreadful documentation of a suicide that took so much from so many. He would never ever reveal those pictures to Jonathan or Mazie, never so much as mention them. Even now, he couldn't forget, couldn't get them out of his head. The blood. So much blood. And his mother's face, pale and perfect in death.

Almost innocent.

He'd seen other photographs, too. That same woman as a child. Laughing. Playing. Carefree. Totally oblivious to the suffering that lay ahead for her.

The transition was horrifying.

Jonathan climbed to the second level, despite the rotting stairs and the broken glass here and there. He flung his pallet on the floor and fell down on his back, his entire body trembling as if he had malaria or some other jungle fever. One moment he was drenched in sweat. The next he wrapped the edges of the sleeping bag around him.

His maternal grandparents had lost two daughters to mental illness. How had they borne the pain? One child was still alive in an institution in Vermont, but she was a shell of herself. After her breakdown, she rarely recognized any of them. She had only fleeting lucid memories of the family she had reared.

Hartley had tried to make his peace with the past by vowing not to perpetuate it. But what now? He had fathered a child. *Sweet Jesus.* And no use asking if the baby was his. Fiona was as guileless and true as any woman who ever lived. He was the one who had pursued her, bedded her again and again, because he couldn't stay away.

He literally had no idea where to go from here.

Eventually, exhaustion claimed him. He slept in snatches, jerked awake again and again by nightmares. The stuffy house and stark, comfortless bed were no more than he deserved.

He had walked out on Fiona. Hadn't said a word.

How much of an ass could a man be and still consider himself a man?

Toward morning, he splashed water on his face and stared into the mottled mirror in despair. The figure looking back at him was a phantom, a ghost. He had searched his heart for hours on end, even in the midst of sleep.

What should he do? What could he say?

If asking forgiveness was all there was, he might figure that out. But he couldn't go back to Fiona unless he was prepared to talk about the baby. Every time he thought about a child that was his, his blood ran cold in his veins. His brain froze. He was no good to Fiona *or her child.* Couldn't she understand that?

Hunger made him faint. He stumbled going back down the stairs. When he grabbed for the railing, a piece of it splintered, slicing his hand. He stared at the blood dripping from his fingertips.

He was dizzy and weak. For a moment, his dread and pain were so overwhelming, he couldn't see a way forward. Was he like his mother after all?

* * *

Fiona had experienced grief many times in her life. Up until now, the worst was a moment long ago when she realized she was too old to be adopted, that she had missed her *window*, that she would never have the family she dreamed about.

She had been luckier than most. Her life had intersected with people who were kind for the most part. There was no memory of abuse to struggle with. No history of alcoholism or drugs. She'd simply been a good kid in an overcrowded governmental system.

Once she was grown, she'd become proud of who she was. She'd created a nest for herself, a niche. Except for brief friendships with a few guys whose faces she barely remembered, she had been content to paint and to draw and to make a living by herself.

She had learned not to dream big dreams, but instead to be satisfied with what she had…who she had become.

Until Hartley Tarleton had burst into her life like a supernova, she believed she *knew* what it was to be content. To be happy.

Like the scene in the *Wizard of Oz* when Dorothy's world morphed from black-and-white into full glorious color, meeting Hartley had shown Fiona feelings and emotions and a whole damned *rainbow* she never knew existed.

Because the climb up the mountain had been so glorious, the fall was brutal. Indescribably agonizing.

She was like two separate women. One exhilarated by the amazing new life she carried. The other crushed by a grief so all encompassing she wanted to hide under the covers.

One day passed. Then two. Then three.

She had believed Hartley would relent. But she had underestimated his pain.

One day bled into the next. She forced herself to eat and exercise and work. Yearning for Hartley was the worst misery she had ever known.

When the one-week mark passed, she knew he wasn't coming. Ever. It became harder to wake up each morning. The only thing that kept her from collapse was knowing she had a responsibility to her child.

It was ten days after the emotional scene in the lawyer's office before she saw Hartley again. By then, she had stopped hoping. She was at work in her studio. When she turned around to get another brush, there he was.

Gaunt and motionless. With a world of agony in his eyes. "I'm sorry," he said gruffly.

She gripped the paintbrush until her knuckles were white. "I didn't need an apology, Hartley. I knew what was going to happen when I told you. I knew it would be bad. I used to imagine scenarios like running away to join the circus. Or taking a different name and starting a new life on the other side of the country. No matter how hard I tried, I couldn't find a way around the obvious. A woman has to tell a man when he has a baby on the way. It's a moral obligation."

Hartley stared at her bleakly. His eyes were almost black in this light. "I'm sorry I made things terrible for you," he said. "You must have been so scared." He stood with his hands in his pockets. His jeans were ancient and torn, not at all the look of a wealthy man, one of Charleston's elite. The navy T-shirt was equally old and stained. Clearly, he had been working on the house he had bought.

"I *was* scared," she said quietly. "But you can't help your feelings. I knew the baby thing wasn't a whim. You were frightened. And rightly so."

He dropped his chin to his chest for a moment and sighed deeply. When he finally lifted his head and tried to smile, it was almost too painful to witness. "I couldn't deal with the news at first," he said. "I knew an apology was worthless until I was willing to talk about the baby."

"And now?"

He swallowed. "I didn't tell you everything. I didn't tell Mazie or Jonathan either."

Her stomach clenched. What more could there be? "Tell me what?" she asked softly.

"My uncle showed me the coroner's photographs. A crime scene. Bloody. Horrifying. Our mother, the woman none of us remember, looked so peaceful and beautiful. But she was dead. By her own hand. And then he showed me pictures from her childhood. A tiny little girl laughing…playing with puppies. A six-year-old wearing a tutu and beaming. The juxtaposition of those pictures was almost incomprehensible. That's when I knew I couldn't bear to father a child. How could I watch him or her grow up, never knowing if the illness that stole my mother lingered beneath the surface?"

Fiona trembled. "All life is a risk, Hartley. None of us can see the future. Some lives are cut short at eighteen. Others stretch out to ninety or a hundred years." Hot tears sprang to her eyes and rolled down her cheeks. She cried the tears he couldn't shed, grieving, lost.

At last, he approached her, perhaps moved by her distress. "Let's go to the living room," he said. "You look exhausted."

Hand in hand they walked down the hall. Simply being with him again was more than she had hoped for, but they were a long way from any kind of resolution.

Hartley released her and sat on one end of the sofa. Did he think she would maintain some kind of distance between them? Not a chance in hell. He was here. With her. She would fight for their happiness.

She curled up beside him and leaned her head on his shoulder. He took her hand in his. The silence was not quite peaceful, but it held gratitude, at least on her part.

She sifted through the words she wanted to say, but ultimately, the decision would have to be Hartley's. "Here's the thing," she said, praying for some kind of divine guidance. "When I was a child, six or seven years old, I lived in an orphanage. It was a nice place. Clean. Safe. But the one thing they couldn't take away was my loneliness. It lived in my bones. I painted a life in my imagination, a life I wanted so very badly. The reality was different."

He grimaced. "It hurts me to think of you like that."

"There came a time when I had to let go of my fantasies and accept that my life couldn't be the imaginary one I craved. But it could be good."

"How did you get there? How did you give up the wanting and the needing and the disappointment?"

She straightened and faced him, her legs crisscrossed. "You'll laugh. It had to do with ice cream."

He blinked. "Ice cream?"

"Yes. For whatever reason, one of the dairies in the area decided to donate ice cream to the orphanage. Every Friday at 3 p.m., a truck would roll up in the driveway, and a big carton packed in dry ice was off-loaded, filled with orange sherbet push-pops."

"I loved those," he said, his smile more genuine this time.

"I still do. In fact, if I see a kid in my neighborhood eating one on the sidewalk, it takes me back to those warm, perfect afternoons."

"I don't understand how ice cream healed your existential crisis."

She chuckled. "Well, first of all, I hadn't a clue that I was having a crisis, existential or otherwise. All I knew was that I was sad. Yet somehow, when I tasted that treat, my sadness went away for a little while. I began to understand that if something as good as orange sherbet push-pops existed in life, then somehow, someday, I was going to be okay."

"That's pretty deep for a kid so young."

Fiona shrugged. "What can I say? I was a wise old soul."

He kissed her temple. "Some of us are more hardheaded than others. I didn't want to see you again, Fee, until I dealt with my mother. I couldn't let her story define mine."

"And now?" She wanted to hold him and kiss him, but this moment was too important. Hope and fear duked it out in her chest. Right now, hope was winning. Barely.

"I adore you, Fiona James. And I won't live in fear," he said firmly. "What happened in the past was a tragedy. My child, our child, may struggle with any number of serious problems. Or maybe he or she will float through life as one of the lucky ones. Either way, I'm going to love you and this baby for the rest of my life."

"Truly?" Her chin wobbled.

He kissed her nose. "Truly. Marry me, Fee. Big wedding. Small one. I don't care. But I don't want to wait."

"Me either." She took his hand and placed it on her slightly rounded tummy. "I've already picked out your wedding gift. It's the only thing I could think of for the man who has everything."

He flattened his hand against her belly, pressing gently, his expression transfixed. "The pregnancy is good? And you? The baby?"

"We're fine. Better than fine." She cupped his face in her hands. "I want you to make love to me, Hartley. I've missed you so much. It's been an eternity since I felt you next to me, skin to skin, heart to heart."

He tugged her to her feet. "I've never had sex with a

pregnant woman." The look in his eyes told her he liked the idea.

"Sure you have," she said, laughing. "You just didn't know it."

In her bedroom, they stood on either side of the bed and stared at each other. When they met in the center of the mattress, kneeling, he brushed the hair from her face, his gaze searching. "No more looking back, my sweet Fee. I swear it. From now on, I'll be under your feet at every turn. You'll never be lonely as long as I have breath in my body."

"I love you, Hartley."

"Not as much as I love you."

He kissed her then, a kiss that started out with relief and thanksgiving for having weathered the storm, but ended up in the same fiery passion that bound them at every turn.

Clothes flew in four directions. Bare skin met bare skin. He entered her carefully, as though she were a fragile china doll.

She clutched his warm muscled shoulders, her breath coming faster, her body arching into his. "I won't break, silly man."

"No, you won't," he said, burying his face in the curve of her neck. "Because if you ever fall, I'll be there to catch you."

"You're mine," she whispered.

"Orange sherbet push-pops, darlin'. For both of us. From now on. I found you, Fee. Against all odds. I'll never let you go."

Then he gave up on words, and showed her that some happiness was even better than ice cream...

Five days later...

"Be careful. Don't tear the paper." Fiona fretted as she and Hartley climbed the steps of J.B. and Mazie's classic home. J.B. had invited half of Charleston for Mazie's kick-ass party.

But first the family was gathering to give her their gifts.

Over punch and cookies and with much laughter and teasing, paper and ribbon fluttered through the air. Lisette and Jonathan had ordered a handmade French baby doll for the woman who had grown up far too soon.

Mazie traced the doll's lifelike lashes and smiled through her tears. "I love it."

Everyone smiled. Then Hartley handed over the next gift. "This is from Fiona and me. Open with care."

Mazie's astonishment when she saw the wedding-day photograph immortalized in oils warmed Fiona's heart. "Hartley commissioned the gift," she said. "It was his idea."

Mazie screeched and hugged them both. "It's incredible," she cried.

Lisette and Mazie looked at each other and smiled. Lisette took Mazie's hand, and they stepped in front of the birthday girl. Lisette took a deep breath. "There's one more present, Mazie. But you'll have to wait a bit for this one."

Fiona nodded. "We didn't want your little one to grow up alone, so Lizzy and I are giving you two cousins, maybe even a birthing room for three if the timing is right."

Mazie's eyes rounded. "Are you serious?"

Hartley studied the pandemonium that followed with a full heart and a happy grin.

Jonathan and J.B. moved to flank him. "We're toast, aren't we?" Jonathan said. "Three pregnant wives? Whew…"

J.B. nodded. "We'll be wrapped around their little fingers. At their beck and call."

Hartley blew a kiss to his precious bride-to-be. "Any complaints, gentlemen?"

The other two shook their heads ruefully. "Not a one," they said in unison.

Hartley felt the world click into sharp focus as joy bubbled in his veins like fine champagne. Today was a new life, a new start. He was a damned lucky man…

* * * * *

A VIRGIN FOR VASQUEZ

CATHY WILLIAMS

CHAPTER ONE

JAVIER VASQUEZ LOOKED around his office with unconcealed satisfaction.

Back in London after seven years spent in New York and didn't fate move in mysterious ways…?

From his enviable vantage point behind the floor-to-ceiling panes of reinforced rock-solid glass, he gazed down to the busy city streets in miniature. Little taxis and little cars ferrying toy-sized people to whatever important or irrelevant destinations were calling them.

And for him…?

A slow, curling smile, utterly devoid of humour, curved his beautiful mouth.

For him, the past had come calling and that, he knew, accounted for the soaring sense of satisfaction now filling him because, as far as offices went, this one, spectacular though it was, was no more or less spectacular than the offices he had left behind in Manhattan. There, too, he had looked down on busy streets, barely noticing the tide of people that daily flowed through those streets like a pulsing, breathing river.

Increasingly, he had become cocooned in an ivory tower, the undisputed master of all he surveyed. He was thirty-three years old. You didn't get to rule the concrete jungle by taking your eye off the ball. No; you kept focused, you eliminated obstacles and in that steady, onward and upward march, time passed by until now...

He glanced at his watch.

Twelve storeys down, in the vast, plush reception area, Oliver Griffin-Watt would already have been waiting for half an hour.

Did Javier feel a twinge of guilt about that?

Not a bit of it.

He wanted to savour this moment because he felt as though it had been a long time coming.

And yet, had he thought about events that had happened all those years ago? He'd left England for America and his life had become consumed in the business of making money, of putting to good use the education his parents had scrimped and saved to put him through, and in the process burying a fleeting past with a woman he needed to consign to the history books.

The only child of devoted parents who had lived in a poor *barrio* in the outskirts of Madrid, Javier had spent his childhood with the driving motto drummed into him that to get out, he had to succeed and to succeed, he had to have an education. And he'd had to get out.

His parents had worked hard, his father as a taxi driver, his mother as a cleaner, and the glass ceiling had always been low for them. They'd managed, but only just. No fancy holidays, no flat-screen tellies for the house, no chichi restaurants with fawning waiters. They'd made do with cheap and cheerful and every single penny had been put into savings for the time when they would send their precociously bright son to university in England. They had known all too well the temptations waiting for anyone stupid enough to go off the rails. They had friends whose sons had taken up with gangs, who had died from drug overdoses, who had lost the plot and ended up as dropouts kicked around on street corners.

That was not going to be the fate of their son.

If, as a teenager, Javier had ever resented the tight controls placed on him, he had said nothing.

He had been able to see for himself, from a very young age, just what financial hardship entailed and how limiting it could be. He had seen how some of his wilder friends, who had made a career out of playing truant, had ended up in the gutter. By the time he had hit eighteen, he had made his plans and nothing was going to derail them: a year or two out, working to add to the money his parents had saved, then university, where he would succeed because he was bright—brighter than anyone he knew. Then a high-paying job. No starting at the ground level and making his way up slowly, but a job with a knockout financial package. Why not? He knew his assets and he had had no intention of selling himself short.

He wasn't just clever.

Lots of people were clever. He was also sharp. Sharp in a streetwise sort of way. He possessed the astuteness of someone who knew how to make deals and how to spot where they could be made. He knew how to play rough and how to intimidate. Those were skills that were ingrained rather than learnt and, whilst they had no place in a civilised world, the world of big business wasn't always civilised; it was handy having those priceless skills tucked up his sleeve.

He'd been destined to make it big and, from the age of ten, he had had no doubt that he would get there.

He'd worked hard, had honed his ferocious intelligence to the point where no one could outsmart him and had sailed through university, resisting the temptation to leave without his Master's. A Master's in engineering opened a lot more doors than an ordinary degree and he wanted to have the full range of open doors to choose from.

And that was when he had met Sophie Griffin-Watt.

The only unexpected flaw in his carefully conceived life plan.

She had been an undergraduate, in her first excitable year, and he had been on the last leg of his Master's, already considering his options, wondering which one to take, which one would work best for him when he left university in a little under four months' time.

He hadn't meant to go out at all but his two housemates, usually as focused as he was, had wanted to celebrate a birthday and he'd agreed to hit the local pub with them.

He'd seen her the second he'd walked in. Young, impossibly pretty, laughing, head flung back with a drink in one hand. She'd been wearing a pair of faded jeans, a tiny cropped vest and a denim jacket that was as faded as the jeans.

And he'd stared.

He never stared. From the age of thirteen, he'd never had to chase any girl. His looks were something he'd always taken for granted. Girls stared. They chased. They flung themselves in his path and waited for him to notice them.

The guys he'd shared his flat with had ribbed him about the ease with which he could snap his fingers and have any girl he wanted but, in actual fact, getting girls was not Javier's driving ambition. They had their part to play. He was a red-blooded male with an extremely healthy libido—and, as such, he was more than happy to take what was always on offer—but his focus, the thing that drove him, had always been his remorseless ambition.

Girls had always been secondary conquests.

Everything seemed to change on the night he had walked into that bar.

Yes, he'd stared, and he'd kept on staring, and she hadn't glanced once at him, even though the gaggle of girls she was with had been giggling pointing at him and whispering.

For the first time in his life, he had become the pursuer. He had made the first move.

She was much younger than the women he usually dated. He was a man on the move, a man looking ahead to bigger things—he'd had no use for young, vulnerable girls with romantic dreams and fantasies about settling down. He'd gone out with a couple of girls in his years at university but, generally speaking, he had dated and slept with slightly older women—women who weren't going to become clingy and start asking for the sort of commitment he wasn't about to give them. Women who were experienced enough to understand his rules and abide by them.

Sophie Griffin-Watt had been all the things he'd had no interest in and he'd fallen for her hook, line and sinker.

Had part of that driving obsession for her been the fact that he'd actually had to try? That he'd had to play the old-fashioned courting game?

That she'd made him wait and, in the end, had not slept with him?

She'd kept him hanging on and he'd allowed it. He'd been happy to wait. The man who played by his own rules and waited for no one had been happy to wait because he'd seen a future for them together.

He'd been a fool and he'd paid the price.

But that was seven years ago and now...

He strolled back to his chair, leant forward and buzzed his secretary to have Oliver Griffin-Watt shown up to his office.

The wheel, he mused, relaxing back, had turned full circle. He'd never considered himself the sort of guy who would ever be interested in extracting revenge but the opportunity to even the scales had come knocking on his door and who was he to refuse it entry...?

* * *

'You did what?'

Sophie looked at her twin brother with a mixture of clammy panic and absolute horror.

She had to sit down. If she didn't sit down, her wobbly legs would collapse under her. She could feel a headache coming on and she rubbed her temples in little circular movements with shaky fingers.

Once upon a time, she'd been able to see all the signs of neglect in the huge family house, but over the past few years she'd become accustomed to the semi-decrepit sadness of the home in which she and her brother had spent their entire lives. She barely noticed the wear and tear now.

'What else would you have suggested I do?' There was complaint in his voice as he looked at his sister.

'Anything but that, Ollie,' Sophie whispered, stricken.

'So you went out with the guy for ten minutes years ago! I admit it was a long shot, going to see him, but I figured we had nothing to lose. It felt like fate that he's only been back in the country for a couple of months, I just happen to pick up someone's newspaper on the tube and, lo and behold, who's staring out at me from the financial pages…? It's not even as though I'm in London all that much! Pure chance. And, hell, we need all the help we can get!'

He gestured broadly to the four walls of the kitchen which, on a cold winter's night, with the stove burning and the lights dimmed, could be mistaken for a cosy and functioning space but which, as was the case now, was shorn of any homely warmth in the glaring, bright light of a summer's day.

'I mean…' His voice rose, morphing from complaint to indignation. 'Look at this place, Soph! It needs so much work that there's no way we can begin to cover the cost.

It's eating every penny we have and you heard what the estate agents have all said. It needs too much work and it's in the wrong price bracket to be an easy sell. It's been on the market for two and a half years! We're never going to get rid of it, unless we can do a patch-up job, and we're never going to do a patch-up job unless the company starts paying its way!'

'And you thought that running to...to...' She could barely let his name pass her lips.

Javier Vasquez.

Even after all these years the memory of him still clung to her, as pernicious as ivy, curling round and round in her head, refusing to go away.

He had come into her life with the savage, mesmerising intensity of a force-nine gale and had blown all her neat, tidy assumptions about her future to smithereens.

When she pictured him in her head, she saw him as he was then, more man than boy, a towering, lean, commanding figure who could render a room silent the minute he walked in.

He had had presence.

Even before she'd fallen under his spell, before she'd even spoken one word to him, she'd known that he was going to be dangerous. Her little clutch of well-bred, upper-middle-class friends had kept sneaking glances at him when he'd entered that pub all those years ago, giggling, tittering and trying hard to get his attention. After the first glance, she, on the other hand, had kept her eyes firmly averted. But she hadn't been able to miss the banging of her heart against her ribcage or the way her skin had broken out in clammy, nervous perspiration.

When he'd sauntered across to her, ignoring her friends, and had begun talking to her, she'd almost fainted.

He'd been doing his Master's in engineering and he

was the cleverest guy she'd ever met in her life. He was so good-looking that he'd taken her breath away.

He'd been also just the sort of boy her parents would have disapproved of. Exotic, foreign and most of all... unashamedly broke.

His fantastic self-assurance—the hint of unleashed power that sat on his shoulders like an invisible cloak— had attracted and scared her at the same time. At eighteen, she had had limited experience of the opposite sex and, in his company, that limited experience had felt like no experience at all. Roger, whom she had left behind and who had been still clinging to her, even though she had broken off their very tepid relationship, had scarcely counted even though he had been only a couple of years younger than Javier.

She'd felt like a gauche little girl next to him. A gauche little girl with one foot poised over an unknown abyss, ready to step out of the comfort zone that had been her privileged, sheltered life.

Private school, skiing holidays, piano lessons and horse riding on Saturday mornings had not prepared her for anyone remotely like Javier Vasquez.

He wasn't going to be good for her but she had been as helpless as a kitten in the face of his lazy but targeted pursuit.

'We could do something,' he had murmured early on when he had cornered her in that pub, in the sort of seductive voice that had literally made her go weak at the knees. 'I don't have much money but trust me when I tell you that I can show you the best time of your life without a penny to my name...'

She'd always mixed with people just like her: pampered girls and spoilt boys who had never had to think hard about how much having a good night out might cost.

She'd drifted into seeing Roger, who'd been part of that set and whom she'd known for ever.

Why? It was something she'd never questioned. Oliver had taken it all for granted but, looking back, she had always felt guilty at the ease with which she had always been encouraged to take what she wanted, whatever the cost.

Her father had enjoyed showing off his beautiful twins and had showered them with presents from the very second they had been born.

She was his princess, and if occasionally she'd felt uneasy at the way he'd dismissed people who were socially inferior to him, she had pushed aside the uneasy feeling because, whatever his faults, her father had adored her. She'd been a daddy's girl.

And she'd known, from the second Javier Vasquez had turned his sexy eyes to her, that she was playing with fire, that her father would have had a coronary had he only known...

But play with fire she had.

Falling deeper and deeper for him, resisting the driving desire to sleep with him because...

Because she'd been a shameless romantic and because there had been a part of her that had wondered whether a man like Javier Vasquez would have ditched her as soon as he'd got her between the sheets.

But he hadn't forced her hand and that, in itself, had fuelled her feelings towards him, honed and fine-tuned them to the point where she had felt truly alive only when she'd been in his company.

It was always going to end in tears, except had she known just how horribly it would all turn out...

'I didn't think the guy would actually agree to see me,' Oliver confessed, sliding his eyes over to her flushed, distressed face before hurriedly looking away. 'Like I said, it was a long shot. I actually didn't even think he'd remember who I was... It wasn't as though I'd met him more than a couple of times...'

Because, although they were twins, Oliver had gone to a completely different university. Whilst she had been at Cambridge, studying Classics with the hope of becoming a lecturer in due course, he had been on the other side of the Atlantic, going to parties and only intermittently hearing about what was happening in her life. He'd left at sixteen, fortunate enough to get a sports scholarship to study at a high school, and had dropped out of her life aside from when he'd returned full of beans during the holidays.

Even when the whole thing had crashed and burned a mere few months after it had started, he had only really heard the edited version of events. Anyway, he had been uninterested, because life in California had been far too absorbing and Oliver, as Sophie had always known, had a very limited capacity when it came to empathising with other people's problems.

Now she wondered whether she should have sat him down when he'd eventually returned to the UK and given him all the miserable details of what had happened.

But by then it had been far too late.

She'd had an engagement ring on her finger and Javier had no longer been on the scene. Roger Scott had been the one walking up the aisle.

It didn't bear thinking about.

'So you saw him...' *What did he look like? What did he sound like? Did he still have that sexy, sexy smile that could make a person's toes curl?* So much had happened over the years, so much had killed her youthful dreams about love and happiness, but she could still remember, couldn't she?

She didn't want to think any of those things, but she did.

'Didn't even hesitate,' Oliver said proudly, as though

he'd accomplished something remarkable. 'I thought I'd have to concoct all sorts of stories to get to see the great man but, in fact, he agreed to see me as soon as he found out who I was...'

I'll bet, Sophie thought.

'Soph, you should see his office. It's incredible. The guy's worth millions. More—billions. Can't believe he was broke when you met him at university. You should have stuck with him, sis, instead of marrying that creep.'

'Let's not go there, Ollie.' As always, Sophie's brain shut down at the mention of her late husband's name. He had his place in a box in her head, firmly locked away. Talking about him was not only pointless but it tore open scabs to reveal wounds still fresh enough to bleed.

Roger, she told herself, had been a learning curve and one should always be grateful for learning curves, however horrible they might have been. She'd been young, innocent and optimistic once upon a time, and if she was battle-hardened now, immune to girlish daydreams of love, then that was all to the good because it meant that she could never again be hurt by anyone or anything.

She stood up and gazed out of the patio doors to the unkempt back garden which rolled into untidy fields, before spinning round, arms folded, to gaze at her brother. 'I'd ask you what he said...' her voice was brisk and unemotional '...but there wouldn't be any point because I don't want to have anything to do with him. He's...my past and you shouldn't have gone there without my permission.'

'It's all well and good for you to get sanctimonious, Soph, but we need money, he has lots of it and he has a connection with you.'

'He has no connection with me!' Her voice was high and fierce.

Of course he had no connection with her. Not unless

you called *hatred* a connection, because he would hate her. After what had happened, after what she had done to him.

Suddenly exhausted, she sank into one of the kitchen chairs and dropped her head in her hands for a few moments, just wanting to block everything out. The past, her memories, the present, their problems. *Everything.*

'He says he'll think about helping.'

'What?' Appalled, she stared at him.

'He seemed very sympathetic when I explained the situation.'

'Sympathetic.' Sophie laughed shortly. The last thing Javier Vasquez would be was sympathetic. As though it had happened yesterday, she remembered how he had looked when she had told him that she was breaking up with him, that it was over between them, that he wasn't the man for her after all. She remembered the coldness in his eyes as the shutters had dropped down. She remembered the way he had sounded when he had told her, his voice flat and hard, that if he ever clapped eyes on her again it would be too soon... That if their paths were ever to cross again she should remember that he would never forget and he would never forgive...

She shivered and licked her lips, resisting the urge to sneak a glance over her shoulder just to make sure that he wasn't looming behind her like an avenging angel.

'What exactly did you tell him, Ollie?'

'The truth.' He looked at his twin defensively. 'I told him that the company hit the buffers and we're struggling to make ends meet, what with all the money that ex of yours blew on stupid ventures that crashed and burned. He bankrupted the company and took us all down with him.'

'Dad allowed him to make those investments, Oliver.'

'Dad...' His voice softened. 'Dad wasn't in the right place to stop him, sis. We both know that. Roger got away with everything because Dad was sick and getting sicker, even if we didn't know it at the time, even if we were all thinking that Mum was the one we had to worry about.'

Tears instantly sprang to Sophie's eyes. Whatever had happened, she still found it hard to blame either of her parents for the course her life had eventually taken.

Predictably, when her parents had found out about Javier, they had been horrified. They had point-blank refused to meet him at all. As far as they were concerned, he could have stepped straight out of a leper colony.

Their appalled disapproval would have been bad enough but, in the wake of their discovery, far more than Sophie had ever expected had come to the surface, rising to the top like scum to smother the comfortable, predictable lifestyle she had always taken for granted.

Financial troubles. The company had failed to move with the times. The procedures employed by the company were cumbersome and time-consuming but the financial investment required to bring everything up to date was too costly. The bank had been sympathetic over the years as things had deteriorated but their patience was wearing thin. They wanted their money returned to them.

Her father, whom she had adored, had actually buried his head in his hands and cried.

At the back of her mind, Sophie had stifled a spurt of anger at the unfairness of being the one lumbered with these confidences while her brother had continued to enjoy himself on the other side of the world in cheerful, ignorant bliss. But then Oliver had never been as serious as her, had never really been quite as responsible.

She had always been her father's 'right-hand man'.

Both her parents had told her that some foreigner blown in from foreign shores, without a penny to his name, wasn't going to do. They were dealing with enough stress, enough financial problems, without her *taking up with someone who will end up being a sponge, because you*

*know what these foreigners can be like... The man prob-
ably figures he's onto a good thing...*

Roger was eager to join the company and he had inherited a great deal of money when his dear parents had
passed away. And hadn't they been dating? Wasn't he already like a member of the family?

Sophie had been dumbstruck as her life had been
sorted out for her.

Yes, she had known Roger for ever. Yes, he was a perfectly okay guy and, sure, they had gone out for five minutes. But *he wasn't the one for her* and she'd broken it off
even before Javier had appeared on the scene!

But her father had cried and she'd never seen her dad
in tears before.

She had been so confused, torn between the surging
power of young love and a debt of duty towards her parents.

Surely they wouldn't expect her to quit university when
she was only in her first year and loving it?

But no. She'd been able to stay on, although they hoped
that she would take over the company alongside Roger,
who would be brought on board should they cement a
union he had already intimated he was keen on.

He was three years older than her and had experience
of working for a company. He would sink money into
the company, take his place on the board of directors...

And she, Sophie had read between the lines, would
have to fulfil her obligations and walk up the aisle with
him.

She hadn't been able to credit what she had been hearing, but seeing her distraught parents, seeing their shame
at having to let her down and destroy her illusions, had
spoken so much more loudly and had said so much more
than mere words could convey.

Had Roger even known about any of these plans? Was

that why he'd been refusing to call it quits between them even though they'd been seeing one another for only less than eight months before she had left for university? Had he already been looking to a future that involved her parents' company?

She had called him, arranged to see him, and had been aghast when he had told her that he knew all about her parents' situation and was keen to do the right thing. He was in love with her, always had been...

With no one in whom to confide, Sophie had returned to university in a state of utter confusion—and Javier had been there. She had mentioned nothing but she had allowed herself to be absorbed by him. With him, she could forget everything.

Swept along on a heady tide of falling in love, the panic she had felt at what was happening on the home front had been dulled. Her parents had not mentioned the situation again and she had uneasily shoved it to the back of her mind.

No news was good news. Wasn't that what everyone said?

She surfaced from the past to find a drink in front of her and she pushed it aside.

'I've got another appointment to see the bank tomorrow,' she said. 'And we can change estate agents.'

'For the fourth time?' Oliver gave a bark of laughter and downed his drink in one gulp. 'Face it, Soph. The way things are going, we'll be in debt for the rest of our lives if we're not careful. The company is losing money. The house will never sell. The bank will take it off our hands to repay our overdraft and we'll both be left homeless. It's not even as though we have alternative accommodation to return to. We don't. You bailed university to get married and moved into the family pile with Roger. I may have stayed on to get my diploma, but by the time I got back here everything had changed and we were both in it together. Both here, both trying to make the company work…' His voice had acquired the bitter, plaintive edge Sophie had come to recognise.

She knew how this would go. He would drink away his sorrows and wake up the following morning in a blurry, sedated haze where all the problems were dulled just enough for him to get through the day.

He was, she had been forced to accept, a weak man not made for facing the sort of situation they were now facing.

And she hated that she couldn't do more for him.

He was drinking too much and she could see the train coming off the tracks if things didn't change.

Did she want that? Wasn't there too much already on her conscience?

She shut down that train of thought, shut down the deluge of unhappy memories and tried hard to focus on the few bright things in her life.

She had her health.

They might be struggling like mad trying not to drown but at least Mum was okay, nicely sorted in a cottage in Cornwall, far from the woes now afflicting herself and her brother.

It might have been a rash expenditure given the dire financial circumstances, but when Gordon Griffin-Watt had tragically died, after a brief but intense period of absolute misery and suffering, it had seemed imperative to try to help Evelyn, their mother, who was herself frail and barely able to cope. Sophie had taken every spare penny she could from the scant profits of the company and sunk it all into a cottage in Cornwall, where Evelyn's sister lived.

It had been worth it. Her mother's contentment was the brightest thing on the horizon, and if she was ignorant about the extent of the troubles afflicting her twins, then that was for her own good. Her health would never be able to stand the stress of knowing the truth: that they stood to lose everything. One of the sweetest things Gordon Griffin-Watt had done had been to allay her fears about their financial situation while dealing with his own disastrous health problems, which he had refused to tell his wife about. She had had two strokes already and he wasn't going to send her to her grave with a third one.

'Vasquez is willing to listen to what we have to say.'

'Javier won't do a thing to help us. Trust me, Ollie.' *But he would have a merry time gloating at how the mighty had fallen, that was for sure.*

'How do you know?' her brother fired back, pouring himself another drink and glaring, challenging her to give him her little lecture about staying off the booze.

'Because I just do.'

'That's where you're wrong, sis.'

'What do you mean? What are you talking about? And should you…be having a second drink when it's not yet four in the afternoon?'

'I'll stop drinking when I'm not worrying 24/7 about whether I'll have a roof over my head next week or whether I'll be begging in the streets for loose change.' He drank, refilled his glass defiantly, and Sophie stifled a sigh of despair.

'So just tell me what Javier had to say,' she said flatly. 'Because I need to go and prepare information to take with me to the bank tomorrow.'

'He wants to see you.'

'He…*what*?'

'He says he will consider helping us but he wants to discuss it with you. I thought it was pretty decent of him, actually…'

A wave of nausea rushed through her. For the first time

ever, she felt that at the unseemly hour of four in the afternoon she could do with a stiff drink.

'That won't be happening.'

'You'd rather see us both living under a bridge in London with newspapers as blankets,' Oliver said sharply, 'rather than have a twenty-minute conversation with some old flame?'

'Don't be stupid. We won't end up *living under a bridge with newspapers as blankets…*'

'It's a bloody short drop from the top to the bottom, Soph. Can take about ten minutes. We're more than halfway there.'

'I'm seeing the bank tomorrow about a loan to broaden our computer systems…'

'Good luck with that! They'll say no and we both know that. And what do you think is going to happen to that allowance we give Mum every month? Who do you think is going to support her in her old age if we go under?'

'Stop!' Never one to dodge reality, Sophie just wanted to blank it all out now. But she couldn't. The weight of their future rested on her shoulders, but Oliver…

How could he?

Because he didn't know, she thought with numb defeat. What he saw was an ex who now had money and might be willing to lend them some at a reasonable rate for old times' sake. To give them a loan because they had nowhere else to turn.

She could hardly blame him, could she?

'I told him that you'd be at his office tomorrow at six.' He extracted a crumpled piece of paper from his pocket and pushed it across the table to her.

When Sophie flattened it out, she saw that on it was a scribbled address and a mobile number. Just looking at those two links with the past she had fought to leave behind made her heart hammer inside her.

'I can't make you go and see the man, Sophie.' Oliver stood up, the bottle of whisky in one hand and his empty glass in the other. There was defeat in his eyes and it pierced her heart because he wasn't strong enough to take any of this. He needed looking after as much as their mother did. 'But if you decide to go with the bank, when they've already knocked us back in the past and when they're making noises about taking the house from us, then on your head be it. If you decide to go, he'll be waiting for you at his office.'

Alone in the kitchen, Sophie sighed and rested back in the chair, eyes closed, mind in turmoil.

She had been left without a choice. Her brother would never forgive her if she walked away from Javier and the bank ended up chucking her out. And her brother was right; the small profits the company was making were all being eaten up and it wouldn't be long before the house was devouring far more than the company could provide. It was falling down. Who in their right mind wanted to buy a country mansion that was falling down, in the middle of nowhere, when the property market was so desperate? And they couldn't afford to sell it for a song because it had been remortgaged...

Maybe he'd forgotten how things had ended, she thought uneasily.

Maybe he'd changed, mellowed. Maybe, just maybe, he really would offer them a loan at a competitive rate because of the brief past they'd shared.

Maybe he'd overlook how disastrous that brief past had ended...

At any rate, she had no choice, none at all. She would simply have to find out...

CHAPTER TWO

SOPHIE STARED UP at the statement building across the frenzied, busy street, a soaring tower of glass and chrome.

She'd never had any driving desire to live in London and the crowds of people frantically weaving past her was a timely reminder of how ill-suited she was to the fierce thrust of city life.

But neither had she ever foreseen that she would be condemned to life in the tiny village where she had grown up, out in rugged Yorkshire territory. Her parents had adored living there; they'd had friends in the village and scattered in the big country piles sitting in their individual acres of land.

She had nothing of the sort.

Having gone to boarding school from the age of thirteen, her friends were largely based in the south of England.

She lived in a collapsing mansion, with no friends at hand with whom she could share her daily woes, and that in itself reminded her why she was here.

To see Javier.

To try to pursue a loan so that she could get out of her situation.

So that she and her brother could begin to have something of a life free from daily worry.

She had to try to free herself from the terror nibbling away at the edges of her resolute intentions and look at the bigger picture.

This wasn't just some silly social visit. This was...*a business meeting.*

She licked her lips now, frozen to the spot while the crowds of people continued to swerve around her, most of them glaring impatiently. There was no time in London to dawdle, not when everyone was living life in the fast lane.

Business meeting. She rather liked that analysis because it allowed her to blank out the horrifying personal aspect to this visit.

She tried to wipe out the alarming total recall she had of his face and superimpose it with the far more manageable features of their bank manager: bland, plump, semi-balding...

Maybe he had become bland, plump and semi-balding, she thought hopefully as she reluctantly propelled herself forward, joining the throng of people clustered on the pavement, waiting for the little man in the box to turn green.

She had dressed carefully.

In fact, she wore what she had planned to wear to visit the bank manager: black knee-length skirt, crisp white blouse—which was fine in cool Yorkshire, but horribly uncomfortable now in sticky London—and flat black pumps.

She had tied her hair back and twisted it into a sensible chignon at the nape of her neck.

Her make-up was discreet and background: a touch of mascara, some pale lip gloss and the very sheerest application of blusher.

She wasn't here to try to make an impression. She was here because she'd been pushed and hounded into a corner and now had to deal with the unfortunate situation in a brisk and businesslike manner.

There was no point travelling down memory lane because that would shatter the fragile veneer of self-confidence she knew she would need for this…*meeting*.

Another word she decided she rather liked.

And, at the end of the day, Oliver was happy. For the first time in ages, his eyes had lit up and she'd felt something of that twin bond they had shared when they'd been young but which seemed to have gone into hiding as their worries had begun piling up.

She took a deep breath and was carried by the crowd to the other side of the road as the lights changed. And then she was there, right in front of the building. Entering when most of the people were heading in the opposite direction because, of course, it was home time and the stampede to enjoy what remained of the warm weather that day was in full swing.

She pushed her way through the opaque glass doors and was disgorged into the most amazing foyer she had ever seen in her entire life.

Javier, naturally, didn't *own* the building, but his company occupied four floors at the very top and it was dawning on her that when Oliver had labelled him a 'billionaire' he hadn't been exaggerating.

You would have to have some serious money at your disposal to afford to rent a place like this, and being able to afford to rent four floors would require *very* serious money.

When had all that happened?

She'd reflected on that the evening before and now, walking woodenly towards the marble counter, which at six in the evening was only partially staffed, she reflected on it again.

When she'd known him, he hadn't had a bean. Lots of

ambition, but at that point in time the ambition had not begun to be translated into money.

He had worked most evenings at the local gym in the town centre for extra cash, training people on the punching bags. If you hadn't known him to be a first-class student with a brain most people would have given their right arm for, you might have mistaken him for a fighter.

He hadn't talked much about his background but she had known that his parents were not well off, and when she had watched him in the gym, muscled, sweaty and focused, she had wondered whether he hadn't done his fair share of fighting on the streets of Madrid.

From that place, he had gone to...*this*: the most expensive office block in the country, probably in Europe... A man shielded from the public by a bank of employees paid to protect the rich from nuisance visits...

Who would have thought?

Maybe if she had followed his progress over the years, she might have been braced for all of this, but, for her, the years had disappeared in a whirlpool of stress and unhappiness.

She tilted her jaw at a combative angle and squashed the wave of maudlin self-pity threatening to wash away her resolve.

Yes, she was told, after one of the women behind the marble counter had scrolled down a list on the computer in front of her, Mr Vasquez was expecting her.

He would buzz when he was ready for her to go up.

In the meantime...she was pointed to a clutch of dove-grey sofas at the side.

Sophie wondered how long she would have to wait. Oliver had admitted that he had had to wait for absolutely ages before Javier had deigned to see him and she settled in for the long haul. So she was surprised when, five minutes later, she was beckoned over and told that she could take the private lift to the eighteenth floor.

'Usually someone would escort you up,' the blonde woman told her with a trace of curiosity and malicious envy in her voice. 'I suppose you must know Mr Vasquez...?'

'Sort of,' Sophie mumbled as the elevator doors pinged open and she stepped into a wonder of glass that reflected her neat, pristine, sensible image back at her in a mosaic of tiny, refracted detail.

And then, thankfully, the doors smoothly and quietly shut and she was whizzing upwards, heart in her mouth, feeling as though she was about to step into the lion's den...

She was on her way up.

Javier had never been prone to nerves, but he would now confess to a certain tightening in his chest at the prospect of seeing her in a matter of minutes.

Of course he had known, from the second her brother had entered his offices with a begging bowl in his hand, that he would see Sophie once again.

As surely as night followed day, when it came to money, pride was the first thing to be sacrificed.

And they needed money. Badly. In fact, far more badly than Oliver had intimated. As soon as he had left, Javier had called up the company records for the family firm and discovered that it was in the process of free fall. Give it six months and it would crash-land and splinter into a thousand fragments.

He smiled slowly and pushed his chair back. He linked his fingers loosely together and toyed with the pleasurable thought of how he would play this meeting.

He knew what he wanted, naturally.

That had come as a bit of a surprise because he had

truly thought that he had put that unfortunate slice of his past behind him, but apparently he hadn't.

Because the very second Oliver had opened his mouth to launch into his plaintive, begging speech, Javier had known what he wanted and how he would get it.

He wanted *her*.

She was the only unfinished business in his life and he hadn't realised how much that had preyed on his mind until now, until the opportunity to finish that business had been presented to him on a silver platter.

He'd never slept with her.

She'd strung him along for a bit of fun, maybe because she'd liked having those tittering, upper-class friends of hers oohing and aahing with envy because she'd managed to attract the attention of the good-looking bad boy.

Didn't they say that about rich, spoilt girls—that they were always drawn to a bit of rough because it gave them an illicit thrill?

Naturally, they would never *marry* the bit of rough. That would be unthinkable!

Javier's lips thinned as he recalled the narrative of their brief relationship.

He remembered the way she had played with him, teasing him with a beguiling mixture of innocence and guileless, sensual temptation. She had let him touch but he hadn't been able to relish the full meal. He'd been confined to starters when he had wanted to devour all courses, including dessert.

He'd reached the point of wanting to ask her to marry him. He'd been offered the New York posting and he'd wanted her by his side. He'd hinted, saying a bit, dancing around the subject, but strangely for him had been too awkward to put all his cards on the table. Yet she must have suspected that a marriage proposal was on the cards.

Just thinking about it now, his insane stupidity, made

him clench his teeth together with barely suppressed anger.

She was the only woman who had got to him and the only one who had escaped him.

He forced himself to relax, to breathe slowly, to release the cold bitterness that had very quickly risen to the surface now that he knew that he would be seeing her in a matter of minutes.

The woman who had…yes…*hurt him.*

The woman who had used him as a bit of fun, making sure that she didn't get involved, saving herself for one of those posh, upper-class idiots who formed part of her tight little circle.

He was immune to being hurt now because he was older and more experienced. His life was rigidly controlled. He knew what he wanted and he got what he wanted, and what he wanted was the sort of financial security that would be immune to the winds of change. It was all that mattered and the only thing that mattered.

Women were a necessary outlet and he enjoyed them but they didn't interrupt the focus of his unwavering ambition. They were like satellites bobbing around the main planet.

Had he only had this level of control within his grasp when he'd met Sophie all those years ago, he might not have fallen for her, but there was no point in crying over spilt milk. The past could not be altered.

Which wasn't to say that there couldn't be retribution…

He *sensed* her even before he was aware of the hesitant knock on the door.

He had given his secretary the afternoon off. He'd been in meetings all afternoon, had returned to his offices only an hour previously, and something in him wanted to see Sophie without the presence of his secretary around.

He had brought Eva back with him from New York.

A widow in her sixties, originally from the UK anyway with all her family living here, she had been only too glad to accompany him back to London. She could be trusted not to gossip, but even so...

Seeing Sophie after all this time felt curiously *intimate*.

Which was something of a joke because *intimacy* implied some level of romance, of two people actually wanting to be in one another's company...

Hardly the case here.

Although, if truth be told, he was almost *looking forward* to seeing the woman again, whilst she...

He settled back in his leather chair and mused that *he* was probably the last person in the world *she* wanted to see.

But needs must...

'Enter.'

The deep, controlled tenor of that familiar voice chilled Sophie to the bone. She took a deep breath and nervously turned the handle before pushing open the door to the splendid office which, in her peripheral vision, was as dauntingly sophisticated as she had mentally predicted.

She had hoped that the years might have wrought changes in him, maybe even that her memory might have played tricks on her. She had prayed that he was no longer the hard-edged, proud, *dangerous* guy she had once known but, instead, a mellow man with room in his heart for forgiveness.

She'd been an idiot.

He was as *dangerous* as she remembered. More so. She stared and kept on staring at the familiar yet unfamiliar angles of his sinfully beautiful face. He'd always been incredibly good-looking, staggeringly exotic with finely chiselled features and lazy dark eyes with the longest eyelashes she had ever seen on a guy.

He was as sinfully good-looking as he had been then,

but now there was a cool self-possession about him that spoke of the tough road he had walked to get to the very top. His dark, dark eyes were watchful and inscrutable as she finally dragged her mesmerised gaze away from him and made her way forward with the grace and suppleness of a broken puppet.

And then, when she reached the chair in front of his desk, it dawned on her that she hadn't been invited to sit down, so she remained hovering with one hand on the back of the chair, waiting in tense, electric silence...

'Why don't you sit down, Sophie?'

He looked at her, enjoying the hectic colour in her cheeks, enjoying the fact that she was standing on shaky legs in front of him, in the role of supplicant.

And he was enjoying a hell of a lot more than that, he freely admitted to himself...

She was even more beautiful than the image he had stored in his mind carefully, as he had discovered, wrapped in tissue paper, waiting for the day when the tissue paper would be removed.

He couldn't see how long or short her hair was but it was still the vibrant tangle of colour it had been when he had first met her. Chestnut interweaved with copper with strands of strawberry blonde threaded through in a colourful display of natural highlights.

And she hadn't put on an ounce over the years. Indeed, she looked slimmer than ever. Gaunt, even, with smudges of strain showing under her violet eyes.

Financial stress would do that to a person, he thought, especially a person who had been brought up to expect the finest things in life.

But for all that she was as beautiful as he remembered, with that elusive quality of hesitancy that had first attracted him to her. She looked like a model, leggy, rangy and startlingly pretty, but she lacked the hard edges of someone with model looks and that was a powerful source of attraction. She had always seemed to be ever so slightly puzzled when guys spun round to stare at her.

Complete act, he now realised. Just one of the many things about her that had roped him in, one of the many things that had been fake.

'So...' he drawled, relaxing back in his chair. 'Where to begin? Such a long time since we last saw one another...'

Sophie was fast realising that there was going to be no loan. He had requested an audience with her *because he could*, because he had *known* that she would be unable to refuse. He had asked to see her so that he could send her away with a flea in her ear over how he thought he had been treated by her the last time they had been together.

She was sitting here in front of him simply because revenge was a dish best served cold.

She cleared her throat, back ramrod-straight, hands clutching the bag on her lap, a leftover designer relic back from the good old days when money, apparently, had been no object.

'My brother informs me that you might be amenable to providing us with a loan.' She didn't want to go down memory lane and, since this was a business meeting, why not cut to the chase? He wasn't going to lend them the money anyway, so what was the point of prolonging the agony?

Though there was some rebellious part of her that was compelled to steal glances at the man who had once held her heart captive in his hand.

He was still so beautiful. A wave of memories washed over her and she seemed to see, in front of her, the guy who could make her laugh, who could make her tingle all over whenever he rested his eyes on her; the guy who had lusted after her and had pursued her with the sort of intent and passion she had never experienced in her life before.

She blinked; the image was gone and she was back in the present, cringing as he continued to assess her with utterly cool detachment.

'Tut-tut-tut, Sophie. Don't tell me that you seriously expected to walk into my office and find yourself presented with a loan arrangement all ready and waiting for you to sign, before disappearing back to...remind where it is... the wilds of Yorkshire?' He shook his head with rueful incredulity, as though chastising her for being a complete moron. 'I think we should at least relax and chat a bit before we begin discussing...*money*...'

Sophie wondered whether this meant that he would actually agree to lend them the money they so desperately needed.

'I would offer you coffee or tea, but my secretary has gone for the day. I can, of course...' He levered himself out of the chair and Sophie noted the length and muscularity of his body.

He had been lean and menacing years ago, with the sort of physical strength that can only be thinly hidden behind clothes. He was just as menacing now, more so because he now wielded power, and a great deal of it.

She watched as he made his way over to a bar, which she now noticed at the far side of his office, in a separate, airy room which overlooked the streets below on two sides.

It was an obscenely luxurious office suite. All that was missing was a bed.

Heat stung her cheeks and she licked her lips nervously. For all she knew, he was married with a couple of kids, even though he didn't look it. He certainly would have a woman tucked away somewhere.

'Have a drink with me, Sophie...'

'I'd rather not.'

'Why not?'

'Because…' Her voice trailed off and she noted that he had ignored her completely and was now strolling towards her with a glass of wine in his hand.

'Because…what?' Instead of returning to his chair, he perched on the edge of his desk and looked down at her with his head tilted to one side.

'Why don't you just lay into me and get it over and done with?' she muttered, taking the drink from him and nursing the glass. She stared up at him defiantly, her violet eyes clashing with his unreadable, dark-as-night ones. 'I knew I shouldn't have come here.'

'Lay into you?' Javier queried smoothly. He shrugged. 'Things happen and relationships bite the dust. We were young. It's no big deal.'

'Yes,' Sophie agreed uneasily.

'So your brother tells me that you are now a widow…'

'Roger died in an accident three years ago.'

'Tragic. You must have been heartbroken.'

'It's always tragic when someone is snatched away in the prime of their life.' She ignored the sarcasm in his voice; she certainly wasn't going to pretend to play the part of heartbroken widow when her marriage had been a sham from beginning to end. 'And perhaps you don't know but my father is also no longer with us. I'm not sure if Ollie told you, but he suffered a brain tumour towards the end. So life, you see, has been very challenging, for me and my brother, but I'm sure you must have guessed that the minute he showed up here.' She lowered her eyes and then nervously sipped some of the wine before resting the glass on the desk.

She wanted to ask whether it was okay to do that or whether he should get a coaster or something.

But then, really rich people never worried about silly little things like wine glass ring-marks on their expensive wooden desks, did they?

'You have my sympathies.' Less sincere condolences had seldom been spoken. 'And your mother?'

'She lives in Cornwall now. We…we bought her a little cottage there so that she could be far from… Well, her health has been poor and the sea air does her good… And you?'

'What about me?' Javier frowned, eased himself off the desk and returned to where he had been sitting.

'Have you married? Got children?' The artificiality of the situation threatened to bring on a bout of manic laughter. It was surreal, sitting here making small talk with a guy who probably hated her guts, even though, thankfully, she had not been subjected to the sort of blistering attack she had been fearing.

At least, not yet.

At any rate, she could always walk out…although he had dangled that carrot in front of her, intimated that he would indeed be willing to discuss the terms and conditions of helping them. Could she seriously afford to let her pride come in the way of some sort of solution to their problems?

If she had been the only one affected, then yes, but there was her brother, her mother, those faithful employees left working, through loyalty, for poor salaries in the ever-shrinking family business.

'This isn't about me,' Javier fielded silkily. 'Although, in answer to your question, I have reached the conclusion that women, as a long-term proposition, have no place in my life at this point in time. So, times have changed for you,' he murmured, moving on with the conversation. He reached into his drawer and extracted a sheet of paper, which he swivelled so that it was facing her.

'Your company accounts. From riches to rags in the space of a few years, although, if you look carefully, you'll see that the company has been mismanaged for somewhat longer than a handful of years. Your dearly departed husband seems to have failed to live up to whatever promise there was that an injection of cash would rescue your family's business. I take it you were too busy playing the good little wife to notice that he had been blowing vast sums of money on pointless ventures that all crashed and burned?'

Sophie stared at the paper, feeling as though she had been stripped naked and made to stand in front of him for inspection.

'I knew,' she said abruptly. *Playing the good little wife? How wrong could he have been?*

'You ditched your degree course to rush into marriage with a man who blew the money on…oh, let's have a look…transport options for sustainable farmers…a wind farm that came to nothing…several aborted ventures into the property market…a sports centre which was built and then left to rot because the appropriate planning permission hadn't been provided… All the time your father's once profitable transport business was haemorrhaging money by the bucketload. And you knew…'

'There was nothing I could do,' Sophie said tightly, loathing him even though she knew that, if he were to lend them any money, he would obviously have to know exactly what he was getting into.

'Did you know where else your husband was blowing his money, to the tune of several hundred thousand?'

Perspiration broke out in a fine, prickly film and she stared at him mutinously.

'Why are you doing this?'

'Doing what?'

'Hanging me out to dry? If you don't want to help, then please just say so and I'll leave and you'll never see me again.'

'Fine.' Javier sat back and watched her.

She had never lain spread across his bed. He had never seen that hair in all its glory across his pillows. He had felt those ripe, firm breasts, but through prudish layers of clothes. He had never tasted them. Had never even *seen* them. Before he'd been able to do any of that, before he'd been able to realise the powerful thrust of his passion and his *yearning*, she had walked away from him. Walked straight up to the altar and into the arms of some little twerp whose very existence she had failed to mention in the months that they had been supposedly going out.

He had a sudden vision of her lying on his bed in the penthouse apartment, just one of several he owned in the capital. It was a blindingly clear vision and his erection was as fast as it was shocking. He had to breathe deeply and evenly in an attempt to dispel the unsettling and unwelcome image that had taken up residence in his head.

'Not going to walk out?' Javier barely recognised the raw lack of self-control that seemed to be guiding his responses.

He'd wanted to see her squirm but the force of his antipathy took him by surprise because he was realising just how fast and tight she had stuck to him over the years.

Unfinished business. That was why. Well, he would make sure he finished it if it was the last thing he did and then he would be free of the woman and whatever useless part of his make-up she still appeared to occupy.

'He gambled.' Sophie raised her eyes to his and held his stare in silence before looking away, offering him her averted profile.

'And you knew about that as well,' Javier had a fleeting twinge of regret that he had mentioned any of this. It had been unnecessary. Then he remembered the way she had summarily dumped him and all fleeting regret vanished in a puff of smoke.

She nodded mutely.

'And there was nothing you could have done about that either?'

'I don't suppose you've ever lived with someone who has a destructive addiction?' she said tightly. 'You can't just sit them down for a pep talk and then expect them to change overnight.'

'But you *can* send them firmly in the direction of professional help.' Javier was curious. The picture he had built of her had been one of the happily married young wife, in love with Prince Charming, so in love that she had not been able to abide being away from him whilst at university—perhaps hoping that the distraction of an unsuitable foreigner might put things into perspective, only for that gambit to hit the rocks.

Then, when he had inspected the accounts closely, he had assumed that, blindly in love, she had been ignorant of her loser husband's uncontrolled behaviour.

Now...

He didn't want curiosity to mar the purity of what he wanted from her and he was taken aback that it was.

'Roger was an adult. He didn't want help. I wasn't capable of manhandling him into a car and driving him to the local association for gambling addicts. And I don't want to talk about...about my marriage. I... It's in the past.'

'So it is,' Javier murmured. When he thought about the other man, he saw red, pure jealousy at being deprived of what he thought should have been his.

Crazy.

Since when had he considered any woman *his possession*?

'And yet,' he mused softly, 'when is the past ever *really* behind us? Don't you find that it dogs us like a guilty conscience, even when we would like to put it to bed for good?'

'What do you mean?'

'You ran out on me.'

'Javier, you don't *understand*…'

'Nor do I wish to. This isn't about understanding what motivated you.' And at this point in time—this very special point in time when the tables had been reversed, when she was now the one without money and he the one with the bank notes piled up in the coffers—well, she was hardly going to tell the whole truth and nothing but the truth when it came to motivations, was she? Oh, no, she would concoct some pretty little tale to try to elicit as much sympathy from him as she could…

'I'm not asking you to give me money, Javier. I…I'm just asking for a loan. I would pay it all back, every penny of it.'

Javier flung back his head and laughed, a rich, full-bodied laugh that managed to lack genuine warmth. 'Really? I'm tickled pink at the thought of a Classics scholar, almost there but never graduated, and her sports scholarship brother running any company successfully enough to make it pay dividends, never mind a company that's on its last legs.'

'There *are* directors in the company…'

'Looked at them. I would ditch most of them if I were you.'

'You *looked at them*?'

Javier shrugged. His dark eyes never left her face. 'I probably know more about your company than you do. Why not? If I'm to sink money into it, then I need to know exactly what I will be sinking money into.'

'So…are you saying that you'll help?'

'I'll help.' He smiled slowly. 'But there's no such thing as a free lunch. There will be terms and conditions…'

'That's fine.' For the first time in a very long time, a cloud seemed to be lifting. She had underestimated him. He was going to help and she wanted to sob with relief. 'Whatever your terms and conditions, well, they won't be a problem. I promise.'

CHAPTER THREE

'PERHAPS WE SHOULD take this conversation somewhere else.'

'Why?' The suggestion of leaving with him for *somewhere else* sent little shivers of alarm skittering through her. She could scarcely credit that she was sitting here, in this office, facing this man who had haunted her for years. All the things that had happened ever since that first tentative step as a young girl falling hopelessly in love with an unsuitable boy lay between them like a great, big, murky chasm.

There was just so much he didn't know.

But none of that was relevant. What was relevant was that he was going to help them and that was enough.

'Because,' Javier drawled, rising to his feet and strolling to fetch his jacket from where it lay slung over the back of one of the expensive, compact sofas in the little sitting area of the office, 'I feel that two old friends should not be discussing something as crass as a business bailout within the confines of an office.'

Two old friends?

Sophie scrutinised the harsh angles of his face for any inherent sarcasm and he returned her stare with bland politeness.

But his bland politeness made her feel unaccountably uneasy.

He'd never been polite.

At least, not in the way that English people were polite. Not in the middle-class way of clinking teacups and saying the right things, which was the way she had been brought up.

He had always spoken his mind and damned the consequences. She had occasionally seen him in action at university, once in the company of two of his lecturers, when they had been discussing economics.

He had listened to them, which had been the accepted polite way, but had then taken their arguments and ripped them to shreds. The breadth and depth of his knowledge had been so staggering that there had been no comeback.

He had never been scared of rocking the boat. Sometimes, she wondered whether he had privately relished it, although when she'd once asked him that directly, he had burst out laughing before kissing her senseless—at which point she had forgotten what she had been saying to him. Kissing him had always had that effect on her.

A surge of memories brought a hectic flush to her cheeks.

'Is this your new way of dressing?' he asked and Sophie blinked, dispelling disturbing images of when they had been an item.

'What do you mean?'

'You look like an office worker.'

'That's exactly what I am,' she returned lightly, following him to the door, because what else could she do? At this point, he held all the trump cards, and if he wanted to go and have their business chat sitting on bar stools in the middle of Threadneedle Street, then so be it. There was too much at stake for her to start digging her heels in and telling him that she felt more comfortable discussing business in an office.

She had come this far and there was no turning back now.

This floor was a sanctum of quiet. It was occupied by CEOs and directors, most of whom were concealed behind opaque glass and thick doors. In the middle there was a huge, open-plan space in which desks were cleverly positioned to allow for maximum space utilisation and minimum scope for chatting aimlessly.

The open space was largely empty, except for a couple of diligent employees who were too absorbed in whatever they were doing to look up at them as they headed for the directors' lift.

'But it's not exactly where you wanted to end up, is it?' he asked as the lift doors quietly closed, sealing them in together.

It didn't matter where she looked, reflections of him bounced back at her.

She shrugged and reluctantly met his dark eyes.

'You don't always end up where you think you're going to,' she said tersely.

'You had big plans to be a university lecturer.'

'Life got in the way of that.'

'I'm sure your dearly departed husband wouldn't like to be seen as someone who got in the way of your big plans.'

'I don't want to talk about Roger.'

Because the thought of him no longer being around was still too painful for her to bear. That thought struck Javier with dagger-like precision. The man might have been a waste of space when it came to business, and an inveterate gambler who had blown vast sums of money that should have been pumped into saving the company, yet she had loved him and now would have nothing said against him.

Javier's lips thinned.

He noted the way she scurried out of the lift, desperate to put some physical distance between them.

'When did you find out that the company was on the brink of going bust?'

Sophie cringed. She wanted to ask whether it was really necessary to go down that road and she knew that she had to divorce the past from the present. He wasn't the guy she had loved to death, the guy she had been forced to give up when life as she knew it had suddenly stopped. That was in the past and right now she was in the company of someone thinking about extending credit to the company. He would want details even if she didn't want to give them.

But there was a lot she didn't want to tell him. She didn't want his contempt or his pity and she knew she would have both if she presented him with the unadorned truth. That was if he believed her at all, which was doubtful.

'I knew things weren't too good a while back,' she said evasively. 'But I had no idea really of just how bad they were until…well, until I got married. '

Javier felt the dull, steady beat of jealousy working its poisonous way through his body.

He was painfully reminded of the folly of his youth, the naivety of imagining that they would have a future together. The poor foreigner working his way up and the beautiful, well-spoken, impeccably bred English girl who just so happened to be the apple of her father's adoring and protective eye.

At the time, he had thought himself to be as hard as nails and immune to distraction.

He'd set his course and he had been cocky enough to imagine that no ill winds would come along to blow him off target.

Of all the girls on the planet, he had found himself blown off target by one who had set her course on someone else and had been playing with him for a bit of fun, stringing him along while her heart belonged to someone else.

'And then…what?'

'What do you mean?' She nervously played with her finger, where once upon an unhappy time there had been a wedding ring.

She hadn't paid much attention to where they were going, but when he stood back to push open a door for her, she saw that they were at an old pub, the sort of pub that populated the heart of the City.

She shimmied past him, ducking under his outstretched arm as he held the door open for her. She was tall at five foot ten, but he was several inches taller and she had a memory of how protected he had always made her feel. The clean, masculine scent of him lingered in her nostrils, making her feel shaky as she sat down at a table in the corner, waiting tensely while he went to get them something to drink. She knew she should keep a clear head and drink water but her nerves were all over the place. They needed something a little stronger than water.

Outside it was hot and she could glimpse a packed garden but in here it was cool, dark and relatively empty.

The sun worshippers were all drinking in the evening sun.

Trying to elicit details about her past was not relevant. Javier knew that and he was furious with himself for succumbing to the desire to know more.

Just like that, in a matter of minutes, she had managed to stoke his curiosity. Just like that, she was back under his skin and he couldn't wait to have her, to bed her, so that he could rid himself of the uncomfortable suspicion that she had been there all along, a spectre biding its time until it could resurface to catch him on the back foot.

For a man to whom absolute control was vital, this slither of susceptibility was unwelcome.

He realised that when he tried to think of the last woman he had slept with, a top-notch career woman in New York with legs to her armpits, he came up blank. He couldn't focus on anyone but the woman sitting in front of him, looking at him as though she expected him to pounce unexpectedly at any minute.

She had the clearest violet eyes he had ever seen, fringed with long, dark lashes, and the tilt of them gave her a slightly dreamy look, as though a part of her was on another plane. He itched to unpin her neat little bun so that he could see whether that glorious hair of hers was still as long, still as unruly.

'Well?' Javier demanded impatiently, hooking a chair with his foot and angling it so that he could sit with his long legs extended. He had brought a wine cooler with a bottle of wine and one of the bartenders placed two glasses in front of them, then simpered for a few seconds, doe-eyed, before reluctantly walking back to the bar.

'Well…what?'

'What was the order of events? Heady marriage, fairy-tale honeymoon and then, lo and behold, no more money? Life can be cruel. And where was your brother when all this was happening?'

'In America.' She sighed.

'By choice, even though he knew?' With the family company haemorrhaging money, surely it would have been an indulgence for Oliver to have stayed in California, enjoying himself…

'He didn't know,' Sophie said abruptly. 'And I don't know why…how all this is relevant.'

'I'm fleshing out the picture,' Javier said softly. 'You've

come to me with a begging bowl. What did you think I was going to do? Give you a big, comforting hug and write out a cheque?'

'No, but...'

'Let's get one thing straight here, Sophie.' He leant forward and held her gaze. She couldn't have said a word even if she had wanted to. She could hardly breathe. 'You're here to ask a favour of me and, that being the case, whether you like it or not, you don't get to choose what questions to answer and what questions to ignore. Your private life is your business. Frankly, I don't give a damn. But I need to know your levels of capability when it comes to doing business. I need to know whether your brother is committed to working for the company, because if he was left to enjoy four years of playing sport in California, then I'm guessing he wouldn't have returned to the sick fold with a cheerful whistle. Most of the directors of the company aren't worth the money they're being paid.'

'You know how much they're being paid!'

'I know everything worth knowing about your crippled family company.'

'When did you get so...so...*hard*?'

Roughly around the same time I discovered what sort of woman I'd been going out with, Javier thought with the sour taste of cynicism in his mouth.

He leant back and crossed his legs, lightly cradling the stem of the wine glass between his long fingers.

'You don't make money by being a sap for sob stories,' he informed her coolly, keen eyes taking in the delicate bloom of colour in her cheeks. 'You've come to me with a sob story.' He shrugged. 'And the bottom line is this— if you don't like the direction this conversation is going, then, like I said before, you're free to go. But of course, we both know you won't, because you need me.'

He was enjoying this little game of going round the houses before he laid all his cards on the table, before she knew exactly what the terms and conditions of her repayment would be.

It wouldn't hurt her to realise just how dangerously close the company was to imploding.

It wouldn't hurt her to realise just how much she needed him...

'If you knew about your husband's hare-brained schemes and addiction to gambling, and you allowed it to go under the radar, then are you a trustworthy person to stand at the helm of your company?'

'I told you that there was nothing I could do,' she said with a dull flush.

'And if your brother was so clueless as to what was happening on the home front, then is *he* competent enough to do what would need to be done should I decide to help you out?'

'Ollie...doesn't have a huge amount of input in the actual running of things...'

'Why?'

'Because he's never been interested in the company and, yes, you're right—he's always resented the fact that he had to finally return to help out. He's found it difficult to deal with not having money.'

'And you've found it easy?'

'I've dealt with it.'

Javier looked at her narrowly and with a certain amount of reluctant admiration for the streak of strength he glimpsed.

Not only had she had to face a tremendous fall from the top of the mountain, but the loss of her husband and the father she had adored.

Yet there was no self-pity in the stubborn tilt of her chin.

'You've had a lot to deal with, haven't you?' he murmured softly and she looked away.

'I'm no different from loads of people the world over who have found their lives changed in one way or another. And, now that you've got the measure of the company, will you lend us some money or not? I don't know if my brother told you, but the family house has been on the market for over two years and we just can't seem to sell it. There's no appetite for big houses. If we could sell it, then we might be able to cover some of the expenses...'

'Although a second mortgage was taken out on it...'

'Yes, but the proceeds would go a little way to at least fixing certain things that need urgent attention.'

'The dated computer systems, for example?'

'You really did your homework, didn't you? How did you manage that in such a small amount of time? Or have you been following my father's company over the years? Watching while it went downhill?'

'Why would I have done that?'

Sophie shrugged uncomfortably. 'I know you probably feel... Well, you don't understand what happened all those years ago.'

'Don't presume to think that you know what goes on in my head, Sophie. You don't. And, in answer to your preposterous question, I haven't had the slightest clue what was going on in your father's company over the years, nor have I cared one way or the other.' He saw that the bottle was empty and debated whether or not to get another, deciding against it, because he wanted them both to have clear heads for this conversation.

When he knew that he would be seeing her, he had predicted how he would react and it hadn't been like this.

He'd thought that he would see her and would feel nothing but the acid, bilious taste of bitterness for having been played in the past and taken for a chump.

He'd accepted that she'd been in his head more than he'd ever imagined possible. A Pandora's box had been opened with her brother's unexpected appearance at his office. Javier had recognised the opportunity he had been given to put an end to her nagging presence, which, he now realised, had been embedded in him like a virus he'd never managed to shake off.

He would have her and he had the means to do so at his disposal.

She needed money. He had vast sums of it. She would take what was offered because she would have no choice. His *terms and conditions* would be met with acquiescence because, as he had learned over the years, money talked.

He had slept with some of the world's most desirable women. It had followed that whatever she had that had held him captive all those years ago, she would lose it when he saw her in the flesh once again. How could she compete with some of the women who had clamoured to sleep with him?

He'd been wrong.

And that was unbelievably frustrating because he was beginning to realise that he wanted a lot more from her than her body for a night or two.

No, he *needed* a lot more from her than her body for a night or two.

He wanted and needed *answers* and his curiosity to pry beneath the surface enraged him because he had thought himself above that particular sentiment when it came to her.

Nor, he was discovering, did he want to take what he knew she would have no choice but to give him in the manner of a marauding plunderer.

He didn't want her reluctance.

He wanted her to come to him and in the end, he reasoned now, if revenge was what he was after, then wouldn't that be the ultimate revenge? To have her want him, to take her and then to walk away?

The logical part of his brain knew that to want revenge was to succumb to a certain type of weakness, and yet the pull was so immensely strong that he could no more fight it than he could have climbed Mount Everest in bare feet.

And he was enjoying this.

His palate had become jaded and that was something he had recognised a while back, when he had made his first few million and the world had begun to spread itself out at his feet.

He had reached a place in life where he could have whatever he wanted and sometimes having everything at your fingertips removed the glory of the chase. Not just women, but deals, mergers, money…the lot.

She wasn't at his fingertips.

In fact, she was simmering with resentment that she had been put in the unfortunate position of having to come to him, cap in hand, to ask for his help.

He was a part of her past that she would rather have swept under the carpet and left there. He was even forced to swallow the unsavoury truth that he was probably a part of her past she bitterly regretted ever having gone anywhere near in the first place.

But she'd wanted him.

That much he felt he knew. She might have played with him as a distraction from the main event happening in her life somewhere else, or maybe just to show off in front of her friends that she had netted the biggest fish in the sea—which Javier had known, without a trace of vanity, he was.

But perhaps she hadn't actually banked on the flare of physical attraction that had erupted between them. She had held out against him and he had seen that as shyness, youthful nerves at taking the plunge… He'd been charmed by it. He'd also been wrong about it, as it turned out. She'd held out against him because there had been someone else in her life.

But she'd still fancied him like hell.

She'd trembled when he'd traced his finger across her collarbone and her eyes had darkened when their lips had touched. He hadn't imagined those reactions. She might have successfully fought that attraction in the end and scurried back to her comfort zone, but, for a brief window, he'd taken her out of that comfort zone...

Did she imagine that she was now immune to that physical attraction because time had passed?

He played with the thought of her opening up to him like a flower and this time giving him what he had wanted all those years ago. What he wanted now.

He wondered what she would feel when she found herself discarded.

He wondered whether he would really care or whether the mere fact that he had had her would be sufficient.

He hadn't felt this *alive* in a long time and it was bloody great.

'I was surprised when your brother showed up on my doorstep, so to speak, in search of help.'

'I hope you know that I never asked him to come to see you.'

'I can well imagine, Sophie. It must cut to the quick having to beg favours from a man who wasn't good enough for you seven years ago.'

'That's not how it was.'

Javier held up one hand. 'But, as it happens, to see you evicted and in the poorhouse would not play well on my conscience.'

'That's a bit of an exaggeration, don't you think?'

'You'd be surprised how thin the dividing line is between the poor and the rich and how fast places can be swapped. One minute you're on top of the world, the ruler of everything around you, and the next minute you're lying on the scrap heap, wondering what went wrong. Or I could put it another way—one minute you're flying upwards, knocking back all those less fortunate cluttering your path, and the next minute you're spiralling downwards and the people you've knocked back are on their way up, having the last laugh.'

'I bet your parents are really sad at the person you've become, Javier.'

Javier flushed darkly, outraged at her remark, and even more outraged by the disappointed expression on her lovely face.

Of course, in those heady days of thinking she was his, he had let her into his world, haltingly confided in her in a way he had never done with any woman either before or since. He had told her about his background, about his parents' determination to make sure he left that life behind. He had painted an unadorned picture of life as he had known it, had been amused at the vast differences between them, had seen those differences as a good thing, rather than an unsurmountable barrier, as she had. If she'd even thought about it at all.

'I know you've become richer than your wildest dreams.' She smiled ruefully at him. 'And you always had very, very wild dreams…'

The conversation seemed to have broken its leash and was racing away in a direction Javier didn't like. He frowned heavily at her.

'And now here we are.'

'You once told me that all your parents wanted was for you to be happy, to make something of your life, to settle down and have a big family.'

Javier decided that he needed another drink after all.

He stood up abruptly, which seemed to do the trick, because she started, blinked and looked up at him as if suddenly remembering that she wasn't here for a trip down memory lane. Indeed, that a trip down memory lane was the very last thing she had wanted.

He'd forgotten that habit of hers.

He was barely aware of placing his order for another bottle of wine at the bar and ordering some bar snacks because they were now both drinking on fairly empty stomachs. He hadn't a clue what bar snacks he ordered, leaving it to the guy serving him to provide whatever was on the menu.

She was filling up his head. He could feel her eyes on him even as he stood here at the bar with his back to her.

Whatever memories he'd had of her, whatever memories he'd kidded himself he'd got rid of and had buried, he was now finding in a very shallow grave.

She'd always had that habit of branching out on a tangent. It was as if a stray word could spark some improbable connection in her head and carry her away down unforeseen paths.

There were no unforeseen paths in this scenario, he thought grimly as he made his way back to the table, where she was sitting with the guarded expression back on her face.

The only unforeseen thing—and it was something he could deal with—was how much he still wanted her after all this time.

'I should be getting back,' she said as he poured her a glass of wine and nodded to her to drink.

'I've ordered food.'

'My ticket…'

'Forget about your ticket.'

'I can't do that.'

'Why not?'

'Because I'm not made of money. In fact, I'm broke. There. Are you satisfied that I've said that? I can't afford to kiss sweet goodbye to the cost of the ticket to get me down here to London. You've probably forgotten how much train tickets cost, but if you'd like a reminder, I can show you mine. They cost a lot. And if you want to do a bit more gloating, then go right ahead.' She fluttered her hand wearily. 'I can't stop you.'

'You'll need to pare down the staff.'

'I beg your pardon?'

'The company is top-heavy. Too many chiefs and very few Indians.'

Sophie nodded. It was what she had privately thought but the thought of sitting down old friends of her parents and handing them their marching orders had been just too much to contemplate. Oliver couldn't have done that in a million years and, although she was a heck of a lot more switched on than he was, the prospect of sacking old retainers, even fairly ineffective old retainers, still stuck in her throat.

Few enough people had stuck by them through thin times.

'And you need to drag the business into this century. The old-fashioned transport business needs to be updated. You need to take risks, to branch out, to try to capture smaller, more profitable markets instead of sticking to having lumbering dinosaurs doing cross-Channel deliveries. That's all well and good but you need a lot more than that if your company is to be rescued from the quicksand.'

'I...' She quailed at the thought of herself and Oliver, along with a handful of maybe or maybe not efficient directors, undertaking a job of those proportions.

'You and your brother are incapable of taking on this challenge,' Javier told her bluntly and she glared at him even though he had merely spoken aloud what she had been thinking.

'I'm sure if you agree to extend a loan,' she muttered, 'we can recruit good people who are capable of—'

'Not going to happen. If I sink money into that business of yours, I want to be certain that I won't be throwing my money into a black hole.'

'That's a bit unfair.' She fiddled with the bun which, instead of making her feel blessedly cool in the scorching temperatures, was making her sweaty and uncomfortable. As were the formal, scratchy clothes, so unlike her normal dress code of jeans, tee shirts and sneakers.

She didn't feel like the brisk, efficient potential client of someone who might want to extend a loan. She felt awkward, gauche and way too aware of the man looking at her narrowly, sizing her up in a way that made her want to squirm.

This wasn't the guy she had known and loved. He hadn't chucked her out of his office but, as far as feelings went, there was nothing there. There wasn't a trace of that simmering attraction that had held them both mesmerised captives all those years ago. He wasn't married but she wondered whether there was a woman in his life, someone rich and beautiful like him.

Even when he'd had no money, he could have had any woman he wanted.

Her mind boggled at the thought of how many women would now fall at his feet because he was the guy who had the full package.

A treacherous thought snaked into her head...

What if she'd defied her parents? What if she'd carried on seeing Javier? Had seen where that love might have taken them both?

It wouldn't have worked.

Despite the fact that she had grown up with money,

had had a rich and pampered life, money per se was not what motivated her. For Javier, it was the only thing that motivated him.

She looked at him from under her lashes, taking in the cut of his clothes, the hand-tailored shoes, the mega-expensive watch around which dark hair curled. He *breathed* wealth. It was what made him happy and made sense of his life.

She might be stressed out because of all the financial worries happening in her life, but if those worries were removed and she was given a clean slate, then she knew that she wouldn't really care if that slate was a rich slate or not.

So, if she'd stayed with him, she certainly wouldn't have been the sort of woman he'd have wanted. She might talk the talk but her jeans, tee shirts and sneakers would not have been found acceptable attire.

They'd had their moment in time when they'd both been jeans and tee shirts people but he'd moved on, and he would always have moved on.

The attraction, for him, would have dimmed and finally been snuffed out.

The road she'd taken had been tough and miserable and, as things had turned out, the wrong one. But it would be silly to think that she would have been any happier if she'd followed Javier and held the hand he'd extended.

'We can go round the houses discussing what's fair and what's unfair,' he said in a hard voice. 'But that won't get us anywhere. I'm prepared to sink money in, but I get a cut of the cake and you abide by my rules.'

'Your rules?' She looked at him in bewilderment.

'Did you really think I'd write a cheque and then keep my fingers crossed that you might know what to do with the money?' He'd had one plan when this situation had first arisen—it had been clean and simple—but now he didn't want clean and simple. He needed to get more immersed in the water…and he was looking forward to that.

'I will, to spell it out, want a percentage of your business. There's no point my waiting for the time when you can repay me. I already have more money than I can shake a stick at, but I could put your business to some good use, branch out in ways that might dovetail with some of my other business concerns.'

Sophie shifted, not liking the sound of this. If he wanted a part of their business, wouldn't that involve him *being around*? Or was he talking about being a silent partner?

'Does your company have a London presence at all?' Javier was thoroughly enjoying himself. Who said the only route to satisfaction was getting what you wanted on demand? He'd always been excellent when it came to thinking outside the box. He was doing just that right now. Whatever he sank into her business would be peanuts for him but he could already see ways of turning a healthy profit.

And as for having her? Of course he would, but where was the rush after all? He could take a little time out to relish this project…

'Barely,' she admitted. 'We closed three of the four branches over the years to save costs.'

'And left one open and running?'

'We couldn't afford to shut them all…even though the overheads are frightening.'

'Splendid. As soon as the details are formalised and all the signatures are in place, I will ensure that the office is modernised and ready for occupation.'

'It's already occupied,' Sophie said, dazed. 'Mandy works on reception and twice a week one of the accountants goes down to see to the various bits of post. Fortunately nearly everything is done by email these days…'

'Pack your bags, Sophie. I'm taking up residence in your London office, just as soon as it's fit for habitation, and you're going to be sitting right there alongside me.'

Not quite the original terms and conditions he had intended to apply, but in so many ways so much better...

CHAPTER FOUR

'I DON'T KNOW what you're so worried about. His terms and conditions seem pretty fair to me. In fact, better than fair. He's going to have a percentage interest in the company but at least it'll be a company that's making money.'

That had been Oliver's reaction when she had presented him, a fortnight ago, with the offer Javier had laid out on the table for her to take or reject.

He had been downright incredulous that she might even be hesitating to eat from the hand that had been extended to feed her. In a manner that was uncharacteristically proactive for him, he had called an extraordinary meeting of the directors and presented them with Javier's plan, and Sophie had had to swallow the unpalatable reality that her past had caught up with her and was now about to join hands with her present.

Since then, with papers signed and agreements reached at the speed of light, the little office they had kept open in Notting Hill had been awash with frantic activity.

Sophie had refused to go. She had delegated that task to her brother, who had been delighted to get out of Yorkshire for a couple of weeks. He had reported back with gusto at the renovations being made and, inside, Sophie had quailed at the way she felt, as though suddenly her life was being taken over.

She knew she was being ridiculous.

Javier had agreed to see them because of their old connection but there had been nothing there beyond that historic connection. He had made no attempts to pursue any conversations about what had happened between them. He had been as cool as might have been expected given the circumstances of their break-up and she was in no doubt that the only reason he had agreed to help them was because he could see a profit in what was being offered.

Money was what he cared about and she suspected that he would be getting a good deal out of them. They were, after all, in the position of the beggars who couldn't be choosers.

Hadn't he greeted her with all the information he had accumulated about the company?

He had done his homework and he wouldn't be offering them a rescue package if he wasn't going to get a great deal out of it.

She brushed her skirt, neatened her blouse and inspected herself in the mirror in the hallway, but she wasn't really seeing her reflection. She was thinking, persuading herself that his attitude towards her made everything much easier. For him, the past was history. What he had with her now was a business deal and one that had fallen into his lap like a piece of ripe fruit that hadn't even needed plucking from the tree.

Maybe in some distant corner of his mind there was an element of satisfaction that he was now in a position to be the one calling the shots, but if that was the case, he would have to have cared one way or another about her and he didn't.

The effect he still had on her was not mutual. And even her responses to him were an illusion, no more than a reminder of the power of nostalgia, because truthfully her heart was safely locked away, never again to be taken out to see the light of day.

She blinked and focused on the tidy image staring back at her. Everything in place. In a few minutes the taxi would come to take her to the station. A month ago, she would have hit the bus stop, which was almost a mile away, but he had deposited a large advance of cash in the company account to cover expenses and to ensure that everyone on the payroll was compensated for the overtime which they had contributed over the months and which had not been paid.

She would take the taxi to the station and then the train down to London so that she could see the final, finished product, the newly refurbished offices in which she would be stationed for as long as it took to get things up and running.

'How long do you think that's going to take?' she had asked Javier on day one, heart thumping at the prospect of being in an office where, on a whim, he could descend without warning.

He had shrugged, his dark-as-night eyes never leaving her face. 'How long is a piece of string? There's a lot of work to do with the company before it begins to pull its weight. There's been mass wastage of money and resources, expenditures that border on criminal and incompetent staff by the bucketload.'

'And you're going to…er…be around, supervising…?'

His eyes had narrowed on her flushed face. 'Does the prospect of that frighten you, Sophie?'

'Not in the slightest,' she had returned quickly. 'I would just be surprised if you managed to take time off from being the ruler of all you surveyed to help out an ailing firm. I mean, don't you have minions who move in when you take over sick companies?'

'I think I might give the minions a rest on this particular occasion,' he had murmured softly.

'Why?' Sophie had heard the thread of desperation in her voice. She couldn't be within five feet of him without her body reliving the way he had once made it feel, playing stupid games with her mind.

'This is a slightly more personal venture for me, Sophie,' he had told her, leaning across the boardroom table where both of them had remained after the legal team had exited. 'Maybe I want to see that the job is done to the highest possible standard given our...past acquaintanceship.'

Sophie hadn't known whether to thank him or quiz him, so she had remained silent, her eyes helplessly drifting down to his sensual mouth before sliding away as heat had consumed her.

With a little sigh, she grabbed her handbag as she heard the taxi circle the gravelled forecourt, and then she was on her way, half hoping that Javier wouldn't be there waiting at the office when she finally arrived, half hoping that he might be, and hating herself for that weakness.

She had no idea what to expect to find. The last time she had visited this particular office had been two years previously, when she and Oliver had been trying to decide which of the offices to shut. She remembered it as spacious enough but, without any money having been spent on it at all, it had already been showing telltale signs of wear and tear. That said, it had been the biggest and the least run-down, so they'd been able to amalgamate the diminishing files and folders there from the other offices.

Not for the first time, as she was ferried from north to south, she thought about how clueless she had been about the groundbreaking changes that had been happening right under her nose.

Ollie, at least, had had the excuse of being abroad, because he had left on his sports scholarship two years before she had gone to Cambridge. He'd been a fresh-faced teenager wrapped up in his own life, with no vision of anything happening outside it.

But she had still been living at home, in her final years at school. Why hadn't she asked more probing questions when her mother's health had begun to fail? The doctor had talked about stress, and now Sophie marvelled that she hadn't dug deeper to find out what the stress had been all about, because on the surface her mother could not have been living a less stressed-out life.

And neither had she questioned the frequency with which Roger's name had cropped up in conversations or the number of times he'd been invited along to the house for various parties. She had been amused at his enthusiasm and had eventually drifted into going out with him; she had never suspected the amount of encouragement he had got from her parents.

All told, she had allowed herself to be wrapped up in cotton wool. So when that cotton wool had been cruelly yanked off, she had been far more shell-shocked than she might otherwise have been.

Everything had hit her at once. She had been bombarded from all sides and, in the middle of this, had had to wise up quickly to the trauma of discovering just how ill her father was and the lengths he had gone to to protect them all from knowing.

She should have been there helping out long before the bomb had detonated, splintering shrapnel through their lives.

If she had been, then perhaps the company could have taken a different direction. And, if it had taken a different direction, then she wouldn't be here now, at the mercy of a guy who could still send her senses reeling, whatever her head was telling her.

Once in London, Sophie took a black cab to the premises of the office in Notting Hill.

Oliver had told her that things were coming along brilliantly but he had undersold just how much had been done in the space of a few days. It wasn't just about the paint job on the outside or the impressive potted plants or the newly painted black door with its gold lettering announcing the name of the company.

Standing back, Sophie's mouth fell open as she took in the smart exterior. Then the door opened and she was staring at a casually dressed Javier, who, in return, stared back at her as he continued to lounge indolently against the door frame. Arms folded, he was already projecting the signs of ownership so that, as she took a few tentative steps towards him, she felt herself to be the visitor.

'Wow.' She hovered, waiting for him to step back, which he did after a couple of seconds, taking his time to unfold his gloriously elegant body and then stand aside so that she had to brush past him, immediately turning around and establishing a safe physical distance between them. 'It's completely changed on the outside.'

'There's no point having an office that repels potential clients,' Javier said drily.

Yet again, she was in work attire. The sort of clothes that drained her natural beauty.

'Why have you shown up wearing a suit?' he asked, strolling past her and expecting her to follow, which she duly did. 'And where is your bag? You do realise that you will be relocating to London for the foreseeable future?'

'I've been giving that some thought…'

Javier stopped and turned to look at her. 'Forget it.'

'I beg your pardon?'

'Remember the terms and conditions? One of them is that you relocate down here so that you can oversee the running of the London arm of the business.'

'Yes, but—'

'No *buts*, Sophie.' His voice was cool and unyielding. He hooked his fingers on the waistband of his black jeans, which sat low on his lean hips, and held her stare. 'You don't get to dip in and out of this. You're on the letterhead, along with your brother, and of course myself. Don't think that you're going to reap the rewards without doing any of the hard graft. I intend to oversee proceedings initially but I need to be assured that you and your brother won't run the company back into the ground the second my back's turned. Don't forget, this isn't a charity gesture of goodwill on my part. I'm not parting with cash if I don't think that there will be a decent return on my investment.'

Sophie thought that she'd been right. It was all about the money for him. Yes, there was a personal connection, but the animosity of their break-up wasn't paramount in his decision to help them. What mattered was that he was being handed a potentially very profitable business with an age-old reputation at a very cheap price because she and Oliver were desperate.

She imagined that, once the company was sorted, its reputation would not only be repaired but would ensure gold-plated business and a return of all the customers they had sadly lost over the years.

Right now, Oliver had an interest in a third of the company, but he would quickly lose interest and, she foresaw, would cash in his shares, take the money and head back to California, where he could continue his sporting career in a teaching capacity.

In due course, Javier would have invested in a very worthwhile project at a very good price.

And their past history did not figure in the calculations. In fact, she wondered whether he felt anything at all about what had happened between them.

'I thought I might commute down.'

Javier burst out laughing before sobering up to look at her with a gimlet-eyed warning. 'I wouldn't even entertain that notion if I were you,' he informed her in the sort of voice that did not expect contradiction. 'In the first few weeks there will probably be a great deal of overtime, and hopping on and off a train to try to get the work done just isn't going to cut it.'

'I have nowhere to stay here.' Once upon a time, there had been a snazzy apartment in Kensington but, she had discovered, that had been mortgaged up to the hilt when the company had started shedding customers and losing profit. It had been sold ages ago.

'Your brother has stayed in a hotel when he's been down.' Javier's eyes roved over her flushed face. 'But,' he mused with soft speculation, 'as you're going to be here for considerably longer, I have already made arrangements for you to have use of one of my apartments in Notting Hill. You'll be within convenient walking distance of the company. No excuse for slacking off.'

'No!' She broke out in clammy perspiration.

'Reason being…?'

'I…I can't just decamp down here to London, Javier!'

'This isn't something that's open to debate.'

'You don't understand.'

'Then enlighten me.' They hadn't even stepped foot into the renovated office and already they were arguing.

He couldn't credit that he had originally played with the thought of helping her in return for having her. He couldn't think of anything less satisfying than having her blackmailed into coming to him as a reluctant and resentful partner when he wanted her hot, wet and willing…

He also couldn't credit that he had simplistically imagined that one scratch would ease this itch that had surfaced with such surprising speed the second her brother had opened that door back into the past. The more he saw of her, the more he *thought* of her, the more dangerously deep his unfinished business with her felt. One or two nights wasn't going to be enough.

'I have to keep an eye on the house,' she said with obvious reluctance.

'What house?'

'The family home.'

'Why? Is it in imminent danger of falling down if you're not at hand with some sticking plaster and masking tape?'

Bitter tears sprang to her eyes and she fought them down as a red mist of anger swirled through her in a tidal rush.

'Since when did you get so arrogant?' she flung at him. They stared at one another in electric silence before she broke eye contact to storm off, out of the beautiful reception area, which she had barely noticed at all, and into the first set of offices.

It took a couple of seconds before Javier was galvanised into following her.

Being accused of *arrogance* was not something he was accustomed to. Indeed, being spoken to in that accusatory, critical tone of voice was unheard of. He caught her arm, tugging her to face him and then immediately releasing her because just the feel of her softness under his fingers was like putting his hand against an open flame. It enraged him that she could still have this effect on him. It enraged him that, for the first time in living memory, and certainly for the first time in many, many years, his body was refusing to obey his mind.

'Are you sure it's the house you need to be close to?' he growled.

'What are you talking about?'

'Maybe there's a man lurking in the background...'

Javier was disgusted to realise that he was fishing. Did he care whether there was some lame boyfriend in the background? She wasn't married and that was the main thing. He would never have gone near any woman with a wedding ring on her finger, but if she had a boyfriend somewhere, another one of those limp–public school idiots who thought that a polished accent was all that it took to get you through life, well…

All was fair in love and war…

Sophie reddened. The dull prickle of unpleasant memories tried to surface and she resolutely shoved them back where they belonged, in the deepest corners of her mind.

'Because, if you have, then he'll just have to take a back seat for…however long it takes. And word of warning— my apartment is for sole occupation only…'

'You mean if there was a guy in my life, and I happened to be living in one of your apartments, I wouldn't be allowed to entertain him?'

Javier looked at her appalled expression and swatted away the uncomfortable feeling that he was being pigeon-holed as some kind of dinosaur when that couldn't have been further from the truth. Having reached the soaring heights the hard way, he made a conscious effort to ensure that the employees of his company were hand-picked for all the right reasons: talent, merit and ability. He made sure that there were no glass ceilings for women, or for those who had had to struggle to find their way, as he had.

He was not the sort of guy who would ever have dreamt of laying down pathetic rules about men being kept apart from women, like teenagers in boarding schools overseen by strict house masters.

So what was he doing right now? And how was it that he had no intention of doing otherwise?

'I mean you're probably going to be working long hours. The distraction of some man who wants you back home to cook his meal by five-thirty isn't going to work' was the most he would offer.

Sophie laughed shortly. If only he knew...

'There's no man around to distract me,' she said in a low voice. 'And, yes, as a matter of fact the house *is* falling down, and Oliver won't be there because he's been dispatched to France to see what's happening to the company over there...'

'Your house is falling down?'

'Not literally,' Sophie admitted. 'But there's a lot wrong with it and I'm always conscious of the fact that if it springs a leak and I'm not there to sort it out, well...'

'Since when has your house been falling down?'

'It doesn't matter.' She sighed and began to run her fingers through her hair, only to realise that she had pinned it up, and let her hand drop to her side. She looked around her but was very much aware of his eyes still on her, and even more aware that somehow they were now standing way too close for comfort.

'You've done marvellous things with the space.' She just wanted to get away from the threat of personal quizzing. She took a few steps away from him and now took time really to notice just how much *had* been done. It was not just a paint job; everything seemed very different from what she remembered.

It seemed much, much larger and that, she realised, was because the space within the first-floor office block had been maximised. Partitions had been cleverly put in where before there had been none. The dank carpeting had been replaced with wooden floors. The desks and furniture were all spanking new. She listened and nodded as he explained the dynamics of the place being manned and who should be working the London office. The client list would have to be updated. The sales team would need to be far more assertive. He had identified useful gaps in the market that could be exploited.

Everything was perfect. There were two private offices and she would be occupying one. Again she nodded because, like it or not, she was going to be here, in London.

'But,' she said when the tour had been concluded and they were in the pristine, updated kitchen, sitting at the high-tech beaten metallic table with cups of steaming coffee in front of them, 'I still don't feel comfortable leaving the house and I don't want to live in one of your apartments.' *He would have a key... He would be able to walk in unannounced at any given time... She could be in the shower and he could just stroll in...*

Her nipples tightened, pushing against her lacy bra and sending tingles up and down, in and out and through her from her toes to her scalp. She licked her lips and reminded herself that if he felt anything towards her at all it would be loathing because of what had happened between them in the past. Although, in reality, he couldn't even be bothered to feel such a strong emotion. What he felt was…indifference.

So if he were to let himself in, which he most certainly wouldn't, the shower would be the last place he would seek her out. Her responses were all over the place and it wouldn't be long before he started to realise that she wasn't as immune to him as she was desperately trying to be.

'I'll bring your brother back over.'

'No! Don't…'

'Why not?' Javier raised his eyebrows expressively, although he knew the reason well enough. Oliver didn't want to be stuck in Yorkshire and he didn't see his future with the family business. He resented the penury into which they had been thrust and, although he recognised the importance of rebuilding what had fallen into disrepair, he really thought no further than what that personally meant for him. Given half a chance, he would have cashed in his shares and headed for the hills. In due course he would, which would be interesting should Javier decide he wanted more than he had. That was unlikely, because once he was done with getting what he wanted, he would be more than happy to disappear and leave the running of the business to an underling of his choice.

'He's enjoying being in Paris.'

'And that's how it's always been, isn't it?' Javier asked softly and Sophie raised translucent violet eyes to look at him with a frown.

'What do you mean?'

'I remember how you used to talk about your twin.' He had resolved not to go down any maudlin, reminiscing roads but now found that he couldn't help himself. 'The party animal. Off to California while you stayed behind to do your A levels. Praised for being sporty and indulged at a time when most kids that age would have had their head in textbooks to make sure they passed exams. When he came down to see you, he barely stayed put. He managed to make friends in five seconds and then off he went to see what nightclubs there were. He had his fun, enjoyed Mummy and Daddy's money and never had to face up to any grim realities because by then he was in California on his sports scholarship...

'I bet no one ever filled him in about the reality of the company losses, not even you...not even when they were glaringly obvious. I'll bet he only found out the extent of the trouble when you couldn't hide it from him any longer. Did your beloved ex-husband likewise conspire to keep your immature brother in the dark?'

'I told you.' Sophie stiffened at the mention of her ex-husband. 'I don't want to talk about Roger.'

Javier's lips tightened. The more she shied away from

all mention of her ex, the more his curiosity was piqued. He was bitterly reminded of his pointless *wondering* when she had dumped him, when she had told him that she was destined to marry someone else... When she had married a guy whom he had found himself researching on the Internet even though it had been an exercise in masochism.

He had learned strength from a very young age. It had taken a great deal of willpower to avoid the pitfalls of so many of his friends when he had been growing up in poverty in Spain. The easy way out had always been littered with drugs and violence, and that easy way had been the popular route for many of the kids he had known. He had had to become an island to turn his back on all of that, just as he had had to develop a great deal of inner strength when he had finally made it to England to begin his university career. He had had to set his sights on distant goals and allow himself to be guided only by them.

Sophie had taken his eye off the ball, and here she was, doing it again.

The sooner he got her out of his system, the better.

'So your brother stays in Paris,' he said, with the sort of insistence that made her think of steamrollers slowly and inexorably flattening vast swathes of land. 'I could get someone to house-sit and daily look for walls falling down...'

'You might think it's funny, Javier, but it's not. You might live in your mansion now, and you might be able to get whatever you want at the snap of a finger, but it's just not funny when you have to watch every step you take because there might just be a minefield waiting to explode if you put your foot somewhere wrong. And I'm surprised you have no sympathy at all, considering you... you were...'

'I was broke? Penniless? A poor immigrant still trying to get a grip on the first rung of that all-important ladder? I feel it's fair to say that our circumstances were slightly different.'

'And, in a way, you probably have no idea how much worse it makes it for me.' She swung her head away. Her prissy, formal clothes felt like a straitjacket and her tidy bun nestled at the nape of her neck was sticky and restricting.

Without thinking, she released it and sifted restless fingers through the length of her tumbling hair.

And Javier watched. His mouth went dry. Her hair cascaded over her shoulders and down her back, a vibrant wash of colour that took his breath away. He had to look away but he knew that he was breathing fast, imagining her naked, projecting how her body would feel were he to run his hands along its shapely contours.

'You're right. Oliver has always been protected,' she told him bluntly. He might very well be the first person she was telling this to. It was a truth she had always kept to herself because to have voiced it would have felt like a little betrayal. 'He only found out about…everything when Dad's illness was finally revealed, and even then we didn't tell him that the company was on its last legs. In fact, he returned to California and only came back after the…the accident when… Well, he came back for Dad's funeral, and of course Roger's, and by then he had to be told.

'But his heart isn't in getting the company up and running. His heart isn't in the house either. Mum's now living in Cornwall and, as far as Ollie is concerned, he would sell the family home to the highest bidder if there was anyone around who was in the slightest bit interested. He doesn't give a hoot if it all falls down in a pile of rubble just so long as we got some money for the rubble. So, no, he wouldn't be at all happy to leave Paris to house-sit.'

She took a deep, shaky breath. 'The house hasn't been maintained for years. It always looked good on the outside, not that I ever really *looked*, but it turned out that there were problems with the roof and subsidence that had never been sorted. There's no money left in the pot to sort that stuff out, so I keep my eyes peeled for anything that might need urgent attention. The worse the house is, the less money we'll get, if we ever manage to sell at all. I can't afford for a leak to spring in the cellar and start mounting the stairs to the hallway.' She sighed and rubbed her eyes.

'Why did you let him get away with it?' It was more of a flat, semi-incredulous statement than a question and Sophie knew exactly who he was talking about even though no name had been mentioned.

'I don't want to talk about that. It's in the past and there's no point stressing about the stuff you can't change. I just have to deal with the here and now...'

'Oliver,' Javier ploughed on, 'might be indifferent and clueless when it comes to business, but you clearly have the capacity to get involved, so why didn't you? You knew what was happening.'

'Mum wasn't in good health. Hadn't been for ages. And then Dad's behaviour started getting weird...erratic... Suddenly everything seemed to be happening at the same time. We found out just how ill he was and then, hard on the heels of that, the full repercussions of...of Roger's gambling and all the bad investments began coming to light. There was no one at the helm. All the good people were leaving. Lots had already left, although I didn't know that at the time, because I'd never been involved in the family business. It was...chaos.'

Even in the midst of this tale of abject woe, Javier couldn't help but notice that there was no condemnation of her scoundrel husband. Loyalties, he thought with a sour taste, were not divided.

'So I'll get a house-sitter,' he repeated and she shook

her head. He had already infiltrated her life enough. She wasn't sure she could cope with more.

'I'll come here,' she conceded, 'and go home at the weekends.' She breathed in deeply. 'And thank you for the use of an apartment. You have to let me know...I don't have a great deal of disposable income, as you can imagine, but please let me know how much rent I will owe you.'

Javier sat back and looked at her from under sinfully long lashes, a lazy, speculative look that felt like a caress.

'Don't even think of paying me rent,' he told her silkily. 'It's on the house...for old times' sake. Trust me, Sophie, I want you...' he paused fractionally '...there at the helm while changes are taking place, and what I want, I usually get...whatever the cost.'

CHAPTER FIVE

SOPHIE LOOKED AROUND her and realised guiltily that, after two weeks' living in the apartment Javier had kindly loaned her, refusing to countenance a penny in payment, she was strangely *happy*.

The apartment was to die for. She still found herself admiring the décor, as she was doing right now, having just returned from the office and kicked off her stupid pumps so that she could walk barefoot on the cool, wooden floor.

She had expected minimalist with lots of off-putting glossy white surfaces, like the inside of a high-tech lab. Images of aggressive black leather and chrome everywhere had sprung to mind when she had been handed the key to the apartment by his personal assistant, who had accompanied her so that the workings of the various gadgets could be explained.

She had assumed that she would be overwhelmed by an ostentatious show of wealth, would be obliged to gasp appropriately at furnishings she didn't really like and would feel like an intruder in a foreign land.

The Javier of today was not the teasing, warm, sexy, funny guy she had once known. The today Javier was tough, rich beyond most people's wildest dreams, ruthless and cutting edge in his hand-tailored suits and Italian shoes. And that would be reflected in any apartment he owned.

She'd been surprised—shocked, even—when she was shown the apartment.

'It's had a makeover,' the personal assistant had said in a vaguely puzzled voice, but obviously far too well-trained to comment further. 'So this is the first time I'm seeing the new version...'

Sophie hadn't quizzed her on what it had been like previously. Tired and in need of updating, she had assumed. He'd probably bought a bunch of apartments without even seeing them, the way you do when you have tons of money, and then paid someone handsomely to turn them into the sort of triple-A, gold-plated investments that would rent for a small fortune and double in value if he ever decided to sell.

Whoever had done the interior design had done a great job.

She padded towards the kitchen, which was cool, in shades of pale grey with vintage off-white tiles on the floor and granite counters that matched the floor.

Everything was open-plan. She strolled into the living room with a cup of tea and sank into the cosy sofa, idly flicking on the television to watch the early-evening news.

It was Friday and the work clothes had been dumped in the clothes hamper. Javier had told her that it was fine to dress casually but she had ignored him.

Keep it professional; keep it businesslike... she had decided.

Jeans and tee shirts would blur the lines between them...at least for her...

Not, in all events, that it made a scrap of difference how she dressed, because, after the first day, he had done a disappearing act, only occasionally emailing her or phoning her for updates. A couple of times he had visited the branch when she had been out seeing customers, trying to drum up business, and she could only think that he had timed his arrivals cleverly to avoid bumping into her.

He didn't give a passing thought to her, whilst she, on the other hand, couldn't stop thinking about him.

She didn't think that she had ever really stopped thinking about him. He'd been in her head, like the ghost of a refrain from a song that wouldn't go away.

And now she couldn't stop thinking about him. Worse than that, she spent every day at the office anticipating his unexpected arrival and was disproportionately disappointed when five-thirty rolled round and he'd failed to make an appearance.

Her heart skipped a beat when she opened up her emails and found a message from him waiting for her.

Her throat went dry when she heard the deep, sexy timbre of his voice on the end of the line.

She was in danger of obsessing over a guy who belonged to her past. At least, emotionally.

He'd suddenly reappeared on the scene, opening all sorts of doors in her head, making her think about choices she had made and bringing back memories of the horror story that had followed those choices.

He made her think about Roger. He was curious about her ex. She sensed that. Perhaps not curious in a personal way, but mildly curious, especially because so many things didn't quite add up. Why, he had asked her, hadn't she intervened when she'd known that he was blowing vast sums of money gambling? When she'd discovered the scale of the financial problems with the company? Why hadn't she acted more decisively?

But, of course, that was the kind of person he was. Someone who was born and bred to act decisively. He could never begin to understand how easy it was just to get lost and find yourself in a fog, with no guiding lights to lead you out.

She had grown up a lot since then. She had had to. And, in the process of taking charge, she had realised just how feeble her brother was when it came to making decisions and taking difficult paths.

When she looked back at herself as she had been seven years ago, it was like staring at a stranger. The carefree girl with a life full of options was gone for ever. She was a woman now with limited options and too many bad memories to deal with.

Was that why she was now obsessing over Javier, someone she had known for such a short space of time? Was it because he reminded her of the girl she used to be? Was it obsession by association, so to speak?

He made her think things she would rather have forgotten but he also made her heart skip a beat the way it once used to when she'd been with him.

And more than that, he made her body feel alive the way it hadn't for years. Not since him, in fact. He made her feel young again and that had a very seductive appeal.

With an impatient click of her tongue, she raised the volume of the television, determined not to waste the evening thinking about Javier and remembering what life had been like when they had been going out.

She almost didn't hear the buzz of the doorbell, and when she did, she almost thought that she might have made a mistake because no one could possibly be calling on her.

Since she had moved to London, she had kept herself to herself. She knew a couple of people who had relocated from the northern branch but the London crew, all very able and super-efficient, were new and she had shied away from making friends with any of them.

For starters, although it wasn't advertised and in all

probability none of them knew, she was more or less their boss. And also…did she really want anyone knowing her backstory? It was just easier to maintain a healthy distance, so there was no way whoever had buzzed her from downstairs was a colleague on the hunt for a Friday night companion.

She picked up the intercom which allowed her to see her unexpected visitor and the breath left her in a whoosh.

'You're in.' Javier had come to the apartment on the spur of the moment. Since she'd started at the London office, he had seen her once, had spoken to her six times and had emailed her every other day. He had purposefully kept his distance because the strength of his response to her had come as a shock. Accustomed to having absolute control over every aspect of his life, he had assumed that her sudden appearance in his highly ordered existence would prove interesting—certainly rewarding, bearing in mind he intended to finish what had been started seven years previously—and definitely nothing that he wouldn't be able to handle.

Except that, from the very minute he had laid eyes on her, all that absolute certainty had flown through the window. The easy route he had planned to take had almost immediately bitten the dust. He'd had every intention of coolly trading his financial help for the body he had been denied, the body he discovered he still longed to touch and explore.

She'd used him and now he'd been given a golden opportunity to get his own back.

Except, he'd seen her, and that approach had seemed worse than simplistic. It had seemed crass.

There was no way he was going to pursue her and showing up at the workplace every day would have smelled a lot like pursuit, even though he had every right to be there, considering the amount of money he was sinking into the failing company.

He wanted her to come to him but staying away had been a lot more difficult than he'd dreamed possible.

Like someone dying of thirst suddenly denied the glass of ice-cold water just within his reach, he had found himself thinking about her to the point of distraction, and that had got on his nerves.

So here he was.

Sophie frantically wondered whether she could say that she was just on her way out. His unexpected appearance had brought her out in a nervous cold sweat. She had been thinking about him, and here he was, conjured up from her imagination.

'I...I...'

'Let me in.'

'I was just about to...have something to eat, actually...'

'Perfect. I'll join you.'

That wasn't what she'd had in mind. What she'd had in mind was a lead-up to a polite excuse and an arrangement to meet when she had some sort of defence system in place. Instead, here she was, hair all over the place, wearing jogging bottoms and an old, tight tee shirt bought at a music festival a dozen years ago and shrunk in the wash over time.

'Come on, Sophie! I'm growing older by the minute!'

'Fine!' She buzzed him in, belatedly remembering that it was actually *his* apartment, so he had every right to be here. And not only was it *his* apartment, but she wasn't paying a penny towards the rent, at his insistence.

She scrambled to the mirror by the front door, accepted that it was too late to start pinning her hair back into something sensible, and even though she was expecting him, she still started when he rapped on the door.

He'd obviously come straight from work, although, *en*

route, he had divested himself of his tie, undone the top couple of buttons of his shirt and rolled his sleeves to his elbows. Her eyes dipped to his sinewy forearms and just as quickly back to his face.

'You look flustered,' Javier drawled, leaning against the door frame and somehow managing to crowd her. 'I haven't interrupted you in the middle of something pressing, have I?' This was how he remembered her. Tousled and sexy and so unbelievably, breathtakingly *fresh*.

And *innocent*.

Which was a bit of a joke, all things considered.

Dark eyes drifted downwards, taking in the outline of her firm, round breasts pushing against a tee shirt that was a few sizes too small, taking in the slither of flat belly where the tee shirt ended and the shapeless jogging bottoms began. Even in an outfit that should have done her no favours, she still looked hot, and his body responded with suitable vigour.

He straightened, frowning at the sudden discomfort of an erection.

'I haven't managed to catch much of you over the past couple of weeks.' He dragged his mind away from thoughts of her, a bed and a heap of hurriedly discarded clothes on the ground. 'So I thought I'd try you at home before you disappeared up north for the weekend.'

'Of course.'

There was a brief pause, during which he tilted his head to one side, before pointedly looking at the door handle.

'So…' He looked around him at his apartment with satisfaction. He'd had it redone. 'How are you finding the apartment?'

Some might say that he'd been a little underhand in the renovating of the apartment, which had been in perfectly good order a month previously. He'd walked round it, looking at the soulless, sterile furnishings, and had been able to picture her reaction to her new surroundings: disdain. He had always been amused at her old-fashioned tastes, despite the fact that she had grown up with money.

'I imagine your family home to be a wonder of the most up-to-the-minute furnishings money can buy,' he had once teased, when she'd stood staring in rapt fixation at a four-poster bed strewn with a million cushions in the window of a department store. She'd waxed lyrical then about the romance of four-poster beds and had told him, sheepishly, that the family home was anything but modern.

'My mum's like me,' she had confessed with a grin. 'She likes antiques and everything that's old and worn and full of character.'

Javier had personally made sure to insert some pieces of character in the apartment. He, himself, liked modern and minimalist. His impoverished family home had been clean but nearly everything had been bought second-hand. He'd grown up with so many items of furniture that had been just a little too full of character that he was now a fully paid-up member of all things modern and lacking in so-called character.

But he'd enjoyed hand-picking pieces for the apartment, had enjoyed picturing her reaction to the four-poster bed he had bought, the beautifully crafted floral sofa, the thick Persian rug that broke up the expanse of pale flooring.

'The apartment's fine.' Sophie stepped away from him and folded her arms. 'Better than fine,' she admitted, eyes darting to him and then staying there because he was just so arresting. 'I love the way it's been done. You should congratulate your interior designer.'

'Who said I used one?' He looked at her with raised eyebrows and she blushed in sudden confusion, because to picture him hand-picking anything was somehow… *intimate*. And of course he would never have done any such thing. What über-rich single guy would ever waste time hunting down rugs and curtains? Definitely not a guy like Javier, who was macho to the very last bone in his body.

'I'm afraid there's not a great deal of food.' She turned away because her heart was beating so fast she could barely breathe properly. His presence seemed to infiltrate every part of the apartment, filling it with suffocating, masculine intensity. This was how it had always been with him. In his presence, she'd felt weak and pleasurably helpless. Even as a young guy, struggling to make ends meet, he'd still managed to project an air of absolute assurance. He'd made all the other students around him seem like little boys in comparison.

The big difference was that, back then, she'd had a remit to bask and luxuriate in that powerful masculinity. She could touch, she could run her fingers through his springy, black hair and she'd had permission to melt at the feel of it.

She'd been allowed to want him and to show him how much she wanted him.

Not so now.

Furthermore, she didn't *want* to want him. She didn't *want* to feel herself dragged back into a past that was gone for good. Of course, foolish love was gone for good, and no longer a threat to the ivory tower she had constructed around herself that had been so vital in withstanding the years spent with her husband, but she didn't want to feel that pressing, urgent *want* either...

She didn't *want* to feel her heart fluttering like an adolescent's because he happened to be sharing the same space as her. She'd grown up, gone through some hellish stuff. Her outlook on life had been changed for ever because of what she'd had to deal with. She had no illusions now and no longer believed that happiness was her right. It wasn't and never would be. Javier Vasquez belonged to a time when unfettered optimism had been her constant companion. Now, not only was the murky past an unbreachable wall between them, but so were all the changes that had happened to her.

'I wasn't expecting company.' She half turned to find him right behind her, having followed her into the kitchen.

The kitchen was big, a clever mix of old and new, and she felt utterly at home in it.

'Smells good. What is it?'

'Just some tomato sauce. I was going to have it with pasta.'

'You never used to enjoy cooking.' Yet again, he found himself referring to the past, dredging it up and bringing it into the present, where it most certainly did not belong.

'I know.' She shot him a fleeting smile as he sat down at the table, angling his chair so that he could extend his long legs to one side. 'I never had to do it,' she explained. 'Mum loved cooking and I was always happy to let her get on with it. When she got ill, she said it used to occupy her and take her mind off her health problems, so I never interfered. I mean, I'd wash the dishes and tidy behind her, but she liked being the main chef. And then...'

She sighed and began finishing the food preparation, but horribly aware of those lazy, speculative eyes on her, following her every movement.

Javier resisted the urge to try to prise answers out of her. 'So you learned to cook,' he said, moving the conversation along, past the point of his curiosity.

'And discovered that I rather enjoyed it.' She didn't fail to notice how swiftly he had diverted the conversation from the controversial topic of her past, the years she had spent after they had gone their separate ways. His initial curiosity was gone, and she told herself that she was very thankful that it had, because there was far too much she could never, would never, tell him.

But alongside that relief was a certain amount of disappointment, because his lack of curiosity was all wrapped up with the indifference he felt for her.

She suddenly had the strangest temptation to reach out and touch him, to stroke his wrist, feel the familiar strength of his forearm under her fingers. What would he do? How would he react? *Would he recoil with horror or would he touch her back?*

Appalled, she thrust a plate of food in front of him and sat down opposite him. She wanted to sit on her treacherous hands just in case they did something wildly inappropriate of their own accord and she had to remind herself shakily that she was a grown woman, fully in control of her wayward emotions. Emotions that had been stirred up, as they *naturally* would be, by having him invade her life out of the blue.

She heard herself babbling on like the village idiot about her culinary exploits while he ate and listened in silence, with every show of interest in what she was saying.

Which was remarkable, given she had just finished a lengthy anecdote about some slow-cooked beef she had tried to cook weeks previously, which had been disastrous.

'So you like the apartment,' Javier drawled, eyes not leaving her face as he sipped some wine. 'And the job? Now that the work of trying to repair the damage done over the years has begun?'

'It's…awkward,' Sophie told him truthfully.

'Explain.'

'You were right,' she said bluntly, rising to begin clearing the table, her colour high. 'Some of the people my father trusted have let the company down badly over the years. I can only think that employing friends was a luxury my father had when he started the company, and he either continued to trust that they were doing a good job or he knew that they weren't but found it difficult to let them go. And then…'

'And then?' Javier queried silkily and Sophie shrugged.

'Getting rid of them never happened. Thankfully the majority have now left, but with generous pension payments or golden handshakes…' Yet more ways money had drained away from the company until the river had run dry.

'The company is in far worse shape than even I imagined…'

Sophie blanched. She watched as he began helping to clear the table, bringing plates to the sink.

'What do you mean?'

'Your father didn't just take his eye off the ball when he became ill. I doubt his eye had ever really been fully on it in the first place.'

'You can't say that!'

'I've gone through all the books with a fine-tooth comb, Sophie.' He relieved her of the plate she was holding and dried it before placing it on the kitchen counter, then he slung the tea towel he had fetched over his shoulder and propped himself against the counter, arms folded.

Javier had always suspected that her father had been instrumental in her decision to quit university and return to the guy she had always been destined to marry. Even though she had never come right out and said so; even though she had barely had the courage to look him in the face when she had announced that she'd be leaving university because of a family situation that had arisen.

He had never told her that he had subsequently gone to see her parents, that he had confronted her father, who had left him in no doubt that there was no way his precious daughter would contemplate a permanent relationship with someone like him.

He wondered whether the old man's extreme reaction

had been somehow linked to his decline into terminal ill health, and scowled as he remembered the heated argument that had resulted in him walking away, never looking back.

This was the perfect moment to disabuse her of whatever illusions she had harboured about a father who had clearly had little clue about running a business, but the dismay on her face made him hesitate.

He raked his fingers uncomfortably through his hair and continued to stare down at her upturned face.

'He was a terrific dad,' she said defensively, thinking back to the many times he had taken the family out on excursions, often leaving the running of the company to the guys working for him. 'Life was to be enjoyed' had always been his motto. He had played golf and taken them on fantastic holidays; she recognised now that ineffective, relatively unsupervised management had not helped the company coffers. He had inherited a thriving business but, especially when everything had gone electronic, he had failed to move with the times and so had his pals who had joined the company when he had taken it over.

In retrospect, she saw that so much had been piling up like dark clouds on the horizon, waiting for their moment to converge and create the thunderstorm of events that would land her where she was right now.

Javier opened his mouth to disabuse her of her girlish illusions and then thought of his own father. There was no way he would ever have had a word said against him, and yet, hadn't Pedro Vasquez once confessed that he had blown an opportunity to advance himself by storming out of his first company, too young and hot-headed to take orders he didn't agree with? The golden opportunity he had walked away from had never again returned and he had had to devote years of saving and scrimping to get by on the low wages he had earned until his retirement.

But Javier had never held that weak moment against him.

'Your father wouldn't be the first man who failed to spot areas for expansion,' he said gruffly. 'It happens.'

Sophie knew that he had softened and something deep inside her shifted and changed as she continued to stare up at him, their eyes locked.

She could scarcely breathe.

'Thank you,' she whispered and he shook his head, wanting to break a connection that was sucking him in, but finding it impossible to do so.

'What are you thanking me for?'

'He was old-fashioned, and unfortunately the people he delegated to were as old-fashioned as he was. Dad should have called a troubleshooter in the minute the profits started taking a nosedive, but he turned a blind eye to what was going on in the company.'

And he turned a blind eye to your ex as well...

That thought made Javier stiffen. Her father had been old-fashioned enough to hold pompous, arrogant views about *foreign upstarts*, to have assumed that some loser with the right accent was the sort of man his daughter should marry.

But that wasn't a road he was willing to go down because it would have absolved Sophie of guilt and the bottom line was that no one had pointed a gun to her head and forced her up the aisle.

She had *wanted* to take that step.

She had *chosen* to stick with the guy even though she knew that he was blowing up the company with his crazy investments.

She had *watched* and *remained silent* as vast sums of vitally needed money had been gambled away.

She had *enabled*. And the only reason she had done that was because she had loved the man.

He turned away abruptly, breaking eye contact, feeling the sour taste of bile rise to his mouth.

'The company will have to be streamlined further,' he told her curtly. 'Dead wood can no longer be tolerated.' He remained where he was, hip against the counter, and watched as she tidied, washed dishes, dried them and stayed silent.

'All the old retainers will end up being sacked. Is that it?'

'Needs must.'

'Some of the old guys have families… They're nearing retirement—and, okay, they may not have been the most efficient on the planet, but they've been loyal…'

'And you place a lot of value on loyalty, do you?' he murmured.

'Don't you?'

'There are times when common sense has to win the battle.'

'You're in charge now. I don't suppose I have any choice, have I?'

Instead of soothing him, her passive, resentful compliance stoked a surge of anger inside him.

'If you'd taken a step back,' he said with ruthless precision, 'and swapped blind loyalty for some common sense, you might have been able to curb some of your dear husband's outrageous excesses…'

'You truly believe that?' She stepped back, swamped by his powerful, aggressive presence, and glared at him.

The last thing Javier felt he needed was to have her try to make feeble excuses for the man who had contributed to almost destroying her family business. What he really felt he needed right now was something stiff to drink. He couldn't look at her without his body going into instant and immediate overdrive and he couldn't talk to her without relinquishing some of his formidable and prized self-control. She affected him in a way no other woman ever had and it annoyed the hell out of him.

'What else is anyone supposed to believe?' he asked with rampant sarcasm. 'Join the dots and you usually get an accurate picture at the end of the exercise.'

'There was no way I could ever have stopped Roger!' Sophie heard herself all but shout at him, appalled by her outburst even as she realised that it was too late to take it back. 'There were always consequences for trying to talk common sense into him!'

The silence that greeted this outburst was electric, sizzling around them, so that the hairs on the back of her neck stood on end.

'Consequences? What consequences?' Javier pressed in a dangerously soft voice.

'Nothing,' Sophie muttered, turning away, but he reached out, circling her forearm to tug her back towards him.

'You don't get to walk away from this conversation after you've opened up a can of worms, Sophie.'

There were so many reasons this was a can of worms that she didn't want to explore. On a deeply emotional level, she didn't want to confront, yet again, the mistakes she had made in the past. She'd done enough of that to last a lifetime and she especially didn't want to confront those mistakes aloud, with Javier as her witness. She didn't want his pity. She didn't want him to sense her vulnerability. He might no longer care about her, but she didn't want to think that he would be quietly satisfied that, having walked out on him, she had got her comeuppance, so to speak.

'It's not relevant!' she snapped, trying and failing to tug her arm out of his grasp.

'Was he…? I don't know what to think here, Soph…'

That abbreviation of her name brought back a flood of memories and they went straight to the core of her, burning a hole through her defence mechanisms. Her soft mouth trembled and she knew that her eyes were glazing over, which, in turn, made her blink rapidly, fighting back the urge to burst into tears.

'He could be unpredictable.' Her jaw tightened and she looked away but he wouldn't allow her to avoid his searching gaze, tilting her to face him by placing a finger gently under her chin.

'That's a big word. Try breaking it down into smaller components…'

'He could be verbally abusive,' she told him jerkily. 'On one occasion he was physically abusive. So there you have it, Javier. If I'd tried to interfere in his gambling, there's no accounting for what the outcome might have been for me.'

Javier was horrified. He dropped his hand and his fingers clenched and unclenched. She might have fancied herself in love with the guy but that would have been disillusionment on a grand scale.

'Why didn't you divorce him?'

'It was a brief marriage, Javier. And there is more to this than you know…'

'Did you know that the man had anger issues?' Javier sifted his fingers through his hair. Suddenly the kitchen felt the size of a matchbox. He wanted to walk, unfettered; he wanted to punch something.

'Of course I didn't, and that certainly wasn't the case when… You don't get it,' she said uneasily. 'And I'd really rather not talk about this any more.'

Javier had been mildly incredulous at her declaration that her descent into penury had been tougher to handle than his own lifetime of struggle and straitened circumstances. She, at least, had had the head start of the silver spoon in the mouth and a failing company was, after all, still a company with hope of salvation. The crumbling family pile was still a very big roof over her head.

Now there were muddy, swirling currents underlying

those glib assumptions, and yet again, he lost sight of the clarity of his intentions.

He reminded himself that fundamentally nothing had changed. She had begun something seven years ago and had failed to finish it because she had chosen to run off with her long-time, socially acceptable boyfriend.

That the boyfriend had failed to live up to expectation, that events in her life had taken a fairly disastrous turn, did not change the basic fact that she had strung him along.

But he couldn't recapture the simple black-and-white equation that had originally propelled him. He wondered, in passing, whether he should just have stuck to his quid pro quo solution: 'you give me what I want and I'll give you what you want'.

But no.

He wanted so much more and he could feel it running hot through his veins as she continued to stare at him, unable to break eye contact.

Subtly, the atmosphere shifted. He sensed the change in her breathing, saw the way her pupils dilated, the way her lips parted as if she might be on the brink of saying something.

He cupped her face with his hand and *felt* rather than heard the long sigh that made her shudder.

Sophie's eyelids felt heavy. She wanted to close her eyes because if she closed her eyes she would be able to breathe him in more deeply, and she wanted to do that, wanted to *breathe him in*, wanted to touch him and scratch the itch that had been bothering her ever since he had been catapulted back into her life.

She wanted to kiss him and taste his mouth.

She only realised that she was reaching up to him when she felt the hardness of muscled chest under the palms of her flattened hands.

She heard a whimper of sheer longing which seemed to come from her and then she was kissing him...tongues entwining...exploring...easing some of the aching pain of her body...

She inched closer, pressed herself against him and wanted to rub against his length, wanted to feel his nakedness against hers.

She couldn't get enough of him.

It was as if no time had gone by between them, as if they were back where they had been, a time when he had been able to set fire to her body with the merest of touches. Nothing had changed and everything had changed.

'No!' She came to her senses with horrified, jerky panic. 'This is...I am *not* that girl I once was. I... *No!*'

She'd flung herself at him! She'd practically assaulted the man like a sex-starved woman desperate to be touched! He didn't even care about her! She'd opened up and on the back of that had leapt on him and had managed to surface only after damage had been done!

Humiliation tore through her. She went beetroot-red and stumbled backwards.

'I apologise for that.' She immediately went on the attack. 'It should never have happened and I don't know what came over me!' She ran her fingers through her hair and tried to remain calm but she was shaking like a leaf. 'This isn't what we're about! Not at all.'

Javier raised his eyebrows and her colour deepened.

'There's only business between us,' she insisted through clenched teeth. 'I must have had...I don't normally drink...'

'Now, isn't that the lamest excuse in the world?' Javier murmured. 'Let's blame it on the wine...'

'I don't care what you think!' How could he be so *cool and composed* when she was all over the place? Except, of course, she knew how. Because she was just so much more affected by him than he was by her and she could see all her pride and self-respect disappearing down the plug hole if she didn't get a grip on the situation *right now.*

She cleared her throat and stared, at him and through him. 'I… We have to work alongside one another for a while and…this was just an unfortunate blip. I would appreciate it if you never mention it again. We can both pretend that it never happened, because it will never happen again.'

Javier lowered his eyes and tilted his head to one side as if seriously considering what she had just said.

So many challenges in that single sentence. Did she really and truly believe that she could close the book now that page one had been turned?

He'd tasted her and one small taste wasn't going to do. Not for him and not for her. Whatever her backstory, they both needed to sate themselves with one another and that was what they would do before that place was inevitably reached where walking away was an option.

'If that's how you want to play it.' He shrugged and looked at her. 'And from Monday,' he said with lazy assurance, 'bank on me being around most of the time. We both want the same thing, don't we…?'

'What?' Confused, the only thought that came to her was *each other*—that, at any rate, was the thing that *she* wanted, and she could *smell* that it was what he wanted as well.

'For us to sort out the problems in this company as quickly as possible,' he said in a voice implying surprise that she hadn't spotted the right answer immediately. 'Of course…'

CHAPTER SIX

'No.'

'Give me three good reasons and maybe I'll let you get away with that response.'

Sophie stared at Javier, body language saying it all as she supported herself on her desk, palms flattened on the highly polished surface, torso tilted towards him in angry refusal.

True to his word, he had more or less taken up residence in the premises in Notting Hill.

He wasn't there *all* the time. That would actually have been far easier for her to deal with. No, he breezed in and out. Sometimes she would arrive at eight-thirty to find him installed at the desk which he had claimed as his own, hard at it, there since the break of dawn and with a list of demands that had her on her feet running at full tilt for the remainder of the day.

Other times he might show up mid-afternoon and content himself with checking a couple of things with members of staff before vanishing, barely giving her a second glance.

And there had been days when he hadn't shown up at all and there had been no communication from him.

After six weeks, Sophie felt as though she had been tossed in a tumble dryer with the speed turned to high. She had been miserable, uncertain and fearful when she had had to deal with the horrendous financial mess into which she had been plunged. After her marriage, that had just felt like a continuation of a state of mind that had become more or less natural to her.

Now, though...

She was none of those things. She was a high-wire walker, with excitement and trepidation fighting for dominance. She leapt out of bed every morning with a treacherous sense of anticipation. Her pulses raced every time she took a deep breath and entered the office. Her blood pressure soared when she glanced to the door and saw him stride in. Her heart sang when she saw him stationed at his desk first thing, with his cup of already tepid black coffee on the desk in front of him.

Life was suddenly in technicolor and it scared the living daylights out of her. It had become obvious that she'd never got him out of her system and she seemed to have no immunity against the staggering force of his impact on all her senses. Her heart might be locked away behind walls of ice but her body clearly wasn't.

'I don't have to give you any reasons, Javier.' She was the last man standing and had been about to leave the office at a little after six when Javier had swanned in and stopped her in the act of putting on her jacket.

'Quick word,' he had said, in that way he had of presuming that there would be no argument. He'd then proceeded to lounge back in his chair, gesturing for her to drop what she was doing and take the seat facing him across his desk.

That had been half an hour ago.

'You do, really.' He looked at her lazily. Despite the fact that the largely young staff all dressed informally, Sophie had stuck it out with her prissy work outfits, which ranged from drab grey skirts and neat white blouses to drab black skirts and neat white blouses, all worn with the same flat black pumps. The ravishing hair which he had glimpsed on the one occasion when he had surprised her weeks ago at the apartment had gone back into hiding. Woe betide she actually released it from captivity between the hours of eight-thirty and five-thirty!

'Why?'

'Because I think it would work.'

'And of course, because *you* think it would work, means *I* have to agree and go along with it!'

'How many of the programmes that I've set in motion over the past couple of months have failed?'

'That's not the point.'

'Any? No. Is the company seeing the start of a turn-around? Yes. Have the sales team been reporting gains? Yes.' He folded his hands behind his head and looked at her evenly. 'Ergo, this idea makes sense and will gener-ate valuable sales.'

'But I'm not a model, Javier!'

'That's the point, Sophie. You're the face of your com-pany. Putting your image on billboards and in advertis-ing campaigns will personalise the company—half the battle in wooing potential customers is making them feel as though they're relating to something more than just a name and a brand.'

She stared at him mutinously and he gazed calmly back at her.

The waiting game was taking longer than he had an-ticipated and he was finding that he was in no rush to speed things up. He was enjoying her. He was enjoying the way she made him feel and it wasn't just the reaction of his body to her. No, he realised that the years of hav-ing whatever he wanted and whoever he chose had jaded him. This blast from the past was...*rejuvenating*. And who didn't like a spot of rejuvenation in their lives? Of course, he would have to hurry things along eventually, because bed was the conclusion to the exercise before normal service was resumed and he returned to the life from which he had been taking a little holiday.

But for the moment…

He really liked the way she blushed. He could almost forget that she was the scheming young girl who had played him for an idiot.

'So we just need to talk about the details. And stop glaring. I thought all women liked to show off their bodies.'

Sophie glared. 'Really, Javier? You really think that?'

'Who wouldn't like to be asked to model?'

'Is that the message you've got from…from the women you've been out with?'

Javier looked at her narrowly because this was the first time she had ventured near the question of his love life. 'Most of the women I've been out with,' he murmured, 'were already catwalk models, accustomed to dealing with the full glare of the public spotlight.'

She'd wondered. Of course she had. Now she knew. Models. Naturally. He certainly wouldn't have dated normal, average women holding down normal, average jobs. He was the man who could have it all and men who could have it all always, but always, seemed to want to have models glued to their arm. It was just so…*predictable*.

'You've stopped glaring,' Javier said. 'Which is a good thing. But now there's disapproval stamped all over your face. What are you disapproving of? My choice of woman?'

'I don't care what your choice of girlfriends has been!'

'Don't you?' He raised his eyebrows. 'Because you look a little agitated. What's wrong with models? Some of them can be relatively clever, as it happens.'

'Relatively clever…' Sophie snorted. Her colour was high and the look in his sinfully dark eyes was doing

weird things to her, making her feel jumpy and thrillingly excited.

Making her nipples tighten...stoking a dampness between her thighs that had nothing to do with her scorn for his choice of dates, whoever those nameless dates had been.

Instant recall of that kiss they had shared made her breath hitch temporarily in her throat.

Just as she had stridently demanded, no mention had been made of it again. It was as though it had never happened. Yes, that was exactly what she had wanted, but it hadn't stopped her constantly harking back to it in her head, reliving the moment and burning up just at the thought of it. How could a bruised and battered heart take second billing to a body that seemed to do whatever it felt like doing?

'You used to tell me that you liked the fact that I had opinions!'

'Many models have opinions—admittedly not of the intellectual variety. They have very strong opinions on, oh, shoes...bags...other models...'

Sophie felt her mouth twitch. She'd missed his sense of humour. In fact, thinking about it, he'd been the benchmark against which Roger had never stood a chance. Not that he had ever been in the running...

In fact, thinking about it, wasn't he the benchmark against which every other man had always been set and always would be? When would that end? How could she resign herself to a half-life because she was still wrapped up in the man in front of her? Because that intense physical reaction just hadn't died and could still make itself felt through all the layers of sadness and despair that had shaped the woman she was now.

She hadn't looked twice at any guy since she'd been on her own. Hadn't even been tempted!

Yet here she was, not only wanting to look but wanting to touch…

Why kid herself? Telling herself to pretend that that kiss had never happened didn't actually mean that it had disappeared from her head.

And telling herself that she should feel nothing for a guy who belonged to her past, a guy who wasn't even interested in her, didn't actually mean that she felt nothing for him.

Lust—that was what it was—and the harder she tried to deny its existence, the more powerful a grip it seemed to have over her.

And part of the reason was because…he *wasn't* indifferent, was he?

Heart racing, she looked down and gave proper house room in her head to all those barely discernible signals she had felt emanating from him over the past few weeks.

For starters, there had been *that kiss*.

She'd felt the way his mouth had explored hers, hungry and greedy and wanting more.

And then, working in the same space, she'd lodged somewhere in the back of her head those accidental brushes when he had leant over her, caging her in in front of her computer so that he could explain some detail on the screen.

She'd committed to memory the way she had occasionally surprised his lazy dark eyes resting on her just a fraction longer than necessary.

And sometimes…didn't he stand just a little too close? Close enough for her to feel the heat from his body? To smell his clean, masculine scent?

Didn't all of that add up to something?

She didn't know whether he was even aware of the dangerous current running between them just beneath the surface. If he was, then it was obvious that he had no intention of doing anything about it.

And then, one day, he would no longer be around.

Right now, he was making sure that his investment paid off. He had sunk money into a bailout, and he wasn't going to see that money flushed down the drain, so he was taking an active part in progressing the company.

But soon enough the company would be on firmer ground and he would be able to retreat and hand over the running of it to other people, herself included.

He would resume his hectic life running his own empire.

And she, likewise, would return to Yorkshire to take up full-time residence in the family home, which she would be able to renovate at least enough to make it a viable selling proposition.

They would part company.

And she would be left with this strange, empty feeling for the rest of her life.

She felt guilty enough about the way they had broken up. On top of that, he would remain the benchmark against which no other man would ever stand a chance of competing for ever.

She should have slept with him.

She knew that now. She should have slept with him instead of holding on to all those girlish fantasies about saving herself for when that time came and she knew that they would be a permanent item, for when she was convinced that their relationship was made to stand the test of time.

If she'd slept with him, he would never have achieved the impossible status of being the only guy capable of turning her on. If she'd slept with him, she might not feel so guilty about the way everything had crashed and burned.

Was it selfish now to think that, if she righted that oversight, she might be free to get on with her life? Things were being sorted financially but what was the good of that if, emotionally, she remained in some kind of dreadful, self-inflicted limbo?

She wasn't the selfish sort. She had never thought of herself as the kind of pushy, independent type who took what she wanted from a man to satisfy her own needs.

The opposite!

But she knew, with a certain amount of desperation, that if she didn't take what she wanted now she would create all sorts of problems for herself down the line.

She wondered whether she could talk to her mother about it and immediately dismissed that thought because, as far as Evelyn Griffin-Watt was concerned, Javier was a youthful blip who had been cut out of her life a long time ago, leaving no nasty scars behind.

Besides, her mother was leading an uncomplicated and contented life in Cornwall; was it really fair to bring back unpleasant memories by resurrecting a long, involved conversation about the past?

'Okay.'

'Come again?'

'I'll do it.'

Javier smiled slowly. In truth, the whole modelling idea had sprung to mind only the day before, and he had anticipated defeat, but here she was…agreeing after a pretty half-hearted battle. At least, half-hearted for her.

'Brilliant decision!'

'I was railroaded into it.'

'Strong word. I prefer *persuaded*. Now, I have a few ideas…'

Sophie peeped through a crack in the curtains and looked down into the courtyard which had been tarted up for the day into a vision of genteel respectability.

The shoot had been arranged in the space of a week, during which time Sophie had spoken to various media types and also to various stylists. She imagined that they were being paid a phenomenal amount for the day because they had all bent over backwards to pay attention to what she had said.

Which hadn't been very much because she had no idea what questions to ask other than the obvious one: *How long is it all going to take?*

Javier hadn't been at any of those meetings, choosing instead to delegate to one of the people in his PR department, but that hadn't bothered Sophie.

In a way, she'd been glad, because she had a plan and the element of surprise was a big part of the plan.

Except, the day had now arrived and the courtyard was buzzing with cameramen, the make-up crew, the director, producer and all the other people whose roles were, quite frankly, bewildering. And where was Javier? Nowhere to be seen.

It was today or it was not at all.

She dropped the curtain and turned to the full-length mirror which the stylist had installed in the bedroom because the small one on the dressing table *'just won't do, darling!'*

The brief which she had agreed on with Javier would have her standing next to a gleaming articulated lorry bearing the company logo, in dungarees, a checked shirt and a jaunty cowboy hat on her head.

Sophie had decided to take it up a notch and the reflection staring back at her had dumped the dungarees in favour of a pair of shorts with a frayed hem. The checked shirt remained the same, but it was tied under her breasts so that her flat stomach was exposed, and there was no jaunty cowboy hat on her head. Instead, she had slung it on her back so that her hair was wild and loose.

Javier had vaguely aimed for something wholesome and appealing, a throwback to the good old days of home-baked bread and jam, which was some of the cargo transported in the lorries. He'd suggested that it would be a nice contrast to the new face of the business, which was streamlined and fully up to spec on the technological front, which it hadn't been before. Something along the lines of the home-baked bread getting from A to B before it had time to cool from the oven and Sophie's image was going to sell the absolute truth of that.

She had taken it up a notch from wholesome to wholesome *and sexy*.

It had been her brainwave when she had sat there, numbly recognising that she would never, ever get over him if she didn't sleep with him, if she didn't seduce him into bed. He'd been in her head for years and she couldn't think of another way to make sure that he was knocked off the position he occupied there.

She'd never seduced anyone in her life before. Just thinking about doing something like that was terrifying, but when it came to her emotions, she had to be proactive. As proactive as she had been dealing with the mess she'd been left to clear up in the company.

She wasn't a simpering teenager any more, seeing the future through rose-tinted specs and believing in happy-ever-after endings.

She was an adult, jaded by experience, who would be left nursing regret for the rest of her life if she didn't give this a shot. And so what if she failed? What if he looked at her get-up and burst out laughing? So, she might have a moment's humiliation, but that would be worth the life-time she would have had thinking about an opportunity that had passed her by, an opportunity to claim what she knew could have been hers all those years ago.

The time had come to take a chance.

Except, it didn't look as though the wretched man was going to show up!

Her nerves were shot, her pulses were racing and she hadn't eaten since lunchtime the previous day because of the shot nerves and the racing pulses...

She was a mess and it was all going to be for nothing because Javier had obviously had his brainwave and then allowed his minions to realise it while he stepped back from the scene of the action.

She slunk down to the courtyard with a white bathrobe over her screamingly uncomfortable outfit and was immediately appropriated by a host of people whose only function seemed to be to get her ready for *the shoot*.

She allowed herself to be manoeuvred while disappointment cascaded through her in waves.

No Javier. No big seduction. It had taken absolutely everything out of her. And there was no way she was going to do this again. She wasn't going to set herself the task of staging seductive scenes in the hope of igniting something that probably wasn't there for him anyway, whatever stupid signals she thought she'd read!

A mirror was brought for her to inspect herself. Sophie barely glanced at the fully made-up face staring back at her. After the tension of the past couple of days, and the nervous excitement of earlier this morning as she had got dressed, she now felt like a balloon that had been deflated before it had made it to the party.

She was aware of orders being shouted and poses she was being instructed to adopt.

No one had questioned the slight change in outfit. She was Javier's personal pet project and no one dared question her for fear that she would report unfavourably back to their boss.

She was supposed to turn up in denim and a checked top with a cowboy hat and they knew what the direction of the shoot should be. The outfit was daring, though, and the poses were therefore slightly more daring than perhaps originally choreographed.

She had her back to the camera team, one hand resting lightly on the shining lorry, looking over her shoulder with a smile, when she heard his roar from behind her.

She'd given up on Javier coming.

But before she'd clocked his absence, she had somehow imagined him standing amongst the crew, goggle-eyed as he looked at her, wanting her as much as she wanted him and knowing that he had to have her. She'd pictured him waiting impatiently until the crew had packed up and gone and then...

Her wanton thoughts had not formulated much beyond that point. There would be a lot of ground to cover before the scene shifted from impatient seduction to the satisfied aftermath.

'What the hell is going on here?'

Sophie stumbled back against the lorry and the entire assembled crew stared at Javier in growing confusion, aware that they had done something wrong but not quite sure what.

Javier strode forward through them like a charging bull, face as black as thunder.

'You!' He pointed to the director of the shoot, who jumped to attention and began stammering out his consternation, puzzled as to what the problem was. The shoot was going very well. Indeed, if Javier wanted, he could see what was already in the bag. It was going to do the job and sell the business like hot cakes straight from the oven. Sophie was a brilliant model. No temper tantrums and no diva pouting. She was perfect for the job and the fact that she was part-owner of the company was going to be a nice touch. They'd make sure they got that in in the backdrop...

Javier held up one cold, imperious hand. 'This was not what I wanted!' he snapped. He looked across to Sophie with a scowl and she folded her arms defensively.

'They have no idea what you're going on about, Javier,' she said sweetly, strolling towards him although she was quaking inside, unable to tear her eyes away from his strident masculinity. He dominated the space around him, a towering, forbidding figure who clearly inspired awe, fear and respect in equal measure.

It was an incredible turn-on to think that this was the guy who had once teased her, told her that she made him weak, the guy whose eyes had flared with desire whenever they had rested on her.

The guy she wanted so much that it hurt.

The guy she was prepared to risk humiliation for.

'Consider this shoot over for the day.' He directed the command at the director but his eyes were focused on Sophie as she moved to stand right in front of him.

He cursed the overseas phone call that had held him up and then the traffic on the motorways and B-roads that wound their way to her family home. If he'd arrived when he had originally planned, he would have...

Made sure that she didn't step one delicate foot out of the house dressed in next to nothing.

He was shocked by his sudden regression to a Neanderthal, which was the very opposite of the cool composure he prided himself on having.

Hands thrust deep into his pockets, he continued to stare at her with ferocious intent while the entire assembled crew hurriedly began packing their equipment and disappearing fast.

Sophie heard the gravelly chaos of reversing cars and SUVs but she was locked into a little bubble in which the only two people who existed were herself and Javier.

'That wasn't the outfit we agreed on.' His voice was

a low, driven snarl and she tilted her chin at a mutinous angle.

'Checked shirt…*tick*. Denim…*tick*. Stupid cowboy hat…*tick*. Trainers…*tick*…'

'You know what I mean,' Javier gritted, unable to take his eyes off her.

'Do I?' She hadn't realised how chilly it was and she hugged herself.

'You're cold,' he said gruffly, removing his jacket and settling it around her shoulders. For a second, she just wanted to close her eyes and breathe in the scent from it.

And this was what it was all about. This *hunger* that had never gone away, but which *had* to go away, because if it didn't it would eat away at her for ever. And there was only one way of it just *going away and leaving her alone*.

'Tell me,' she pressed huskily. 'Why are you so furious? It wasn't fair of you to send all those poor people packing. They were only doing their job.'

'That's not the way I see it,' Javier growled. The jacket, way too big, drowned her and it was really weird the way that just made her look even sexier. He shifted in an attempt to ease the discomfort of his erection. Was she wearing a bra? He didn't think so and that made him angry all over again.

'How do you see it?'

'The brief was for you to look wholesome!' He raked his fingers through his hair and shook his head. This was the first time he had ventured to her family home but he hadn't noticed a single brick. His entire focus was on her. She consumed him. 'The attractive girl next door! Not a sex siren out to snag a man! How the hell is *that* supposed to sell the company?'

'I thought that sex sold everything?'

'Is that why you did it? Was that your concept of positive input? Dressing up in next to nothing and draping yourself over that lorry like a hooker posing in a motorbike shot?'

'How *dare you*?' But she flushed and cringed and knew that there was some justification for that horrible slur. She barely stopped to think that in summer there were many, many girls her age who went out dressed like this and thought nothing of it. She just knew that it wasn't *her*.

'The entire crew,' he delineated coldly, 'must have had a field day ogling you. Or maybe that was what you had in mind. Is that it? Has living in London kick-started an urge to push the limits? Have you realised how much tamer your life up here was?'

'I didn't do this so that any of the crew could *ogle me*.' She fought to maintain his cool, disapproving stare and took a deep breath. 'I did this so that...' Her voice faltered. Her hands were clammy and she licked her lips as the tension stretched and stretched between them.

'So that...?' Javier prompted softly.

'So that *you* could ogle me...'

CHAPTER SEVEN

THIS WAS WHAT he had been waiting for, the slow burn until the conflagration, because he knew that it would be a conflagration. She oozed sex appeal without even realising it. And she had come to him. He hadn't been mistaken about those invisible signals his antennae had been picking up and he marvelled that he had ever doubted himself.

Of course, he would have to make it clear to her that this wasn't some kind of romance, that whatever they did would be a purely physical animal act. They'd had their window for romance once and she'd put paid to that. Romance was definitely off the cards now.

He smiled slowly, his beautiful, sensuous mouth curving as he lazily ran his eyes over her flushed face, taking in everything from the slight tremor of her hands to the nervous tic in her neck, a beating pulse that was advertising what she wanted as loud and as clear as if it had been written in neon lettering over her head.

Him.

She wanted him.

The wheel had turned full circle, and having walked away from him, she was now walking back.

That tasted good and it would taste even better when he laid down his conditions.

'Is that so?' he breathed huskily, his erection threatening to hamper movement.

Sophie didn't say anything in response to that. She read the satisfaction in his gleaming eyes and a primal lust that was so powerful that it easily swept aside any nagging doubt that she might be embarking on the wrong course of action.

He caught the lapels of his jacket and drew her a few inches towards him. 'There were less complicated ways of getting my attention, Soph…' he murmured. 'A simple *I want you* would have done the trick.'

The fact that he made no attempt to kiss her or touch her acted as an unbearably powerful aphrodisiac. Her heart was beating so fast that it felt as though it was going to explode and she was melting everywhere. She licked her lips and Javier followed that tiny movement with such intense concentration that it made her blood heat up even further.

'That would have been…too much,' she breathed. 'It was tough enough…' She gestured down to her lack of outfit and Javier half-smiled, remembering how shy she had once been, despite the fact that she had the face and figure that could turn heads from a mile away.

'Getting into your skimpy little get-up? Let's go inside. It's getting breezier out here.' He kept his distance but the electricity crackled between them. He wasn't touching her and he hardly dared because one touch and he would have to have her at once, fast and hard, up against a wall.

He didn't want that. He wanted slow and leisurely. He wanted to explore every inch of the woman who had escaped him. Only then would he be able to walk away satisfied.

Walking towards the house, he really noticed the signs of disrepair which he had failed to see when he had arrived earlier. He paused and looked critically at the façade and Sophie followed the leisurely and critical inspection, marvelling at the damage that had been done over a handful of years.

She longed to reach out and touch him. She longed to link her fingers through his in the same careless gesture of ownership to which she had once been privy. She reminded herself that times had changed since then. This was something quite, quite different.

'You're right,' Javier said drily, stepping back as she pushed open the front door. 'The place is falling down.'

'I know.' Sophie looked around her, seeing it through his eyes. He was now used to the best that money could buy. The apartment loaned to her was pristine, like something from the centre pages of a house magazine. This house, on the other hand...

They were in a cavernous hall. Javier could see that this would have been an enormous and elegant country estate once upon a time but the paint was peeling, the once ornate ceiling was cracked and he was sure that further exploration would reveal a lot more problems.

'I'm sorry,' he said gravely and Sophie looked at him, startled.

'What for?'

'You told me that penury was harder for you than it ever had been for me and you were probably right. I knew no better and things could only go up. You knew better and the journey down must have been swift and painful. But...' he tilted his head to one side and looked at her '...you coped.'

'I didn't have a choice, did I?' She suddenly felt shy. Should they be heading up to the bedroom? What was the etiquette for two people who had decided that they are going to sleep together? Not in the 'clutching one another while stumbling up the stairs' kind of way, but in the manner of a business transaction. At least that was what it felt like—two people putting an end to their unfinished business.

They wanted each other but neither of them liked it.

'Show me the rest of the place.'

'Why?' She was genuinely puzzled.

'I used to wonder what it was like. You talked about your home a lot when we were…going out. At the time, it had sounded like a slice of paradise, especially compared to where I had grown up.'

'And I bet you're thinking, *how the mighty have fallen…*' She laughed self-consciously because all of a sudden she was walking on quicksand. This was the man she had fallen in love with—a man who was interested, warm, curious, empathetic… For a minute, the cynical, mocking stranger was gone and she was floundering.

'No. I'm not,' he said quietly. 'I'm thinking that it must have taken a lot of courage not to have cracked under the strain.'

Sophie blushed and began showing him through the various rooms on the ground floor of the house. There were a lot of them and most of them were now closed with the heating off so that money could be saved. When she and Oliver had realised the necessity of putting the house on the market, they had made an effort to do a patch-up job here and there, but not even those dabs of paint in some of the rooms could conceal the disintegrating façade.

The more she talked, the more aware she was of him there by her side, taking it all in. If this was his idea of foreplay, it couldn't have been more effective, because she was on fire.

Talking…who would have thought that it could have changed the atmosphere between them so thoroughly?

Her nipples were tight and tingling and the ache between her thighs made her want to moan out loud. She could *feel* him, could feel herself warming to him, and she had to fight the seductive urge to start mingling the past with the present, confusing the powerful, ruthless man he had become with the man she had once known.

When they were through with the ground floor, she gazed up the sweeping staircase before turning to him and clearing her throat.

'The bedrooms are upstairs.' She wanted to sound controlled and adult, a woman in charge of a situation she had engendered. Instead, she heard the nervous falsetto of her voice and inwardly cringed.

Javier lounged against the door frame, hoping that it wouldn't collapse under his weight from dry rot or termites. He folded his arms and looked at her as she fidgeted for a few seconds before meeting his gaze.

'Why are you so nervous?' he enquired, reaching out to adjust the collar of the jacket which she was still clutching around her, and then allowing his hands to remain there, resting lightly on her. 'It's not as though you haven't felt the touch of my lips on yours before...'

Sophie inhaled sharply.

She had got this far and now realised that she hadn't actually worked out what happened next. Yes, on the physical level, terrifying and exciting though that was, her body would simply just take over. She knew it would. She remembered what it had felt like to be touched by him, the way he had made her whole body ignite in a burst of red-hot flame.

How much more glorious would it feel to actually *make love* with him...?

She was nervous, yes, thrillingly so at the prospect of making love with him. But there were other things... things that needed to be discussed...and now that the time had come she wondered whether she would be able to open up to him.

'I'm... I'm not nervous about...about...'

'Going to bed with me? Being touched all over by me? Your breasts and nipples with my tongue? Your belly...?' He loved the fluttering of her eyes as she listened, the way her tongue darted out to moisten her lips and the way she was breathing just a little faster; tiny, jerky breaths that were an unbelievable turn-on because they showed him what she was feeling. He doubted that she could even put into words what she was feeling because...

Because of her inherent shyness. It almost made him burst out laughing because she was far from shy. She was a widow who had been through the mill.

'I'm not nervous about any of that!' Sophie glared at him. 'Not really.'

'You're as jumpy as a cat on a hot tin roof, Sophie. If that's not nerves, then I don't know what is.'

'I need to talk to you,' she said jerkily and watched as the shutters instantly came down over his beautiful eyes.

'Is this the part where you start backtracking?' he asked softly. 'Because I don't like those sorts of games. You did a runner on me once before and I wouldn't like to think that I'm in line for a repeat performance...'

Sophie chewed her lip nervously. To open up would expose so much and yet how could she not?

How else would she be able to explain away the fact that she was still a virgin?

A virgin widow. It wasn't the first time that she'd wanted to laugh at the irony of that. Laugh or cry. Maybe both.

Would he even notice that she was a virgin? He would know that she lacked experience but would he really notice just how inexperienced she truly was?

Could she pretend?

'I'm not backtracking.' She glanced up the stairs and then began heading up, glancing over her shoulder just once. At the top of the staircase, she eased the jacket off and slung it over the banister. 'If I didn't want to do this...' she half-smiled '...would I be doing *this*?'

Javier looked at her long and hard and then returned that half-smile with one of his own.

'No, I don't suppose you would be,' he murmured, taking the steps two at a time until he was right by her, crowding her in a way that was very, very sexy.

He curved his big hand behind the nape of her neck and kissed her.

With a helpless whimper, Sophie leant into him. She undid a couple of his shirt buttons and slipped her hands underneath the silky cotton and the helpless whimper turned into a giddy groan as she felt the hard muscle of his chest.

This was what she had dreamed of and it was only now, when she was touching him, that she realised just how long those dreams had been in her head, never-ending versions of the same thing...*touching him*.

Javier eventually pulled back and gazed down at her flushed face.

'We need to get to a bed.' He barely recognised his own voice, which was thick with desire, the voice of someone drunk with *want*. 'If we don't, I'm going to turn into a caveman, rip off your clothes right here on the staircase and take you before we can make it to a bedroom...'

Sophie discovered that she was wantonly turned on by the image of him doing that.

'My bedroom's just along the corridor,' she whispered huskily, galvanising her jelly-like legs forward.

There were numerous bedrooms on the landing and most of the doors were shut, which led Javier to assume that they were never used. Probably in as much of a state of disrepair as some of the rooms downstairs which had been sealed off.

Her bedroom was at the very end of the long, wide corridor and it was huge.

'I keep meaning to brighten it up a bit,' she apologised,

nervous all over again because, now that they were in the bedroom, all her fears and worries had returned with a vengeance. 'I've had some of the pictures on the walls since I was a kid and now, in a weird way, I would feel quite sad to take them down and chuck them in the bin…'

He was strolling through the bedroom, taking in absolutely everything, from the books on the bookshelf by the window to the little framed family shots in silver frames which were lined up on her dressing table.

Eventually he turned to face her and began unbuttoning his shirt.

Sophie tensed and gulped. She watched in fascination as his shirt fell open, revealing the hard chest she had earlier felt under her fingers.

He shrugged it off and tossed it on the ground and her mouth went dry as he walked slowly towards her.

'There's…there's something I should tell you…' she stammered, frozen to the spot and very much aware of the great big bed just behind her.

Javier didn't break stride.

Talk? He didn't think so. The marriage she had hoped for and the guy she had ditched him to be with hadn't gone according to plan. That changed nothing. She still remained the same woman who had strung him along and then walked away because, when you got right down to it, he had not been good enough for her.

'No conversation,' he murmured, trailing his finger along her collarbone until she sighed and squirmed and her eyelids fluttered.

'What do you mean?'

'No confidences, no long explanations about why you're doing what you're doing. We both know the reason that we're here.' He hooked his fingers under the checked shirt and circled her waist, then gently began to undo the buttons on the shirt. 'We still want one another,' he murmured, nibbling her ear.

'Yes…' Sophie could barely get the word out. Her body tingled everywhere and his delicate touch sent vibrations racing through her. She rubbed her thighs together and heard him laugh softly, as if he knew that she was trying to ease the pain between them.

'This is all there is, Soph.' There was a finality to stating the obvious which, for some reason, set his teeth on edge, although he didn't quite understand why when it was pretty straightforward a situation. He was propelling her very gently towards the bed; she realised that only when she tumbled back, and then he leant forward, propping himself up on either side of her, staring down at her gravely.

Sophie couldn't have uttered a word if she'd tried. She was mesmerised by the compelling intensity of his expression, the soft, sexy drawl of his voice, the penetrating, opaque blackness of his eyes.

Somehow he had managed to undo every last button of her shirt and the cool air was a sweet antidote to the heat that was consuming her.

He stood up and paused for a few seconds with his fingers resting loosely on the zipper of his trousers.

She could see the bulge of his erection and half closed her eyes when she thought about the mechanics of something so impressively large entering her.

But no talking, he'd said…

No talking because he wasn't interested in what she had to say.

As though reading the anxious direction of her thoughts, he dropped his hand and joined her on the bed, manoeuvring her onto her side so that they were lying stomach to stomach, then she flopped over onto her back and stared up at the ceiling.

'Look at me, Soph.' He framed her face with his hand so that she was forced to look at him. His breath was warm on her cheek and she wanted to evade the deadly seriousness of his gaze. 'Whatever it is you want to tell me, resist, because I'm not interested.' He felt a sharp jab of pain deep inside him but pressed on, because this had to be said, and wasn't this all part of that wheel turning full circle? That she'd come to him and now, with her in the palm of his hand, he could reduce her to humility? That he could let her know, without even having to vocalise the obvious, that the shoe was firmly on the other foot?

That he was the one calling the shots?

He had the uncomfortable feeling that it should have felt more satisfying than it did.

'This is something we both have to do, wouldn't you agree? If you hadn't ended up back in my life in a way neither of us could ever have predicted, well, we wouldn't be here now. But we're here and...' He smoothed his hand over her thigh and felt her shudder, wishing she wasn't wearing clothes because he was itching to feel all of her, naked, supple and compliant. 'We have to finish this. But finishing it doesn't involve tender sharing of our life histories. This isn't a courtship and it's important for you to recognise that.'

Sophie felt the hot crawl of colour seep into her cheeks. Of course, he was just being honest. Of course, this was just about the sex they should have had all those years ago. Nothing more. If she could, she would have slid off the bed, looked at him with haughty disdain and told him to clear off, but what her body wanted and *needed* was calling the shots now.

'I know that,' she assured him in a calm voice which was not at all how she was feeling inside. 'I'm not on the lookout for a courtship! Do you really think that I'm the same idiotic young girl you knew all those years ago,

Javier? I've grown up! Life has…flattened me in ways you couldn't begin to understand.' Right now, she didn't feel very grown up. Indeed, she felt as unsure and uncertain as a teenager.

But she really wasn't the same girl she had once been. That much, at least, was true.

Javier frowned. Her words were the words of a cynic altered by circumstance, but the tenor of her voice…the soft tremble of her mouth…seemed to be saying something different, which was, of course, ridiculous.

'Good,' he purred. 'So we understand one another.'

'A one-night stand,' she murmured, flattening her hand against his chest as a tingle of unbridled excitement rippled through her. She'd never been a one-night stand kind of girl but a one-night stand with this man would be worth the final demolishing of all her girlhood, or whatever remnants remained in some dark closet at the very back of her mind.

Javier was a little piqued at the speed with which she had accepted the brevity of what they were about to embark on but he was done with thinking.

His erection was so rock-hard it was painful and he took her hand and guided it to his trousers.

'If you don't hold me hard,' he muttered, 'I'm not going to be able to finish what's been started the way it should be finished.'

'What do you mean?'

'I mean it's time to stop talking.'

He stood up in one fluid movement and began undressing. She marvelled at his utter lack of self-consciousness. He looked at her and held her fascinated gaze as he removed his trousers, tossing it on the ground, where it joined his shirt, leaving him in his low-slung silk boxers, which did nothing to conceal the evidence of his arousal.

She did this to him!

Hard on the heels of that thought came another, less welcome one.

How many other women had done this to him? How many women had lain on a bed and watched him with the same open-mouthed fascination with which *she* was now watching him?

He wouldn't have slept with any of *them* because they had started something years ago that needed *to be finished*. He wouldn't have slept with any of them because he'd been *driven to*. He would have slept with them *because he'd wanted to*. The difference felt huge but it was good that she was aware of that, because it would make it easy to walk away when they were finished making love.

It would make it easy to detach.

'I'm really surprised you never got married,' she blurted out and he grinned and slipped onto the bed alongside her.

His erection butted against her thigh and then against her stomach as he angled her to face him.

Javier was accustomed to women who couldn't wait to strip off so that they could show him what was on offer and it was weirdly erotic to be naked and in bed with a woman who was still fully clothed. He couldn't wait to get those clothes off, yet he was reluctant to undress her, wanting to savour the thrill of anticipation.

Once they'd made love, once he'd had her, it would signal the end and where was the harm in delaying that inevitable moment? They had the night to make love and in the morning, with that itch put to rest for ever, he would leave and contrive never to see her again. His relationship with her company would revert to being just another business deal, which would, he knew, be as successful as all the other business deals he had made over the years.

This didn't taste of revenge, not the revenge that he had

seen as his when her brother had first entered his office on a begging mission.

This was a conclusion and it was one over which he had complete control.

He was exactly where he was meant to be and it felt good.

'I don't think marriage and I would make happy bed partners.' He propped himself up on one elbow and began undressing her. 'A successful marriage...' the shirt was off '...requires just the sort of commitment...'

Now she was wriggling out of the shorts, leaving just a pair of lacy briefs that matched her bra. Her breasts were full and firm and he could see the dark circle of her nipples through the lace.

'That I don't have...' He breathed unsteadily. 'Your breasts are driving me crazy, Sophie...' He bent to circle one nipple through the lacy bra with his mouth and she gasped and arched into his questing mouth.

They hadn't even got this far first time round. She had been as prim and as chaste as a Victorian maiden and he had held off, curbing his natural instinct to swoop and conquer. He closed his mind off to the reasons why she had been so damned prim and chaste because the only thing that mattered now was the taste of her.

He didn't unhook the bra. Instead, he pushed it over her breasts and, for a few unbelievably erotic seconds, he just stared. The big, circular discs of her nipples pouted at him. Her breasts were smooth, creamy and soft. He was a teenager again, with a teenager's crazy, wildly out-of-control hormones, trying hard not to come prematurely.

He almost wanted to laugh in disbelief at the extraordinary reaction of his normally well-behaved body.

He licked the stiffened bud of one nipple and then lost himself in something he had dreamed of, suckling and drawing her nipple into his mouth, flicking his tongue over the tip and just loving her responsive body underneath him.

Without breaking the devastating caress, he slid his hand under the small of her back so that she was arched up, writhing and squirming as he moved from nipple to the soft underside of her breast, nuzzling and tasting.

Driving himself mad.

He had to hold off for a few seconds to catch his breath; he had to grit his teeth and summon up all his willpower to withstand the urge of her hand as she reached up, blindly curving the contour of his cheek, desperate for him to resume what he had been doing.

Without his usual finesse, he clumsily ripped the remainder of her clothes off.

How long had he been waiting for this moment? It felt like for ever as he gazed down at her rosy, flushed body, his breathing laboured as if he had just completed a marathon.

She was perfect.

Her skin was silky smooth, her breasts pert, inviting all sorts of wicked thoughts, and as his eyes drifted lower...

The soft, downy hair between her legs elicited a groan that sounded decidedly helpless.

So this was what it felt like...

This heady sense of power as she watched him watching her and losing control.

By the time she had married Roger, she had known the full scale of the mistake she had made, but she had still been young and naïve enough fundamentally to trust that the lectures from her parents about the follies of youth and the transitory nature of her attraction to the wrong man were somehow rooted in truth. She hadn't, back then, been sure enough of herself to resist the wisdom of the two people she trusted and loved.

Surely time would make her see sense and make her

forget Javier and the new, wonderful feelings he had roused in her?

It wasn't as though she didn't *like* Roger, after all…

But it hadn't turned out that way. Neither of them had been able to find a way through all the muddy water under the bridge and she had discovered fast enough how easy it was for loathing to set in, forging a destructive path through affection and friendship.

She hadn't turned him on and he, certainly, had never, ever had the sort of effect on her that Javier was now having.

It was suddenly very, very important that they do this. Would he walk away if he knew that she was a virgin? Was he hoping for someone experienced, as he doubtless assumed she was, who could perform all sorts of exciting gymnastics in bed?

In her head, she balanced the scales.

Alarm and disappointment with her if he found out that he was dealing with someone who might not live up to expectation…versus her embarrassment at having to come clean and tell him the truth about the marriage into which she should never have entered…

Which in turn would lead her down all sorts of uncertain routes. Because how else could she explain away her mistake without letting him know just how much she had felt for him all those years ago, how deeply she had fallen in love with him?

And, in turn, would that lead him to start thinking that she might just go and do the same again, after he had issued his warnings and told her that this was just sex and nothing more—no romance, no courtship and certainly no repeat performance of what they had once had?

'I've never done this before.' She couldn't face the embarrassment of him pulling away, appalled that he had mistaken her for someone else, someone who might prove to be fun in bed instead of a novice waiting to be taught, guided only by instinct.

It took a few seconds for Javier to register what she had just said and he paid attention to her words only because of the tone in which they had been spoken.

He was still confused, though, as he pulled back to stare down at her.

'You mean you've never had a one-night stand with an ex-flame?'

'No.' Face flaming with embarrassment, she wriggled into a sitting position and drew the duvet cover protectively over her, suddenly shy in the face of his probing dark eyes.

'What, then?' He had never talked so much in bed with any woman. Frustrated, he raked his fingers through his hair and sighed. 'Do I need to get dressed to sit this one out?'

'What are you talking about?'

'What I'm asking is…is this going to be a long conversation involving more confidence sharing? Should I make myself a pot of tea and settle down for the long haul?'

'Why do you have to be so sarcastic?' Sophie asked, stung.

'Because,' Javier pointed out coolly, 'this should be a simple situation, Sophie. Once upon a time, there was something between us. Now there isn't—aside, that is, from the small technicality that we never actually made it past the bedroom door. Indeed, we never made it even near the bedroom door. So here we are, rectifying that oversight before going our separate ways. I'm not sure that there's anything much to talk about because it's not one of those *getting to know you* exercises.'

'I know! You've already told me that. Not that you needed to! I don't have any illusions as to why we're here…and *I know* it's not because we're *getting to know one another*!' Which didn't mean that it didn't hurt to have it laid out so flatly. 'I don't *want to get to know you*, Javier!'

Javier frowned. 'What is that supposed to mean?'

'It means that you're not the sort of guy I could ever be interested in now.'

Did that bother him? No. Why should it? 'Explain!' And if he wanted an explanation, it was simply to indulge his curiosity. Perfectly understandable.

'You're arrogant.' She ticked off on one finger. 'You're condescending. You think that, because you have stacks of money, you can say whatever you want and do whatever you please. You can't even be bothered to make a show of being polite because you don't think you ever have to be...'

Javier was outraged. 'I can't believe I'm hearing this!' He leapt out of the bed to pace the floor, glaring at the shabby wallpaper and the crumbling cornices.

Sophie watched him, shocked at what she had just said but in no way having the slightest intention of taking any of it back. She had to keep her eyes glued to his face because that glorious body of his was still doing things to her, even in the middle of the sudden squall that had blown up between them.

'That's because I bet no one has the courage to ever criticise you.'

'That's ridiculous! I *invite* openness from my staff! In fact, I welcome positive criticism from everyone!'

'Maybe you forgot to tell them.' Sophie glared. 'Because you behave just like someone who has the rack on standby for anyone who dares speak their mind!'

'Maybe...' He strolled towards the bed and then leant over, caging her in, hands on either side of her. 'You're the only one who thinks there's room for improvement in me...'

'Arrogant! Do you honestly think you're *that perfect*?'

'I haven't had complaints,' he purred, suddenly turned on and invigorated by the heat between them. 'Especially from the opposite sex. Stop arguing, Soph. And stop talking…'

There was no way he was going to allow her to dance around this any longer.

And she didn't want to.

She met his eyes steadily and took a deep breath. 'You're not going to believe this…'

'I loathe when people open a sentence with that statement.'

'I've never slept with anyone before, Javier. I'm…I'm still a virgin…'

CHAPTER EIGHT

'DON'T BE RIDICULOUS.' He shot her a look of amused disbelief. 'You can't be.'

Sophie continued to stare at him until he frowned as he continued to grapple with her bolt-from-the-blue remark.

'And there's no need to try to pique my interest by pretending,' he crooned softly. 'My interest is already piqued. In fact, my interest was piqued the second your brother walked through the door with his begging bowl and sob story...'

'What are you saying? Are you telling me that...that...?'

'I suddenly realised what had been missing for the past seven years—completion.'

'You wanted us to end up in bed?'

'I knew we would.'

'Is that why you offered to help us?' Sophie edged away from him, shaking with anger. 'Because you wanted... *completion*?'

'Why are you finding that so hard to believe?' Javier couldn't believe that the tide had turned so swiftly. One minute, he had been touching her, and now here she was, spinning him some tall story about being a virgin and staring at him as though he had suddenly transformed into the world's most wanted.

'I'm surprised...' she said bitterly, grabbing clothes

from the floor and hopping into them, beyond caring that he was watching her dress and wishing that he would follow suit and do the same '...that you didn't try to blackmail me into bed by offering me a deal in return!' Silence greeted this remark and she paused and stared up at him through narrowed eyes that were spitting fire.

'You thought about it, though, didn't you...?' she said slowly.

'This is a ridiculous conversation.' Javier slipped on his boxers and moved to stand by the window, arms folded, his expression thunderous.

'Did you pick all that stuff for the flat? I wondered about that, wondered how come everything seemed to have a personal touch when you didn't actually live there. When your taste, judging from your office, didn't run to old-fashioned... Did you think that shoving me into free accommodation where I'd be surrounded by stuff that made me feel at home was a good way to butter me up into sleeping with you, so that you could have your *completion*?'

Javier flushed darkly and glowered. 'Since when is it a criminal offence to choose what to put in your own property?'

'I'm going to add *manipulative and underhand* to *arrogant and full of yourself*!' He was all those things *and more*, yet she still couldn't tear her eyes away from his masculine perfection as he remained standing with his back to the window, which just went to show how downright *unfair* fate could be.

She should throw him out of the house, tell him what he could do with his deal and order him never to darken her doors again.

Instead, the awful truth was sinking in...

She still wanted him, still wanted to sleep with him, and for her it wasn't all about completion, even though that was what she had told herself, because that was the acceptable explanation for what she felt.

For her...

A jumble of confused, mixed-up emotions poured through her, weakening her, and she feebly pushed them aside because she didn't want to dwell on them.

Javier walked slowly towards her, half-naked, bronzed, a thing of such intense beauty that it took her breath away.

'So I weighted the scales in my favour,' he murmured. 'Where's the crime in that?' He was standing right in front of her now and he could almost *feel* the war raging inside her. Flee or stay put?

She wasn't running.

Because, like it or not, she wanted him as much as he wanted her and getting all worked up about the whys and hows didn't make a scrap of difference. The power of lust.

'I'm accustomed to getting what I want and I want you. And, yes, I did consider holding the offer of financial help over your head in exchange for that glorious body that has disturbed far too many of my nights, but I didn't.'

'Arrogant...' Sophie muttered. But she reluctantly had to concede that at least he wasn't trying to economise with the truth and the fact that he had used whatever ploys he had at hand to get what he wanted was all just part and parcel of his personality. There wasn't a scrap of shame or sheepishness in his voice.

He shrugged and smiled. 'Tell me you don't like it.'

'No one likes arrogance.' Her heart was beating madly. In the space of a heartbeat, the atmosphere had shifted right back to the sexy intimacy they had been sharing only moments earlier, before everything had gone downhill.

Before she had told him that she was a virgin.

'I've always been arrogant and you weren't complaining seven years ago. Why did you tell me that you were a virgin?'

'Because it's the truth,' she whispered stiltedly. 'I know you probably find that hard to believe.'

'Try impossible.'

'Roger…he…'

She wasn't lying or making up something to try to pique his interest. She was telling the truth. He could see it in her face and hear it in the clumsy awkwardness of her voice.

'Sit down.'

'Sorry?'

'You look as though you're about to collapse.' He guided her away from the bed with all its heated connotations of sex towards a chair that was by the window, facing into the room. Perhaps she sat there in the light evenings and read a book. It was the sort of thing he could picture her doing.

What he *couldn't* picture her doing was marrying some man only to spend her married life in a state of frustrated virginity.

Who the hell did something like that?

'You hadn't slept with the man before you…agreed to walk up the aisle with him?' This when she was sitting on the chair like a fragile wooden doll and he had dragged over the only other chair in the room, which had been in front of the oversized, dark mahogany dressing table.

'He…I…' The weight of all those nagging thoughts that she had temporarily pushed aside surged forward in a rush that made her breath hitch in her throat. She couldn't even remember what she had expected from her doomed marriage to Roger. She had half believed her parents when they had told her that her feelings for Javier were just an adolescent crush, the result of being away from home, being free for the first time in her young life. It happened to everyone, they had insisted, and it would blow over in due course. She would gravitate back towards someone on her own level, from her own social class, and the thrill of the unknown would fade away in time.

They had been very convincing, and as all those other reasons for marrying Roger had piled up, so had the tug of war going on inside her intensified.

But had she ever foreseen a satisfying sex life with the man she should never have wed?

Had she properly considered what married life was going to be like for her? Had she simply assumed that forgetting Javier would be as easy as her parents had said it would be and so all those feelings would, likewise, be easily replaced, transferred to Roger? What a complete idiot she had been! Foolish and naïve.

She now knew that what she had felt for Javier hadn't been a passing crush. She had fallen in love with him and he had been spot on when he had told her, just then, that his arrogance had never bothered her when they had been going out.

It was just something else she had adored about him. That and his utter integrity, his dry wit, his sharp intelligence and his sense of fair play.

She was still in love with him and all those traits that should have turned her off him but didn't. He had become the billionaire he had quietly always known he would end up being, and of course he had changed in the process. How could he not? But underneath the changes was the same man and she was still in love with him.

And just acknowledging that appalled and frightened her.

Because things might have stayed the same for her but they hadn't stayed the same for him.

He really did want completion. He hadn't stayed celibate over the years. He was a powerful, wealthy man now who could have any woman on the planet with a snap of his fingers. She was the one who'd got away, and he was determined to put that right, so he was having a little time out with her.

He didn't love her and whatever feelings he had had for her in the past had disappeared over the years. He'd made that perfectly clear. But she still loved him and that was a dreadful state of affairs.

Whilst one part of her realised that she must look very strange, just sitting with a blank expression on her face, another part recognised that there was nothing she could do about that because she couldn't control the racing whirlpool of her thoughts.

One thing was emerging very fast, though. She couldn't let him know how she felt. If he could be cool and controlled, then she must be as well. There was no way that she would allow him to see just how weak and vulnerable she was inside.

'There's no need to explain,' Javier said gently. He was beginning to feel all sorts of things and top of the list was intense satisfaction that he was going to be her first. He'd never thought that he was the sort of primal guy who would actually be thrilled to the core by something like that but he had clearly underestimated his own primitive side. Under the civilised veneer, he was as untamed as they came.

'What…what do you mean?' Sophie stammered. Of course, he had no insight into her murky past, but she still had a moment of wondering whether he had somehow worked everything out, including her feelings for him.

'I don't suppose you ever anticipated entering into a sexless marriage.'

Sophie went beetroot-red and didn't snatch back her hand when he reached out and idly played with her fingers.

'I…er…I…'

'No.' He stopped her mid awkward sentence. 'Like I said, there's no need to explain because I understand.'

'You do?'

'You were young. You weren't to know that it takes all sorts to make the world go round and some men find it harder than others to face their sexuality.'

'Sorry?'

For the first time in living memory, Javier wasn't seeing red when he thought about the loser she had tossed him over for. In many ways, he felt sorry for her. With financial problems surfacing on the home front, and a man with control over purse strings her family needed, she had failed to see that he had his own agenda and had tied the knot in the expectation that life would be normal.

She'd been sorely mistaken.

Javier shunted aside thorny questions about whether she had loved the guy or not. That was then and this was now and, in the interim, she sure as hell had had her wake-up call on that front.

A virgin widow and now here she was. Here they both were...

Sophie was reeling from the series of misunderstandings and misinterpretations. Red-blooded alpha male that Javier was, he had jumped to the simplest conclusion. She was good-looking, she and Roger had married... The only possible reason they might not have consummated their marriage would be because he physically hadn't been able to, and the only reason that might have been the case would be because he just wasn't attracted to women.

End of story.

Was she going to set him straight on that count? Was she going to tell him the series of events that had led to her sexless union? The depth of feeling she had carried for him, Javier? Was she going to risk him knowing how madly in love with him she had been and then finding the link and working out just how madly in love she still was with him?

'Roger, gay…' He might as well have been for the amount of notice he had paid her.

'Key thing here is this, Soph—it was nothing you did.'

'Really?' She very much doubted that but Javier nodded briskly.

'I went out with a functioning alcoholic a couple of years ago,' he confided, drawing her closer to him and liking her lack of resistance. 'You would never have guessed that she drank her daily intake of calories. She was a model with an erratic, hectic lifestyle and she was very careful.'

'Didn't you suspect anything?' Sophie stared at him, round-eyed. It was a relief to have the conversation off her for a moment.

'We were both busy, meeting in various foreign locations either where she was modelling or where I happened to be. I only twigged when she started having more ambitious plans for our…relationship.'

'What does that mean?'

'It means she decided that meeting in various foreign locations wasn't enough. She wanted something of a more permanent arrangement.'

'Poor woman,' Sophie said with heartfelt sympathy.

'Misplaced sympathies,' Javier said wryly. 'She knew the game before it started. Not my fault if somewhere along the line she forgot the rules.'

She knew the game the way I know the game, Sophie thought, *and I'd better make sure I don't forget the rules or else…*

And with a finger in the family company—frankly more than just a finger—parting company might be a little more difficult than he would want. Not just a simple case of ignoring calls and text messages after signing off with a bunch of flowers and a thanks-but-no-thanks farewell note...

'So how did you, er, find out that there was a problem?'

'She surprised me by inviting me over to her place in London for dinner.'

'And it was the first time you'd been there?'

'Like I said, the rules of the game...they don't include cosy domestic scenes.'

'You eat out all the time?'

Javier shrugged. 'It works. I'm only interested in the bedroom when it comes to any woman's house.'

Sophie thought that he'd seen more than just the bedroom of this particular house, but then, she knew, circumstances weren't exactly typical even though the ground rules would be exactly the same.

'But I went along and it didn't take me long to see just how many bottles of alcohol there were in places where food should have been stored. And it took even less time to unearth the mother lode because there had been no reason for her to hide any of it as she didn't share the flat with anyone. When I confronted her, she tried to make me believe that it was somehow my fault that she drank as much as she did, because I wouldn't commit to her. She clung and cried and said that her drinking had gone through the roof because she was depressed that our relationship wasn't going anywhere. Of course, I left her immediately and then got in touch with a private counsellor specialising in people with alcohol-related addictions. But the point I'm making is that there are just some people who won't face up to their own shortcomings and will take every opportunity to shift the blame onto other people.'

'And you think that, er, that Roger...'

'I think nothing.' Javier gestured in a way that was exotically foreign and then leant in closer to her. 'It would be a tough call for a man to find the courage to face up to his own sexual inclinations when those sexual inclinations risk putting him outside his comfort zone and alienating him from the people he has grown up with.'

'Roger was certainly a coward,' Sophie said bitterly.

'But all that is in the past.' He waved his hand elegantly. 'We find ourselves here and I'm glad you felt comfortable enough to bare all to me.'

'You would have found out anyway,' she said vaguely.

'You shouldn't have put your clothes back on. Now I'm going to have to strip them off you all over again. No, scrap that—what I'd really like is for you to take them off for me, bit by slow bit, a piece at a time, so that I can appreciate every delectable bit of your glorious body...'

'I...I can't do that.'

'You're shy...' Had she ever undressed in front of her husband? he wondered. Was all of this completely new to her? He confessed to himself that he was tickled pink and turned on like hell by the thought of that, the thought of him being the absolute first on so many counts.

Shy but unbelievably turned on...

She liked the way his dark, appreciative eyes roved over her like a physical caress. She liked the way he made her feel. She had never done any kind of striptease for a man before but now she began undressing as he had asked, very slowly, eyes never leaving his as she removed her clothing.

He made her feel safe and she knew why. It was because she loved him. She knew that he could hurt her beyond repair—knew that her love would never be returned and, after tonight, she would be left with only the memory of making love and the knowledge that what she wanted would never happen—but none of that seemed to matter. She'd thought that her heart could never again be made to beat but she'd been wrong. Her love overrode common sense and she couldn't fight it.

And what was the point of fighting anyway? She lived with enough regret on her shoulders without adding to the tally. If she had this one opportunity to grasp a bit of happiness, then why shouldn't she take it? She would deal with the aftermath later.

She unhooked her bra, stepped out of her undies and then walked slowly towards him, sashaying provocatively and seeing for herself the effect she was having on him.

Javier held his erection through his boxers, controlling the wayward effects of his surging libido. He breathed deeply and tried to think pleasant, pedestrian thoughts so that he could gather himself sufficiently to do justice to the situation.

No rushing.

'You look tense,' Sophie murmured. She was amazed at how at ease she was with her nakedness. Indeed, she was positively basking in it. She delicately stroked the side of his face with one finger and Javier grabbed it and sucked it, watching her with smouldering passion so that every bone in her body seemed to go into meltdown.

'*Tense* isn't quite the word I would use...' He drew her close to him so that their bodies were lightly pressed together and, eyes still locked to hers, he eased his hand over her hip, along her thigh and then between them.

Her wetness on his finger elicited a moan of pure satisfaction from him.

Sophie couldn't breathe. Her eyelids fluttered. There was something so erotic about them both standing, looking at one another while he rubbed his finger against the small, tight bud of her clitoris, rousing sensations like little explosions and fireworks inside her. She shifted and moaned softly.

'This is just the appetiser,' Javier murmured, kissing

her on her mouth, small, darting kisses that left her breathless. 'And there will be lots of those to enjoy before the main course.'

'I want to pleasure you too...'

'You already are. Trust me—just touching you is giving me more pleasure than you could even begin to understand.'

In one fluid movement, he swept her off her feet and carried her to the bed as easily as if she weighed nothing. He deposited her as gently as if she were a piece of priceless porcelain and then he stood back and looked at her, and Sophie looked back at him, eyes half-closed, her breathing shallow and jerky. The outline of his impressive erection made her heart skip a beat.

She realised that she had never actually considered the dynamics of sexual intercourse; how something so big would fit into her...

'Your face is as transparent as a sheet of glass,' Javier told her drily. 'There's no need to be nervous. I am going to be very gentle.'

'I know you will.' And she did. He might be ruthless on the battlefield of high finance, but here in the bedroom he was a giver and utterly unselfish. That was something she sensed.

Javier decided that he would leave the boxers on. He didn't want to scare her. He was a big boy and he had seen that flash of apprehension on her face and interpreted it without any difficulty at all. He'd said he was going to be gentle and he would be; he would ease himself into her and she would accept his largeness without anything but sheer, unadulterated pleasure.

He had forgotten that this single act was supposed to be about revenge.

He positioned her arms above her head and she shifted into the position so that her breasts were pointing at him.

Hunkering over her, he delicately circled one rosy nipple with his tongue until she was writhing in response.

'No moving,' he chastised sternly. 'Or else I might have to tie those hands of yours together above your head...'

'You wouldn't.' But now that he had put that thought in her head, she found that she rather enjoyed playing around with it in her mind.

Maybe another time, she thought with heated contentment only to realise that there wouldn't *be* another time. This was it. This was all he wanted. A night of fun so that he could get the *completion* he felt he deserved.

She felt a sharp, searing pain as she pictured him walking away from her, taking his sense of completion with him, returning to the queue of beautiful, experienced women patiently waiting for him.

She squeezed her eyes tightly shut, blocking out the intrusive, unwelcome image and succumbing to the riot of physical sensations sparked as he trailed kisses along her collarbone, down to her pouting, pink nipple.

He took his time. He drew her aching nipple into his mouth so that he could caress the tip with his tongue in firm, circular movements that had her gasping for breath. Every time she lowered her arm to clutch his hair, he pushed it back up without pausing in his devastating caress.

'Now let's try this another way,' he murmured, rising up and staring down at her flushed, drowsy face.

'I'm not pleasing you...' Sophie's voice was suddenly anxious and her eyes expressed concern that she was taking without giving anything in return.

'Shh...' Javier admonished. 'Like I said, you're doing more for me than you can ever imagine possible.' *Doing more than any woman had ever done before.*

She made him feel young again. He was no longer the boy who had grown into a man whose only focus was

forging the financial stability he had grown up wanting.
He was no longer the tycoon who had made it to the top,
who could have anything and anyone he wanted. He was
young again, without the cynicism invested in him by his
upwards journey.

'Straddle me,' he commanded, flipping her so that their
positions were reversed, and she was now the one over
him, her full breasts dangling like ripe fruit, swinging
tantalisingly close to his face. 'And move on me…move
on my thigh…let me feel your wetness…'

Sophie obeyed. It was wickedly decadent. She moved
against his thigh, slowly and firmly, legs parted so that
she could feel the nudge of an orgasm slowly building.

She didn't care that he could see the naked, open-
mouthed lust on her face or hear the heavy, laboured
breathing which she could no longer get under control.

She didn't care if he watched her, in her most private
moment, come against his leg.

She was so turned on, she could scarcely breathe. She
gasped when he held her breasts, massaging their fullness,
drawing her down towards him so that he could suckle on
first one, then the other, while she continued to pleasure
herself against him, hands pinned on either side of him.

As limp as a rag doll, she lay for a while on him, taking
time out to quell the rise of an impending orgasm because
she wanted to have it all. She didn't want to come like this.
She wanted to feel him moving hard in her.

The apprehension she had earlier felt when she had
seen his impressive size had faded completely.

He was in no rush. He stroked her spine and then, when
she propped herself up once again, he kissed her slowly,
tasting every morsel of her mouth. Her hair fell around
her and he pushed his hand through its tangle and gazed
at her in perfect, still silence.

'You're beautiful, Sophie.'

Sophie blushed, unused to compliments. She felt as though she had given away her carefree youth somewhere along the line and that single compliment had returned it to her for a little while.

'I bet you say that to all the women you get into bed with.' Her voice was soft and breathless and he quirked an eyebrow in amusement.

'Is that the sound of someone fishing for compliments?'

Sophie thought that actually it was the sound of someone trying to be casual when in fact she was eaten up with jealousy over lovers she had never met or seen.

'It's been a very long time since anyone paid me a compliment,' she told him truthfully and for a few moments Javier stared at her seriously.

'Weren't you tempted to get some sort of life of your own after your husband died? Or even when he was alive, given the extraordinary circumstances?'

Sophie felt a distinct twinge of guilt that she had allowed him to believe something that couldn't have been further from the truth. But then she reminded herself that she was simply avoiding opening a can of worms and where was the harm in a very small white lie? It hardly altered the fact that she was a virgin, did it?

She decided to completely skirt around the whole thorny business of life as she had known it when she had been married to Roger.

'By the time my husband died,' she said instead, snuggling against him, 'I was so snowed under with financial problems, I barely had time to eat a meal and brush my teeth, never mind launch myself into the singles scene and start trying to find a man.'

'And you must have been pretty jaded with the male sex by then,' Javier offered encouragingly.

'Um…with life in general,' she returned vaguely.

'And with your husband specifically,' Javier pressed.

'Understand one hundred percent—he lied and used you and on top of that managed to ruin what was left of your family company.'

Sophie sighed. Put like that, she marvelled that she had had the strength to go on after her mother had moved down to Cornwall. She marvelled that she just hadn't thrown in the towel and fled to the furthest corners of the earth to live on a beach somewhere.

She had been raised to be dutiful and responsible, however, and she could see now, looking back on her life, that those two traits, whilst positive, had in fact been the very things that had taken her down the wrong road. At the age of just nineteen, she had been dutiful and responsible enough to put herself last so that she could fall in line with what everyone else seemed to want from her.

'Let's not talk about all that,' she said gruffly, sensing the tears of self-pity not too far away. What a fantastic start to her one big night that would be—snotty nosed, puffy eyed and blubbing like a baby in front of him!

It enraged Javier that she still couldn't seem to find it in herself to give the man the lack of due credit and respect he so richly deserved, even with a string of unpalatable facts laid out in front of her. But, he thought with harsh satisfaction, who was she here with now? Him! And he was going to take her to such heights that by the time he walked away from her he would be the only man in her head. No one forgot their first lover.

'You're right,' he breathed huskily, expertly reversing positions so that he was the dominant one now, on top of her. 'I've always found talking superfluous between the sheets...'

Sophie sadly thanked her lucky stars that she had ended her rambling conversation before she could really begin to bore him witless. If he didn't care for women talking when they were in bed with him, then she shuddered to think what he might feel if she began weeping like a baby and clutching him like a life jacket flung into stormy seas to a drowning man.

Javier lowered himself and began to kiss her. He started with her mouth and he took his time there, until she was whimpering and squirming, then he moved to her succulent breasts, nibbling and nipping and suckling. Her skin was like satin, velvety smooth and warm. When he began to lick her stomach, her sides, the path down to her belly button, she moaned with fevered impatience.

She reached down compulsively and tangled her fingers in his hair.

'Javier!'

Sophie met his darkened gaze and blushed furiously. 'What…are you doing?'

'Trust me,' he murmured roughly. 'I'm taking you to heaven…' He gently pushed her thighs open and she fell back, then sucked in a shocked breath. The delicate darting of his tongue as he explored her was agonisingly, explosively erotic.

She moved against his mouth, rocking and undulating her hips, and groaning so loudly that it was a blessing the house was empty. She arched up, pushing herself into that slickly exploring tongue, and cried out when two fingers, gently inserted into her wetness, ratcheted up the wildly soaring sensations racing through her as fast as quicksilver.

'I'm going to…' She could scarcely get the words out before a shattering orgasm ripped through her and she clutched the sheets, driving herself upwards as his big hands supported her tightened buttocks.

It was an orgasm that went on and on, taking her to heights she had never dreamed possible, before subsiding, returning her gently back to planet Earth.

She scrambled onto her elbows, intent on apologising

for being so selfish, but Javier was already out of the bed and rooting through his trousers.

It was only when he began putting on protection that it dawned on her what he was doing.

The last thing he would want was a pregnancy.

She barely had time to register the treacherous stab of curiosity that filled her head... *What would a baby created by them look like?*

'Lie back,' he urged with a wolfish grin. 'The fun is only beginning...'

CHAPTER NINE

SOPHIE QUIVERED WITH anticipation but this time it was her decision to take things slowly. He had pleasured her in the most intimate and wonderful way possible and now it was her turn to give.

She wriggled so that she was kneeling and gently pushed him so that he was lying down. His initial expression of surprise quickly gave way to one of wicked understanding that she wanted the opportunity to take the reins instead of leaving it all to him.

'No touching,' she whispered huskily.

'That's going to be impossible.'

'You're going to have to fold your hands behind your head.' She grinned and then looked at him with haughty reprimand. 'It's only what *you* asked *me* to do.'

'Well, then,' he drawled, 'I'd better obey, hadn't I?' He lay back, arms folded behind his head. He could have watched that glorious body for ever, the shapely indent of her waist, the full heaviness of her breasts, the perfect outline of her nipples, the scattering of freckles along her collarbone, that tiny mole on the side of her left breast…

Her eyes were modestly diverted but he knew that she was aware of him with every ounce of her being and that was a real turn on for him.

He'd never felt so *alive* to the business of making love.

Somehow, he was functioning on another level, where every sensation was heightened to almost unbearable limits.

Was it because he was finally making love to the one woman who had escaped him? Was this what it felt like finally to settle old scores?

Would he be feeling this had he had her the first time round? No. That was a given. However crazy he'd been about her, he knew far more about himself now than he had back then. He knew that he wasn't cut out for permanence. If they had slept together, carried on seeing one another, if circumstances hadn't interrupted their relationship, it still wouldn't have lasted. Because, whether he liked it or not, he'd been focused on one thing and one thing only—the acquisition of the sort of wealth that would empower him, afford him the financial security he had never had growing up.

He no longer questioned his motivation, if indeed he ever had. Some things were ingrained, like scores from a branding iron, and that was one of them.

He had no burning desire for children and not once, over the years, had any of the women he had dated given him pause for thought. He expected that if he ever married—and it was a big *if*—it would be a marriage of convenience, a union years down the road with a suitable woman who would make him an acceptable companion with whom to see in his retirement. A woman of independent means, because the world was full of gold-diggers, who enjoyed the same things he enjoyed and would make no demands on him. He would look for a harmonious relationship.

Harmony in his fading years would be acceptable. Until then, he would make do with his string of women, all beautiful, all amenable, all willing to please and all so easily placated with jewellery and gifts if he ended up being unreliable.

They were all a known quantity and, in a life driven by ambition, it was soothing to have a private life where there were no surprises.

Except, right now, Sophie was the exception to the rule, and a necessary exception.

And he was enjoying every minute of her.

She straddled him and he looked down, to the slickness between her legs, and then up as she leant over him so that she could tease his hungry mouth with her dangling breasts.

He was allowed to lick, but only for a while, and allowed to suckle, but only for a while.

And he wasn't allowed to touch, which meant he had to fight off the agonising urge to pull her down so that she was on top of him and take her.

She did to him what he had done to her. She explored his torso with her mouth. She kissed the bunched muscles of his shoulders and then circled his flat, brown nipples with her mouth so that she could drizzle her tongue over them with licks as dainty as a cat's.

She could feel the demanding throb of his erection against her but it was only when she moved lower down his body that she circled its massive girth with her hand, pressing down firmly and somehow knowing what to do, how to elicit those groans from him, how to sharpen his breathing until each breath was accompanied by a shudder.

Instinct.

Or something else. Love. Love that had been born all those years ago and had forgotten that it was supposed to die. Like a weed, it had clung and survived the worst possible conditions so that now it could resume its steady growth. Against all odds and against all better judgement.

Well, worse conditions loomed round the corner, but before she encountered those she would enjoy this night to the absolute fullest.

She straightened, eyes dark with desire, and half-smiled with a sense of heady power as she registered his utter lack of control. She might be the inexperienced one here, but when it came to the power of *lust* she wasn't the only one to be in its grip. She wasn't the only one who was out of control.

And that balanced the scales a bit.

Hot and consumed with a sense of recklessness she would never have thought possible, she sat astride him so that he could breathe in the musky scent of her, positioning herself over him so that he could explore between her legs with his flicking tongue.

She breathed in sharply as he found her sensitive clitoris and probed it with the tip of his tongue.

He still wasn't touching her, still had his hands behind his head, as she had her fists clenched at her sides.

But the heat between them was indescribable all the more so because of the tantalising promise of fulfilment that lay ahead.

She let him taste her until she could stand it no longer, until her breathing was so fractured that she wanted to scream. She could move against his mouth but there was no way she was going to come again, not like this...

She worked her way down him until she was the one tasting him. The solid steel of his erection fascinated her. She took it into her mouth, sucked on the tip, played with it with her hands, tasted it and loved the way it tasted.

She explored his hard six-pack with the flat of her hand as she sucked, enjoying the hard, abrasive rub of muscle and sinew under her palm.

'Okay.' Javier rose onto his elbows to tangle his hand

in her tumbling hair. 'Enough. My blood pressure can't take any more.'

Sophie glanced at him from under her lashes.

'You're a witch,' he breathed huskily. 'Come here and kiss me.'

Their kiss was a mingling of scents and Sophie lost herself in it. She wanted to wrap her arms around him and never let him go. She wanted to be needy, clingy and demanding, and all those awful things that would have him running for the hills without a backwards glance.

She wanted to be open and honest, tell him how she felt and declare her love for him, and the fact that there was no way that she could do that felt like an impossible weight on her shoulders.

She sighed, rolling as he propelled her gently onto her back. Balancing over her, he looked at her seriously.

'Still nervous?'

'A little,' she admitted. She could have admitted a lot more. She could have admitted that what really made her nervous was the prospect of what happened when this glorious night was over and they both returned to their own little worlds. There was no way she would duck away from this but the aftermath still made her nervous.

She didn't think he would like to hear about that.

'Don't be,' he murmured. 'Trust me.'

He nudged her with the tip of his erection, felt her wetness and gently, slowly eased himself in.

She was beautifully tight. Would he have guessed that she had never made love before? Probably. She would have winced, given her inexperience away. That said, he was pleased that she had thought to confide in him and more than pleased that he was going to be her first lover.

Whatever feelings still lingered for the creep who had married her for all the wrong reasons, *he* would be the man who would be imprinted in her head for the rest of her life. Not her ex-husband. When she lay in bed, the loser she still refused to hold in contempt would no longer dominate her thoughts. No. Instead, *he* would be in her head now, and the memory of this first night spent together.

Sophie inhaled and tensed but she was already so turned on that the tension quickly evaporated. Nor did she want him treating her like a piece of china that could shatter into a thousand pieces if he happened to be just a little too rough.

She wanted him to thrust long and deep into her. She wanted his *urgency*.

'Move faster...' she moaned.

It was all the invitation Javier needed. He was unbelievably aroused. Holding on had required a superhuman feat of willpower because having her touch him had driven him wild.

He began moving with expert assurance, felt her wince as he drove deeper, then gradually relax as he picked up pace until their bodies were moving in harmony, as sweet as the coming together of the chords of a song.

Still, he refused to satisfy himself at her expense, waiting until her rhythm was inexorably building and he could feel her fingers dig into the small of his back and knew that she had raised her legs, wrapped them around his waist, all the better to receive him...

Sophie came, spinning off to a different world where nothing existed but her body and its powerful, shattering responses. She was distantly aware of Javier arching up, his whole body tensing as he reached orgasm.

Apart yet inextricably joined. She had never felt closer to anyone in her entire life. And it wasn't just because of the sex. Somewhere in the core of her she knew that it was what it was because of what she felt. She couldn't disentangle her emotions from her responses. The two were inextricably linked.

Not good. Yet so right. She couldn't imagine feeling anything like this for anyone else, ever, and that scared her because when this was over she would have no choice but to pick up the pieces and move on. She would have to put him behind her and one day find herself a partner because she couldn't envisage spending the rest of her life on her own.

She was lying in the crook of his arm, both of them staring upwards. His breathing was thick and uneven and with a little chuckle he swung her onto her side so that they were now facing one another, their bodies pressed together.

Somewhere along the line he had disposed of the condom. He was a very generously built man, however, and even with his erection temporarily subsided she was still aware of his thick length against her, stirring her, although she was aching a little and as tired as if she had run a marathon at full tilt.

She wondered what the protocol was for a one-night stand. She couldn't leap out of bed, stroll to get her clothes and head for the door, having thanked him for a good time, because it was her house. Which meant that she would have to rely on him to make the first move, and that made her feel a little awkward, because she didn't want him to imagine that she was hanging around, waiting for an encore.

She was afraid to carry on being intimate, in these most intimate of circumstances, because she didn't want him to guess the depth of her feelings for him.

She wanted to maintain her dignity. It wasn't just a case of self-preservation, but on a more realistic level: he now had a slice of the family company. He might decide to take a back seat now that they had made love and *completion* had been established, might disappear never to be seen again, but on the small chance that she bumped into him at some point in the future the last thing she needed was for him to know her feelings. If she bumped into him, she wanted him to think that she had been as detached from the whole experience, on an emotional level, as he had been. She wanted to be able to have a conversation with him, with her head held high, and preferably with a man on her arm.

'So,' Javier drawled, breaking the silence and stroking her hair away from her face.

'So…' Sophie cleared her throat and offered him a bright smile. 'That was very nice.'

Javier burst out laughing. 'That's a first,' he informed her wryly. 'I've never had a woman tell me afterwards that the sex was "very nice".'

Sophie didn't want to think about the women he had bedded or what sexy little conversations they had had post–making love.

'You don't have to tell me that.' She was going to keep it light, brace herself for when he levered himself out of bed and began getting dressed. She didn't think he'd be spending the night.

'No?'

'I already have a picture in my head of the sort of women you, er, entertain and I guess they'd be busy telling you how great you were and offering to do whatever you wanted…'

'Did you think I was great?'

Sophie blushed a vibrant red.

'Is that a *yes*…?' He nuzzled her neck and then absently rested his hand between her legs.

'What happens about the shoot?'

'I don't want to talk about the shoot. I want to talk about how great you found me between the sheets.'

Sophie didn't want to laugh but her lips twitched because there was just something so incredibly endearing and boyish about his arrogance.

'I'm glad we made love,' she told him truthfully. 'I...'

'Don't go there, Soph.' He fell onto his back and gazed upwards because this was what he didn't want. Any sort of half-hearted, limp excuses and explanations for the choices she had made seven years ago. She'd already told him enough. He knew enough. He wasn't interested in hearing any more.

'Don't go where?'

'This isn't the point where we pick up sharing our life histories.' He gathered her into him, his arm draped loosely around her. He could touch her nipple with his fingers and he liked that. He liked the way the little bud stiffened in response to the gentle pressure of his fingers rolling it. And he liked what that did to his body, the way it made him feel as though he could keep going indefinitely, his body resting between bouts of lovemaking only long enough to build back up the vigour to carry on.

After sex, no matter how good the sex had been, his instinct had always been to get out of bed as fast as he could and have a shower, his mind already racing ahead to work and business, deals that had to be done.

He'd never been one for hanging around between the sheets, chewing the fat and talking about a future that wasn't going to happen.

But he wanted to hang around between the sheets now. Minus the chat.

He'd managed, just, to relegate her loser ex-husband to a box somewhere in his head that he could safely ignore. The last thing he wanted was for her to begin recapping her past, forcing him to confront the unpalatable truth that, whether she had come to him a virgin or not, she had still ditched him for someone else and probably still loved that someone else, even though the man in question had failed to deliver.

'No,' she agreed quickly. 'I was simply going to say

that it's probably a good idea if you head back now. Un-fortunately...' she gave a derisive laugh '...the guest bed-rooms aren't exactly made up for visiting crowds. No crisp white sheets and fluffy towels, I'm afraid.'

She began to slip her legs over the side of the bed and he tugged her back against him.

He wasn't ready for her to leave just yet. He hadn't quite got his fill of her. Surprising, all things considered, but nevertheless true. And he didn't want to give her time to think things over. He wanted her warm, ripe and soft like she was now; yielding.

'I'm not sure I can face the horror story of a long drive back to London,' he murmured, curving his big body against hers and pushing his thigh between her legs.

'There are hotels,' Sophie told him as her heart gave a silly little leap in her chest.

She didn't want him to go. It was exhausting pretend-ing that she didn't care one way or another.

'This may be the back of beyond for you,' she carried on, 'compared to London, but we still have our fair share of excellent hotels. All come complete with mod cons like clean sheets, windows that open and no lingering smell of mustiness from being shut up for too long.'

Javier burst out laughing. He'd forgotten how funny she could be and that was something that hadn't been ap-parent over the past few weeks.

Probably over the past few years, he thought, sober-ing up.

'Bit of a trek going to a hotel,' he murmured. 'That would entail me getting up, getting dressed...and who's to say that they aren't all full?'

'What are you saying?'

'I could always save myself the hassle and spend the night here,' he told her.

'Some of the bedrooms... Well, I guess I could make

up the one at the end of the corridor. It's shocking to think how fast things have gone downhill here...' She sighed. 'It's as if the whole place was glued together with sticking plaster and then, one day, someone tugged some of the plaster off and everything else just came down with it. Like a house of cards being toppled. I can't imagine the stress my dad had been living under for ages. It's as well he's not alive to see the way the house has gone downhill. And it's a blessing that Mum is down in Cornwall. She honestly doesn't know the half of what's been going on here.' She pulled back and looked at him gravely. 'Sorry. I forgot you don't like conversing between the sheets.'

'That's not what I said,' Javier felt constrained to mutter. But she had hit the nail on the head. It was all tied in with his driving need to focus on the essentials—work and financial security. For the first time, he found himself projecting to places beyond those confines, the sort of places most people seemed ridiculously keen to occupy, places which he had shunned as irrelevant. 'How can your mother not know what's been happening here?' he found himself asking. 'How often do you go down to Cornwall to visit her? She surely must return here on occasion?'

'Are you really interested? Because you don't have to ask a load of questions just because you happen to be staying on here for a few more hours.'

'So you're going to put me up?'

Sophie shrugged. 'It's no bother for me.'

'Good, because I'd quite like to have a look around the house in the morning—see how bad it is in the unforgiving light of day.'

'Why?' She propped herself up on one elbow and stared down at him.

'Curiosity. You were explaining the mystery of how it is that your mother doesn't know the situation here.'

'Would you like something to eat? To drink?'

'I'm fine here.'

But, even to her, chatting like this in bed felt weirdly intimate and she could understand why he avoided doing it. It would be easy to find herself being seduced into all sorts of cosy, inappropriate feelings, into thinking this was more than it actually was.

'Well, I'm starved,' she declared briskly, disentangling herself from him and scrambling for the door so that she could head to the bathroom for a shower.

Caught on the back foot, Javier frowned as he watched her hastily departing figure.

Since when did women turn down invitations from him to stay in bed—*talking*?

Actually, since when had he made a habit of issuing invitations to women to stay in bed, talking?

He levered himself out and strolled to the bathroom which was a couple of doors along. He was surprised that the bedrooms weren't all en suite and then surmised that the house predated such luxuries and, somewhere along the line, it had become too costly to have them installed.

He pushed open the door to the succulent sight of her bending over the bath to test the water.

Her hair was swept over one shoulder, the tips almost touching the water in the bath. She had one hand on the mixer tap, the other gripping the side of the cast-iron claw-foot bath. He could see the low hang of one breast swinging as she adjusted the temperature of the water, and he moved to stand behind her, grinning as she gave a little squeak when he straddled her from behind, cupping both breasts with his hands.

'Couldn't resist,' he murmured into her hair as she straightened and leant into him so that her back was pressed against his torso.

He massaged her breasts and bent to nibble and kiss the

slender column of her neck. With a sigh of contentment, Sophie closed her eyes and covered his hands with hers.

'What are you doing?' she asked thickly.

'Is there any doubt?'

'I was just going to have a bath...then maybe get something for us to eat.'

'I have all I want to eat right here, right now...'

Sophie moaned softly at the provocative image that hoarsely spoken statement planted in her head.

They hadn't talked at all. Not really. Not about the one thing they needed to talk about. Which was *what happened next*. She knew that she shouldn't be sinking into his arms like this, should be maintaining some distance, but her body was turning to liquid as he continued to assault her senses.

She could have locked the door, of course, but somehow that would have felt silly and childish after they had just finished making love.

And maybe, she thought weakly, there was a part of her that wouldn't have wanted to stop him from coming into the bathroom anyway.

She breathed in sharply as his wicked hand drifted lower. Now he was just caressing one breast, playing with the pulsing, pink nipple while his other hand roamed over her ribcage, exploring downwards at a leisurely pace.

'Spread your legs,' he instructed softly and Sophie obeyed, as weak as a kitten.

She knew what he was going to do, yet she still gasped as he immediately found the swollen bud of her clitoris with the flat of his finger.

He knew just how to rub her there, applying just the right amount of pressure. His fingers were devastating. She could feel her wetness on his hand, and she reached behind her to hold his erection, although the angle was awkward and she couldn't begin to do half as much as she would have liked to.

And she didn't have time.

Because the rhythm of his touching grew faster, his fingers sending a million darting sensations flowing through her body until she was rocking under the impact of an orgasm, bucking against his hand, unable to contain her low groaning cries as she reached the point of utter physical fulfilment.

She spun round, blindly kissed his neck, just as he had done to her only minutes previously, and then she knelt in front of him, tossing her hair behind her, and took his rock-hard bigness into her mouth.

He tasted...like heaven.

She sucked him and he curled his fingers into her hair. She could feel his loss of self-control as she continued, sucking and licking him at the same time, her slender fingers gripping his erection, moving and massaging, working her own rhythm.

Javier had never felt so wildly out of control before. She was exciting him in ways no other woman ever had and he could no more control his own orgasm than he could have stopped the sun from rising or setting.

Spent, he pulled her back to her feet and for a few seconds their bodies were entwined into beautiful, sated pleasure, the aftermath of their physical satisfaction.

'I might have to share that oversized bath with you,' he murmured, tilting her face so that he could gently kiss her on her mouth.

Sophie smiled, as content as a cat in possession of a full tub of cream.

This was just the sort of thing he might take for granted, think nothing of, but she was so scared of taking yet another step into *him*...into losing herself in a non-relationship that wasn't going anywhere and never would.

But what was the harm in having a bath with him? What was the harm in another first experience?

'Okay.'

'And then you can cook something for me to eat.' He had never uttered those words to any woman before.

'Don't expect cordon bleu food,' Sophie warned him in alarm and he laughed.

'Beans on toast would be fine.'

Sophie lowered herself into the water a little self-consciously, drawing her knees up as he took the other end. It was an enormous bath, easily accommodating the both of them, and he made a few approving noises as he settled into the water, pulling her legs out to tangle with his, looking for the inevitable signs of deterioration in the fabric of the building as he was now accustomed to doing after only a short space of time.

'Really?' she couldn't help but ask drily. Once upon a time, perhaps, but he was no longer a 'beans on toast' kind of guy.

'And then you can tell me about your mother and how you've managed to keep this situation from her.'

He stroked her calf, which sent a frisson rippling through her body. She literally couldn't seem to get enough of him and she marvelled at her body's capacity to rouse itself at the speed of light, from satiated, pleasant torpor to wakening hunger to be touched again.

'And then we can talk about this house, which appears to be on the point of collapse. But before all that you can wriggle up and turn round so that I can begin soaping you…'

Sophie looked at the newspaper spread out on the kitchen table in front of her.

It had been *that* easy to become accustomed to having him around. It had felt so natural. Working in London, having him in and out of the office, going through paperwork with him, sitting in on interviews, being consulted on absolutely everything to do with the company...

And then, when they were on their own, those precious times when they would talk, laugh, make love...

The company had picked up in the space of just a few short months. Swept along on the coat-tails of Javier and his remarkable reputation, business that had been lost to competitors was gradually returning and returning customers were treated to reward schemes that secured their loyalty.

Little changes had been incremental and she marvelled at how simple some of the solutions were to turn the company around.

With profit came money to start working on the house. And the profits had also secured Oliver's release from the work he had never enjoyed doing.

He had returned to America to become a sports teacher at one of the prestigious private schools.

Everything had slotted into place and, of course, she had grown complacent.

Who wouldn't have?

She had actually begun secretly to see a future for them, even though he never, ever made plans; never, ever mentioned doing anything with her at some point in the future.

The one-night stand had grown into a relationship that was now almost four months old.

They hadn't talked about Christmas but she could envisage them spending at least a part of it together.

All told, hope, that dangerous emotion, had begun to take root. Loving him had taken away her objectivity, made her vulnerable to all kinds of foolish thoughts about them having a proper relationship, a relationship in which he might actually be persuaded to try to make a go of it, persuaded to think about commitment.

It was her own fault for not listening to the dictates of common sense…

No sooner had she told herself that she had to maintain some sort of emotional distance than she had hurled herself headlong into a relationship that was the equivalent of a minefield.

And this was where it had got her.

She was driven to stare at the picture occupying a large portion of the tabloid newspaper she had bought on the spur of the moment from the local newsagent. Lord knew, she wasn't much of a newspaper reader. She had an app on her mobile that kept her fully updated with what was happening in the world.

The picture had been taken at a London gallery opening. She hadn't even known that Javier had been invited. Ensconced in Yorkshire, where she had been for the past couple of weeks, getting the local offices in order and supervising decorating and refurbishment, she had seen him in fits and starts.

She looked forward to his arrivals with eager, edge-of-seat anticipation. She dressed in clothes she imagined him ripping off. She no longer felt constrained to hide how much he turned her on. Lust and the physical side of things were the only things that were out in the open between them.

She knew how much he wanted her and he knew how much she wanted him.

And he was going to be arriving any minute now. She had cooked and could smell it wafting aromatically from the kitchen, which had seen recent updates and now functioned the way it once had, with everything working and in spanking new condition.

She neatly folded the paper and then hovered until, at

seven promptly, she heard the insistent buzz of the doorbell. She closed her eyes and breathed in deeply to calm
her shaky nerves.

She found that she'd even memorised the way he rang
the doorbell, as if he couldn't wait to stride into the house,
shedding his coat even as he reached to scoop her towards him.

She still hadn't become accustomed to that first sight
of him. Even if she'd seen him the evening before, even if
she'd seen him five minutes before, he still always blew
her mind and took her breath away.

As always when he drove up north—quitting work earlier than he normally would because, he had confessed,
those few hours behind the wheel of his car afforded him
a certain amount of freedom which he deeply valued—he
arrived still in his suit.

Minus jacket, which, she knew, he would have flung
into the back seat of the car, oblivious to the fact that what
he treated with such casual indifference had cost more
than most people earned in a month.

'Have I told you that I missed you...?' Javier growled,
closing the space between them in one fluid stride.

He had. It had been three days and he'd gone to sleep
every evening with an erection and woken up with one.
Not even those sexy phone calls late at night to her had
been able to do the trick. There was only so much pleasure to be had satisfying himself.

He kissed her thoroughly, so thoroughly that Sophie
forgot that this wasn't going to be the sort of evening they
had both been anticipating: an evening of chat, food and
lots of very satisfying sex. No, things were going to be
different this evening because of that picture.

She pushed ever so slightly against him but immediately weakened as he plundered her mouth, driving her
back until she was pressed against the wall.

She'd stopped wearing a bra in the house, liking the fact that he could touch her whenever he wanted without the bother of removing it, and she hadn't thought to put one on this evening. Her head fell back as he pushed up her long-sleeved tee shirt to feel her.

He'd thought of nothing but her on the drive up and now to touch her breast, feel the tautness of her nipple between his fingers, was almost indescribable.

'I want to take you right here,' he confessed unsteadily. 'I don't even think I can make it to the bedroom. Or *any* room...'

'Don't be silly,' Sophie returned breathlessly. She *needed* to talk to him. She knew that it wasn't going to be a comfortable conversation, but talking couldn't have been further from her mind as he dragged at the waistband of her jeans, fumbling to undo the button and pull down the zipper.

She rested her hands on his broad shoulders and her mind went completely blank, swamped by the powerful churn of sensation. Her tee shirt was still over her breasts and she could feel the air cooling her heated nipples. She wanted him to lick them, suckle at them, but, like him, she was frantic for them to unite, to feel him moving in her, free and unencumbered, because she was now on the pill, so there was no need for him to reach for protection.

She helped with the jeans, tugging them down and then somehow wriggling out of them, while he, likewise, dealt with his trousers and boxers.

When she opened drugged eyes, she saw that his white shirt was unbuttoned all the way down, revealing a broad slither of bronzed chest, and he had dispensed with his shoes and socks. When had that happened? Her socks were tangled up with her trousers.

They'd barely closed the front door and here they were,

practically naked in the hall, unable to keep their hands off one another.

Hands balled tightly behind her back, she literally couldn't keep still as he crouched in front of her and began tasting her, savouring her. She planted her legs apart to accommodate his questing mouth, barely able to breathe. When she glanced down to see his dark head moving between her legs, she felt unspeakably turned on.

'You need to come in me *now*!'

She heard his low laugh and then he was lifting her up and she was wrapping her legs around him, clinging to him as he began thrusting hard inside her, his hands supporting her bottom, her breasts bouncing as they moved together.

It was fast, furious, *raw* and earth-shattering. And utterly draining. For a short while, Sophie was transported to another place, another dimension, one in which difficult, awkward conversations with unpredictable outcomes didn't have to take place.

But as soon as she was back on her feet, hurriedly snatching clothes to put them on, her mind returned to what it had been chewing over before and she edged away from him, horrified at how easily she had dumped all her worries the second he had touched her.

And that was the essence of the problem, wasn't it? He did things to her, turned her to putty in his hands. He put her in a position where she couldn't seem to say *no* to him, which meant that this could go on until he got bored, and then he would chuck her aside and move on and where would her precious dignity be when that happened?

She was so cautious about never revealing the depth of her feelings for him, so fearful that he might gaze back into the past, understand how much she had meant to him then and work out how much he meant to her now. She was just so damned careful to play the adult game of keeping it cool, matching his control with control of her own.

She'd still be a mess when he decided that it was time to move on and he'd spot that in an instant.

The mere fact that she was about to tell him about that picture said it all but she didn't care because she had to find out.

'There's something I want to show you,' she told him in a rush, having put some vital distance between them. 'Well, something I want to ask you.' She sighed on a deep breath. 'Javier, we need to talk…'

CHAPTER TEN

'WHAT ABOUT?' HE TOOK his time getting dressed while she watched him from the door, arms folded, her expression revealing nothing. 'There's nothing more guaranteed to kill a good mood than *a talk*.'

'Are you speaking from personal experience?' Sophie asked coolly. She held up one interrupting hand even though he hadn't said anything. 'Of course you are. I suppose some of those women you went out with might have wanted a bit more from you than sex on tap.'

'Is that what this talk of yours is going to be about?' Javier's voice was as cool as hers, his expression suddenly wary and guarded.

Sophie spun round and began walking towards the kitchen. She could feel stinging colour washing over her because, in a way, this *was* about that. This *was* about more than just sex on tap.

'Well?' He caught up with her and held her arm, staying her, forcing her to turn to look at him. 'Is that what this *talk* of yours is going to be about? Wanting more?' He hadn't worked out the exact time scale, but it hit him that he had been seeing her now for several months, virtually on a daily basis, and he wasn't tiring of her. Immediately he felt his defences snap into position.

'I'm not an idiot,' Sophie lied valiantly. 'You'd have to be completely stupid to want *more* from a man like you!'

She yanked her arm free and glared at him. Her heart was thumping so hard and so fast in her chest that it felt as though it might explode.

She wanted to snatch the conversation back, stuff it away, take back wanting to *talk*. She wanted to pretend that she hadn't seen a picture of him at a gallery opening with some beautiful model clinging like a limpet to his arm, their body language saying all sorts of things she didn't want to hear.

'You're not capable of giving anyone anything more than sex,' she fumed, storming off towards the kitchen and the offending picture that she intended to fling in his face as proof of what she was saying.

'You weren't complaining five minutes ago,' he pointed out smoothly.

Below the belt, Sophie thought, but her face burnt when she thought about how her talk had taken a back seat the second he had touched her. He was right. She hadn't been complaining. In fact, at one point she remembered asking for more.

'I don't want more from you, Javier,' she gritted, reaching for the paper with shaking hands and flicking it open to the piece in the centre section. She tossed it to him and then stood at the opposite end of the table with her arms folded, nails biting into the soft flesh of her forearms. 'But what I *do* want is to know that you're not running around behind my back while we're an item!'

Javier stared down at the picture in front of him. He remembered the occasion distinctly. Another boring opening, this one at an art gallery. It had been full of just the sort of types he loathed—pretentious, champagne-drinking, caviar-scoffing crowds who had never given a penny to charity in their lives and had all attended top private schools courtesy of their wealthy parents. He could have given them a short lecture on the reality of being poor, but instead he had kept glancing at his watch and wondering what Sophie was doing.

As always, mixing in the jabbering, wealthy intellectual crowd was the usual assortment of beautiful hangers-on dressed in not very much and on the lookout for men with money. He had been a target from the very second he had walked through the door. He had shaken them off like flies, but by the end of the evening he had more or less given up and that was when the photographer had obviously seen fit to take a compromising snap.

In under a second, Javier could understand why Sophie had questions. He couldn't even remember the woman's name but he knew that she was a famous model and the way she was looking at him...the way she was holding on to his arm...

She didn't look like a woman on the verge of being cast aside by an indifferent stranger. Which she had been.

And snapped when, for five seconds, his attention had been caught by something the guy standing next to her had said to him and he was leaning into her, the very image of keen, while the guy to whom he had been speaking had been artfully cropped from the photo.

Not for a second was Javier tempted to launch into any kind of self-justifying speech. Why should he? He looked at her angry, hurt face and he ignored the thing inside him that twisted.

'Are you asking me to account for my actions when I'm not with you?'

'I don't think that's out of order on my part!'

'I have never felt the need to justify my behaviour to anyone. Ever.'

'Maybe you should have! Because when you're sleeping with someone, you are, actually, travelling down a two-way street whether you like it or not!'

'Meaning what?'

'Meaning it's not all about your world and what you want.'

'And maybe that will be the case one day, when I decide that I want more than a passing…situation with a woman.'

Sophie recoiled as though she had been physically struck. Suddenly all her anger seeped out of her and she was left feeling empty, hollow and utterly miserable.

Of course he would account for his behaviour one day. When he had met the right woman. In the meantime, he was having fun, and that was all that mattered. He wasn't tied to her any more than he had been tied to any of the women he had dated in the past, so if someone else came along and he was feeling energetic, then he probably thought, *why not?*

Facing up to that was like being kicked in the stomach. She literally reeled from the truth but she faced it anyway, just as she had faced the fact that she was still in love with him.

What was the point hiding from the truth? It didn't change anything. Having to deal with the mess her father had made of the company and the horror of her doomed marriage had taught her that, if nothing else.

'Did you sleep with that woman?'

'I'm not going to answer that question, Sophie.' Javier was incensed that, picture or no picture, she dared question his integrity. Did she think that he was the sort of man who couldn't control his libido and took sex wherever he found it?

He was also annoyed with himself for the way he had drifted along with this to the point where she felt okay about calling him to account. He'd been lazy. This had never been supposed to end up as anything more than an inconvenient itch that needed scratching. This had only ever been about finishing unfinished business.

'And maybe,' he said carefully, 'it's time for us to re-assess what's going on here.'

Sophie nodded curtly. The ground had just fallen away from under her feet, but she wasn't going to plead or beg or hurl herself at him, because they really *did* need to 're-assess', as he put it.

'Your company is pretty much back on its feet.' He gave an expansive gesture while she waited in hopeless resignation for the Dear John speech he would soon be delivering.

She was too miserable to think about getting in there first, being the first to initiate the break-up. It didn't matter anyway. The result was going to be the same.

'Your brother's disappeared back across the Atlantic and there's no need for you to continue taking an active part in the running of the company. The right people are all now in the right places to guide the ship. You can do whatever you want to do now, Sophie. Go back to uni-versity…get another job…disappear across the Atlantic to join your brother…'

Sophie's heart constricted because that was as good as telling her what he thought of her and she could have kicked herself for having been lulled into imagining that there was ever anything more to what they had.

'Or France.'

'Come again?'

'I've been thinking about it for a couple of weeks.'

Javier was at a loss as to what she was talking about. 'Thinking about…what, exactly?'

'Ollie's job is still up for grabs,' she said, thinking on her feet. 'And it's dealing with marketing, which is some-thing I've found I rather like and I'm pretty good at.'

'You've been thinking about going to France?'

Sophie straightened. Did he think that she wasn't good enough for the job? Or did he think that she was always going to hang around until he got fed up with her, without giving any thought at all to life beyond Javier?

'Pretty much decided in favour of it,' she declared firmly. 'The house has found a buyer, as you know, who's happy to take it on and complete the renovations I've started, so there's literally nothing keeping me here. Aside, that is, from Mum. And I think she'd be overjoyed to come and visit Paris once a month. And, of course, I can easily get to Cornwall to see her.'

'So you're telling me that you've been concocting this scheme behind my back for weeks?'

'It's not *a scheme*, Javier.' The more she thought about it, the better it sounded. How else would she get over him if she didn't put as much distance as she possibly could between them? Affairs were in order here. Why not? Too much of her life had been taken up having other people make decisions on her behalf. 'I wasn't sure exactly when, but seeing that picture of you in the newspaper...'

'For God's sake!' He tried hard to temper his voice. 'What the hell does some half-baked picture in a sleazy tabloid have to do with anything?'

'It's made me realise that it's time for me to take the next step.'

'Next step? What next step?' Javier raked his fingers through his hair and wished she would settle on one topic and stick there. He felt as though the carpet had been yanked from under his feet and he didn't like the feeling. 'Of course you can't go to bloody France! It's a ludicrous idea!'

'You can do what you like with whoever you want to... er...do it with, Javier, but it's time for me to get back into the dating scene, meet someone I can share my life with.' She tried to visualise this mystery man and drew a blank. 'I feel like my youth has been on hold and now I have a great opportunity to reclaim it.'

'In France?' He laughed scornfully.

'That's right.'

'And what if you'd never seen that picture?' He stopped just short of doing the unthinkable and telling her that he'd never met that woman in his life before and had no intention of ever meeting her again. Because his head was too wrapped up with *her*.

Unthinkable!

'It was just a question of time,' Sophie said truthfully. 'And that time's come.'

'You're telling me, after the sex we've just had, that you want out…' He laughed in disbelief and Sophie wanted to smack him because it was just the sort of arrogant reaction she might have expected.

'I'm telling you that the time has come when it has to be more than just the sex. So I'm going to find my soulmate,' she added quickly.

'You're going to find your *soulmate*?' Javier hated himself for prolonging this conversation. As soon as she had started kicking up a fuss about that picture, he should have told her that it was over. He didn't need anyone thinking that they had claim to him. Never had, never would, whatever he had told her about a woman coming along who could tame him. Wasn't going to happen.

Except… *She hadn't been trying to claim him, had she?*

She'd just reasonably asked him if there was anything going on with the airhead who had been dripping off his arm at a forgettable gallery opening and, instead of laughing and dismissing the idea, he had returned to his comfort zone, dug his heels in and stubbornly refused to answer.

And it was too late now to do anything about that.

Not that it would have made any difference, considering she had been making all sorts of plans behind his back.

For the best, he decided. So he'd become lazy but in truth the itch had been scratched a long time ago.

'Fine.' He held up both hands and laughed indulgently. 'Good luck with that one, Sophie. Experience has taught me that there's no such thing. I'm surprised given your past that you haven't had the same learning curve.'

'Just the opposite.' She felt nauseous as she watched him start heading for the door. 'Life's taught me that there are rainbows around every corner.'

'How…kitsch.' He saluted her and she remained where she was as he strode out of the kitchen.

And out of her life for good.

From Spain to France.

When you thought about it, it was a hop and a skip and it made perfect sense. He had had no input in Sophie's company for over three months. He had delegated responsibility to his trusted CEO and withdrawn from the scene.

He'd done his bit. He'd taken over, done what taking apart had needed doing and had put back together what had needed putting back together. The company was actually beginning to pull itself out of the quagmire of debt it had been languishing in for the past decade, and it was doing so in record time.

It was a success story.

He'd moved on and was focused on another takeover, this time a chain of failing hotels in Asia.

He was adding to his portfolio and, furthermore, branching out into new terrain, which was invigorating. By definition, branching out into anything new on the business front was going to be invigorating!

He had also just had a good holiday with his parents and had persuaded them to let him buy them a little place on the beach in the south of France, where they could go whenever they wanted to relax. He had pulled the trump card of promising that he would join them at least three times a year there and he had meant it.

Somehow, he had learnt the value of relaxation.

So what if he hadn't been able to relax in the company of any woman since he had walked out of Sophie's life?

He'd been bloody busy, what with his latest takeover and various company expansions across Europe.

But he was in Spain.

France seemed ridiculously close...

And he really ought to check, first hand, on the progress being made in the Parisian arm of a company which, all told, he part-owned...

And, if he *was* going to go to Paris, it made sense to drop in and see what Sophie was up to.

He knew that she had been working there for the past six weeks. It was his duty, after all, to keep tabs on the company. Everything was easily accessible on the computer, from the salary she was pulling in to where she lived and the apartment she was renting near Montmartre.

He was surprised that she hadn't headed off to more fulfilling horizons, leaving the running of the company to the experts, as her brother had.

His decision was made in moments. Already heading away from the first-class desk, he walked briskly back, ignoring the simpering blushes of the young girl who had just seen him.

A ticket to Paris. Next flight. First class.

Sophie let herself into her apartment, slamming the door against the fierce cold outside.

She was dressed in several layers but, even so, the biting wind still managed to find all sorts of gaps in those layers, working their way past them and finding the soft warmth of her skin.

Her face tingled as she yanked off the woolly hat, the scarf and the gloves, walking through her studio apartment and luxuriating in the warmth.

She had been incredibly lucky to have found the apartment that she had. It was small but cosy, comfortable and conveniently located.

And Paris was, as she had expected, as beautiful as she remembered it from the last time she had been there nearly ten years ago.

She had wanted to leave her comfort zone behind and she had! She had climbed out of her box and was now living in one of the most strikingly beautiful cities on the planet. Her mother had already been to visit her once and was determined to come again just as soon as the weather improved.

All in all, there were loads of girls her age who would have given their right arm to be where she was now!

And if she happened to be spending a Friday night in, with plans to curl up with her tablet in her flannel pyjamas and bedroom socks, then it was simply because it was just so cold!

When spring came, she would be out there, jumping right into that dating scene, as she had promised herself she would do before she had left England.

For the moment, she was perfectly happy just chilling.

And expecting no one to come calling because, although she had been out a few times with some of the other employees in the small arm of the company in Paris, she had not thus far met anyone who might just drop by on a Friday evening to see what she was up to.

That would come in time.

Probably in spring.

So when the doorbell went, she didn't budge. She just assumed it was someone selling something and she wasn't interested.

She gritted her teeth as the buzzer kept sounding and eventually abandoned all pretence of Zen calm as she stormed to the door and pulled it open, ready to give her uninvited caller a piece of her mind.

Javier had kept his finger on the buzzer. She was in. She had a basement apartment and he could see lights on behind the drawn curtains. He wondered whether she knew that basement apartments were at the highest risk of being burgled.

Since leaving Spain, he hadn't once questioned his decision to spring this visit on her, but now that he was here, now that he could hear the soft pad of footsteps, he felt his stomach clench with an uncustomary attack of nerves.

He straightened as she opened the door and for a few seconds something bewildering seemed to happen to him: he lost the ability to think.

'You're here…' he said inanely. Her long hair was swept over one narrow shoulder and she was wearing thick flannel bottoms and a long-sleeved thermal vest. And no bra. 'Do you always just open your door to strangers?' he continued gruffly, barely knowing where this unimaginative line of conversation was coming from.

'Javier!' Temporarily deprived of speech, Sophie could just blink at him, owl-like.

She'd pretended that she'd moved on. She was in Paris, she was enjoying her job, meeting new people…

How could she *not* have moved on? Hadn't that been the whole point of Paris?

But seeing him here, lounging against the door frame in a pair of faded black jeans and a black jumper, with his coat slung over his shoulder…

She was still in the same place she'd been when she'd watched him stroll out of her flat without a backwards glance.

How dared he just show up like this and scupper all her chances of moving on?

'What are you doing here? And how the heck did you find out where I live!'

'Computers are wonderful things. You'd be shocked at the amount of information they can divulge. Especially considering you work for a company I part-own...' Javier planted himself solidly in front of her. He hadn't given much thought to what sort of welcome he was likely to receive but a hostile one hadn't really crossed his mind.

Since when were women hostile towards him?

But since when was she just *any woman*?

She never had been and she never would be and, just like that, he suddenly felt sick. Sick and vulnerable in a way he had never felt before. Every signpost that had ever guided him, every tenet he had ever held dear, disappeared and he was left groping in the dark, feeling his way towards a realisation that had always been there at the back of his mind.

'Go away. I don't want to see you.'

Javier placed his hand on the door, preventing her from shutting it in his face. 'I've come...'

'For what?' Sophie mocked.

'I...'

Sophie opened her mouth and shut it because she didn't know what was going on. He looked unsettled. Confused. *Unsure.* Since when had Javier *ever* looked unsure?

'Are you all right?' she asked waspishly, relenting just enough to let him slip inside the apartment, but then shutting the door and leaning against it with her hands behind her back.

'No,' Javier said abruptly, looking away and then staring at her.

'What are you saying?' Sophie blanched. 'Are you...?

Are you ill...?' Fear and panic gripped her in equal measure.

'Can we go sit somewhere?'

'Tell me what's wrong!' She was at his side in seconds, her small hand on his forearm, her eyes pleading for reassurance that he was okay because, whatever he was, he wasn't himself and that was scaring her half to death.

And if he saw that, she didn't care.

'I've missed you.' The words slipped out before Javier could stop them in their tracks. He had put everything on the line and he felt sick. He wondered why he hadn't thought to down a bottle of whisky before embarking on this trip.

'You've missed me?' Sophie squeaked.

'You asked what was wrong with me,' Javier threw at her accusingly.

'Is missing me wrong?' Something inside her burst and she wanted to laugh and cry at the same time. She had to tell herself that no mention had been made of love, and if he was missing her, then chances were that he was missing her body. Which was something else entirely.

She walked on wooden legs into the sitting room, where she had been watching telly on her tablet, and watched as he sat down, briefly glancing around him before settling those dark, dark eyes on her.

'Missing...' he sat down, arms loosely resting on his thighs, his body leaning towards hers '...isn't something I've ever done.'

'Then it's a good thing,'

'I couldn't focus,' he admitted heavily. Now that he had started down this road, he had no alternative but to continue, although she hadn't chucked him out and that was a good thing. 'I couldn't sleep. You got into my head and I couldn't get you out of it.'

Sophie's heart was singing. She didn't want to speak. What if she broke the spell?

'I wanted you, you know...' He looked at her gravely. 'I don't think I ever really stopped wanting you, and when your brother showed up at my office, I figured I'd been handed the perfect way of putting that want to bed for good. Literally. I was going to just...go down the simple "exchange for favours" road. Cash for a little fun between the sheets, but then I decided that I wanted more than that...I didn't want a reluctant lover motivated for the wrong reasons.'

'You're assuming I would have given you your fun between the sheets because I needed money!' But she couldn't fire herself up to anger because her heart was still singing. She itched to touch him but first she wanted to talk.

'I'm arrogant.' He shot her a crooked smile. 'As you've told me a million times. I thought that it would be a one-night stand, simple as that, and then when you told me that you were a virgin...that the ex was gay...'

'Um, about that...'

'Sleeping with you that first time was...mind-blowing.'

'Er...'

'And it wasn't just because I'd never slept with a virgin before. It was because that person was *you*...'

'I should tell you something.' Sophie took a deep breath and looked him squarely in the eyes. So what if he hadn't said anything about love? He had opened up and she could tell from the way he was groping with his words that this was a first for him. A big deal. Her turn. It would be a bigger deal, but so be it.

'He wasn't gay. Roger wasn't gay. The opposite. He was one hundred percent straight as an arrow.'

Javier stared at her, for once in his life lost for words. 'You said...'

'No, Javier, *you* said.' She sighed wearily and sifted her fingers through her hair. 'It's such a long story and I'm sorry if I just let you think that Roger…'

Javier just continued staring, his agile brain trying and failing to make connections. 'Tell me from the beginning,' he said slowly.

'And you won't interrupt?'

'I promise nothing.'

Sophie half-smiled because why would this proud, stubborn, utterly adorable man ever take orders from anyone, even if it happened to be a very simple order?

'Okay…' Javier half-smiled back and a warm feeling spread through her 'I as good as half promise.'

'I'd been sort of going out with Roger by the time I went to university,' Sophie began, staring back into the past and not flinching away from it as she always did. 'I honestly don't know why except he'd been around for ever and it was something I just drifted into. It was cosy. We mixed in the same circles, had the same friends. His mother died when he was little and he and his father spent a good deal of time at our place. When his father died, he became more or less a fixture. He was crazy about me…' she said that without a trace of vanity '…and I think both my parents just assumed that we would end up getting married. Then I left home to go to university and everything just imploded.'

'Tell me,' Javier urged, leaning forward.

'Roger didn't want me to go to university. He was three years older and hadn't gone. He'd done an apprenticeship and gone straight into work at a local company. His parents had been very well off and he'd inherited everything as an only child, so there was no need for him to do anything high-powered and, in truth, he wasn't all that bright.'

She sighed. 'He wanted to have fun and have a wife

to cater to him. But as soon as I went to university it hit me that I didn't love him. I liked him well enough but not enough to ever, ever consider marrying. I told him that but he wasn't happy and then I met you and…I stopped caring whether he was happy or not. I stopped caring about anyone or anything but you.'

'And yet you ended up marrying him. Doesn't make sense.'

'You promised you wouldn't interrupt.'

Javier raised both his hands in agreement. In truth, he was too intrigued by this tale to ask too many questions.

'My father summoned me back home,' she said. 'I went immediately. I knew it had to be important and I was worried that it was Mum. Her health hadn't been good and we were all worried for her. I never expected to be told that the family was facing bankruptcy.' She took a deep breath, eyes clouded. 'Suddenly it was like every bad thing that could happen at once had happened. Not only was the company on the verge of collapse but my father admitted that he had been ill—cancer—and it was terminal. Roger was presented to me as the only solution, given the circumstances.'

'Why didn't you come to me?'

'I wanted to but it was hard enough just fighting your corner without presenting you to my parents. They wanted nothing to do with you. They said that Roger would bring much-needed money to the table, money that would revitalise the company and drag it out of the red. Dad was worried sick that he wouldn't be around long enough to do anything about saving the company. He was broken with guilt that he had allowed things to go down the pan but I think his own personal worries, which he had kept to himself, must have been enormous.

'They told me that what I felt for you was…infatuation. That I was young and bowled over by someone who would be no good for me in the long run. You weren't in my social class and you were a foreigner. Those two things would have been enough to condemn you but, had it not been for what was happening in the company, I don't think they would have dreamt of forcing my hand.'

'But they persuaded you that marrying Roger was vital to keep the family business afloat,' Javier recapped slowly. 'And, with your father facing death, there wasn't time for long debates…'

'I still wouldn't have,' Sophie whispered. 'I was so head over heels in love with you, and I told Roger that. Pleaded with him to see it from my point of view. I knew that if he backed me up, Mum and Dad might lay off the whole convenient marriage thing, but of course he didn't back me up. He was red with anger and jealousy. He stormed off. At the time, he had a little red sports car…'

'He crashed, didn't he?'

Sophie nodded and Javier picked up the story.

'And you felt…guilty.'

'Yes. I did. Especially because it was a very bad accident. Roger was in hospital for nearly two months and, by the time he was ready to come out, I had resigned myself to doing what had to be done. I'd even come to half believe that perhaps Mum and Dad were right—perhaps what I felt for you was a flash in the pan, whereas my relationship with Roger had the weight of shared history, which would prove a lot more powerful in the long run.'

Javier was seeing what life must have been like for her. In a matter of a few disastrous weeks, her entire future and a lot of her past had been changed for ever. She hadn't used him. He had simply been a casualty of events that had been far too powerful for her to do anything about but bow her head and follow the path she had been instructed to follow.

Not old enough to know her own mind, and too attached to her parents to rebel, she had simply obeyed them.

'But it didn't go according to plan...' he encouraged.

'How did you guess? It was a disaster from the very start. We married but the accident had changed Roger. Maybe, like me, he went into it thinking that we could give it a shot, but there was too much water under the bridge. And there had been after-effects from the accident. He very quickly became addicted to painkillers. He used to play a lot of football but he no longer could. Our marriage became a battleground. He blamed me, and the more he blamed me, the guiltier I felt. He had affairs, which he proudly told me about. He wreaked havoc with the company. He gambled. There was nothing I could do because he could quickly turn violent. By the time he died, I'd... I'd grown up for ever.'

Javier looked at her long and hard. 'Why did you let me believe that he was gay?'

'Because...' She took a deep breath. 'I thought that if you knew the whole story, you would know how much you meant to me then and you would quickly work out how much you mean to me now.' She laughed sadly. 'And, besides that, I've always felt ashamed—ashamed that I let myself be persuaded into doing something I really didn't want to do.'

'When you say that I *mean something to you now...*'

'I know what this is for you, Javier. You believed that I ran out on you, and when you had the chance, you figured you would take what should have been yours all those years ago.'

Javier had the grace to flush. What else could he do?

'And, for a while, I kidded myself that that was what it was for me too. I'd dreamt about you for seven years and

I'd been given the chance to turn those dreams into reality, except for me it was much more than that. You won't want to hear this but I'll tell you anyway. I never stopped loving you. You were the real thing, Javier. You'll always be the main event in my life.'

'Sophie...' He closed the distance between them but only so that he could sit closer to her, close enough to thread his fingers through hers. His throat ached. 'I've missed you so much. I thought I could walk away, just like I thought that sleeping with you would be a simple solution to sorting out the problem of you being on my mind all the time through the years. There, at the back of my mind like a ghost that refused to go away. You'd dumped me and married someone else. It didn't matter how many times I told myself that I was well rid of someone who used me for a bit of fun until she got her head together and realised that the person she really wanted to be with wasn't me...I still couldn't forget you.'

Sophie thought that this was one of those conversations she never wanted to end. She just wanted to keep repeating it on a loop, over and over and over.

'We slept together, Sophie, and just like that my life changed. Not having you in it was unthinkable. I didn't even register that consciously until you presented me with that picture and I suddenly realised that I had succumbed to all the things I'd thought I'd ruled out of my life. You'd domesticated me to the point where I didn't want to be anywhere unless you were there, and I hadn't even realised it. I took fright, Soph. I suddenly felt the walls closing in and I reacted on instinct and scarpered.'

'And now that you're back...' She had to say this. 'I can't have a relationship with you, Javier. I can't go back to living from one day to the next, not knowing whether you'll decide that you're bored and that you have to take off.'

'How could I ever get bored with you, Sophie?' He lightly touched her cheek with his fingers and realised that he was trembling. 'And how can you not see what I need to tell you? I don't just want you, but I need you. I can't live without you, Sophie. I fell in love with you all those years ago and, yes, you're the main event in my life as well and always will be. Why do you think I came here? I came because *I had to*. I just couldn't stand not being with you any longer.'

Sophie flung herself at him and he caught her in his arms, laughing because the chair very nearly toppled over.

'So, will you marry me?' he whispered into her hair and she pulled back, smiling, wanting to laugh and shout all at the same time.

'You mean it?'

'With every drop of blood that flows through my veins. Let me show you how great marriage can be.' He laughed. 'I never thought I'd hear myself say that.'

'Nor did I.' She kissed him softly and drew back. 'And now that you have, I won't allow you to take it back, so, yes, my darling. I'll marry you…'

* * * * *